I dedicate this book to my children:
Lidia, Danylo, Nicole and *Mark*.

Infinity

Serhii Adamenko

Contents

The Wolf

Preface

Dear readers,

I am pleased to present the "Infinity" trilogy, a revised version of books you may have already heard of. These are "The Flight of the Butterfly", "The Gaze of the Raven", and "The Step of the Wolf". The decision to publish all three books in a single edition came to me when all three had already been printed in Ukrainian and English. I decided it would be more convenient for readers to follow the characters and easier to grasp what I wanted to convey to my audience.

Questions about life after death, the transmigration of souls, and other mystical events have intrigued me since childhood. Only in adulthood was I able to formulate my vision and find answers to my questions. Perhaps my time at war and personal mystical experiences prompted me to write these books. I cannot answer that. However, I can confidently state that the writing of these books was influenced by forces unknown to me. The titles of the books, the characters, and the plots seemed to have been suggested to me by someone. In some stories, I described my own experiences. I even dedicated a separate chapter to one of the characters, a monk. A long time ago, I read Lobsang Rampa's book *The Third Eye*, which left a profound impression on me at that time. Later, when I began writing my second book, I remembered what had moved me so deeply then. So, I decided to describe his life in one of the chapters of this book, basing it on his narratives. His personal experiences and teachings strangely coincided with my contemporary views on reincarnation and life after death.

I can say one thing: writing these books changed my attitude toward the Church and religion, my views on spiritual life, and my life as a whole. I left Christianity and embraced paganism, which, in my opinion, closely connects a person to the Universe and is unjustly forgotten. Having been born in Ukraine and spent considerable time living in Ireland, I devoted much time to researching the ancient traditions of the Slavs and Celts. To my surprise, I found a great deal in common between them. Simply put, I discovered a new world for myself.

In this book, you will read about the journey of three individual souls toward Eternity through reincarnation. Along their path, these souls will cross each other's lives. There will be many repetitions and similarities in the stories, with some events recurring in dreams. You will read about love, patriotism, mysticism, déjà vu experiences, the meeting of kindred souls, dream journeys, reflections on the meaning of life, and much more. Some moments described here are tied to real events but do not correspond to historical truth. I deliberately did not specify the countries or nationalities of the characters because, in God's eyes, all people are equal as His creations. Nevertheless, from certain details, you will be able to identify the countries where certain events took place.

Once I realised that life is cyclical, I decided to close that circle with the third book. Thus, the final lines of the book will take you back to its beginning. I hope you will enjoy this book. Perhaps it will help you find answers to some questions you have not yet resolved. Do not judge me harshly for my vision. It is mine and mine alone.

I wish you a pleasant time with "Infinity".

Serhii Adamenko

Ireland, 2025

The Butterfly

The Butterfly

It's very dark and cramped, but he knows it's time to see the light. It won't be easy, but gradually, making his way to the exit, the butterfly finally recognises the light after several hours of struggle. It feels so unusual to be outside the cocoon. It's like you're being expanded from within, ready to embrace the whole world. The wings are still very weak, but the butterfly senses them increasingly unfolding and gaining strength. Soon, very soon, he will be able to flap them for the first time and soar upward. Then he will finally see everything he dreamed of when he was still a caterpillar. The butterfly will feel new scents and taste new flavours. A wonderful life awaits him, full of bright experiences and unforgettable encounters.

Shortly the moment came when he flapped his wings and detached from the green bush where he spent several long winter months. This morning was special, every second of his new life thrilled the little hero. Perhaps because it was the first morning, he was able to fly. The butterfly saw the sunrise over the mountains with his own eyes. He saw the forest that seemed endless and mysterious, emanating both charm and danger. This impenetrable forest lured and enchanted him at the same time. The butterfly felt its inner power and it excited him to catch his breath.

Illustration by Oleksand Prodan

Sunbeams pierced through the leaves of trees and fell onto clearings, creating islands of light. The swarms of insects were swirling in these sunny areas. They flew in flocks, individually creating intricate patterns in the air with their colourful bodies. It seemed like a kind of dance of their delicate souls, breaking free and feeling complete freedom. It all resembled a joyful celebration, and the butterfly was dizzy with excitement.

Several days passed. He drank delicious nectar, flitted from flower to flower, danced in the air, basked in the sunlight, and thought this 'celebration of life' would never end.

In a little while the butterfly saw Her. She was sitting on a flower with her wings spread, resembling a flower herself. Two iridescent spots on her back shimmered with all the colours of the rainbow and magically attracted him. The butterfly couldn't take his eyes off such a beauty and, subsequently, never left her side. They flew together from flower to flower, from petal to petal, rising high into the sky circling endlessly in a unique dance. The beauty responded to him in kind, and this feeling quickened his breathing.

Thunder rumbled and it started raining. They took shelter under a huge burdock leaf. They sat together, huddled, and watched as raindrops slid off the protective leaf, causing them no harm. Then it seemed to the butterfly that the whole world was contained here, under this burdock leaf. In those moments, he felt like he could move mountains. Those mountains towered over the edge of the forest.

Illustration by Oleksand Prodan

Days went by, they loved each other, enjoying every moment spent together, and dreaming for it to last forever. But that day came, the same day when she didn't waken. The butterfly flew in despair around his beloved, trying to wake her. He touched her with his legs hoping she would come to life and fly again into the heavenly heights. But she had entered an eternal slumber, and no one could revive her. On that day, colours disappeared for the butterfly, and the whole world darkened. It felt like a part of his soul went into oblivion along with her. The butterfly sat next to her, folded his wings, and waited. He looked at the colourful spots on her back, and it seemed she was looking at him, that she would soon move her wings. But all was in vain, and he understood that. Hours passed, maybe even days and then came the morning. The same dawn when the butterfly couldn't see the sunrise anymore. That morning eternal sleep overtook him.

Jonathan

"Hey, blackie! Don't you know it's strictly forbidden for blacks to walk on this side of the street?"

A group of six young men, aged 20-25, was approaching Jonathan. He felt a chill inside, as he recognized them. They were members of the local gang that hunted down black residents of the city.

"I always walk here," replied Jonathan. "Nobody told me we couldn't move around on this side of the street."

"Of course not," one of the gang members sneered. "Explain to every darkie that this side of the street is only for whites."

Jonathan was the eldest child in a family of former slaves, Gary and Dolores, who belonged to the local owner of a cotton plantation, Hugh Rogers. He had two younger brothers and twin sisters. Born a year before the start of the war between the North and South, Jonathan did not remember slavery, though he was born a slave. However, he remembered how his father, who served in General Lee's army, returned home hoping for a new life.

Although slavery was legally abolished, the lives of black people did not improve significantly. They still faced humiliation and discrimination, much like before the war. Finding work was difficult, and education wasn't readily available. The white population still considered former slaves as second-class citizens. Members of the newly-formed racist organization, the Ku Klux Klan, openly and with impunity persecuted black people.

Jonathan's family lived in a small house on the outskirts of town. His mother earned meagre wages doing laundry and cleaning for a wealthy family who were relatively kind to black people. His father worked as a dock worker, hauling bales of cotton and other goods. The work was hard, and the wages barely covered the expenses of a large family. Gary had been wounded in the war, walking with a limp, but trying not to show the pain. He feared losing his job, which would have made things even harder for them. Dolores' earnings barely covered bread, and the children were growing up, always needing something. Fortunately, Dolores knew how to sew, and they saved on clothes that way. Recently, she had sewn lovely dresses for the twins, Maria and Elizabeth, using an old but decent outfit given to them by the mistress. As Dolores sat sewing, Gary tended to his leg with ointment provided by the same mistress. She knew he had fought for the South, had been wounded, captured, escaped and re-enlisted. But the war was nearing its end, and after the surrender, he came home. Out of respect for him, the mistress occasionally helped the children, but didn't publicise it.

Gary didn't like to talk about the war, especially about that unfortunate captivity. He had only spent one night as a prisoner of war, but it left an indelible impression on him. On April 1, 1865, during the battle at Five Forks, their convoy was attacked by Union soldiers. They repelled the first attack, but the enemy regrouped, flanked them and attacked again. This time luck deserted the Confederates. Among the first casualties was the captain in charge of the convoy, which threw their ranks into disarray, exploited by the attackers. Several people died, many were wounded, including Gary. Fate spared some, but they had no choice but to surrender. After receiving first aid, they were put on wagons with other prisoners and sent deep into Union territory. There, they were placed in a barn under guard.

What struck Gary the most was that the raiding party was led by a black corporal, and many of them were black. This corporal had ordered his men to provide first aid to the wounded enemy soldiers. Gary had a leg wound after a bullet tore a chunk of flesh from his thigh. Although not serious he had lost a fair amount of blood. While bandaging his thigh, one of the black soldiers said to Gary: "Here we are, both black, yet fighting against each other. I fight for freedom! I want to be free, to live in my country and have the same rights as whites. So, tell me, what do you fight for?"

Momentarily, Gary couldn't answer that question. But he thought about it all night: "Indeed, what was he fighting for? For his family and little son? For the Confederacy? For his cotton plantation owner?"

While everyone slept soundly, Gary was nudged in his shoulder. Eyes stared at him and a white row of teeth gleaming even in the dark. It was the soldier who had helped him. He silently put a finger to his lips and quietly beckoned Gary to follow him. In the corner of the barn, behind a pile of hay, was a small hole, but large enough to crawl through. His nocturnal guest crept through first, then helped Gary squeeze out gesturing him to follow silently.

It was dark, but his new friend knew the area and carefully navigating the route to Gary's freedom. They walked in silence for a while. Gary could barely keep up because his leg still bled and was painful. On several occasions the corporal stopped and waited for him to catch up. He found a sturdy stick and quietly handed it to Gary to support himself. It made walking much easier. The moon emerged from behind the clouds, illuminating everything around them.

His new friend stopped and, pointing towards the woods, said: "That's it, you go on alone from here. Your units are over there."

Then added: "Remember what I told you yesterday. The war will soon be over. You no longer have the strength or resources to continue fighting us. It's up to each of us to decide the country in which we'll live: a country of slaves and masters or a free country. It's hard for you, southern black people to understand us. But remember, once you taste freedom, you'll never want to be a slave again and I'm ready to die for that. Alright, go, brother. God willing, we'll see each other after the war."

He turned and quickly walked away towards his unit.

"What's your name?" Gary shouted after him.

"Nathaniel. My name is Nathaniel," he heard from the darkness.

Illustration by Oleksand Prodan

In the morning, Gary made his way to his army's position. As a wounded soldier he was sent to the rear for treatment. After a month, Gary decided to return to his unit, but not to continue fighting. He saw that the war was coming to an end and sought an opportunity to meet Nathaniel and thank him. His leg would heal only occasionally reminding him of the pain he had endured. The commander didn't take Gary back into the unit, everyone understood that the war was lost. A few days later, General Lee surrendered. The Confederacy ceased to exist and, subsequently, slavery was abolished.

Gary returned to his hometown, where his wife and young son awaited him. He barely remembered his parents because they were separated from him when Gary was still little and he hadn't heard anything about them. He was raised by others and, from childhood, became accustomed to serving white people.

Two years before the war began, he met Dolores and they quickly became lovers, meeting secretly before deciding to marry. Since they were slaves, they had to ask their respective masters' permission to marry. Fortunately, permission was granted and they married in a local church where a black pastor served. The birth of their first child was a true celebration for the couple. Although they understood that their son was born a slave, they nurtured a hope that he would have a happy, opportunity-filled life ahead. They believed that their son would grow up free, unlike his parents, and would never remember slavery.

Jonathan grew up a clever boy. From early childhood, he helped his parents with farm work. Then Nathaniel appeared, and a year later, Christopher was born. As the older brother, Jonathan always helped his mother care for the babies. He fed, changed and taught them to take their first steps when the time came. Jonathan paid special attention to this, because he believed that a person becomes a human when they start walking on their own. The birth of the twins, Mary and Elizabeth, was such a significant event for him that everyone in the house immediately understood: the girls had a real protector who wouldn't let anyone hurt them. In their turn the girls gravitated towards him, feeling his affection and love. Dolores smiled indulgently when the younger siblings rushed to Jonathan.

He studied at a school for black children only, but didn't pay an attention about it. The main thing for him was he had the opportunity to learn, so he eagerly absorbed knowledge. Their teacher, Mr Jenkins taught literacy, mathematics, history and geography. Jonathan was fascinated by him. He always wondered how much the teacher knew and how easily he imparted his thoughts to the students, who sat and listened to him in awe. Jonathan wanted to learn as much as possible and dreamed of continuing his education after finishing school to become a doctor. But he kept his ambition a secret from everyone and diligently and joyfully studied hard. His commitment to his studied was rewarded when he was deservedly considered the best student in school. Simultaneously, he started taking banjo lessons from his neighbour, a black carpenter named Billy, who lived alone without children and was happy to teach Jonathan.

Illustration by Oleksand Prodan

Jonathan's parents initially treated his enthusiasm without much interest, there was always enough trouble in the house without it. But one day, Gary passed by the local church and saw a crowd of adults and children joyfully singing to the sounds of music. How surprised he was to see his son sitting on the steps and singing a song to the accompaniment of a banjo. Jonathan noticed his father and momentarily hesitated, but seeing approval in his eyes, he played with even greater fervour.

That evening, they talked for a long time, sitting on the cart behind the house. There was a small bundle of fragrant hay left there and, setting comfortably, they communicated for the first time like two adult men. The sky was incredibly starry that evening, and these two kindred souls spoke to each other, looking at the stars, as if addressing the universe. Jonathan was only fifteen, but for his age, he expressed himself quite wisely. Therefore, Gary was pleasantly surprised to hear the reflections of his son. Due to his work, he couldn't devote enough attention to raising his children. Dolores took care of this, as she spent most of her time at home. Now, listening to how maturely and adult-like Jonathan talked about his vision of life and future plans, Gary was overjoyed with parental love for having such a wonderful son.

Illustration by Oleksand Prodan

"Remember, son," Gary said towards the end of their conversation. "The most important thing for a person is freedom. It's something that cannot be measured. It's something you can't see or touch. It's the breath for our soul. For a person born free, it's very difficult to grasp that they possess an invaluable treasure – freedom. They take it for granted. But I spent most of my life in slavery and can tell you, there is nothing sweeter in the world than freedom. Treasure it, son, and don't let anyone encroach upon it."

The next day, they found Jonathan in the woods nearby. He was hanging by his feet from an old tree. Beneath him was a large puddle of blood swarming with flies. The sheriff arrived and ordered the men present to take down the body and lay it on the ground. Everyone was silent, waiting for the sheriff to speak. Those standing around the body knew those responsible, but none uttered a word.

"Take him to his parents. Let them bury him as they see fit. Also I would like to ask you to keep your tongues still!" the sheriff stated loudly before swiftly turning his horse and riding off.

Gary and Dolores stood silently beside the freshly dug grave. Bitter tears rolled down their cheeks, and a lump formed in their throats. Unbearable pain turned them into stoic statues. The death of their firstborn struck such a blow that it robbed them both of speech.

"We will go to live in the North," Gary broke the silence first. "I will find Nathaniel, and he will help us settle. I don't want to lose the rest of our children."

"But what about Jonathan?" Dolores asked, looking at the grave.

"He's already home. He no longer needs anything from us," Gary replied.

"In this country, we have no place. We will always be second-class citizens," Dolores responded sadly.

"No, I believe that one day everyone will have equal rights, regardless of skin colour or beliefs. No one will ever speak of slavery again," Gary said, clenching his fists in pain.

By morning, the wagon loaded with their modest belongings, was already rolling northward along the road. They were heading towards a new life, to a place where free people lived.

Vaino

"Get up, the court is in session!" a stern voice boomed across the packed courtroom and people rose silently.

Vaino also stood up without haste. He was prepared for the court's decision, aware of the sentence he would now hear and thus, surveyed the audience with indifference. Looking out the window where the bright June sun shone, he thought about how soon he would not be able to enjoy this ordinary phenomenon anymore. Everyone treated sunrise as something mundane. No one ever thought that there would come a day when you would see the sunrise for the last time. It is one thing not to know that day is coming, but another when you know it is.

He had no doubt for a moment that the judge would give him the death sentence. Vaino's throat was dry, he wanted a drink of water, but couldn't ask anyone, as everyone was listening intently to the judge address the court. Fragments of the accusation reached him: "due to aggravating circumstances," "with cruelty," and the like, but he couldn't concentrate on the accusation. He kept thinking about the sunrise, its enchanting and unique beauty. Also he thought about Luisa. The one who managed to touch his soul and stir up deep emotions in him.

"What happened to her? How is she? Did the police harm her because of me? Since I was arrested, I haven't heard a word from her. I wish I could see her one more time," he thought.

Young man also felt very ashamed because during all the time they spent together, he never once revealed his real name. Vaino flinched. The judge's voice went from monotone to clear and sharp.

"In the name of the Republic, the defendant is sentenced to death by hanging. The sentence is final and not subject to appeal, to be carried out on the third day after the sentence is pronounced," said the judge, closing the file and, glancing disdainfully at Vaino, left the room.

"I have three days," thought Vaino. "That's so much time."

He scanned the courtroom and suddenly, he saw a woman wearing a headscarf and sunglasses. It was her, Luisa. She took off her sunglasses, looked at him, and whispered something. Vaino understood what she had said. Those were the three cherished words that he heard from a woman for the first time and that warmed his soul so much.

"I love you too, Luisa! Farewell!" Vaino managed to shout and then the guards approached, placed handcuffs on his wrists before escorting to the car that transferred him to court from prison earlier that morning.

Vaino committed his first murder at the age of seventeen. Back then, in a street fight, he hit that guy so hard that he fell and hit his head on a concrete curb. Vaino immediately realised what had happened. The guy twitched oddly and froze, and a dark red stain began to spread from under his head. Vaino was scared and disappeared from the city. He went to his grandmother's village for three weeks. Luckily, she always waited for him and was incredibly happy to see him. His grandfather had long passed away, and his grandmother lived alone. She was delighted to see him despite the unannounced visit. Old woman was unaware of his criminal background and did not ask him awkward questions. She cherished every minute of his presence and was happy to cook

Illustration by Oleksand Prodan

his favourite childhood food. He especially liked her fish soup, its taste and smell. Vaino never ate anything tastier than his grandmother's fish soup again.

After three weeks hiding from the authorities at his grandmother's home, Vaino decided to visit the city where he had committed the murder. To his surprise, nobody was looking for him. It was quiet at his mother's house, but she was, unsurprisingly, drunk again. Mom was unaware he had been gone for three whole weeks. That evening, he met his friends, and they told him that the police were investigating the murder, but they hadn't identified him as the killer. Throughout his life, that guy had caused enough trouble for the police and it was clear they preferred to slow things down rather than investigate the circumstances of his death thoroughly.

Vaino stopped worrying about it and returned to normality living life as a street thug. He did not want to study or work. Youngster did odd jobs, before being offered his first "real" job. Walking home one evening after a game of cards stranger approached him.

"How are you, Vaino? Is your mother still drinking?" the nondescript man wearing a grey suit inquired.

"What's it to you?" Vaino replied, clenching his fists and moving towards the uninvited guest.

"Hey, easy there, friend," the stranger smiled.

"I've heard you're a hot-blooded guy! But look, don't act rashly. Everything needs to be approached with a cool head. Otherwise, you might end up killing someone else," the man smirked slyly and winked at him.

Inside, Vaino felt a chill and looked around anxiously. But there was no one else on the street besides them.

"Don't worry, I'm not from the police," said the stranger. "I need to talk to you."

"About what?" Vaino asked nervously, barely moving his dry lips.

"We've been observing you for a while. We need someone for special assignments. Your lifestyle, ambition, unconventional thinking and physical abilities perfectly meet our requirements. You can earn well. You'll help your mother recover from alcoholism and your grandmother also needs your help. It's hard for her to live alone in the village."

The stranger winked again and Vaino realised this meeting wasn't coincidental.

"Who are you?" Vaino finally asked.

"You shouldn't know who we are," replied the stranger. "I'll find you in a few days and you'll give me an answer."

"I agree," replied Vaino, not understanding why he agreed so quickly. Perhaps his innate adventurous spirit pushed him to make such a decision. He was always drawn to danger and mystery. Without adrenaline in his blood, he couldn't live.

A second meeting with the nameless person took place. The stranger told him what he wanted him to do, how they would communicate, he would receive a generous advance payment for each assignment. That's how Vaino started his new dangerous but financially rewarding life. A life known only to him. He no longer roamed the streets with friends. He enrolled in jiu-jitsu lessons with a renowned master who had spent many years in the East studying this martial art. He disappeared into the library, studying books on criminology. He was intrigued by everything related to methods of killing and erasing crime scenes.

Vaino prepared and awaited his first task. Once the instructions and details were outlined to him he carried it out efficiently and with ease. His second and third tasks followed swiftly and were executed professionally. He always improvised and approached each job as a creative process, if murder could be called creativity. For each victim, he determined the method and tools of murder. His arsenal included firearms, strangulation and poisons. But he had a particular passion for cold weapons, considering them the most reliable and silent murder tools. His jiu-jitsu trainer had told him a lot about how ancient warriors treated cold weapons, how they used them and what types of weapons existed. He even showed him his collection of swords brought from the East.

Vaino was particularly fascinated by small throwing knives, shurikens, which resembled snowflakes. He had a special fondness for them. They fitted easily in the palm and, seemingly harmless, turned into a ruthless and silent weapon when skilfully flung. Vaino disliked noise, so he always tried to complete tasks while attracting as little attention as possible. He always attached a silencer to a pistol if a gun was required for an execution. The only thing he didn't like about his work were dogs. Once, in his childhood, he was severely bitten by a stray mutt. Since then, he avoided them. Now they interfered with his work. One day, to access his client, Vaino had to poison his dog. The huge Doberman didn't let anyone near its owner. Vaino did everything at a time when the dog's owner, overwhelmed by the death of his beloved pet, lost his vigilance.

Gradually, the young man got used to his role. He never repeated himself and constantly perfected his skills. Money became plentiful and Vaino was able to send his mother to treatment at a private clinic. He visited his grandmother infrequently, though he loved her with his childhood affection and enjoyed being with her. To him, she was the keeper of childhood memories. His grandmother categorically refused to take money from her grandson. Therefore, he arranged with neighbours to look after the old lady and left them money for various needs.

Months and years passed. Vaino became a professional in his trade. The geography of his orders expanded beyond the borders of the republic. The clients were satisfied and, sometimes, he felt like he had become an arbiter of human destinies. This lifestyle might have continued for an exceptionally long time but love intervened. One summer's day he met Luisa.

Walking passed a flower kiosk he heard a woman's lively and carefree voice targeting passing potential customers. Vaino was intrigued and decided to investigate. Having spotted the girl with red hair and green eyes enthusiastically selling flowers he froze on the spot. Vaino stood and watched her until she noticed him nearby coyly observing her.

"Well, are we just standing here not buying flowers?" she asked.

Illustration by Oleksand Prodan

"Or maybe there's no special person to buy flowers for such a shy guy?" she added, laughing sincerely.

Young man was surprised by her openness, and although his confusion lasted briefly, it seemed like an eternity to him. The girl herself was like a flower among flowers. Besides her, he saw no one around. He bought all the flowers on her stall and in an automatic romantic gesture, gave them back to her. Then it was her turn to be surprised because she had never had such customer before. That's how they met and started dating.

Vaino didn't know what was happening to him. His was a whirlwind romance. The well-established singleton's life began to crumble, but he didn't mind. He ran to Luisa for dates like a boy and always parted from her with regret. He knew that in his profession romantic attachment was unacceptable. Vaino always worked alone. Throughout the year, he wore leather gloves to avoid leaving fingerprints accidentally. He regularly moved residence, changed his appearance and his daily habits, never using the services of the same mistress twice. But here everything was different. Vaino's soul seemed to blossom, and he undoubtedly enjoyed this feeling. He continued to receive orders, but each time, it became harder for him to leave her. Vaino began to think about stepping away from his line of work. Fortunately, he had more than enough money, so buying a house was not a problem. Just choose a country to your liking.

That morning, he awoke earlier than her. Sunlight filled the room. The open window ensured a steady flow of fresh air and the curtains moved back and forth in the gentle breeze. Birds tweeted energetically in advance of a new near perfect day. Vaino couldn't take his eyes off Luisa, sleeping peacefully. He ran his hand over her supple chest, traced his finger around her nipple and joyfully noticed how she smiled in her sleep. He loved waking her up this way and she loved it too. Vaino continued to caress her body, but he felt troubled. Over the past few weeks, he couldn't shake the feeling that something was slipping out of his control. He tried to distract himself from these thoughts, but they kept returning to him.

"Damn it!" Vaino shouted to himself. His hand froze on Luisa's stomach. "Damn. What an idiot I am. They've been tracking me. I should have paid attention to that beggar homeless man on the street corner. He was never there before. I'm sure that's the same beggar who met me on the street when I was leaving the communicator with the next assignment."

Seconds of confusion turned into cold calculation.

"Yes, I need to leave urgently. I won't wake Luisa. I don't think they will touch her. Also what can she say? She doesn't even know my real name."

Vaino quietly got out of bed, dressed quickly and walked to the door.

"The street is probably under surveillance. I need to go through the back door," he told himself. Closing it behind him he purposefully walked to the exit in the backyard. He knew how to move silently and could see well in the dark, like a cat. There was no light in the hallway, but he passed through it without any problems. He opened the door to the street and at the same time as the sunbeam that blinded him, he received a powerful blow to the head. Then someone pounced on him, pressing hard between his shoulder blades and clicked handcuffs on his hands.

"Well, that's it. Sorry, Luisa," thought Vaino before losing consciousness.

Before his execution, Vaino was placed in a windowless, unlit cell. For him, this was an unbearable torture. He couldn't watch the sunrise through the prison window, so morning blurred into evening, and he lost track of time. Moreover, he hardly slept and spent all his time thinking. His thoughts were not about approaching death, but about childhood. Vivid images flashed by when he spent time in a fishing village with his grandparents. He often walked with his grandmother to the dock to see off his grandfather. Then they would come back and wait on the shore for his return, staring at the horizon. It was the happiest time in his life.

The latch clanked and the creaking cell door opened. Accompanied by a guard, a priest entered, Bible in hand.

"Son, today you will stand before our Heavenly Father. Wouldn't you like to confess your sins?" asked the priest.

Vaino silently sat up from the cot and looked him in the eye.

"No, holy Father. I don't need intermediaries in my communication with God. Since I will meet Him today, I will personally tell Him everything," Vaino smiled unconvincingly.

"Well, as you wish, my son," said the priest, exiting quickly.

At the door, he turned and said: "When you see Him, give my regards."

"Okay, I will," said Vaino wryly. His attempt at sarcasm fooled nobody.

"Father, may I ask you to fulfil one request? A final request?"

"Yes, my son, ask."

"Do you have a paper and a pencil?"

"No, but I will ask the guard," replied the priest.

He returned to the cell and handed over a sheet of paper and a pencil. Vaino wrote a few words. He folded the paper and said: "At the corner of the main street, near the park entrance, there is a flower kiosk. The florist there is called Luisa. Please give this note to her."

"Very well, I will do as you ask," said the priest and disappeared through the door.

Instead, the prosecutor entered the cell. He produced a copy of the verdict and began to read it aloud. After announcing it, he said: "According to our rules, the poison will be brought to you. You will be left alone for one hour. If you choose to go voluntarily, you may drink the poison. If not, the sentence will carried out by hanging as soon as the time expires."

The prosecutor returned to the door and signalled to the guard. He brought in a cup with a clear liquid and a burning candle and placed everything on the table. The door closed and darkness filled the cell. Vaino stared at the cup, in which the flame of the candle flickered, and thought: "Nothing is eternal on this earth. Now my last hour has come."

He reached out towards the table but could not bring himself to take the poison.

"You coward. It's one thing to kill others, but a whole different matter to kill oneself."

He stood in front of the table for the hour, looking at the flickering candle. Upon hearing the sound of the bolt and cell door opening, he looked away from the candle and the cup. The prison warden and two guards stood at the threshold.

"No one has ever used this privilege in my memory," said the prison warden. Then added: "Follow me."

Accompanied by the guards, Vaino went out into the prison yard. An imposing wooden platform with a pole and a crossbar dominated the area. A thick rope with a noose dangled from the crossbar.

"What time is it now?" Vaino asked the guard.

"Six thirty."

"Morning or evening?"

"Morning," the guard answered, not surprised at all.

"So, this is my last sunrise," the sentenced thought, watching the sun's rays piercing through the clouds over the prison yard.

"How good that I was able to see it one last time."

The guards led him to the platform, tied his hands behind his back, put a cloth bag over his head, and then pulled the noose over it. One of the guards checked if the noose was securely placed around his neck and nodded satisfactorily to the other guard. The latter tied the end of the rope to the hook on the pole and stood behind the lever next to the platform.

"I should have read some prayer if I knew any," Vaino thought, but at that moment the prison warden gave the signal and one of the guards raised

Illustration by Oleksand Prodan

the lever upwards. A trapdoor opened under the condemned man's feet and his body plummeted down.

On a sunny Sunday morning, Luisa prepared for work, arranging freshly cut flowers in vases. She loved her job and had been involved in floral cultivation for a long time. But lately, she had been coming to work without enthusiasm. Her whole life had been turned upside down. She had fallen in love with a hired killer, responsible for dozens of lives. A person who was to be hanged today. A person whose real name she only learned when he ended up in prison. She genuinely loved him, but the feeling of being deceived and betrayed wouldn't let her go.

"Luisa?" someone called out to her.

She looked up. A priest stood before her.

"Yes, it's me. What do you need, Father? Are you looking for flowers?"

He silently approached and handed her a folded piece of paper.

"May the Lord accept his soul," he said and, turning around, walked into the park.

Luisa unfolded the note, her heart pounding with excitement.

"Forgive me, my love! I owe you an apology. You were the same beam of light that illuminated my path in the darkness. I want you to live your life happily and safely. Do you remember that little house by the sea? In the windowsill, where the flowers stood, you'll find everything you need. Farewell! See you in another life. Your Matias."

Thomas

"Thomas, you beast, did you steal the sausage again? I'm going to kill you! Where are you?" the hysterical scream of the mistress suddenly rang out from the kitchen.

"Oh-oh-oh!" thought the cat and decided to get out of harm's way. He jumped out the window and went to the backyard, while the mistress's screams were still coming from the window.

"Well, think about it, a piece of sausage. Why is she yelling like that? By the way, why did she leave it unattended? Doesn't she know I have a soft spot for sausage?" Thomas tried to justify himself to himself.

"Well, here we are, brought into the world. I wonder how many of us are there? Judging by the voices, there are six of us, including me. How many brothers and sisters? It's so dark around. I'll have to endure until my eyes open. My brothers and sisters probably think it will always be like this for them, destined to live in darkness. But I know there's another life, full of colours and sensations. It's one thing when you see nothing and get used to it. It's another when you know it won't always be like this. Because you know this other life. Well, all that later. Now I need to crawl to mom and look for a nipple. Shouldn't I starve here?" The little one crawled towards the sound of gentle purring in the direction of the mother, bumping into his restless and constantly meowing brothers and sisters.

"Look, he threw something in the water!" shouted one of the boys playing on the riverbank.

He pointed at a man who was quickly walking away from the river.

"Let's fish it out and see," another exclaimed.

The boys rushed into the water. The object floating down the river began to sink gradually and had almost sunk when the quickest boy dived under and retrieved it. He held a canvas sack, tightly tied with a rope, holding it above water and swimming towards the shore. He put the bag on the sand and, breathing heavily, with help of his friends opened the bag. The scene horrified them.

"They are so small," said one of the boys.

At the bottom of the sack lay six motionless fluffy kittens. The boys silently watched them, holding their breath. Everyone knew that unwanted kittens were often drowned, but it's one thing to hear about it, and another to be an unwitting witness to murder. Now, having seen it with their own eyes, each one reflected on their own.

"Look, this ginger one is moving!" another boy shouted.

Illustration by Oleksand Prodan

Indeed, one of the kittens showed signs of life. The boy who had pulled the sack out of the water carefully picked it up and placed it between his palms, trying to warm it up in this way. The kitten, feeling someone's attention, turned its blind little face towards the sound and gave a faint squeak.

"I'll take it home," the rescuer said. "Let's bury the others here, on the shore by that willow tree."

The boys dug a small grave, gently laid the dead kittens to rest and covered them with soil. They put a stick on top of the grave, stood quietly for a while before going home.

That's how the little one ended up in this family. The boy's mother did not scold him and allowed the kitten to stay. She found an old baby bottle with a nipple in a storeroom, gave it to her son and said: "Now, this is your responsibility. I used to feed you from this bottle. Now you feed your little son."

The mother smiled and stroked her son on the head. She was glad that her only son was growing up to be a kind and caring person. The boy's father had left them when he was only three years old, and since then she had been raising her son alone, trying to instil the best human qualities in him. Now, watching her son take care of the kitten with caution and responsibility, she was secretly happy and thought about how she had succeeded in raising a decent person.

The days passed and the boy diligently cared for his new friend. He was fascinated to watch it suck milk from the bottle and make its first attempts to stand on its weak legs.

Finally, the moment came when through a half-open slit in its eyes, the kitten saw the light.

"At last," it thought. "I can't stand this darkness anymore".

A few days later, its eyes fully opened, and through the haze, it could make out its rescuer, whom it had already recognised by voice.

"So that's what you are like. It is you I owe my life to?" it said to itself, staring into the boy's face.

The boy was immensely happy to see the kitten looking at him.

"I will name you Thomas," said the boy. "I like that name."

"Why Thomas and not, for example, Nathaniel?" the kitten tried to protest, but the boy stuffed a bottle of milk into its mouth and the kitty eagerly began to suckle the milk, purring with pleasure. Weeks passed, followed by months. Thomas grew and often caused his mistress trouble. Sometimes he would dig up the dirt in the flowerpot, steal something from the table, or tear the curtains. The woman scolded him, but she never hit him. The cat knew she loved him, so he preferred to wait somewhere until her anger subsided. Then he would appear and start rubbing against her legs, hoping for leniency.

At first, she would mutter something like: "What, you came, you scoundrel? I'll teach you a lesson. You'll learn not to misbehave."

But Thomas knew that in a few minutes, she would pick him up and start tenderly stroking behind his ear. In that moment, the cat would have given anything for such pleasure. Thomas often slept with her in bed. He especially liked sleeping on her chest. Listening to the calming beat of her heart and the breasts rising with her breathing excited him. He didn't understand what exactly excited him at that moment. Thomas felt that he had touched a woman's breasts before.

This elastic softness and scent revealed pleasant thoughts. The cat began to purr and think about the little feline he had seen recently. She had just appeared in the neighbourhood. Her owners had moved to their street just a few days ago. Once, returning from another 'inspection' of his territory, he noticed her. She was lying on the porch, basking in the sun. Thomas froze for a moment when he saw her. She looked at him with her emerald eyes, and they seemed to magnetically draw him in. It felt like he was falling into an abyss. Since then, Thomas thought only of this fluffy, green-eyed neighbour. He didn't know how to approach her. With other cats, it was simple, and he never lingered his attention on any of them. Thomas's offspring had long been running around the outskirts, but he wasn't particularly bothered by that. This one was special; he felt awkward around her. Thomas wasn't afraid to fight with the neighbouring cats, sometimes even engaging in fights with dogs, including the neighbour's Doberman who fiercely hated him. But here, his bravery disappeared. Thomas felt like the same helpless kitten his owner's son had rescued from the river.

Despite his tough image, Thomas was very romantic and sentimental. But he tried to hide this from those around him. After all, he was the master of the adjacent territory and needed to maintain the image of a hard guy. So, no one had any idea that his favourite activity was watching butterflies in the backyard of the house where he lived.

Illustration by Oleksand Prodan

There, the mistress had created a kind of earthly paradise. She loved to grow flowers and was very good at it. Her flowers bloomed from early spring to late autumn. As some faded, others began to bloom right away, creating a continuous cycle of flowering. The garden attracted a large number of insects. Here, bees collected nectar, intently working over the blossoming flowers. Bumblebees also visited, buzzing heavily, slowly and solemnly moving from plant to plant. But what particularly fascinated Thomas were the butterflies. There were countless numbers of them. Large and small, colourful and monochrome, their aerial dances created an illusion of tranquillity.

It was so mesmerizing that Thomas could watch them forever. He felt he too could fly and any moment soar above the flower bushes. Once the cat was so engrossed in watching them that he didn't notice when a large butterfly landed right on his nose. Taken by surprise, he was so flustered that he stopped breathing for a moment. The butterfly fluttered its patterned wings. The cat looked at it closely appearing like a mythical dragon about to open its maw and scorch him with fiery breath. But after a short while, the butterfly took off and flew high up into the sky.

Having watched enough butterflies, Thomas decided to approach the green-eyed kitty. He walked leisurely, dreaming about how he would go up and talk to her, tell her everything he had been thinking about these days. Then, he would invite her to his backyard and watch the dance of the butterflies together. An unstoppable desire to meet her filled Thomas's soul. He could think of nothing but her. As he walked, he was unaware that just yesterday, a neighbour, whose yard Thomas crossed, had acquired another Doberman, and these two had entirely different plans for the brazen redhead who so boldly roamed their yard.

Illustration by Oleksand Prodan

Taro

Everything was prepared for the ritual of seppuku[1]. Taro decided that he would conduct it tomorrow, at the first rays of the morning sun. His comrade Yoshiro Matsumoto agreed to be his kaishaku[2]. In the morning, he would hand him his katana[3], the one his father had given him before being sent to the front, which in turn had been passed down to him from his grandfather, and his grandfather from his great-grandfather. His grandfather, Ketsuo Ishikawa, commanded a destroyer in His Imperial Majesty's fleet and during the war of 1904-1905, his ship sank an enemy cruiser and damaged several other vessels. The Emperor awarded him the Order of the Rising Sun. Taro paused for a moment. He would not disgrace the honour of his ancestors and would leave life with dignity. They would be proud of him, for honour was above everything else for their family. But all this would happen tomorrow. For now, Taro sat on a mat in the corner of the caponier, closed his eyes, and remembered his childhood and youth.

---

[1] Seppuku, also known as hara-kiri, is a ritual of suicide among samurais, in which the person performing it cuts their stomach with a special knife or sword.
[2] Kaishaku — an assistant to the one performing seppuku.
[3] Katana — a samurai sword.

Taro was born into a family of hereditary military men. He was the eldest son, so a military career was never in doubt. From childhood, he prepared for a job in the army and was not interested in anything else. Unlike his ancestors, who were exclusively naval officers, Taro decided to become an officer in His Imperial Majesty's land forces. When he told his father, after some thought, he said: "You are a man and it is up to you to make independent decisions. Be worthy of the glory of your ancestors and serve our Emperor faithfully. I will send you to the cadet corps. There you will go through a good school and gain the skills and knowledge necessary to enter the Imperial Army Academy."

At twelve years old, Taro crossed the threshold of the cadet corps, where he wore a military uniform for the first time. He vividly remembered that sunny day. Cadets and their instructors were lined up in the courtyard. The corps commander, Takeshi Nakamura, welcomed everyone to the start of the academic year, wished them success, and expressed hope that the cadets would withstand all upcoming tests with honour. Taro was overwhelmed with pride, and the excitement made his head spin. Thus began his challenging journey toward his dream. The Way of the Warrior.

At fourteen years of age, his father came to visit and said: "It's time to learn something new."

With permission from the school's headmaster, he took Taro and they drove to the outskirts of the city. Soon, they stopped in front of tall gates and his father knocked on the door. They were quickly opened, and a small man in a kimono appeared on the doorstep.

"We have come to see Sensei Keitashi," his father announced.

The man silently bowed and let them into the courtyard. A moment later, a tall man in an elegant kimono came out. He wore leather zōri[4] on his feet.

"Good afternoon, Sensei," the father and the man bowed to each other.

"This is my son Taro. He is studying at the cadet school and intends to become an army officer. I want you to teach him to master the sword."

---

[4] Zōri — a sandals made of cloth, leather, or woven from straw.

"Very well," the sensei replied. "My servant will take him to the armoury and we will go inside the house."

He gave a signal to the man who had opened the door and beckoned Taro to follow him. Taro followed the servant to the back of the house before entering a door on the south side. Inside Taro stopped in amazement. The room turned out to be quite large, more like a spacious living room, with various weapons hanging on the walls. There were crossbows and bows made of bamboo, arrows of different lengths and various tips, as well as primitive firearms used in the middle ages: three-metre muskets fired from fortress walls, arquebuses with a side ignition for firing and various modifications of flintlock pistols. Along one wall was an array of spears and pikes. There were regular yari spears, kama-yari spears resembling a sickle, three-bladed jumonji-yari, curved moon-shaped naginata, shortened nagamaki and much more.

A special place was occupied by the smallest, but no less dangerous weapon – shuriken. These throwing blades came in various shapes and were widely used in ancient times. But most of all, there were swords – adorning an entire wall.

Along the wall on mats stood tables and on them, on special stands, lay swords. There were several dozens of them including a nagamaki with an extremely long handle and a gigantic two metres long odachi sword. The tachi sword attracted attention for its majesty and beauty. Not much shorter were the o-tachi and saya-mati-no-tachi swords. Beside them, the aikuchi knives, tanto and kusungobu seemed toy-like. But the main collection consisted of katanas and their younger brothers – wakizashis.

Among the several dozen swords, no two were alike, as they all differed in the colour of the scabbards, the weaving of the handle, and the pattern of the blade. Wooden bokken swords, mainly used for training, stood there as well. In the corner of the room, Taro saw a mannequin dressed in samurai armour. It wore a helmet with a mask that hid the face, had two swords tucked into its belt, a short one in front and a long one behind, and in its hands, the mannequin held a long naginata halberd, resembling a sword blade mounted on a long pole. The leather and metal plates of its armour showed dents from impacts.

Taro even imagined hearing the sounds of battle: the thudding and neighing of horses, the clinking of swords, the groaning of wounded and dying warriors. It seemed to him that any moment now, the mannequin would come to life and shout its battle cry: "Banzai!"

He was so engrossed that he did not notice when the sensei and his father entered the room.

"Every week, in your free time from classes, you will come here to learn to master the sword," his father said. "You have chosen the path of a warrior and the sword is its soul."

They both bowed to the sensei and left.

Taro eagerly awaited the moment each week when he would return to the sensei. On his first day, the boy approached the sacred gates, the familiar servant admitted him and silently led the boy to a small room where he gestured to change clothes. They proceeded to the familiar armoury room, where Master Keitashi awaited him. The teacher had a katana tucked into his belt. Taro bowed in greeting and stood in anticipation.

"What is the most important thing in swordsmanship?" the master asked at the start of the training.

The boy thought for a moment and replied: "Strength and reaction?"

"These are important qualities," the master agreed. "But the most critical aspect of swordsmanship is the technique of drawing the sword from the scabbard."

He nodded to the servant, who brought a katana and, bowing, handed it to Taro. Taro, also bowing, accepted it and tucked it into his belt as the sensei had shown.

The teacher continued: "It is also important how you stand. Your back must be straight, your legs slightly bent, and your arms relaxed, hanging down and ready to act. You must be able to draw the sword quickly from

Illustration by Oleksand Prodan

any position: whether you are standing, kneeling, or even sitting. Now the servant will clap his hands, and at that signal, we will draw our swords, standing opposite each other."

The servant clapped his hands. Taro had just grasped the handle when he saw the blade of the sensei's sword in front of his nose.

"Whoever draws the sword faster, wins, remember this," Master Keitashi said.

Weeks and months of training passed. Taro could not remember how many times he had drawn his sword from its scabbard, probably thousands.

But the day came when his speed satisfied the master, and they moved on to training fights with swords. For this, they used wooden bokken. At first glance, this sword seemed like a child's toy, but in skilled hands, it transformed into a formidable weapon. Taro understood this during his first training session when he received several painful hits with the bokken. Over time, they began training with real combat weapons, and when he entered the military academy, Taro was a master of the sword. The young man constantly improved his skills under the sensei's supervision, for which the usually sparing-with-praise Keitashi often commended him for his diligence and achievements. Taro invented new exercises for himself. He particularly liked sitting on the ground, tossing a cherry above him, and then jumping up to split it in half. The juice of the berry remained on the blade of his sword, and it seemed to him like the traces of an enemy's blood.

Immediately after finishing the cadet corps, Taro was admitted to the military academy of the Imperial army. There, he was to study for two years before being sent to the troops. Then, after serving eight months, he would continue his studies to receive, after twenty months, the rank of senior sergeant and an assignment to a permanent post.

Learning came easily to him. The skills acquired in the cadet corps greatly helped him here. These cadets notably stood out from other students who came after finishing general education schools. He absorbed knowledge like a sponge: drill and firearms training, fortification and sapper work, foreign languages and hand-to-hand combat – everywhere Taro tried to be among the best. This did not go unnoticed by the academy's command.

He was one of the first to be prematurely granted the rank of sergeant. Taro was respected not only by his classmates but also by the upper-class men who had returned to finish their studies after serving in the army.

Taro spent a lot of time with his friend from the senior course, Makoto Nakagawa. Makoto had already served eight months in the army, and Taro always eagerly asked him about his service. Makoto, two years Taro's senior, gladly shared his experiences and was drawn to his younger comrade, noticing his extraordinary abilities and strong character.

When Taro turned eighteen, Makoto suggested visiting a tea house. This proposal was unexpected for Taro, but he agreed. On one of their free days from studying, they went to the eastern part of the city, where tea houses were located. Makoto walked confidently; it was evident that he had been there more than once. They quickly approached the right place. Huge heavy gates were open, and they walked inside. There, in a small house serving as an anteroom, they changed their shoes. Then, along a path laid with stones of various shapes and colours, they walked deeper into the garden, where the chashitsu – the tea house – was located.

The path meandered among various bushes and trees. An incredible fragrance filled the air, as many flowers were in bloom and, at one moment, Taro felt as if this was the road to Paradise. Finally, in the depths of this wonder garden, the little house appeared. On the threshold stood Mistress Katsumi – the hostess of the establishment who, bowing slightly, led the guests into a room enclosed by paper screens. The young men sat down on small cushions and waited. After a few minutes, the paper doors opened, and two girls entered the room. They bowed politely and one moved to a corner of the room where the equipment for the tea ceremony was set up on the floor. The other girl, after bowing again, sat down next to them. Everything happened in complete silence. But if there had been any sounds, Taro probably wouldn't have heard them. He was mesmerized, watching this girl and unable to look away. She was so beautiful that he found himself forgetting to breathe. Her elegant, brightly coloured kimono, the flawless hairstyle woven with flowers, makeup that could be considered a work of art, and those enchanting black eyes. Taro felt like he was drowning in them and had no desire to be saved. But then the tea was ready, the girl stood up and went to the corner of the room. Taro followed her with his eyes. Her kimono was wrapped with an obi[5], painted in mother-of-pearl colours, tied in a special knot at the back – darari[6]. Meanwhile, the ends of the belt hung almost to the ground, resembling butterfly wings when they swayed as she walked. The girl moved in small steps, as if floating above the floor. Her feet were shod in okobo[7] sandals with little bells. As she moved, they tinkled softly, filling the room with a carefree calm. She brought the first cup of tea for Makoto and returned for the second one – for Taro. He took the cup from the beauty's hands, accidentally touching her fingers. The excitement made the young man's face flush with red. The girl noticed this and smiled slightly.

The evening flew by unnoticed. They walked back through the dark streets of the city, each lost in their thoughts. All of Taro's thoughts were about Netsumi, that was the girl's name. He had never felt such excitement before. It seemed to him that he had been in a fairy tale, in some other life existing parallel to the real one. From then on, every morning upon waking, he would say her name, which meant Summer Beauty. Later, Taro dared to visit the tea house again, this time without accompaniment, hoping to see Netsumi again. But that evening, the girl was not there. The hostess explained that Netsumi did not live at the tea house permanently, but rented accommodation elsewhere and told him when to come to meet Netsumi.

---

[5] Obi – a geisha's belt, tied in different styles at the back depending on the tradition and school.
[6] Darari – a knot style where the ends of the belt hang down.
[7] Okobo – a sandals with a wooden base to which bells are attached.

That day, in the morning, Taro woke up an hour before reveille. Indeed, today he would see her! All day during classes the boy thought only of Netsumi and was reprimanded by his teacher for not paying attention. He constantly glanced at the clock and mentally hastened time.

Finally, he was sitting on the mat again with his heart pounding, waiting for the paper doors to open and for her to enter the room. Taro heard the geisha approaching with the tinkle of bells, and his heart almost leaped from his chest. Netsumi entered, bowed to him, and headed to the corner of the room to prepare the tea.

When the tea was ready she handed him a cup of tea: "Thank you for coming, Taro-san."

Taro accepted the cup, his hands trembling slightly.

"Thank you for seeing me again, Netsumi-san. I couldn't stop thinking about our last meeting,"

"It is my pleasure, Taro-san. I hope our time together will bring you some peace before your journey to the army," Netsumi smiled gently.

For a brief moment, they quietly sipped their tea. The warmth of the drink eased Taro's nerves. Netsumi noticed the mix of determination and apprehension in his eyes.

"Mistress Katsumi told me that you were looking to meet me," she said while handing him another cup of tea.

He accepted it with a slight nod.

"Yes, I wanted to see you," Taro replied. "Ever since I met you, I can't think about anything else. All my thoughts are with you."

"Wow, quite the confession for such a young boy. Even an adult man doesn't always dare to say something like that," she said.

"I like the feeling that has arisen within me, but I don't know what to do with it. I will soon be going to the army. Our country is on the brink of war," desperate responded Taro.

They spent the entire evening sitting across from each other, talking. Netsumi proved to be a very interesting conversationalist. Taro could discuss any topic with her.

Before leaving, Netsumi said to him: "If you want to see me, come to my home. I don't live with the other girls. My landlord rents a small house for me nearby."

She explained in detail how to find her place and as a farewell added: "When you see an ikebana with an orchid in the window, it means I am home and waiting for you."

Taro returned home, barely feeling his feet beneath him. Now all his thoughts were about the upcoming meeting with Netsumi. He still smelled her scent, which took his breath away. He spent the entire week as if in a fog. His friends started to look at him worriedly. Only Makoto knew the reason for such striking changes in his behaviour.

One day, meeting Taro in the academy courtyard, he tried to snap his friend back to reality: "I understand you. But you must remember, here we are trained to defend our Homeland and our Emperor, and overly strong emotions hinder this. So remember what is said in the code of Bushido[8]."

Taro understood everything, but he couldn't help himself and ran to the outskirts of the city every free day to the cherished little house to see if there was an ikebana with an orchid in the window. He still remembers the excitement he felt when he first saw that orchid. The young man hesitated for a long time, but finally mustered the courage to knock.

The door opened almost immediately, as if Netsumi was standing behind it, waiting for him.

"Please come in and seat down," said Netsumi. "I will prepare some tea."

Taro walked in deeper and sat down on the mat. He watched the girl without taking his eyes off her. She was wearing the same kimono he had seen

---

[8] Bushido – the code of honour of the samurai.

Illustration by Oleksand Prodan

her in for the first time, but this time everything was different. Taro actually saw a giant butterfly on the girl's back.

Holding his breath, Taro waited, expecting the butterfly to straighten its wings and soar into the sky with Netsumi. He shook his head and surveyed the small, yet very cosy room. The walls were adorned with paintings, and variously shaped and coloured lamps hung from the ceiling. Flowers in diverse arrangements were placed everywhere. Through a large window that opened to the courtyard, a small but well-maintained garden was visible.

"Do you like it here?" Taro jumped, surprised by her question.

"Yes, very much! It's so cosy here. Do you understand flowers, right?"

"I love creating ikebana: each arrangement conveys a mood. Through flowers, you can express your feelings. It's a real science, and I studied it for a long time when I was a maiko[9] at our geisha school. Look, for example, the one you saw in my window. With that ikebana, I wanted to say that this home is happy to see you!" Netsumi laughed.

They drank tea and chatted for a long time. Taro was constantly amazed by the girl's erudition and sharp wit. It seemed there was no topic they couldn't discuss. It was getting dark when Netsumi moved closer to him and ran her hand over his face.

Then she looked him straight in the eyes and said: "You are still very young and you've never had a woman."

It was not a question, but a statement. At these words, Taro's heart began to beat so loudly that she must have heard it too.

"Let's go, I'll show you something," Netsumi whispered, taking the young man by the hand and leading him to the bedroom.

Taro did not remember how he returned to the barracks. Along the way, he bumped into pedestrians several times. Everything was like a fog, as if he

---

[9] Maiko – a geisha apprentice. Distinguished from geisha by a shortened kimono sleeve and a bright red lower collar.

was in another reality. Everything that happened that evening felt like a dream or a hallucination.

Thus, Taro began seeing Netsumi. He spent every weekend with her, except on days when there was no orchid ikebana in the window. Then he walked back disheartened. He knew that Netsumi was kept by a high-ranking official and could do nothing about it. Despite his blind infatuation, Taro well understood that his main goal was to finish the academy. Netsumi also forbade any talk about their future. This went on for four months. Then for several weeks in a row, Taro stopped seeing the desired bouquet in the window. He didn't understand that and was very upset. The young man kept walking around the familiar house, hoping to see the orchid in the window.

One day someone called out to Taro, and he turned toward the voice.

"Are you the one called Taro?" a girl in a fancy kimono clarified.

"Yes, that's me and who are you?" asked Taro.

The girl did not give her name, silently approached the young man, bowed, and handed him a piece of paper rolled into a tube. Then she quickly turned and scurried away along the street. Taro eagerly unrolled the paper and began to read.

"My dear boy, the time has come for us to part ways. Do you remember when I told you about the sakura blossoms? Each year they fade only to bloom again the next. Love is the same: keep it in your heart and in time it will flourish once more. Forgive me for leaving without warning. My master received a promotion and moved to the capital. I must go with him. He has done much for me, for which I am endlessly grateful. Do not look for me. Walk your path with honour. You are the best thing that has ever happened in my life. Yours, Netsumi."

Taro walked home, his tears obscuring his vision. The fairy tale had ended almost before it began.

For some time after Netsumi's disappearance, the young man felt a complete apathy, losing interest in everything.

Makoto watched him closely and one day, when they were alone on the street, grabbed him by the lapels of his uniform and shook him vigorously: "Pull yourself together. You're about to be sent to the army. How will you appear before your commander? Do you want to disgrace your lineage?"

The words of his friend acted like a cold shower on Taro.

"No, anything but that," he thought.

He redoubled his efforts in his studies, trying to make up for lost time, and by the time he was dispatched to the army, no trace of his melancholy remained. Just before being sent to his unit, Taro received a letter. He was surprised, as he seldom received mail. His father sometimes came to visit him and talk with the instructors. His mother sent gifts and letters through him. His fellow cadets were not in the habit of writing.

"My dear boy!"—Taro's heart pounded just as it once had in the tea house, *"I know you will soon be going to the army. Since I left, I haven't forgotten about you for a single minute. All my thoughts were about you, my boy. I will pray for you every day and will always be invisibly by your side. Kisses, your Netsumi."*

He kept that letter until his last day. The letter from his first and only love.

A week later, Taro went to his military unit based on the islands. Six months later, his country entered the war.

In the final year of the war, Taro commanded a unit defending the southern coast of the island. He already held the rank of captain and had been awarded several medals for bravery and courage. There was little strength left, but no one was prepared to surrender. Only about half of his unit remained alive, some wounded, others shell-shocked. However, they managed to repel several enemy amphibious assaults. Each attack began after a massive air raid. They had no air superiority, so all their hopes were pinned on the anti-aircraft batteries. Concrete structures still reliably protected the soldiers, but with each raid, the situation became increasingly difficult. The soldiers dug deeper into the earth, understanding that it was the only way to survive the terrifying air strikes. The fighters battled bravely, but Taro had long understood that victory was not in sight. He had felt this since the first year of the war when, after deciphering their command's plan, the enemy sank four aircraft carriers. This happened when all the planes had taken off to carry out a mission, and the carriers were left almost defenceless. At that time, the enemy directed their bombers and virtually annihilated the floating airfields without opposition. Hundreds of aircraft were destroyed. Pilots, unable to land on the carriers, ditched their planes in the water and died by the dozens. Thus, the elite of the military aviation was decimated, and they never regained air superiority. Even the numerous kamikaze[10], who piloted aircrafts or kaiten torpedoes, could not turn the tide of the war. The enemy was strong and numerically superior and, most importantly, they had practically inexhaustible resources, a constant deficiency for his country.

Yet, the soldiers did not lose spirit. Each time, to repel the enemy, Taro rallied the remnants of his troops for a counterattack. He remembered one of the laws of Bushido – never defend, always attack first. Afterwards, they aided the wounded, collected the bodies of the fallen, and finished off any surviving enemies. Because there could be no mercy for the foes.

Then a nuclear bomb destroyed the city of his childhood. Three days later, there was a second bombing, and it became clear that continuing the war was pointless. A few days after that, an order from the Emperor arrived to cease fire and lay down arms. Hearing about the capitulation, Taro decided to spend the night in prayer and reflection, and the next day, at dawn, to do what he must to preserve his dignity and the honour of his lineage. He would remain faithful to his Emperor until the end.

---

[10] Kamikaze – a suicide warriors who piloted planes, boats, and kaiten torpedoes, directing them at enemy targets.

Just before dawn, Taro took out a small bamboo box. He knew well what lay inside.

Before being sent to the army, his father had handed him the box with the words: "Here lies what will help you preserve the honour of our family. Open it only in the utmost need and not frivolously, for once opened, you can never do so again."

Later, his friend Yoshiro Matsumoto entered the bunker. He had been a loyal comrade and good friend, fittingly as his name meant "good son." Taro handed Yoshiro his will and his sword. They left the bunker. The comrade drew the sword from its sheath and stood behind in the corner of a half-collapsed trench. Taro sat down on the ground, placed the box in front of him, unbuttoned his uniform, and bared his abdomen. The morning star was rising over the ocean.

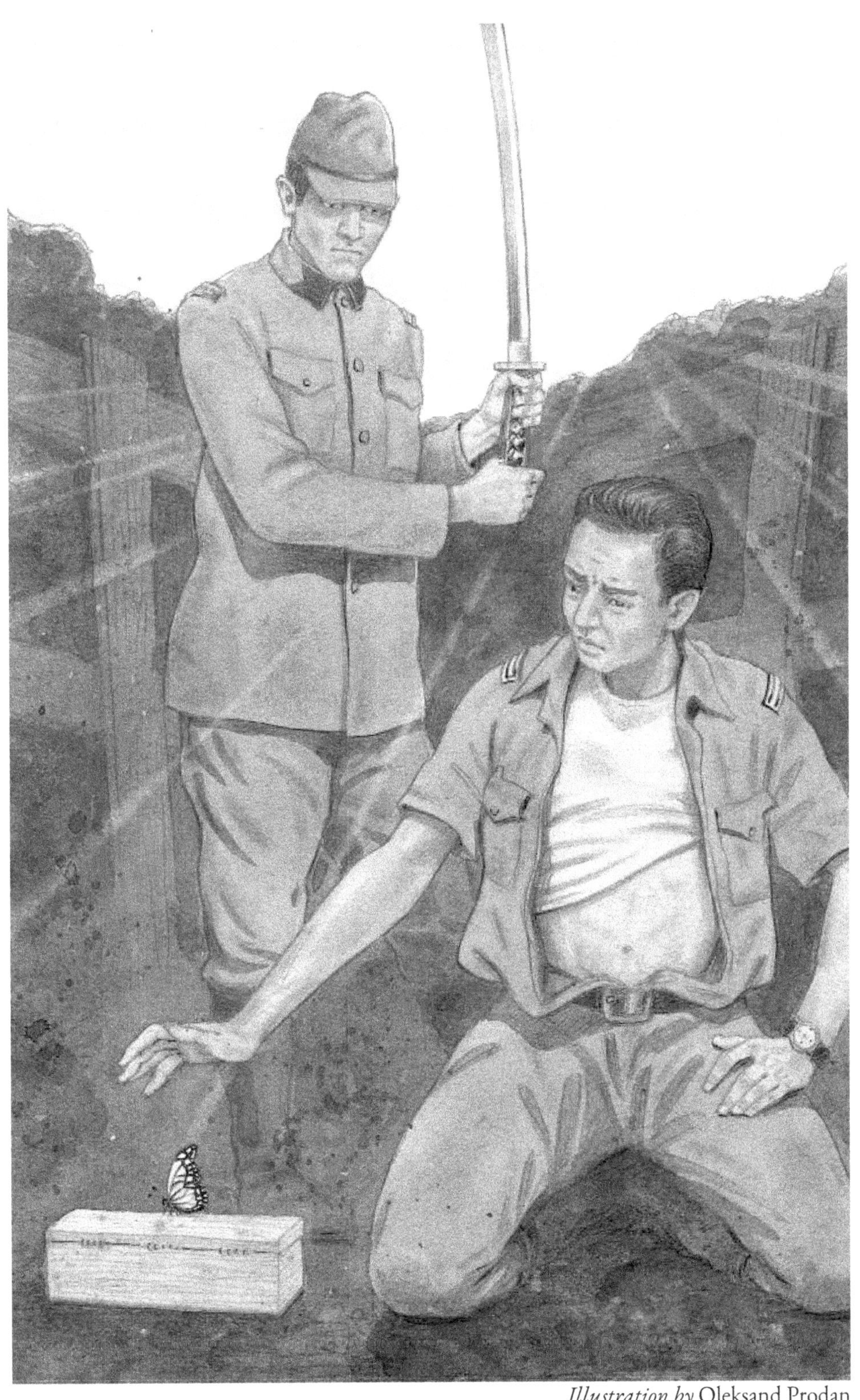

Illustration by Oleksand Prodan

Yoshiro raised the sword and paused in anticipation. Taro reached out to the bamboo box, but unexpectedly, a butterfly landed on it. Taro was surprised, as butterflies usually sleep at this hour, and they were rarely seen during combat operations. The butterfly was large and beautiful. Its wings, shimmering with nacre, reminded Taro of something, but he couldn't quite grasp what. Taro didn't shoo the butterfly away but waited until it flapped its wings and flew to the edge of the parapet, and then he opened the box. Yes, it was it – the sacred kusunigobu knife[11]. Taro drew it from its sheath and waited. As the sun rose from the horizon and the sky lit up with the first rays, Taro placed the knife against the left side of his abdomen, then with force, thrust it into himself and drew it to the right, and, fainting, jerked the knife upwards. Without letting out a breath, he began to lean forward. At that moment, Yoshiro brought down the sword on his neck. The head separated from the torso and, hanging by a piece of skin, fell forward. Taro fell to the ground following it, and a large pool of blood spread beneath him. Then the butterfly, sitting on the parapet, flapped its wings and, making a circle over Taro's body, soared into the heights.

---

[11] Kusunigobu – a special dagger used for performing seppuku.

The baby

"When I come into the world, I will cling to my mommy and listen to her heart, just as I listen now. Its beating lulls me to sleep. I can tell my mom's mood by the beat of her heart. I discern whether she is happy or sad. My mommy is the best in the whole world. I am sure she loves me very much because I am a part of her. I feel how she strokes her belly, and warmth spreads from these touches. Mommy talks to me, and I just smile in response. It's a pity that I cannot yet show her the joy of our communication. It is very cramped here, and I can only nudge her with my little foot or hand, reminding her of my existence. But it's okay – soon I will be born and then I will see her, my mommy, my dear mother!"

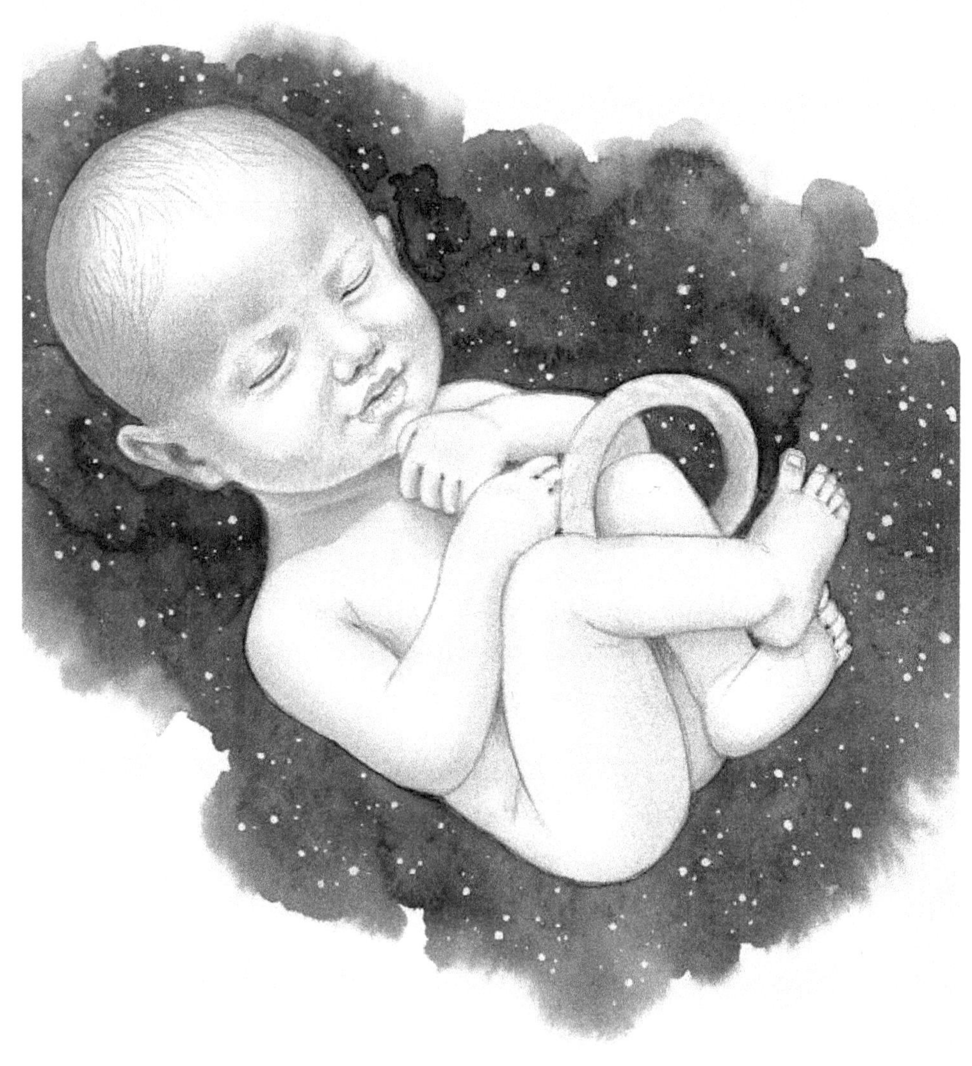

Illustration by Oleksand Prodan

"Paola, hello! Where are you rushing to?" asked the boy on the bicycle.

"Well, Jose is coming back soon, I want to meet him with a tasty dinner. I need to buy some more groceries. You know how much he loves my feijoada and you have asked me for seconds so many times!" laughed Paola and playfully ruffled the boy's hair.

This was Joaquim, her husband's younger brother. Jose loved his brother and was like a father to him. Ever since their parents passed away, he had been raising his brother and the younger one looked up to him. When Jose went to work logging, Joaquim helped Paola around the house. He was ten years younger and did not hide that he was deeply in love with her.

Often at dinner, he would say: "Paola, if Jose ever leaves you, don't worry – I'll marry you!".

Jose would pretend to be jealous and give the little one a light slap and everyone would laugh. Now he saw his sister-in-law and and offered to give her a ride to the market on his bicycle. Paola agreed, since she couldn't get rid of him anyway and would get things done faster.

The shift of forestry workers would soon return after a long stint away from their hometown, and the woman wanted to get everything done before meeting her husband. Jose was deeply missed, so on the days he was home, she tried to make the most of them: taking care and feeding him treats. Often, they would drive from the city to a fishing village where they had a small cottage, an inheritance from Paola's grandfather. There, away from prying eyes, they passionately made love. For what could be better than a sunny morning in bed with your loved one by the ocean? Today she would share the main news with Jose. But first, he needed to be fed, and Paola set about cooking.

"Paola, they're back!" Joaquim yelled through the window, breathless. "I'll go meet them."

"Okay, I'll wait for you," was all Paola managed to say.

She set the table and went outside. In a few minutes, she saw both brothers walking down the street arm in arm. Joaquim was leading his bicycle with his free hand. Jose's bag was hanging on the bicycle. The brothers chatted merrily. She watched them with tenderness. When they reached the house, Joaquim stopped and Jose came over and hugged Paola.

Then he stepped back and, looking into her eyes, quietly said: "How have you been without me, dear? I missed you so much!"

"I've been waiting for you, my love. Come inside. Everything's ready," she replied.

After dinner, Jose asked: "You seem a bit off this time. Is everything alright? Is there anything you want to tell me?"

"You're right, Jose. I have wonderful news for us all," Paola agreed, in turn looking into her husband's eyes. "We're going to have a baby."

Silence descended. Jose froze, staring at his wife, unable to utter a word. The silence was broken by Joaquim: "So I'm going to have a nephew and I can teach him how to play soccer?"

"What if it's a niece?" Jose, smiling, stood up from the table and hugged Paola. "This is the best news I could have heard. I love you, my girl."

That night they didn't sleep until morning. Jose stroked and kissed Paola's belly and whispered funny things to the little person inside, who surely heard them. Paola laughed, and there probably wasn't anyone happier than her in the world. Then they went to the fishing village to enjoy each other's company. Jose was more tender with his wife than ever: he woke up early, prepared breakfast and didn't let her do absolutely anything.

"Now, your main task is our son or, maybe, a daughter," he added thoughtfully.

They sat by the open window, admiring each other.

"What shall we name our boy?" Jose asked.

"Let it be Cristiano and, if it's a girl, then Maria," Paola answered.

"Good, I like that," Jose agreed.

How they wished this could last forever! But the holiday ended and it was time again for parting and waiting for the next meeting. So she lived from one meeting to another.

"I feel how happy my mommy is! Her heart is beating so fast it almost jumps out of her chest. She is so good to me. How lucky I am to have chosen her. I think this man's voice, obviously, belongs to my daddy. I love him too, because without him, I wouldn't exist!" thought the little one, listening to the conversation, *"Oh, how I wish I could see them. But everything has its time. When it comes, I will be able to hug and kiss them. But for now, I must stay in the dark and cramped space."*

"Paola," the doctor paused for a moment. "I have bad news. You have a rare heart disease. It hadn't shown any symptoms until now, but pregnancy has increased the strain on your body. Your child is healthy, but your heart can't handle both. If we don't terminate the pregnancy – you could die and the child will die with you. But this way, at least we can save you."

It was a difficult conversation for the doctor to communicate such devastating news to her.

"Doctor, I want to have this child. I really want to give birth. We've waited for this for so long. How can I look my husband in the eye?" Paola said with a trembling voice.

The doctor shook his head: "I understand everything, but I can't ignore your test results and the cardiogram. You have no chance. The time is also working against you!" He pointed at the clock above his head.

Illustration by Oleksand Prodan

Paola didn't remember how she got home. Everything felt like a dream. Yes, she knew she had the symptoms as described by her physician, but thought it was normal and how all pregnant women felt.

"How will I tell Jose? It would feel like a betrayal," Paola was emotionally shattered at the news she had received and cried helplessly.

Waking up the next morning, Paola decided: "I want this child, no matter what. Jose must not know about the diagnosis. I will pray and ask the Lord to preserve our lives, but if He decides otherwise, then so be it."

With less than two months until Jose's return, Paola decided to change things around the house.

"Everything must be prepared for the baby's arrival," she thought.

So, she threw out all the old things, changed the curtains and asked Joaquim to rearrange the furniture. The house became somehow brighter and cosier. But with each passing day, it became harder for her to manage household chores, she frequently felt short of breath, and rested more often. Joaquim was always ready to help. He didn't need to be asked. Remembering Jose's instructions, he tried to protect his brother's wife from any labour.

However, Joaquim became concerned about her appearance and how tired she had become: "Paola, I don't like how you look. You get tired very quickly, sometimes you're gasping for air. Have you seen a doctor, what did he say?"

"All is well, little brother, it's just how my pregnancy is going. It's normal. Don't worry," Paola reassured him.

"Why don't you run to the market and buy some cassava flour? I'll bake some cakes tomorrow. You love them, right?" she shifted the conversation.

When Joaquim left, Paola placed her hand on her belly. It was already noticeably rounder. She stroked it assuredly: "Everything will be fine, my little one. I love you very much and we all are waiting for you."

The following day Paola woke up feeling anxious. She had nightmares: in her dream she was walking through a forest on a narrow path, carrying some package in her hands, which she somehow believed was a child. Then, at the foot of the mountain, Paola saw a forest glade bathed in sunlight. It was not far to go, but the woman slowed down as if she had stepped into thick mud or even a real swamp because she could barely lift her feet from the ground. Heavy clouds blocked the sunlight, and suddenly horrifying screams emanated from the dense forest.

Paola failed to go back asleep and lay in bed till early morning. As dawn broke, she got up and decided to prepare breakfast for herself and Joaquim.

"I'll bake him some cakes, he loves them so much," thought Paola.

She walked over to the stove, but at that moment the ground under her feet shook and she fell face down on the floor.

"Mommy, what's wrong with you? What happened? Why have you stopped moving? Your little heart is barely beating... Mommy, I feel sick... I can't breathe... Mommy, don't leave me! M-o-o-o-o-m!"

Illustration by Oleksand Prodan

Johan

"That's it, I can't keep silent anymore. Tomorrow I'll confess my love to Jürgen, come what may. I can no longer carry these intense feelings. Of course, he will be shocked, but he needs to know about my affection for him."

Johan kicked through the autumn leaves that thickly carpeted the ground of the city park. The leaves rustled pleasantly underfoot, flipping from one side to the other, creating a unique pattern on the ground.

"Look at these leaves!" Johan thought further. "There are thousands and thousands of them, hundreds of thousands. But you won't find two that are the same: they all differ in colour and shape, even smell differently. Just like people: we are all different and there are no two identical people among us. Even twins differ from each other in character and habits. Yes, I was born different from everyone else and what now? Do I not have the right to love?" Johan pondered.

He knew that not long ago in his country, people like him were sent to "re-education" camps. Few returned alive, let alone re-educated. Though the war had ended almost twenty years ago, in people's minds nothing had changed regarding someone like Johan. He knew he was taking a big risk, but he couldn't hold back anymore. Tomorrow. Everything would be decided tomorrow.

Illustration by Oleksand Prodan

"Jürgen!" Johan called out to the tall blonde young man who was descending the university stairs. "We need to talk."

"Hello!" he replied approaching him.

"What are you doing here? We were supposed to meet at practice! The game is next week. We need to kick those Rainer's guys' asses. It's about the honour of our university. Our honour, you understand?" Jürgen noticed the look of absolute indifference on Johan's face.

"Is everything alright? Did your brother get into trouble with the police again? Parents? What? You look upset."

"Jürgen!" Johan faltered. "Let's walk by the river. I have something to tell you."

"Alright," Jürgen agreed. "But not for long. Practice is in an hour and I still need to go home for my gear."

The friends walked together silently. Jürgen couldn't understand the reason for what he considered Johan's strange behaviour and didn't know what to say. Meanwhile Johan, with horror, realised that his peaceful life might come to an end in a few minutes and there would be no turning back.

The boys reached the promenade and leaned on the railings along the path to the water.

Johan silently looked at the leaves slowly floating on the water and thought: "That's how life flows. The leaves will never swim against the current or return to the branches of the trees. So are our actions. Once you've done something, you no longer have the power to change it. All other actions thereafter are merely consequences of the previous act."

"Jürgen!" Johan straightened his shoulders.

"Jürgen!" he repeated. "I want to tell you that I love you. I've loved you since I first saw you a year ago at the game against the team from the neighbouring town. I've never been interested in basketball. I joined your team just to be near you as often as possible. I know the risks of this confession, but my feelings for you are so strong that I can no longer hide them. I think about you day and night. I wake up and go to sleep with your name on my lips. That's all I wanted to say!" He looked into the blue eyes of his friend and felt a huge relief, as if he had shed a great burden he had been forced to carry for many years.

Jürgen froze and stared at him, unblinking: "Are you one of 'those'? I even asked you to wash my back in the shower after the game and you touched me with your hands?"

He was disgusted.

"Get away from me and never come near again!" Jürgen shouted, then turned sharply and quickly walked away.

Johan was puzzled by his friend's reaction, but remained surprisingly calm. He had done it. Now he could sleep with a clear conscience.

Johan was born in a bomb shelter, where his parents hid during the allied air raids. Their house, like most buildings in the city, was destroyed by bomb strikes. For some time after the war they lived in the basement. Johan was born first and, a few minutes later, Peter was delivered into this world.

They were twins, but different in appearance and temperament. Peter was tall, strongly built, with abrupt movements and a quick speech that had caused quite a few headaches for their parents with his antics from a young age. Upon reaching adolescence, he joined a local gang. By then, the family had to move to another city, as they found no peace from either the neighbours or the police.

Johan, on the other hand, was half a head smaller than his brother. He was calm, sensible and always first to help his troubled parents. He excelled in school and showed great promise at the university's biology department. His mother always looked at him with undisguised joy and, secretly from the father, pampered him. Their dad was a lathe operator in a factory and was equally strict with both sons. He believed that boys should not be coddled; they needed to grow into stern, responsible men who could protect their family if necessary. Despite their differences, the brothers were close. Peter always protected the weaker Johan from local bullies. In turn, Johan took on brother's school assignments, often joking that he had to keep an eye on his younger sibling and be involved in his life.

The next morning, Johan woke up in a wonderful mood: for the first time in a long while, he felt light-hearted. He wasn't troubled by Jürgen's reaction, as he had expected something similar.

"Let him think it over, calm down," Johan comforted himself mentally.

"Jürgen will agree to spend more time with me. After all, I'm not asking for anything more," he hoped, as his heart beat faster.

During breakfast, he thought about the same thing, so his mother, who always watched him closely, asked: "Have you fallen in love, son? Your look is unusual."

"No, mom," Johan said dismissively. "Just remembering childhood, how Peter and I used to steal apples from the neighbours. Oh, did we get it from dad then."

At the mention of Peter, his mother's face darkened.

"He hasn't been home for several nights," she said quietly. "I don't know where he is. I hope we don't have to move again because of him."

"Mom, he promised me he wouldn't go back to his old ways," Johan said reassuringly.

At one time after the family had to move to a new house, Johan had his first serious conversation with his brother about his behaviour.

"Do you see what your actions have led to?" Johan yelled at him. "Don't you care about our parents or me at all? I had to change schools in the middle of the school year. Dad quit his job. All this happened because you got involved with those scoundrels. They'll either kill you or you'll end up in jail! Do you understand?"

Peter remained silent because he knew he was the cause of the family problems, but the easy money and the constant adrenaline rush were too hard to let go. Peter didn't understand why he should work hard from morning to night when he could earn a month of his father's salary in just one evening. Only respect for his parents and love for his brother made him reconsider his behaviour. That evening, Peter promised his brother that he would break with the past and straighten himself out. They then spent a long-time reminiscing about their childhood, friends from their street and various funny incidents that had happened when they still lived in the old city.

Johan finished his breakfast, put the dishes in the sink.

"Mom!" he shouted from the kitchen. "I'll be home late today: I have an important practice. The Rainer's team is mocking us, saying they'll wipe the floor with us. But we've got a few nasty surprises for them. So we need to work hard before the game."

He dressed, kissed his mother, grabbed his leather bag, and went outside. The first thing he saw was a pink heart cut out of paper and stuck on their front door. He knew well what such a sign meant. In the past, the Nazis had marked people like him with pink hearts. His heart sank with trepidation.

Illustration by Oleksand Prodan

"No, he couldn't have done this," Johan thought. "It must be a mistake or a cruel joke."

He ripped off the sticker, crumpled it and put it in his pocket. He looked around, but no one was in sight. A sickening feeling hit him, and his mood instantly soured. But he had to get to class, so he walked up the street. As he approached the university, he saw many students staring at him unusually. Then he spotted Jürgen standing with a group of teammates and glaring in his direction. Jürgen's expression was hostile. The guys walked towards Johan menacingly. The team captain, Hans shouted aggressively: "Listen, sweetheart, we don't need players like you on the team. I don't want to see you here again."

Then he spat at Johan's feet. Everyone laughed and headed to their lectures.

Johan ran up to Jürgen, grabbed his sleeve and asked: "Why?"

Jürgen pulled his hand away and hissed: "Don't touch me ever again. You disgust me!"

He walked quickly to the entrance, where the other team members were waiting.

Johan felt dizzy as if the ground was moving under his feet. Struggling to breathe, he staggered, almost falling before grabbing onto a nearby tree. His negative experience with Jürgen and his friends had just shattered his whole world and faith in mankind. He walked, swaying down the street, seeing nothing, hearing nothing. Jürgen's voice endlessly repeated in his head: "You disgust me!"

Without realising it, Johan found himself at the riverbank. The river wrapped around a rocky mountain on which stood an old, semi-ruined fortress. Once, it had protected the city from attacks, and the townspeople had taken shelter behind its walls. Surrounded on three sides by the river with rocky shores and a high stone wall with a moat separating it from the city, the fortress was nearly impregnable. It had also suffered from bombings by the allied aviation during the war, but the structure was so robust that the walls withstood several direct hits. Now, the city administration was doing everything possible to restore the old fortress to attract tourists.

Johan climbed onto the lookout platform on the southern side of the building above the river, right by the cliff above the river.

The sun had already risen over the city. Its rays cut through small dark clouds and fell on the trees in the city park, creating sunlit clearings where birds swirled in flocks. For a moment, Johan felt as if he had seen this before. He was mesmerised by the dance of the birds, flocking in the sunlight and couldn't look away from the spectacle. With each passing minute, his belief that he had witnessed this scene before grew stronger.

"No, that just can't be. I'm here for the first time and I don't remember anything like this in the old city," the young man rejected the thought.

Then he returned to the reason he was on the fortress wall and frowned.

"How wonderful it would be to fly above the ground, like a bird. To leave all sorrow and worries down below. To be left with only my feelings and the joy of flight."

He approached the very edge of the wall above the rocky shore, stood thinking for a few seconds, then straightened up and, with a strong push, flew into the abyss.

"Forgive me, Jürgen, I love you!" was all Johan could think.

Illustration by Oleksand Prodan

In the evening, after Johan's funeral, Jürgen walked alone through the park. Johan's suicide shocked him and he felt guilty over his death.

"After all, if I had reacted differently to Johan's confession, he might have stayed alive. Johan didn't demand anything from me, he just confessed his feelings. But I told the guys about it, instead of talking to him and figuring out our relationship. I'm a scum. I gave in to fleeting feelings, scared that they'd pin a pink heart on my door. I'm a coward and a traitor. Now I have to live with it. I see the judgment in my friends' eyes. Even although no-one openly blames me, I know they judge me behind my back."

Jürgen walked silently down the dark alley, looking at the ground. Suddenly, a figure of a tall man emerged from the darkness as if appeared from the ground.

"How's your conscience, Jürgen? I've been waiting for you here for a while. I want to pass on a message from your friend, my brother."

At that moment, a knife gleamed in the stranger's hand and he forcefully stabbed the young man on the left side, aiming for the heart. Jürgen groaned and fell on the ground.

"My brother was not like everyone else and it was not his fault, so he was born that way. Johan was an honest, bright person and you killed him. So now you'll die too!" The stranger spat on the ground and disappeared into the night's darkness.

Mia

"Yes, that's enough!" Mia interrupted her husband irritably. "We argue every time you touch on this topic. There is no God. I don't believe he exists. Do you think a kind, bearded old man sits on a cloud watching over everyone? Watching us and punishing those who do wrong? These tales were invented by clerics to keep us in fear and to control us."

"It's better to think about what we're going to name our child. It's not long now," she said and stroked her round belly.

"Alright," Rory conceded. "Let's think about it. Do you, after all, want a boy or a girl?"

"Well, as God wills!" said Mia and they both laughed.

"Alright, if it's a boy, we'll name him Sean," Rory said.

"And if it's a girl, we'll name her Aoife," Mia continued.

"I agree," Rory replied hugging his wife and gently tickling her.

Mia screamed and tried to break free from his embrace. She was ticklish and Rory always tickled her whenever he needed to defuse a situation or shift his wife's attention to something else. Then she would slap him a few times and they would start kissing. Rory was good at kissing. He kissed her in such a way that Mia completely forgot what she was talking about before. Now, he kissed her as tenderly as never before. After all, the heart of a little person, a piece of his soul, was beating in her belly. Mia, realising this, was in heaven with happiness. It's such a joy: to carry a child of a loved one.

Mia came to the capital from the north of the country. There, she enrolled in a medical college. It was the dream of her life. As a child she wanted to be a nurse. She had three younger brothers whom she looked after when her parents were working. They were her first patients. Mia set up a small hospital at home and the children happily played doctors and patients. Whenever someone scraped a knee or cut a finger, Mia was their first aid. Her parents watched tenderly as she cared for her brothers and they did not object to her decision to become a nurse. On the contrary, when it was time to finish school, her father drove her to the southern capital to choose the right college. She could have studied in their city, but her father insisted that she study where there were no religious conflicts. The republic was only half a century old, but life there was improving year by year, unlike the north, where constant clashes occurred between Catholics and Protestants.

Mia was from a Catholic family and her father was her unquestionable authority. Despite his beliefs, he often told her: "God gave people religion so they could find their way to Him with its help, but they use it to control other people."

The family regularly attended Sunday mass at the church. Her younger brothers sang in the church choir and Mia also participated in church activities during holidays. However, the doubts her father planted in her soul grew every day.

Once, while still in school, she asked her father: "Are you sure God exists? Look at all the misery and injustice around. Why do the innocent suffer?"

Her father, after thinking a bit, replied: "God exists, my daughter. We are simply not meant to understand everything that happens and He works in ways incomprehensible to us."

But the conflicting thoughts were so deeply rooted in her consciousness that, over time, while doing her practicum in an oncology hospital, Mia constantly asked herself: "Why do children die? What is their fault? Can't God save them?"

Illustration by Oleksand Prodan

Once, when she was walking in the botanical gardens, Mia noticed a young man who was so engrossed in taking photos that she couldn't help, but admire him. Clearly, the he was completely focused on his task: apart from his subject, whether it was a blooming flower or a cautiously approaching squirrel, nothing else existed in the world.

Mia watched him until he suddenly turned to her and asked: "May I take your photo? You are very beautiful."

Mia was so taken aback that she blushed deeply, feeling as if she were a criminal caught in the act. Seeing her confusion, the young man approached her and said: "I apologise for startling you with my request. You really are very attractive and I could take a lovely portrait. Please agree!"

Mia remained silent for a moment, then spoke: "Please forgive me. I was secretly watching you. You were working so diligently it stirred my curiosity."

"Don't apologise," the young man said, extending his hand. "My name is Rory, and yours?"

"I'm Mia!" she replied, shaking his hand.

"Wow! What a coincidence. I really like your name. My grandmother was named that. Now, let me introduce you to my friend," said Rory, lifting the camera that hung around his neck.

"This is 'Leica', my father gave it to me. He taught me how to take pictures. Photography has a big future. We can't notice everything around us, but photography gives us that opportunity. It's a separate world, wonderful and unexplored."

They walked along the narrow paths of the park. Rory tirelessly explained what shutter speed and aperture were and how to use sunlight for exposure. Mia listened to him and realised she liked this guy. There was just a positive energy emanating from him. She also liked his voice. Low, slightly husky, it had a hypnotic effect on her. She listened without interrupting.

"So, will you let me take your picture before the sun sets?" Rory asked.

Mia realised they had been walking a long time and the sun was about to set.

"Okay," she said. "Maybe here, by this bush with roses?"

Rory loaded a new film and began to shoot. He used the entire film and was very pleased with the results.

"I'll need a couple of days to develop the photos. Where can I find you?"

Mia lived in a rented apartment and gave him the address.

"Great. I work as a bartender at the nearby 'Green Rock' pub. I'll come over the day after tomorrow. Is that okay?"

"We have a deal," said Mia. "Just don't come too late: I have a very strict landlady."

They got to know each other and started dating. Eventually, Mia moved in with him. He lived in an apartment that he had inherited from his grandmother. Since then Rory's life changed. Mia transformed his bachelor flat beyond recognition. The apartment became a cosy, comfortable place for them. Mia was in her final year at nursing college and worked as an intern in various hospitals. She spotted a position in a private clinic while waiting to receive her diploma.

Rory continued working as a barman while pursuing his beloved photography. He managed to sell his works to magazines, which brought in a good income. Both loved travelling and whenever they had free time they headed to the mountains or to the sea.

The only issue they couldn't agree on was religion. Rory was devout and tried to convince Mia that everything on earth is done by God's greater will and everything should be accepted with patience and humility. Mia argued that with so much suffering and injustice around. Why did God do nothing about it? Mia did not want to hear Rory's contrary arguments.

That day, she returned from her parents feeling down. Rory dared not her ask what was wrong. Finally, in the evening, he asked why she was moody: "Is everything okay? Are your parents all right? How are the boys? I can't stand to see you upset. What happened? How can I help?"

Mia was silent for a long time before she spoke: "Do you remember the church where we got married? The one my parents went to, where my brothers sang in the choir?"

"Yes, how could I forget that church and that day? What about it?" he asked apprehensively.

He didn't like where the topic was going.

"The priest who married us has been exposed for..." Mia paused, as if searching for the right words.

"He's been exposed for having an interest in little boys," she finally managed to say.

"You understand, my brothers went to that church and sang in the choir. Father questioned them for a long time and they said that the priest had made indecent proposals to them. They subsequently remained silent all this time. They were afraid to tell not their parents, but also each other. Even though they are so close and usually keep no secrets from one another!" Mia paused and lowered her head.

"If this is true, it's so filthy. Although I find it hard to believe," Rory responded indignantly.

"I didn't want to tell you earlier. Have you ever heard of 'The Magdalene's Laundries'?" Mia asked.

"No, what kind of organisation is that? For the homeless and orphans?" Rory inquired.

"It's an institution run by nuns for women who became pregnant outside marriage or who were raped by family members or other men. The pregnant young women were forced to work hard from morning till late at night. The things that happened there are so horrific, you can't even imagine. It's a purgatory-prison of the twentieth century for sinners, in their understanding of the word. Once their babies were born, they were given up for adoption.

No one knows about it. Do you understand me? Well, somebody know, but they keep their mouths shut. I'm even afraid to tell you everything I've learned. It's so frightening," Mia broke down and cried.

"How did you find out about this?" Rory asked. "If it's true, we need to inform the police."

"The police. I think they are aware," Mia replied. "Six months ago, a girl was brought into our clinic. She was accompanied by two nuns and a police officer in plain clothes. She had a miscarriage and our doctor performed a dilation and curettage. It's not entirely legal and that's why the officer asked for no records to be made. Although it was against our rules, apparently, someone influential from above pressured our doctor to do so. The girl spent the night in our clinic under the supervision of nuns and the next day she was taken away. I was on duty at that time and needed to take her temperature. One nun was sleeping in the neighbouring room and another was dozing off in a chair in the corner. I was with her for about five to seven minutes, during which time the girl managed to tell me quite a lot. I was so shocked by what I heard that I even forgot to record the temperature readings in the journal. This poor girl found a moment to tell me everything and took a great risk because she did not know me and really laid out a terrifying truth to the first person available. I think the girl would have been in big trouble if the nuns had found out what she told me."

At this point, Mia fell silent and stared at her feet.

"So what did she tell you?" Rory asked, being himself in a state of shock from what he heard.

"Her name was Siobhan. She was seventeen years old and got pregnant by her stepfather, who was constantly raping her. The poor girl wanted to seek help from the police and went to the priest looking for advice. He listened and promised to help. Then nuns came for Siobhan, said they knew about her problems and took her away. That's how she ended up in a closed

Illustration by Oleksand Prodan

institution called 'The Magdalene Laundry.' If Heaven and Hell exist, then the latter is here on Earth."

More than six months had passed since that conversation and all this time they had tried to avoid the topic. Rory became more measured in his expressions. He tried to spend as much time as possible with his wife, especially since their family was expecting an addition. He was overjoyed and took on practically all the household chores. Mia resisted this, but he was relentless. The only area where he conceded was in cooking. Here he was a complete novice as his diet comprised sausages, fried potatoes and eggs. But now he understood the importance of proper nutrition and tried to diversify their food as much as possible.

Rory worked longer hours after the birth of Aoife as Mia was on maternity leave. The baby was no problem which pleased her parents.

Mia recalled how her mother struggled with her younger brothers and dreaded sleepless nights. They often stood by their daughter's bed and enjoyed watching her sleep quietly. Sometimes, in her sleep, the baby would make a funny face and then both parents would cover their mouths with their hands to avoid waking her with their laughter. Time passed, the child grew and delighted her parents with her new sounds and movements. Aoife could already stand up by herself, holding onto the back of her crib. When she was seven months old, Mia's milk disappeared and she bought a bottle with a nipple to give her daughter cow's milk. Aoife sat in the corner of the crib and sucked it with pleasure. She looked so busy at that moment that the parents tiptoed around not to distract the child from such an important task.

One morning, while tidying up in the bathroom, Mia noticed a small lump in her left breast. She felt it and, not experiencing any hint of pain, quickly forgot about it.

"Probably because my milk disappeared early," she decided.

Later, Mia arranged with a nanny who lived nearby to take care of Aoife and returned to the clinic. Everyone there had been waiting for her and she had missed work so much. The workdays dragged on and she had the added responsibility of caring for her child. As winter approached, Mia's mother asked them to visit with Aoife. She had knitted a suit and a winter hat for the child and wanted to dress her herself. Mia returned from that trip with a fever that never went away. She tried to treat herself and ignored Rory's pleas to see a doctor, even though she saw him at work every day.

Doctor Seamus, who greatly admired Mia for her professionalism and responsibility, noticed her condition and advised her to get tested. A few days later, he called her to his office and said: "I've arranged for you to have additional tests at the municipal clinic. Don't come to work tomorrow go there and do everything they tell you. You did your practicum there and they remember you well. Dr. Berk will be taking care of you."

"Can you tell me what you suspect? Is it cancer? Really?" Mia asked.

Doctor Seamus lowered his head: "Let's wait for the final results, okay? You can take the rest of the day off."

Mia's condition deteriorated very quickly. Less than two months after her final diagnosis she could hardly take care of herself increasingly needing Rory's help to get dressed and take a shower. She declined the treatment offered, realising that it was a waste of time and money. The disease had progressed too far and she had no chance of survival. Rory insisted that Mia be hospitalised since Dr. Berk said that she only had a matter of days not weeks to live and it would be better for her to be in the hospital under medical supervision.

That day, leaving Aoife with a nanny, Rory rushed to the hospital. He was mentally prepared to be alone with the child, but refused to believe it would come to that. At the hospital, he went to see Dr. Berk and asked about his wife's condition.

"It will happen today, be ready!" the doctor said. "She hardly regains consciousness anymore."

Rory entered the room where Mia was lying in bed. She was semi-conscious and breathing erratically. None of her former beauty remained. Mia lost lots of weight and was almost just skin and bones, barely breathing. Rory bit his lip painfully and cried. He wept, not understanding whom he felt sorrier for: her, the young and once beautiful woman; himself, practically a widower with a small child; or Aoife, who was beginning her life.

Suddenly, Mia opened her eyes and looked at him confusedly.

He leaned towards her and asked: "Do you want anything to drink or eat? Maybe I should take you to the bathroom?"

She shook her head slightly: "I want to eat. Bring me a fish soup."

"Fish soup?" Rory repeated.

"I'll be quick, right now!" he exclaimed and dashed out of the room.

On his way home, he bought fish and vegetables. At home, he quickly made the soup, poured it into a small pot, wrapped it tightly in a towel and ran back to the hospital. Rory was afraid of being too late and he made it. Mia was still alive, but she breathed sparingly and was no longer conscious.

He stood by her bed, holding the bag with the freshly made soup and never took his eyes off her. Young man waited for the last breath of his wife and he did not miss it.

Illustration by Oleksand Prodan

Several days had passed since her funeral. Rory sat on a chair by Aoife's crib, where she was sleeping and thought: "Maybe she was right and there is no God in this world? I don't understand why this child should suffer. She is innocent. Aoife is just starting her life, but she is already doomed to suffer. I don't understand why?"

Rory lifted his tearful eyes and looked at the photograph hanging above the crib. It was the same photograph he had taken on the day they met. In the photo, Mia was smiling and a butterfly fluttered above a rose bush.

Yaroslav

Jazz was gradually regaining consciousness. A ringing buzzed in his head. "What was that?" the youngster asked himself. He tried sitting up but couldn't and almost screamed as excruciating pain shot through his body. Exhausted, he fell back. His legs were pinned under a concrete wall up to his thighs. He could only half-sit, leaning on his hands.

"Legs are broken, that's clear. Just hope there's no bleeding," the young man remembered about the tourniquet and pulled out a first aid kit from behind his back.

"Ok, where's the gun? Probably where my legs are," he thought angrily.

Jazz recalled his grandfather's words that a knife could turn out to be the only friend in a tough moment and felt for his pouch. Only the sheaths were left, tied to the body armour. Jazz bit his lip painfully: "The knife stayed in the door. I forgot to take it out."

The second knife remained under the slab because it was in sheaths attached to the shin. He threw his head back and looked up. Helplessness brought tears to his eyes. Swirls of dust slowly cleared and he saw the sky.

"So? What was that?" Jazz asked himself again.

"The explosion was very powerful. Not from a shell or a missile. They blew up the floor above us," the boy guessed.

"That's why they asked our command to go up! Not to retrieve their wounded, but to mine the entire floor and, by blowing it up, break our resistance. Truly brotherly indeed," he tried to smile.

"Where are our guys? Where is Gwint? Am I really alone? I won't make it out of here. Even if they don't finish me off, I'll freeze to death from the cold," he thought and reached into his inner pocket.

He took out his phone, found the last message from his mother about her dream and wrote: "My dear mom, I love you very much. Forgive me for everything!"

Then he pressed the "Send" button, but received a reply: "Failed to send message. No network coverage. The message will be sent as soon as connection is available."

Cursing to himself, Jazz put the phone back into his chest pocket.

Svitlana was restless. There had been no news from Yaroslav for several days.

"Could there really be no connection at the training ground?" she wondered.

The mother needed to talk to her son because for several nights in a row had the same dream.

She saw Yaroslav standing on the high wall of some fortress, looking into the distance. Her son was facing her, but he did not see his mother. She tried to shout to him, but it was all in vain: he couldn't hear her. Then, from above the clouds, a bright beam of light broke through directly onto Yaroslav. The son pushed off the fortress wall and, spreading his arms like a bird's wings, soared up to the heavens, gliding along the beam like on a path. At this point, Svitlana always woke up and couldn't fall back asleep.

"I'll write to him about this dream. He should be more careful!" the woman thought.

Illustration by Oleksand Prodan

Svitlana took out her phone, quickly wrote a message and pressed the "Send" button. A few minutes later, she checked the status of the message, but it had not changed: "Sent but not delivered." The mother sighed heavily and went to the kitchen to make herself breakfast.

She had been raising her son alone for many years. His father, Oleksiy, served in the Military Mining Rescue Unit and died saving workers during a mining accident. When his rescue squad descended the mine, there was a methane explosion, so none of the shift miners and rescuers survived. They were all buried in closed coffins, thus Svitlana never saw Oleksiy dead. All these years, she shuddered every time someone knocked on the door. She imagined Oleksiy came home, embraced her and said looking into her eyes: "Here I am. How have you been without me?" Then Svitlana would lead him to the kitchen and watch with pleasure as he ate the dinner she had prepared.

Yaroslav was ten years old at the time. The boy remembered his father well, their trips to the forest for mushrooms, night fishing. His father had taught him to drive a car and once, taking his son to work, let him steer a large yellow truck, which had "Military Mining Rescue Unit" written on its side. It was not easy for a ten-year-old boy to handle such a big vehicle, but he managed because his father – the best friend who would come to help at any moment – was by his side.

Every summer, Yaroslav lived in the village at his father's parents' house. Grandfather Petro adored his grandson and allowed him to get up to all sorts of mischief. Grandmother Nastya was strict with them and they feared her. She could tell by looking into grandfather's eyes that he was up to something.

"What, you're going to take your grandson to steal corn again? Don't shame me! How old are you? You are old stump!" she would scold him and he would guiltily look away while secretly winking at Yaroslav. The boy found it interesting to observe the relationship between his grandparents.

Grandma Nastya was younger than her husband, but he listened to her in everything. Despite his advanced age, the grandfather retained a youthful enthusiasm and was always drawn to some adventure. He was popular and respected in the village, but sometimes people laughed about his mishaps. Conversations among the villagers often started with: "Have you heard what Petro did?" or "Petro got it from Nastya again!"

However, Yaroslav's friends considered the grandfather one of their own and often came to him for advice. He was influential and would advise the boys to avoid bad deeds. When such moments arose and he joined their group, the boys would sit with their mouths open all evening, listening to the grandfather's stories. He was an excellent storyteller. Maybe that's why Grandma Nastya loved him. Despite her sternness, she always looked at him with such tenderness that Yaroslav couldn't help but wonder: "Will he, Yaroslav, have a wife who after so many years together look at him with the same love?"

After the death of his only son, the grandfather focused all his attention on his grandson – the last bearer of their family name. In his turn Yaroslav, feeling this love and care, reciprocated in the same manner. Both missed each other and always looked forward to meeting. It was fortunate that the village was very close to the city where Yaroslav was growing up. Thus, it is well-known that the bond between grandchildren and grandparents is much closer than between parents and children.

Due to the circumstances, Yaroslav matured much faster than his peers. He understood that his grandfather wanted to pass on all his experience and knowledge that he had not managed to pass on to his son. The boy was curious about everything and therefore was drawn to his grandfather. The old man knew so much that sometimes Yaroslav felt that a whole lifetime would not be enough to learn everything his grandfather knew.

When Yaroslav was about five or six years old, his grandfather carved him a wooden flute and taught him how to play. Perhaps even then he saw a future musician in him. Soon the little boy was whistling melodies he made up himself. The grandfather also had a mandolin, which somehow had found its way to their country. He showed Yaroslav how to play it and gradually the boy also mastered this instrument.

Despite Yaroslav's progress in music, grandfather Petro tried to raise the boy to be a fighter, believing that every man is a protector and warrior.

For this purpose, the grandfather first made a slingshot and taught him how to shoot from it. Then came a bow and arrows. When Yaroslav grew up, the grandfather showed him how to make a homemade gun and shoot with it. All this was done in great secrecy from grandmother because she was very opposed to such toys.

Grandfather was a jack-of-all-trades and, in his workshop, he could make many interesting things. Petro had a big collection of knives he had made. He instilled in Yaroslav a love for bladed weapons: he showed the boy knife-fighting techniques, taught him how to throw knives from any position. Yaroslav often asked his grandfather where he learned all this, but he always evaded the answer which would satisfy Yaroslav.

The grandfather said: "Never play with a weapon. It does not take jokes lightly and never use it to harm others. But if you decide to use it, do it only for a just cause. Feel the blade with your body, embrace it with your soul, feel the cold of the metal, its weight and its centre of gravity. Never throw a knife into a living tree, because it, like a person, has a soul. In a tough situation, a knife can be your only friend. Never neglect it and always treat it with respect."

That summer he turned fourteen and, as always, he came to the village for the holidays. His grandparents were happy about his arrival. They wouldn't be lonely and he was a good helper. He could ride the bike to the store, bring in the cow and help in the garden. Yaroslav approached everything with enthusiasm.

One evening, while his grandmother went to milk the cow, he tried to recreate a melody by tapping on carved sticks against clay pots and glass jars that his grandmother had hung on the fence. It resembled a drum set. Each vessel produced its own sound. Meanwhile, his grandfather sat on a bench nearby, watching him and smoking his favourite pipe.

He looked at his grandson with kindness, blowing smoke from his mouth through his grey Cossack moustache, which had turned brown from the tobacco. At one moment, Yaroslav got carried away and struck his grandmother's favourite pot too hard. It cracked, split in half and fell to the ground. Startled, the boy crouched down, slowly turned around and looked at his grandfather. Petro took the pipe out of his mouth, rose slightly and stared at his grandson. Just then, the grandmother came out of the barn with a bucket of milk. They both turned their heads towards her, and at that moment, the grandfather yelled: "Run!"

They dashed through the gate and ran to the end of the street. As they ran, they heard the grandmother's screams and tried not to look back. But a few houses down, the grandfather stopped, panting heavily and bent over, resting his hands on his knees: "Son, have some conscience, don't run so fast. I'm almost eighty years old."

"Grandpa, why did you run? It's my fault!" Yaroslav said, also breathing heavily.

The grandfather waved his hand and barely managed to say: "There's a saying, my boy – 'Perish yourself, but save your comrade.'"

"Grandma wouldn't have killed me over that pot! It's not that scary! How are we going to face going home now? Though, it really is a pity about the pot. It was so old! They don't make them like that anymore."

"I don't even know why I started running! Old reflexes, probably," answered Petro.

"So what are we going to do? It's almost night. We have to go home anyway," said Yaroslav.

"Let's go to my godfather's, take some potatoes from him and go to our spot. We'll make a fire and bake them. Look what a beautiful evening it is! Just lie on the ground and look at the sky."

Yaroslav would remember that evening for the rest of his life. They sat by the fire, peeling the blackened potatoes, eating them and burning their lips.

Roasted bacon and bread on the fire, which grandpa's godfather Ivan had also given them. These two friends constantly watching the fire and talking nonstop. Yaroslav could barely keep up with asking questions and that night the grandfather was more open than ever. That's when Yaroslav learned that during the war, his grandfather was in the reconnaissance unit. How he was captured and escaped from captivity. How he made it back to his own people and how they sentenced him to ten years in the camps as a traitor. Yaroslav had never seen his grandfather like this. Recalling all this, his eyes glowed with fury and his hands clenched into fists.

Illustration by Oleksand Prodan

"Grandpa, does God exist?" Yaroslav unexpectedly asked.

The grandfather paused for a moment and replied: "Look at the sky! Do you see how many stars there are? Now, for a moment, imagine the entire Universe. Can you grasp infinity? No," the grandfather answered himself.

"It's the same with God. He exists, I know it, but He is not like how various clergy depict Him. We cannot understand Him just as we cannot imagine this infinity. Although everyone sees it, they can't even touch it."

"But what about Hell and Heaven? Do they exist? What happens to us after death?" Yaroslav couldn't calm down.

"I don't know, my boy," the grandfather calmly replied.

"Someday everyone will find out. As for Heaven or Hell, I can tell you one thing..." here the grandfather paused, as if deciding whether to speak or not. "I have seen so much in my life that it seems to me that Hell is here on Earth and only after our death we will find freedom and eternity."

"Do you believe in life after death?" Yaroslav asked.

"Nobody knows what will happen to us after we leave this life. I just know that the end of anything is the beginning of something else. It's like sunset and sunrise. You watch the sunset and think your day is ending. But for someone else, it's a sunrise and their day is just beginning."

"Grandpa, why are you so afraid of grandma?" Yaroslav ventured to ask.

The grandfather laughed long and hard at this, tears even welling up in his eyes from the laughter.

"I'm not afraid of her. I just love her and respect very much. I love her so much that my heart tightens with tenderness for her. We've been together for over sixty years. She saw me off to war, then travelled with me across the north while I was shuffled between camps. If it weren't for her love, I probably wouldn't have survived. She is like the air to me. I can't breathe without her. So, it's not that I'm afraid of her. Simply because I love my Nastya very much!" The grandfather then fell silent, staring into the blazing fire, lost in thought.

Years later, Yaroslav remembered his words. Grandma Nastya suddenly fell ill and took to her bed. She refused to go to the hospital: apparently, she felt her time was short. Grandfather didn't leave her side for a moment and he was hard to recognise during those days. He seemed to age and weaken rapidly. The sparkle in his eyes was gone, his shoulders slumped. One morning grandmother didn't wake up. Grandfather went to the neighbours and asked them to call Svitlana to inform her of Nastya's death. He then returned to his wife. When the relatives arrived, they found them just like that: grandmother lying on the bed and grandfather sitting by her side, holding her hand. His head rested on her chest and no longer breathing.

"Grandpa, why do we speak different languages?" Yaroslav asked a question that had long intrigued him.

"For three hundred and fifty years during the occupation, our native language was banned many times. Gradually, it was pushed out everywhere and remained only in the villages. We still learned in our native language, allowing it to take a small breath. Your parents caught a bit of that time and then almost all schools switched to a foreign language. Higher education was always taught in another language. It's good that now our country has gained independence and our native language is gradually returning. But it's a very long journey."

"Why was it banned?" Yaroslav asked in surprise.

"Ancient people said that if you want to conquer a nation, you must take away their language," grandfather replied. "So they were right. Our language was almost destroyed as well as our memory, because the genetic code of a people is stored in its language. People without memory are easier to govern. So learn our native language, son. It is our soul and what identifies us as a nation."

"But that was in the past and now we live in peace with them. Also we have a lot in common with them," Yaroslav insisted.

"Remember, son: sooner or later they will go on war against us. I spent twenty long winters there. I know them very well."

"War? Why? What for? What do we have to divide?" Yaroslav was surprised.

"Yaroslav. They are a completely different people. We have nothing in common with them except a bloody history. Everything they have, they stole from us: language, culture, religion, history, traditions. Stolen and appropriated. We forgave them because we forgot our history. But even so, we have not lost our desire for freedom, because freedom is the most valuable thing a person has. I say this as someone who spent ten years in camps. It's like breathing: as soon as you can't breathe, you immediately understand how happy you were before when you could breathe freely. We are a freedom-loving people and they are slaves. A slave who does not want to be freed from slavery will never forgive another slave who has become a free man. He will try to make him a slave again. Understand, he will do everything to make others as enslaved as he is, instead of freeing himself. They are accustomed to living in slavery, it suits them. But we need freedom, we cannot breathe without it."

The grandfather spoke with such fervour that Yaroslav was afraid to interrupt him and listened, holding his breath. The boy sat on a thick log by the fire, gazing at the endless starry sky, feeling as if he had seen and heard it all before. But where it came from, he couldn't figure out. He would remember that evening many times and, when the war started, he understood how right his grandfather had been.

After finishing school, Yaroslav entered a music college, specialising in piano. The studies came easily to him and he simultaneously learned to play other instruments. In his third year, he was offered an internship abroad. It was a good sign and an evaluation of his talents. When he told his mother, she was so overwhelmed that she couldn't utter a word. After all, the son had always been nearby, even though he was studying in another city.

In a while the revolution started. Yaroslav and his friends went to the capital to see everything with their own eyes. He told his mother it would be for a few days. It turned out to be for a lifetime. Events took such a turn that returning was out of the question. Soon there were the first casualties and wounded. After that Yaroslav realised that the country in which he was born no longer existed. The young man witnessed the birth of a new state, felt himself a member of one huge family, where no one was indifferent, where everyone was there for each other.

Recalling that evening conversation with his grandfather, he deliberately switched to his native language and from then on never used a foreign one. Yaroslav occasionally went home, tried to catch up on his studies and help his mother, but all his thoughts were there, at the Maidan[*1], among his new comrades.

Then came the war. At first, it was covert and incomprehensible and then it became overt and cynical. They were attacked by those from whom they never expected it. Confusion passed, replaced by anger and hatred. Many of Yaroslav's Maidan's comrades went to the front, ready to defend their homeland with arms in hand.

Yaroslav tried to continue his studies and somehow managed to finish his third year. An international internship was no longer discussed. His whole heart was with his friends at the front. Eventually, he packed his things and went to the capital, where volunteer battalions were being formed. He told his mother that he had been drafted into the army. To keep her from worrying too much, he said he would spend the first six months on a training ground, so she had nothing to worry about.

Thus, he joined one of the territorial volunteer battalions. He learned military skills on the fly. There was no time to ramp up, as the enemy was pressing on all fronts. This was a strong, motivated and well-equipped enemy. Clearly, they had been preparing for this war for years. They had calculated everything except one thing: they would meet fierce resistance from half-dressed and poorly armed fighters.

[1] Maidan – the Independence Square in Kyiv.

Illustration by Oleksand Prodan

This was his second rotation[2] at the airport. Yaroslav knew some from the first rotation, but most of the fighters were strangers, so during the brief breaks between battles, they got to know each other, talked and asked questions. Yaroslav, wherever he was, always honed his knife-throwing skills. Here, his grandfather's training came in handy. He always carried two knives with him. He set up torn-off doors and practiced his throwing, while the rest of the fighters watched, following the flight of each knife.

"Where did you get the call sign 'Jazz'?" asked a short man named Krit.

"I studied at a music school and was very passionate about jazz. I can play it on the piano, clarinet, or saxophone. Even on drums. My idols have always been Duke Ellington and Louis Armstrong. I can listen to Frank Sinatra for hours," replied Yaroslav.

"Wow!" said Krit. "I only know how to play 'Dog Waltz' on the piano with two fingers."

"Well, at least you can play very well on another 'instrument'!" said Boatswain, nodding towards the SVD[3] that stood by the wall next to Krit.

"I also want to learn to play the banjo! I've only held one once. When I was a kid, my grandpa taught me to play the mandolin. They're somewhat similar, but the banjo has a unique sound and a more complex playing style," mused Yaroslav.

"Why the banjo specifically?" Krit asked, puzzled.

"I don't know, I just do. I can't explain why," shrugged Yaroslav.

"Well, good thing it's not the balalaika!" chimed Gwint from the corner, the known chatterbox. "Otherwise, I wouldn't have understood you."

Everyone laughed together and Yaroslav picked up a small stone from the ground and playfully threw it at Gwint.

---

[2] Rotation – a replacement of personnel in a specific military unit.
[3] SVD — Dragunov Sniper Rifle.

Just then, the commander entered the room and said: "So, soldiers. The other side has requested a ceasefire. They want to retrieve their 200[4]. Command has approved. We won't shoot, but will keep an eye on them. Gwint, take Jazz with you and head to the far post for a shift. Just be very careful. Our guys took down two Monkas[5] in that area yesterday. Don't forget the radio battery and take a couple of RPGs[6]."

"Roger that,[7] Commander," said Gwint.

They both immediately got serious and started preparing. Gwint pulled two RPGs wrapped in cellophane out of the weapon box. He handed one to Yaroslav and took the other for himself.

"Just take off the cellophane," Gwint advised.

Yaroslav used a knife to cut open the package and took out the grenade.

"Wow, I've never shot one of these before," said Yaroslav.

"This is the RPG 26," explained Gwint. "It's simpler to use than the RPG 22. No need to open the front cover. Just raise the sight and you're ready to fire. You can return it to travel position too. Very convenient."

"Got it. Give me another F1[8] for just in case."

They both knew what their former "brothers" did to prisoners, so they had long decided that death was better than suffering in captivity.

Gwint opened the box, took out a grenade together with its fuse and handed it to Yaroslav: "Here is, just be careful."

"Thanks, I know," smiled Yaroslav, fitting a cut-off piece of a plastic syringe to the fuse[9].

---

[4] 200 — military slang for a fallen soldier.

[5] Mon-50 — a directional fragmentation anti-personnel mine.

[6] RPG — Rocket Propelled Grenade. Produced in various modifications like RPG-18, RPG-22, RPG-26, among others.

[7] Roger that — military slang for understood, accepted, agree.

[8] F-1 — a defensive hand grenade.

[9] Fuse – a trimmed syringe is put on the grenade's fuse for additional protection against an accidental explosion.

Gwint looked at him and silently nodded. As the senior shift member and more experienced warrior, he decided to take the young soldier under his wing, as he was quite impressed by him.

The veteran appreciated Jazz's courage and determination. At the same time, he saw that the young soldier never took undue risks, always worked well in a team and constantly learned combat skills. Talking with him was always a pleasure. Jazz was a true wellspring of knowledge. Gwint was always amazed: how could someone so young know so much, so he always listened with interest to Jazz's stories.

Half an hour later, the soldiers reached the post where Slon and Maks were waiting for them. The guys quickly briefed them on the situation and, after changing the radio battery, moved almost silently back to the base. Gwint and Yaroslav took their positions and began monitoring their sector. Gaps in the walls and hanging pieces of rebar complicated surveillance, but it was practically impossible to approach them without making noise. The floor was covered with debris, so any movement was noisy.

"I wonder if the scums will stay where they've been allowed to go?" Gwint said. "They're already all around us."

"Do you know the old joke? – *Sir, we are surrounded! Good. That means we can attack in any direction,*" Yaroslav replied, smiling.

"That's how it is. The former "brothers" are holed up in the basement. We're letting them up now. No matter where you go, they're everywhere. So, we can shoot in any direction," Gwint said quietly.

"We're on our own land, brother. They came to us with weapons and we shouldn't just defend, we should attack. Until we drive them out of here and back to their lair," Yaroslav replied, clenching his fists.

For a while, they sat silently, peering into the semi-darkness, listening for any unusual sounds. The night-time air temperature dropped to minus 30 degrees, complicating their task as they had to sit still for long periods, the cold penetrating their bones meaning any movement was dangerous.

"Jazz, do you hear?" Gwint suddenly said. "Do you have a girlfriend?"

"No, it never worked out," Yaroslav sighed.

"I do, her name is Marina," Gwint said proudly. He handed his phone to Yaroslav, displaying a blonde girl with a bouquet of flowers on the screen.

"She's beautiful," said Yaroslav. "How long have you been together?"

"We were at the same university, different faculties though. I was in the physics and mathematics faculty and she was in the humanities. So we started dating before the war. We've even met each other's parents. Already planned to get married this summer, but we had to postpone it," – Gwint added sadly.

"I've never had anything serious. Went on dates, to movies, cafes, kissed, but nothing serious yet. But you know, I have this strong feeling that I'll meet her very soon. I've had this feeling for a few days now. Though, I don't understand where I could meet her here," Yaroslav said, sweeping his gaze over the ruins.

They fell silent. Gwint checked his watch, picked up the radio, pressed the push-to-talk button[10] and said: "Nora, this is Window. Situation 4.5.0.[11] Do you copy?"

The radio crackled to life: "Window, this is Nora. Understood. End of communication."

Less than an hour remained until the shift change. They were thoroughly frozen and were counting the minutes until they could be relieved when suddenly a terrible explosion sounded.

Steps and muffled voices were heard very close by. Someone was making their way through the rubble.

"Doubt those are ours," Jazz decided and prepared for the worst.

____

[10] Push-to-talk button — a button on the radio used to switch between receiving and transmitting modes.

[11] 4.5.0. — military slang, means that everything is okay.

He glanced into his pouch and pulled out the F1 grenade he had saved for an emergency.

"So, the special occasion has arrived," he thought sadly, looking up at the sky.

With his teeth, he pulled off the homemade safety pin cover from the grenade's fuse. He spat it out, straightened the fuse's 'whiskers' and, clutching the grenade in his hand, pulled the pin. Jazz slipped the ring over the middle finger of his left hand and pulled his coat sleeve down as low as possible to conceal the grenade.

"Oh, this one is still alive," someone's voice rang out nearby.

Approaching him leisurely, three figures in uniforms with the insignia of a fake republic and their rifles ready.

"Search him!" ordered the one who stood furthest away.

A burly soldier approached Jazz, holding his rifle in one hand and began to search him with the other. He took a phone from Jazz's breast pocket and handed it to his commander. Then he turned back to Jazz and asked: *"Well, warrior, got anything else on you? You won't be needing anything anymore."*

The fighters were not local separatists, it was clear from their accent. Jazz looked him in the eyes and said: "Yes, I do have something!"

Then he raised his left hand, where a ring dangled from his middle finger.

He looked at his palm and thought: "So, my lifeline ends here."

Then he turned his palm towards the burly soldier and saw his eyes fill with horror. The next moment, a grenade rolled out from the right sleeve of his coat and fell at his feet.

Illustration by Oleksand Prodan

Svitlana hadn't slept all night. She dreamt again of Yaroslav standing on the fortress rampart, staring into the distance. Then he flapped his arms like wings and soared into the sky, while she stood below calling out to him. After tossing and turning nearly all night, she woke up exhausted and decided to make some coffee. She took the cezve[12], added coffee, poured water and set it on the stove. Just then, her phone signalled a received message. Svitlana unlocked the phone immediately.

"It's from Yaroslav!" the mother rejoiced and opened the message. "My dear Mom, I love you very much. Forgive me for everything." The ground seemed to sway under her feet. The phone slipped from her hands and fell onto the tiled floor. Svitlana fell shortly after. Minutes later, the coffee boiled over and extinguished the flame.

---

[12] Cezve – a small long-handled pot with a pouring lip designed specifically to make Turkish coffee. It is traditionally made of brass or copper, occasionally also silver or gold.

Illustration by Oleksand Prodan

Epilogue

"Now that you have walked your entire path, I want to ask you," the Creator paused momentarily, as if doubting the appropriateness of his question. "Tell me, which life would you want to live again? Which of them do you remember the most?"

"You know, Creator," he replied thoughtfully. "I would prefer to be a butterfly. I've lived nine lives and each was unique, unforgettable. I loved and was loved. I killed and was killed. I experienced joy and sorrow. I found and I lost. But I never felt as light and thrilled as when I was a butterfly. I lived each day as if it were my last. I relished every moment. I loved sincerely and openly and these feelings gave me a sense of exhilaration. They truly energized me. My love was reciprocated in a way it never was afterward. My heart was full of joy and my head spun with the overflow of emotions. Yes, I experienced the bitterness of loss, which I didn't survive. I wanted to go where she went. But I was destined to take a long journey. Finally here I am. All the transitions have passed, but I have retained the feelings I experienced while being a butterfly."

Then, after a short pause, he added: "Actually, I can say that my entire path resembles the life of a butterfly and its flight. Everything is cyclical: Birth – Life – Death – Rebirth. Like the sunrise and sunset. Today, you may be an ugly caterpillar and tomorrow a beautiful butterfly!"

Illustration by Oleksand Prodan

He fell silent and the Creator thought before saying: "Alright, I understand you. Now all your knowledge and experience will be transferred to the Memory Vault. The Guardians will now take you to where you will reside forever. Go, you have completed your mission."

Two Guardians appeared in the foggy corridor and gestured for him to follow them.

"Oh, I almost forgot." He stopped and, turning back to the Creator, said: "The prison priest sends his regards. Good that I remembered!"

"Yes, I know. Thank you. You'll meet him soon too," the Creator replied. "Now go, they are waiting for you!"

The path was short. The Guardians led him to a place filled with fragrances. He had never seen anything like it before. The place resembled a fairy tale. Everything was different from what he was accustomed to seeing during his transitions: different plants, unknown sounds and even the scents were completely unfamiliar and new. Everything was tuned to immense happiness. There he met others like him. They moved slowly, as if gliding over the surface, giving the impression that they were fluttering amidst all this beauty. Suddenly, his attention was drawn to a figure standing with its back to him. There was something painfully familiar about this silhouette. He decided to get closer, and only then did he understand everything. Two small pearly dots on her back were looking at him.

Illustration by Oleksand Prodan

The Raven

Teker

Teker slowly opened his eyelids. The thought that this was his last morning pierced his consciousness. He breathed heavily, drops of sweat trickling down his temples. The old Janissary[1] understood everything and his mind, fogged by illness, cleared instantly.

"My last day has come," thought Teker. "Well, so what? I have lived a long life, and I am not ashamed to stand before Allah".

Then he remembered his dream, which awoke him in a cold sweat. It was indeed a terrible vision. Teker dreamed he was a raven: flying, looking at the ground from above, soaring in the clouds with other birds, black ravens like himself. Suddenly Teker saw people on the ground killing each other. It was a great battle. The entire earth was covered with the bodies of the fallen. There were so many that it was impossible to count. They lay alongside horses, blood flowing from all sides down the hill, small streams gradually merging into raging torrents. After the battle, it was time for the feast. Ravens flew in from everywhere and began their meal. Teker sat on the chest of a young fallen warrior. His face was pale and serene. He appeared to be resting. Teker was

---

[1] The Janissaries — the regular infantry Corps established by the Turkish Sultan Murad I in 1365. This military force comprised boys aged 8 to 16, taken as a tax or captured during military campaigns. Thus, many of the Janissaries were Christians, who were later raised in strict Islamic traditions.

Illustration by Artem Burlyk

about to peck at his eyes when the warrior suddenly opened them and stared intently at the bird. Startled, the raven jumped aside. Horrified, Teker realised it was his son looking at him. The same one whose birth a gypsy had foretold and who would never come into the world.

It was noisy at the slave market. The sun was already nearing its peak. In the busy square, merchants from various countries competed for business trying to outshout each other. Near the entrance, a few beggars with outstretched hands pleaded for alms. The Khan's[2] guards patrolled the rows, keeping order. Here and there, dervishes[3] in tattered robes wandered, occasionally stopping to talk with some of the sellers or buyers. The visitors could buy everything there: handmade carpets, fine silk, spices, kitchen utensils, domestic animals and birds. But the main goods were located in the corner of the square: captives taken during the last raid to the north. Frightened children stood next to the adults guarded by several armed warriors who prevented the crowd from getting too close to the slaves.

For a moment, the market fell silent and then it buzzed differently – the slave trading began. The square was immediately filled with the shouts of sellers and buyers of humans. First, strong young men were selected for the sultan's fleet of galleys[4]. Then, eunuchs[5] took the most beautiful girls aside for the Khan's harem[6]. Elderly captives and young girls were taken by lone buyers who needed workers for their households. The most valuable goods remained – the boys. They huddled together, glancing fearfully at the people surrounding them. When the clamour of the trade died down, a tall blue-eyed warrior in a high hat, with a long white plume hung to his waist and

---

[2] Khan — a medieval sovereign of China and ruler over the Turkish, Tatar, and Mongol tribes.
[3] Dervish — a Muslim monk beggar.
[4] Galley — a ship or boat propelled solely or chiefly by oars.
[5] Eunuchs — a castrated man placed in charge of a harem or employed as a chamberlain in a palace.
[6] Harem — a women's quarter in a Muslim household.

a yataghan at his side, approached the boys. He looked them over carefully and uttered something in a language they did not understand and gestured for them to follow him.

Vasylko, cautiously glancing around, struggled to keep up with his fellow captives who followed the warrior. They moved through the city's narrow streets, revealing to the boy a new world. Onlookers curiously watched the procession.

"Yasir,"[7] — Vasylko heard several times as the captives marched through the crowds. He was fearful as he didn't understand that word. The big warrior kept a close eye on the fearful dozen captives in case they lagged or tried to escape. But the scared boys did not even think of running. They trudged, huddled together, looking around in fear.

As they passed a small square, a young gypsy woman in bright clothing approached Vasylko and placed a bread loaf in his hand. He hesitated for a second but did not let go of the loaf, pressing it to his chest. The woman quickly disappeared into the crowd. Vasylko didn't even have time to look at her closely, as her face was hidden by a scarf. He only remembered her black, coal-like eyes, looking with kindness and pity. Vasylko hid the loaf under his shirt and continued.

Soon the procession reached the port where many different ships were docked. There were fishing boats, small schooners, and galleys. A large frigate was anchored at the entrance to the port. Vasylko had never seen the sea and he gazed in amazement at the endless water. The white seagulls circled above the waves as the scorching sun's rays reflected on the blue waters. There was a large lake near his village, where he went fishing with his father, but the boy could never imagine there could be so much water that its end would not be visible.

---

7 Yasir — a term used to refer to captives taken during military campaigns or raids, who were then sold into slavery for work on galleys or in personal households. Attractive girls were sent to the sultan's harem and boys were trained to become Janissaries.

The procession approached the galley, from which a gangway had been lowered. The blue-eyed warrior stopped to inspect the crowd of boys. They stood huddled together, fearfully looking around. It was clear that not only Vasylko was seeing the sea and ships for the first time. The warrior glanced over the boys and was satisfied. Everyone was present and no one had fallen behind. He jabbered something while pointing to the gangway. The boys, terrified, huddled even closer together and did not move. The warrior shouted again, his face taking on a fierce expression, while he pointed with his hand for the boys to board via the gangway. The eldest of the boys cautiously stepped onto it and began to climb up.

One by one, they climbed aboard, where another warrior similarly dressed awaited them. He said something and, waving his hand, led the boys away. The children, hunched over, walked through a narrow wooden passageway, flanked by rows of half-naked people chained to the oars. Many of them had visible scars from severe wounds on their backs and sides.

Trembling, they passed the rows of oarsmen. No one spoke a word, only the silent gazes of the chained slaves followed them. They descended a staircase into the hold and the hatch closed behind them. The young captives were enveloped in complete darkness. The stifling air reeked of vomit and human excrement. Gradually, their eyes adjusted to the darkness, and they settled on the straw piled in a corner. Exhausted from their ordeal, they fell asleep instantly.

They slept a long time and eventually awoke to the hold's floor creaking from side to side. It became clear to everyone that the galley was sailing on the sea. Faint rays of sunlight penetrated through the cracks in the hatch which enabled them to become familiar with their dark surroundings. They were very hungry and more so thirsty. However, the hatch was closed and no one dared to open it. Then Vasylko remembered the flatbread he had hidden in his shirt and took it out. The smell of bread spread through the hold. His fellow captives looked at him with hungry eyes from the darkness. Vasylko divided the bread into equal parts and gave some to each of the boys. Everyone greedily pounced on the food and at that moment, it seemed that there was nothing tastier in the world than that bread. The feeling of hunger subsided a little, but their thirst only grew stronger.

A while later the hatch opened, and a stranger appeared. He pointed his finger at the eldest boy and gestured to him to come up. The boy slowly climbed the stairs. A few minutes later, he returned, holding a water skin and two large loaves of bread. The bread was again divided equally. Then everyone took turns drinking from the water skin. The cool water gave the captives strength, and they revived a bit.

Time passed and no one disturbed the boys further, so they comfortably settled back to sleep on the straw. They were awakened by loud cries on the deck. Not understanding anything, the boys stood up and stared at the hatch: the only place that connected them to the outside world.

"What is happening?" Vasylko asked, most likely to himself.

"We'll find out soon," the eldest boy responded, glancing around at the others.

In the semi-darkness, their frightened faces were visible. Some of the children did not understand the language Vasylko and the eldest boy were speaking, which made everyone feel more uneasy.

"What's your name?" the teenager asked Vasylko.

"Vasylko. What about yours?"

"Yaroslav," the boy replied. "Stay close to me and don't be afraid. It's always easier together."

Suddenly, the hatch opened, and bright sunlight flooded the hold. The boys squinted and covered their eyes with hands. In the opening, they saw the same warrior who had brought them from the market to the galley. He said something in his language and gestured for the boys to climb up.

The boys headed up, shielding their eyes from the blazing sun. The warrior pointed and they again walked between the rows of slaves chained to the oars. Dozens of eyes wistfully watched the boys as they headed to the shore. The boys felt unbearable pain from these looks, understanding that a grim fate awaited them.

Once more, they filed along the long path through the streets of the unknown, majestic city. The boys looked curiously and fearfully at the fortress walls, clay houses, and tall minarets. Everything was unfamiliar and strange to them. Passing by a crowd of traders, Vasylko heard someone whisper: 'Devshirme'[8]. He did not know what this word meant, but he understood it referred to them. They stopped at the big house and the accompanying warrior led them inside. He pointed to a shaded corner, and they sat on the ground. Their wait was short. Soon, a man in a turban[9] and long robe appeared, clapped his hands, and signalled for the boys to follow him. They stood up and marched down to a basement where they joined other boys who looked at the newcomers with distrust and fear. The new arrivals silently settled on the floor. Vasylko made himself comfortable next to Yaroslav. Closer to night, he spoke to his new friend: "What do you think is going to happen to us?"

"I don't know, but I think we'll find out everything tomorrow morning. In any case, let's stick together," Yaroslav replied.

The long journey had exhausted the boys, and they fell into a deep sleep. Vasylko dreamed of his mother, who was walking through a wheat field carrying a basket of food. She looked at him with tenderness and love.

"I'll feed you now, my little one," she said, but suddenly the sky darkened, and a tremendous hurricane swept in and carried her far beyond the horizon.

Vasylko screamed and woke up. He looked around. It was hard to see in the darkness, but he could hear everyone peacefully snoring, lying sprawled on the floor.

---

[8] Devshirme — in the Ottoman Empire, a form of tax on non-Muslim populations, a system of forcibly recruiting boys from Christian families for future upbringing and service as the Sultan's personal slaves.
[9] Turban (from Persian durband) – a type of headwear based on cloth winding.

In the morning, the basement door opened and the same man in a turban muttering something, gestured for them to get up. One by one, the boys started to go upstairs. Gathering all together, the man led them along. The children found themselves in a long colonnade with a view of a large courtyard. Here, the boys were taken to a corner of the courtyard and told to sit on the ground. Three guards with long bardiches[10] appeared and stood on different sides around the boys. Then two servants arrived: one holding a basket of bread and fruit, the other carrying a large jug of water. The servants distributed the food among the boys, waited for them to finish their meal, and left silently.

Not much time passed before the courtyard began to fill with people. Among them, the giant warrior who had brought the boys from across the sea stood out. He was accompanied by several other warriors. After a brief silence, they approached the boys and said something in their language. The frightened boys huddled together, not understanding what was expected of them. Then one of the warriors demonstrated that they needed to run in a circle within the courtyard. One by one, the boys started to run, gradually picking up speed. The warriors and priests stood by the wall and watched them closely. A command rang out and everyone stopped. Then the children were lined up and instructed to throw a stone. The boys were grouped by height and age. Each group's participants took turns throwing the stone, trying to throw it as far as possible. Then a horse was brought into the courtyard and each of the boys had to ride it. At one time, Vasylko's father had taught him to ride and, despite his short stature, he successfully handled this task.

The trials lasted several hours and at the end of the day, the boys were divided into two groups. The older ones, including Yaroslav, were taken away by the warriors wearing the long white plumes. As Yaroslav was leaving, he turned to Vasylko and shouted: "Don't forget who you are and where you come from! God willing, we'll meet again!"

---

[10] Bardiches — a long pole weapons with a large blade, used by guards and soldiers in medieval Eastern Europe.

"I won't forget!" the boy shouted back.

They didn't know that soon they would be forced to forget not only their lineage but also their names.

In the morning, the remaining boys were taken to the market and assigned to different craftsmen. Therefore for the next few years, the captives would live with their families, learning the language, crafts, traditions, and culture of the local people.

Two oxen slowly pulled the creaking cart along the dusty road. Vasylko gazed into the distance, towards the vast city they had left behind. The boy didn't know where this taciturn man, who had chosen him at the market, was taking him. But he understood that his future now rested in this man's hands. The cart was loaded with hay, so Vasylko, comfortably settled on it, started looking at the sky. It was almost the same as back home. The thought of his homeland brought tears to Vasylko's eyes. His mother had been in the field when the enemies attacked their village. His grandfather had tried to protect him but fell, killed by an arrow. The boy was captured, tied up, and placed on a horse to be taken away. Had his father been there, those bandits would have had a tough time, but he was at the Sich[11] and couldn't help at that moment.

Vasylko remembered when his father visited home, and they went fishing together. A skilled warrior, he often demonstrated his mastery. Vasylko especially loved when they would place a large pumpkin on a pole and his father, galloping on a horse and, shouting "Assa!", would slice it into several pieces. The saber in the cossack's hand moved so fast it was hard to follow its motion.

He had told his son then: "This is how we deal with our enemies and those who betray the faith of our ancestors, my boy."

---

[11] Sich — Sich was an administrative and military center of the Zaporozhian Cossacks in Ukraine in 16th - 18th centuries.

Vasylko was calm about his father but worried about mother. He hadn't seen her on the way south or at the slave market. Was she alive? These heavy thoughts tired him, and he fell asleep on the cart, which swayed rhythmically as it moved. He woke up to the shout of the man driving the oxen. The animals had stopped and Vasylko, getting up on the edge of the cart, saw that they were near a small house. The man, having jumped off the cart, entered the house. A minute later, a woman in a headscarf and a long dress came out, extended her hand to Vasylko, and said something. The man stood behind her, smiling approvingly. The boy climbed off the cart and followed the woman into the house.

Inside, everything was different from his home. A large carpet was spread on the floor, with several pillows scattered on it. The man said something and pointed to the carpet. Vasylko sat at the edge, tucking his legs under him. The master of the house nodded favourably. A minute later, the woman brought them each a bowl of soup and a bread roll. The boy was very hungry but afraid to start eating. The man nodded as if inviting him to eat and the boy eagerly began to eat. The woman stood nearby, watching them eat with emotion.

After lunch, she brought some clothes for Vasylko and explained with gestures that he needed to change. The man waved to him, and they went to another room, where he helped the boy put on the unfamiliar attire. When they returned, there was tea and sweets on a small table. The man again invited him to sit and waited to enjoy the baklava and tea.

Then pointed to himself and said: "Makhmut."

Next, he turned to the woman and spoke: "Aygul."

After that, he extended his finger to the boy: "Teker."

Thus began the new life of the teenager, who became Teker, the son of the village blacksmith Makhmut and his wife Aygul. They had no children of their own, so they devoted all their love to Teker: the boy whom Allah had sent them. At first, Teker struggled to communicate with his new parents, but over time, his fear subsided, and he felt like a member of their family. He accepted Islam and began to learn the language and traditions.

Gradually, he made friends among the village boys, although they did not immediately accept him into their group. Teker liked working in the forge with Makhmut, who was now his father, the most. He took the boy with him every day. Initially, the boy just assisted, watching the fire blaze in the furnace. Then, he was allowed to work with metal for the first time. His new father taught him all the intricacies of blacksmithing and soon Teker forged his first blade. It was like the birth of a firstborn. He put his soul into the weapon and deservedly received praise from the master.

Years passed, Teker grew and progressed. Now, it was hard to distinguish him from the local youths. He had grown, strengthened, and was no longer the frightened boy that Makhmut had brought with him a few years ago. The time soon came and Teker first felt his heartbeat faster when he met the neighbour's daughter Hanum. However, he didn't dare to talk to her for a long time, although he saw that she was also interested in him and joked about him with her friends.

"Who am I and who is she? We will never be together," Teker thought.

But thoughts of the girl never left him for a minute. Hanum came to him in his dreams, where they flew hand in hand like two birds. In these moments, he felt like the happiest person in the world.

Finally, the day came when he mustered the courage to speak to Hanum. She was on her way to the well to fetch water, lost in her thoughts.

"Hanum, I want to talk to you," he called to her.

Startled, the girl flinched and looked around fearfully, covering her face with her scarf.

"You scared me, Teker, What do you want to talk to me about?" she asked.

"You know…," the boy hesitated, but then, looking her in the eyes, continued. "I think about you constantly, you appear in my dreams. This feeling that has arisen in me grows stronger every day. I understand that one day I must leave home and go to serve our Sultan, but I can't imagine my life without you. I want you to become my wife."

"I like you too!" Hanum replied, blushing slightly. "But you have to ask my father if he will allow us to marry."

Teker flew home as if he had grown wings.

"Father! I want to ask you something," he said entering the forge.

Makhmut put the hammer aside and, wiping the sweat from his forehead, asked: "What is it you want to ask me, son?"

"Father, I want to marry Hanum, Akim's daughter," he said.

Makhmut frowned, but after a brief silence replied: "Alright, son. I will talk to her father. He knows our family well and often asks about you. But you must understand that you belong to our Sultan and one day you will go to serve him. Those who become Janissaries are forbidden to marry."

"I know, father. But I hope that through my loyal service, I will earn this right," Teker exclaimed passionately.

As Makhmut promised, he spoke with Hanum's father and one day the blacksmith and his son visited their home. The guests were seated in honoured places and treated to tea and sweets.

"Your father tells me you want to marry my daughter Hanum," Akim began, looking intently at the boy.

"But you will soon leave to serve our Sultan and who knows when you will return. Moreover, Janissaries are not allowed to have families. Things might change in the future, but will my daughter be willing to wait for you all this time?"

"Zarema!" he called his wife. "Bring Hanum, I want to ask her something."

A minute later Akim's wife entered the room with their daughter.

"Hanum, this boy wants to marry you. I have known him for many years, and I like him very much, but he will soon leave to serve. Are you willing to wait for him as long as it takes?" her father asked sternly.

"Yes, father, I will wait for him," she replied demurely.

"Very well," Akim responded. "I give my consent to your marriage, but not now. You must earn the right to marry from our Sultan. Return a hero and we will celebrate your wedding."

From that moment, Teker had a goal he would have to pursue for many years while serving the Sultan.

His parents saw Teker grow up and secretly rejoiced for him. Aygul loved him with all her heart and treated him with such tenderness that one day Makhmut said: "You understand that the time will come when he will leave? It will be painful for you to part with him. He is the Sultan's servant, and we have no right to him."

"Don't you love him yourself?" Aygul asked with tears in her eyes.

Makhmut frowned, lowered his head and, without saying anything, went outside. He tried not to show his feelings, but he admitted to himself that his wife was right. Yes, he had grown to love the boy and now he dreaded the day when their son would be taken from them.

That day finally came. Early in the morning, Makhmut heard the neighing of horses and the bustle of voices outside his house. His heart froze as he listened, hoping they were not the Sultan's envoys. He slowly put on his robe and stepped outside. When he saw the riders, his heart sank: it was indeed them.

"Greetings to you, master, may your days be long," one of them called out. "We have come to take the one who belongs to our great Sultan."

"Peace be upon you, warriors of Allah. You must be tired from your journey. Please, come into the house, rest, and taste our bread. You have a long journey back ahead of you," Makhmut said, bowing his head.

The warriors tied their horses and entered the house, where they saw a frightened Aygul standing in the corner, covering her face with a scarf.

"Aygul," Makhmut said. "Feed our guests and bring Teker. His time has come."

Silently, the woman bowed and left. The guests settled on the carpet, waiting. A moment later, Aygul returned with Teker and then went to the kitchen to prepare refreshments.

"Teker, my son," Makhmut addressed the boy. "The time has come for you to leave our home. These warriors will take you to the capital, where you will serve our Sultan faithfully and truthfully. Over the years, you have become a son to us, and we believe you will uphold the honour of our family. Serve honestly and may Allah protect you."

Teker was a bit confused but received his father's words with dignity.

"Father, you can be at peace. You will never be ashamed of me," said Teker.

After resting and having a meal, the guests prepared to leave. Throughout this time, Aygul stood in the depths of the house, crying. Parting with her son was very difficult for her. When it was time to say goodbye, she hugged Teker to her chest and said: "I will pray for you every day and always wait for you as long as my heart beats."

"Mother, don't worry about me," said Teker. "Thank you for everything. I will visit you when I can. Tell Hanum that I will keep my promise and marry her. It's a pity we didn't get to say goodbye."

He mounted the horse brought by the warriors, waved goodbye and, rode off after the riders.

The dust raised by the horses' hooves had already settled, but Makhmut and Aygul still stood, looking into the distance where their only son had gone.

Upon arrival in the capital, Teker was placed in the preparatory school Acemi Oğlan[12]. There he was to spend seven years before being initiated into the Janissaries. The years were filled with hard and exhausting training under the watchful eyes of demanding instructors. The school maintained strict discipline and any infraction was punished severely. The Sultan's slaves were raised in silent obedience and loyalty to their ruler. At the same time, future Janissaries were granted many privileges:

---

[12] Acemi Oğlan — a preparatory school akin to a cadet school, where young men were trained for service in the Janissary Corps.

they were exempt from the obligatory five daily prayers, were well-fed, and received financial support. Teker understood the importance of his training, so he was very diligent. The students learned archery, horseback riding, fencing, and hand-to-hand combat. Much attention was given to studying foreign languages, literature, theology, law, and calligraphy. In all areas, Teker was among the best in acquiring knowledge. Clerics from the Bektashi Dervish Order[13] did everything to raise future Janissaries as ruthless and cold-blooded warriors, ready to die for their Sultan.

The years of training flew by swiftly. Teker matured significantly. The frightened boy who had been brought to this city on a galley many years ago was gone. When Teker turned twenty-five, he and several other students were initiated into the Janissaries and moved to live in the barracks.

They were personally greeted by the commander of the orta[14], yayabashi[15] Yusuf – a strong and tall warrior without a beard, with long moustaches hanging down to his chin, dressed in an elegant kaftan, shalwars, and boots. The yayabashi's head was adorned with a hat – a yuskiuf[16], with a wooden spoon attached at the front, serving as both a badge and a practical tool.

"Welcome, new Janissaries," Yusuf's deep voice resonated as he inspected the new recruits. "You have completed your training and proven yourselves worthy. Now you are part of the elite Corps of our great Sultan. Serve him with honour and loyalty and you will be rewarded."

The new Janissaries, including Teker, stood tall and proud, feeling the weight of their new responsibilities and the honour bestowed upon them. The

---

[13] The Bektashi Dervish Order — the Janissaries were closely connected with the Bektashi Dervish Order, whose members served as regimental chaplains. The order also significantly influenced the formation of the Janissary Corps' hierarchy. Researchers note a certain resemblance between the Janissaries and European military-religious orders.

[14] Orta — a regiment, a military unit within the Janissary Corps.

[15] Yayabashi — a commander of an orta.

[16] Yuskiuf — a white felt cap with a piece of cloth attached at the back, resembling the sleeve of a Sultan's robe or a ceremonial hat of a Zaporozhian Cossack. A wooden spoon was attached to the front of the cap.

years of rigorous training had transformed them into disciplined and skilled warriors, ready to serve their Sultan with unwavering dedication.

"You are entering the service of our Great Lord Sultan Osman the Second, may Allah prolong his days," Yusuf said. "From now on, you are all brothers and members of our large family. All your possessions belong to the brotherhood, on which you can always rely, both in peace and in war. Betrayal of the brotherhood is punishable by death."

That was the start of a new chapter in the life of the boy-slave, who now belonged to the caste of the chosen, the elite Corps composed of the Sultan's personal slaves.

Three peaceful years passed. Teker diligently served, earning a promotion: he was appointed odabashi[17]. During peacetime, Janissaries had ample personal time, and each used it as they saw fit. Teker primarily used his time to perfect his military skills. Few could match him in saber fencing and in archery, he had no equals. The young Janissary read a lot and even tried his hand at writing poetry.

One day, Teker decided to go to the market to buy himself a new dagger. His love for cold weapons had developed when he worked in his father's forge. Craftsmen from various countries brought their products to the market and Teker, with his knowledge, enjoyed talking with them. Here, one could choose a curved shamshir[18] made of Damascus steel or a strangely shaped kilij[19]. There were countless knives and various daggers, each waiting for its owner. Teker had a particular passion for yataghans[20]. They fit so comfortably in his hand that he felt them to be its extension.

---

[17] Odabashi — an assistant commander of an orta.
[18] Shamshir — a type of Persian sword with a radical curve.
[19] Kilij — a type of one-handed single-edged and curved scimitar used by the Ottoman Empire.
[20] Yataghans — Ottoman short sabers with a double-curved blade, popular among the Janissaries.

One day, as Teker was walking along the market stalls, a gypsy woman called out to him: "Hey, warrior. Do you want me to tell your fortune?"

"No, thank you, I don't believe in fortune-telling. Our lives are all in the hands of Allah," Teker replied.

"I'm not asking for money and it won't take much time," said the gypsy woman, looking intently into his eyes.

"Well, alright, tell my fortune," Teker said, not understanding why he agreed so quickly.

The gypsy woman took his left hand and gazed at it for a while, murmuring to herself. Suddenly, she frowned: "Beware of your father, warrior. He will want to kill you."

"What nonsense are you talking about, woman?" Teker exclaimed angrily, pulling his hand away.

"You will be a great warrior," the gypsy woman continued, ignoring his outburst.

"Also you will have a son, a great warrior like you, but he will die in battle, defending a fortress," she finished with sadness in her voice.

Teker laughed: "What? A son? Don't you know we are forbidden to have families? Foolish woman, you can't earn your bread with such nonsense."

"You can laugh at me, but it is as true as the fact that you still remember the taste of that flatbread I gave you many years ago on the street of the city across the sea," the gypsy woman said and then disappeared into the crowd.

Teker stood there, stunned, as memories flooded back. He remembered the gypsy woman who had given him the flatbread when he was walking by the street together with other boys. The taste of that bread had stayed with him, a small comfort in those dark times. Shaking his head, he continued through the market, but the gypsy's words lingered in his mind, unsettling him.

Illustration by Artem Burlyk

Teker came to his senses after a moment. He remembered everything: the street, the crowd, the tall warrior in the same uniform he wore now, the galley with slaves, and the taste of that bread. He shook his head and looked around, but the gypsy woman was nowhere to be seen. Without buying anything, he wandered back to the barracks, pondering the fortune-teller's words. Troubling thoughts consumed him: "Who am I? Where do I come from? What awaits me in the future? A son? What son? Maybe she's right and I can finally marry Hanum? What nonsense did that crazy woman say? Fear my father? What's so frightening about a simple village blacksmith? But the taste of that bread... I do remember it."

Teker returned to the barracks feeling out of sorts. He felt a mortal fatigue and lay down to rest. The young warrior had a dream, where he was a raven and flew high above a battlefield, watching people killing each other. He circled in the sky with other ravens, like himself, waiting for a feast. When the battle ended, he descended from the sky and started choosing his prey. The bird didn't notice the wounded warrior aiming a crossbow at him. The arrow whizzed and pierced his body. In a moment, flapping his wings, he plummeted down.

Teker woke up from his scream and sat up on the carpet. Cold sweat trickled down his temples.

"What a dream?" he thought.

"Are you alright?" he suddenly heard. It was his close friend Gokhan.

"You screamed so loudly in your sleep that I got scared for you. Were infidels* chasing you?" he laughed.

"No. I dreamed I was flying and then I was killed by an arrow," Teker replied grimly.

"Well, that makes sense," Gokhan said. "No one wants to die. Although dying for our Sultan is a special honour."

A vast army disembarked from ships onto the shore. It seemed endless. There were heavily armed cavalrymen (sipahis), light cavalry (akinjis), artillerymen and archer-azaps. But the most numerous were the Janissaries. Their white plumes on their hats stood out against the general backdrop. The army formed ranks and moved forward, where the enemy awaited. It was so numerous that it seemed like nothing and no one in the world could stop it.

After a few days, the Sultan's army camped before a massive enemy fortress. The enemies were far fewer, but they were heavily fortifying, building defensive structures and installing devices for defence. The Sultan, without delay, ordered an attack. The battle lasted all day, but far from retreating the enemy counter-attacked several times, inflicting irreparable damage on the Sultan's forces. By this time, Teker was already a commander of an orta and personally led his soldiers into battle. Seeing the defenders' tenacity and the losses among his troops, he repeatedly ordered retreats to save his soldiers' lives. Enraged, the Sultan threw more and more forces into the fight. Weeks of siege passed, and the fortress remained impregnable. Teker's orta had been halved, but he continued to lead them into attacks, always at the forefront.

On that fateful night, nothing foretold disaster. The army, exhausted by the siege, rested, campfires burned, and guards patrolled the camp. Suddenly, the sound of horse hooves was heard and as if from the ground, hundreds of horsemen sprang up, charging the camp with wild cries. Teker gave the order to defend, but it was too late. A battle ensued and the camp was overrun. Teker shot one of the attackers with a musket, knocking him off his horse and, drawing his yataghan, he threw himself into the fray. But from the darkness of the night, a rider emerged and, with a cry of "Assa!," charged at Teker. The Janissary tried to defend himself, but the rider, skillfully wielding his saber, struck. The saber slid along Teker's yataghan and slashed the warrior's shoulder. He remembered nothing after that.

Illustration by Artem Burlyk

"Teker, they've overturned the cauldron[21] and are marching to the Sultan's palace," said a breathless Gokhan.

"Stay with them and keep me informed," Teker replied, slowly rising from his cot.

He was still weak but could stand and walk.

"Got it. He'll pay for everything!" shouted Gokhan as he disappeared through the doorway.

Teker was in the infirmary for several weeks, recovering from injuries sustained during the campaign. Osman II's forces had failed to capture the fortress, forcing him to sign an unfavourable and humiliating peace treaty. Upon returning home, the Sultan blamed the Janissaries for his defeat, provoking the righteous anger and resentment of these elite soldiers. The conflict escalated, leading to a rebellion. The Janissaries stormed the palace, killed the guards, and captured the Sultan. He resisted desperately: "You are my slaves! How dare you raise a hand against me?"

But realising that no one was coming to his rescue, he suddenly cowered, whimpering and begging for mercy. However, the Janissaries were not swayed. The Sultan was taken to the square and publicly strangled with a bowstring.

Following this, a council was convened, attended by the highest-ranking Janissaries, elders and clerics. The young and promising Ibrahim was appointed the new Sultan. To appease the Janissaries, he ordered gold items to be melted down and generously rewarded them. Only then did the turmoil cease and life in the country returned to its former course.

Teker was nearly recovered. His left arm was still supported by a sling. The wound had healed, but it sometimes reminded him of its presence with

---

[21] The regimental cauldron — analogous to a regimental flag. During campaigns, it was carried at the front of the unit. Losing the cauldron was severely punished: the unit would be disbanded and those responsible executed. There was also a tradition: if a condemned person managed to hide under the cauldron, they would be pardoned. An overturned cauldron signalled a rebellion.

pain and his arm didn't function as it used to. However, he hoped it would be back to normal over time. Since he couldn't fully perform his duties, he decided to visit his parents, whom he hadn't seen for many years since the Sultan's envoys took him away. But more than anything, Teker wanted to see Hanum, the girl he had kept in his heart all these years and promised to marry.

The long journey led him to his parents' home. From a distance, Teker heard the hammer's clanging in the forge.

"Father is still working," Teker thought joyfully.

At that moment, the door opened and Aygul appeared on the threshold.

"I felt that you would come! I knew it," she said, her voice trembling with tears and she rushed to Teker, but stopped when she saw his bandaged arm.

"What is this? Were you wounded?" she asked anxiously.

"Yes, Mother, but it's all in the past now. Is father in the forge? Let's go visit him," said Teker, embracing her.

Nothing had changed in the forge since he left. The same smells, the same sounds and the same blacksmith standing with his back to them, hammering a new blade on the anvil.

"Makhmut," called Aygul. "Look who has come to see us."

He turned and a smile lit up his face.

"Son! You've come. Praise Allah."

But his face darkened immediately upon seeing the injured arm.

"Father, I kept my word. You and Mother will never be ashamed of me. I'm sorry it took me so long to come. It was Allah's will."

Makhmut stepped forward, his eyes filled with pride and concern.

"Welcome home, son. Your bravery and dedication are evident. Come, let's sit and talk. There's so much to catch up on."

As they made their way inside, Teker couldn't help, but ask: "What about Hanum? How is she? Tell me, is Hanum still here? Has she not married?"

"She's well, my son and been waiting for you, just as you promised each other. She always asks about you and sometimes helps us with the household chores," Aygul smiled.

Teker's heart swelled with hope and anticipation, knowing that the love he held in his heart for so long might soon become a reality.

"I'll go visit her, alright?" he said with impatience in his voice.

"Of course, go ahead," replied mum.

As Teker walked, he felt his legs becoming like jelly. He had never felt this way, not even in the war. Now his courage seemed to have vanished. He spotted Hanum's slender figure from a distance. Once again, like many years ago, she was carrying a pitcher of water on her shoulder.

Teker quickened his pace and caught up with her.

"Do you need help, Hanum?"

Startled, she almost dropped the pitcher. Teker steadied it with his healthy hand to prevent it from breaking.

"You've come?" she exclaimed joyfully. "It's been so long."

But she immediately frowned upon seeing his arm: "Are you wounded?"

Those simple words made Teker's head spin.

"It's alright. Can I help you?"

They carried the pitcher in silence, holding its handles together.

"Are you staying long?" Hanum finally broke the silence.

"For a few days. To visit my parents and, well, you too," Teker said, feeling bashful.

"You're as shy as ever!" Hanum laughed and those words made him wish he could disappear into the ground.

"The new Sultan has issued a decree allowing Janissaries to marry. Now we can get married. Have you changed your mind about marrying me?" Teker asked, already knowing the answer.

"Of course not, I've waited for you all these years," Hanum replied, tears glistening in her eyes.

"We need to inform my father that you have kept your promise and can now marry me. Everything must be done according to the law," she added.

"Shall we take a walk now? Would you mind?" Teker asked hopefully.

"I'd love to. Just let me inform my parents," Hanum replied. "Thank you for helping me carry the pitcher."

Teker only then noticed they had already reached her house.

Hearing voices from the yard, the old Agha[22] came out of the house and greeted Teker.

"Greetings, warrior. I'm glad to see you. I hope you have kept your promise?"

"Yes," Teker replied. "Now I have the right to marry your daughter."

He spent a few endlessly happy days with his parents.

Before his departure, Teker and Hanum walked in the garden and saw a pair of ravens circling high in the sky.

"Do you know that a raven chooses its mate for life?" Hanum asked.

"No, I didn't know that," Teker replied, surprised.

"They're like people. Very intelligent and faithful to each other until death," Hanum said.

At that moment, he remembered his dream where he was a raven and frowned. A feeling of inexplicable anxiety settled in his chest. Hanum noticed the change in his mood but did not dare to ask the reason. She felt good with Teker, even when they simply walked silently, holding hands.

Then came a long farewell and Teker promised to return for her.

---

[22] Agha — an honorific title for a civilian or officer in Ottoman times. In rural communities, this term is used for people who own considerable land and are influential in their community.

The return journey to the capital seemed much shorter to Teker. He flew, buoyed by love and all his thoughts were with the one who had been in his heart all these years.

Sometime later, Teker's life changed drastically. He married Hanum and brought her to the capital. The newlyweds bought a small house and began to set it up. Hanum always tried to please her husband when he returned home from service. In his turn, he rushed home to see the one who had captured his heart many years ago. Soon they had a daughter, Shirin and, two years later, twin girls, Emine and Dilar. Looking at how the girls were growing and flourishing, Teker often thought: "They are so beautiful, and each with a strong character. They should have been born boys, not girls."

Sometimes he pondered the gypsy woman's words, who had foretold the birth of a son: "Could she have been wrong, and I will not have an heir?"

Years passed. The country lived from war to war. The Janissaries always had something to do. If there were no distant campaigns overseas, then at home, rebellions would occasionally flare up, which had to be suppressed. Teker outlived several Sultans, achieved a high military rank, and retired with a well-deserved pension for his loyal service. However, illnesses and injuries sustained in the campaigns had taken a toll on his health. He was slowly dying.

That day, as the sun was setting, casting a golden glow over the city, Teker sat on the bench in the garden of his home. Hanum and his daughters were inside, preparing dinner. He looked up at the sky, watching a pair of ravens flying together and a sense of peace washed over him.

Hanum came out and sat beside him, holding his hand.

"Are you alright?" she asked softly.

"Yes, I am," Teker replied, his voice weak but content. "I have everything I ever wanted. A loving wife, beautiful daughters, and a life filled with honour".

Hanum squeezed his hand, her eyes filled with tears.

"We have been so blessed," she said.

Teker smiled and closed his eyes, feeling the warmth of Hanum's hand in his. He knew his time was near, but he felt no fear. As he drifted into a peaceful sleep, he dreamed once again of flying high above, knowing he would always be remembered by those he loved.

"Hanum," Teker said in a quiet but still strong voice. "Bring me my favourite yataghan. I want it to be with me in my final moments."

Hanum went and soon returned, carrying the yataghan – Teker's beloved and faithful weapon. He remembered every notch on its blade. Countless enemies had met their end by it.

"Place it beside me," Teker said, grasping the hilt of the yataghan with his right hand. "I want you to know that I have always loved you and I never forgot you, even in moments of mortal danger. Take care of yourself and tell our daughters to raise my grandchildren to be honourable people."

Teker paused, the old wounds flaring with unbearable pain.

"Do you remember those ravens we saw high in the sky?" Teker continued. "Well, I was always faithful to you. You were the only one in my heart. Forgive me, if I was ever unfair to you. Now leave me."

Hanum wept and, covering her face, went inside the house. Teker fell into a reverie once more and this time he dreamed of flying towards the sun. He felt light and carefree. The old Janissary soared into infinity, towards his home. He exhaled weakly and his exhausted hand slipped from the hilt of the yataghan.

The Raven

Since she was gone, the raven tried to avoid the nest, the place where everything reminded him of her and where their children had come into the world. He was already quite old, but still strong enough to fend off young and brazen rivals. Every morning, the raven flew high into the sky and circled, observing everything happening on the ground. He enjoyed watching how the earth changed with each season. From the bird's eye view, this was clearly visible. He loved spring the most, the time when everything starts to bloom and spread its fragrance. Life begins in spring. Perhaps he was fond of this season because it was the time of his birth? The old bird didn't know the answer to this question, but he always eagerly awaited the start of nature's awakening. As winter's rest ended, the earth stirred, transforming its colours. The air filled with the chatter of birds and the voices of animals. In summer, life reached its peak. The raven watched with interest as people tended the land and harvested crops. Besides, near humans, there was always something to eat.

Then came autumn with its array of colours. The ground seemed to be covered with a multi-coloured carpet. Leaves began to fall from the trees. The old oak, where they had built their nest, seemed bare and defenceless to him. At the end, the winter came, cold and hungry. The entire land was covered with a white blanket, sharply contrasting with his kin, the other black ravens like him. Winter was hard, but he knew that soon the snow would melt, and life would thrive again. He also knew that early in the spring, they would have children, and they would need to be cared for a few weeks until the little ones became independent and soon left the parental nest forever. Life on earth seemed like an endless cycle. A sort of circle, where the end of one period became the beginning of another. But this spring, for the first time in many years, their little ones would not come into the world. The raven's mate had not survived the long frosty winter. Therefore, he felt sad and lonely. He flew and awaited the moment when he too would go where she had gone.

"Yes, it's probably time to get out of this place! It's so cramped in here," thought the little bird and began to move slowly, trying to make himself more comfortable.

He had grown too much and there was less and less room in the egg.

"Well, my beak is already strong enough, so I should try to break this wall that separates me from the outside world," the chick continued to ponder.

It aimed and started pecking at the eggshell. Long hours of persistent effort brought their first results: a ray of sunlight broke into his dark kingdom.

"Finally! How much longer can I sit in this darkness!" the chick rejoiced.

It pecked even more vigorously and soon the egg cracked in half. The chick was able to stretch its legs and move freely. The first thing it saw were two pairs of eyes watching him closely from above.

"These must be my parents. Well, that's very good! I'm so hungry," it thought and opened its beak as wide as possible.

Illustration by Artem Burlyk

The chick was not alone in the nest. There were four more eggs, but the brothers or sisters were not in a hurry to break free. Therefore, all the parents' attention was focused on him and, consequently, all the food went to him, as he had an excellent appetite!

Days and weeks passed. Now, he had company. Following him, four more chicks hatched, making the nest increasingly cramped each day. From early morning until sunset, the parents flew in search of food to feed their perpetually hungry brood. Over time, the chicks grew feathers, becoming more like their parents, but none of them were in a hurry to leave the home nest, which the pair of ravens built on branches of an old oak tree. When the wind howled and the oak branches banged against the nest with a terrifying rattle, the young ravens would huddle together and gaze fearfully at the sky.

Finally, the day came when the young raven dared to take his first flight. He was scared, but the presence of his father soothed him. The young raven climbed out of the nest onto a sturdy oak branch, flapping his wings to feel his strength before the first flight. He still felt fear, but the desire to fly was stronger than any apprehension. He pushed off and, spreading his wings, soared into the sky. His father flew beside him, encouraging his son. They climbed higher and higher into the sky. The views that the young raven saw from above took his breath away and his heartbeat faster than ever before. He finally saw everything that had been hidden behind the tree branches during all those months in the nest. Father and son flew over endless fields and forests, and the young raven felt as if this flight would never end. The sun stood at its highest beckoning him with its rays. After flying to their heart's content, they returned to the forest.

Months and years passed. The young raven grew stronger and seldom thought about his first flight. Now, he was an adult, skilled at finding food and capable of defending himself when necessary. There were many enemies among birds and animals, but he was mostly wary of humans. He had often seen them kill his fellow ravens and, even more frequently, he had seen them kill each other. The raven couldn't understand why humans acted this way since there was always plenty of food. Why kill each other only to eventually become food for the ravens?

That summer, everything was as usual. Meadows and fields were in bloom, the earth was fragrant and teeming with life. The raven flew and observed everything happening around him. Suddenly, he saw birds attack a young raveness, who was desperately trying to defend herself. He rushed to help drive her attackers away. The raven had plenty of experience in such battles. Then pair flew side by side and that flight made them both realise that from now on they would fly together.

The raven was always by her side, and she was delighted to have a protector. He didn't understand what was happening to him. The excitement he felt during their first meeting didn't fade. He, a former fighter, was unfamiliar with such feelings. When he was with her, it seemed his wings grew as large as a dragon's and his chest swelled with emotions.

He forgot his hobbies and interests, as all his attention was firmly fixed on her. In her turn, she responded with tenderness and care. The time came for them to build their own habitat in a tall oak tree in the forest, not far from a huge fortress. He loved flying there. There was always something to scavenge and the people were friendly. The raven even made friends with some of them after he once saved the town's inhabitants from enemies.

Illustration by Artem Burlyk

It happened early one summer morning. He flew to the fortress as usual, hoping to find something to eat. Suddenly, he saw many armed men sneaking towards the stronghold. They moved quietly and tried not to make any noise. The raven felt these men could threaten those behind the fortress walls. He circled above, thinking desperately about what to do. Then he flew to the lookout post, where the fort's guards were usually stationed. But he was disappointed to find the guards sleeping peacefully on bales of straw. He cawed several times, but no one reacted to his cries. He looked back at the approaching armed men and realised time was running out. He spotted a large stone on the ground, landed, and picked it up with his beak before rising high into the sky. He flew over the sleeping guards and, aiming, dropped the stone on one of them. The stone hit the guard's iron helmet, but the soldier didn't wake up. The alternative was for him to descend onto the chest of the guard and peck him hard on the nose so he would wake up. That plan worked perfectly. The guard cried out in pain and jumped to his feet, grabbing his spear. The raven flew away and perched himself on the edge of the wall.

"I'll show you!" the guard shouted, running to the wall while waving his spear.

The bird flapped his wings and flew towards the approaching attackers. The guard immediately understood everything.

"Alarm! Everyone to the walls!" he shouted.

Seeing the guards awake, the raven cawed again and flew away. The garrison hastily prepared for the impending attack. Thanks to the raven's timely warning, the fortress was ready when the armed men reached the walls. The attackers were repelled, and the townspeople were saved. From that day on, the raven became a respected and welcomed guest in the fortress, as the defenders knew to whom they owed their lives.

So, the place for the nest was not chosen by chance. Spring came and the raveness laid the first four eggs. She sat on them constantly, while the raven ensured she was fed. Gradually, chicks began to hatch from the eggs. They were funny and unlike their parents: featherless, yellow-mouthed, and always hungry. The adult birds had to work hard to feed their growing family.

Soon the chicks started to fly. At first, they didn't fly far and constantly returned home. Then, they began to appear at home less and less frequently. Eventually, the raven and the raveness were left alone, but only until spring brought new chicks. This cycle repeated every year and seemed to them it would last forever. But a harsh and hungry winter arrived. There was no escape from the piercing cold. The birds tried to warm each other with their bodies, but it helped little. One frosty day, the raven flew out of the nest hoping to find some food. People in the fortress were also struggling, but the raven found some offal that the people had discarded as garbage. He flew home, where his mate was weakened by hunger and cold. But it was too late. She died before his return. The raven stood on the edge of the nest and looked at his beloved, hoping for a miracle, but her frozen body showed no signs of life. Only her feathers occasionally rustled in the fierce wind that blew repeatedly.

Because of the shouts of men and the neighing of horses, animals hid in their burrows and birds took refuge in the trees. The battle had been raging on the field for several hours. Cries and groans filled the air with horror. The raven was observing the battle sitting high in a tree. He knew that soon it would all be over and the time for a feast would come. He had seen this many times before, but he still hadn't found an answer to his question: "Why do people kill each other? What do they lack?" Meanwhile, the people below continued to fight with unspeakable fury. Eventually, the moment came when everything went quiet and only the occasional groans of the wounded could be heard. The green field had turned brown with blood and the air was filled with the smell of death. The raven pushed off from the branch and circled above the battlefield. Gradually, other ravens joined him. Soon entire flocks of birds were flying over the field, eyeing their prey. The raven descended lower and lower, having already chosen whom he would feast on. He didn't notice that a wounded soldier was watching him closely. The soldier was pinned down by his horse, but still able to hold his crossbow. When the raven descended within shooting distance, the soldier aimed and pulled the trigger. The arrow pierced the bird's body. He cried out and, folding his wings, plummeted like a stone. Down to where the kingdom of the dead lay.

Laura

"So, you confirm your connection with the devil?" Bishop Antonio asked, staring intently into Laura's pain-clouded eyes.

The executioners stood next to the bleeding girl, waiting for the bishop's signal to tighten the iron clamps on her legs even more.

"Yes, I admit it," Laura groaned and, fainting, dropped her head onto chest.

Her body became heavy and slumped forward. The metal clamps that tightly held her arms, legs and chest prevented her from falling off the chair studded with sharp spikes. The bishop rose and, with a self-satisfied smile, headed for the exit of the dungeon. At the door, he stopped and, turning, ordered the executioners: "Prepare her for tomorrow. Abbot Firenze is coming to visit us. We'll need to put on a real show".

"Laura, where are you?" a voice called out in the garden. "Everyone is waiting for you."

It was Felicia, the older sister.

"I'm here," the girl shouted in response. "Come here. Look what I found."

Felicia approached and opened her mouth in surprise.

"Wow," she exclaimed. "How many of them are there?"

Illustration by Artem Burlyk

Hundreds of colourful butterflies sat, fluttering their wings on the large oak tree in their garden. It seemed like the entire tree trunk was wrapped in a blanket made from patches of various coloured fabric. The girls stood holding hands and it looked to them as if the oak was also alive. That in just another moment it would walk, shaking the earth from its roots.

"Wowww!" Felicia exclaimed. "I've never seen anything like this."

"Me neither," Laura replied. "It's so mesmerizing."

The girls stood a little longer and then quietly, so as not to disturb this paradise that fluttered incessantly, went to the house.

"Aunt Anna Maria has arrived," Felicia announced. "She's asking about you. You know how much she loves you."

"Oh, I've been waiting for her. Last time she promised to bring me a doll just like our cousin Lucia's."

Laughing, both sisters ran into the house, where their parents and their mother's older sister, Anna Maria, were waiting for them.

"Finally," exclaimed their aunt. "I was wondering where you disappeared to. Let me hug you."

The woman rose from the chair, walked towards the girls, and hugged them.

"I didn't come empty-handed."

Anna Maria took a small package from her bag and handed it to Felicia.

She unwrapped it and her heart fluttered with joy. Inside was a chain with a beryl cross.

"How beautiful. I'll wear it to church tomorrow. Father Ignacio will be very pleased. Thank you, auntie," the girl stood on tiptoe to kiss her aunt.

"Well and for you, my little one, I brought what I promised," said Aunt Anna Maria, pulling out a cardboard box.

"I already know what's inside!" Laura shouted joyfully and started jumping up and down, clapping her hands.

Yes, it was the knitted doll with a porcelain face, hands and feet. It looked at the girl with its turquoise eyes and it seemed as if it was about to say something.

"Thank you so much, Auntie. I'm so happy," exclaimed Laura and hugged her.

The parents looked at them tenderly, happy for their girls. They were growing up well-mannered and humble, just as the Holy Church taught them.

"Well, let's go have lunch. But first, let us give thanks to our Creator," said the father and everyone started praying at the family table.

Afterward, they sat for a long time, chatting about family matters, the children and events that had taken place in their towns since they last saw each other. Many years ago, Anna Maria got married and moved to live with her husband in another province. But the sisters tried to see one another as often as possible and visited whenever they could.

"Have you heard? They caught the witch who cast a spell so that all the cows in our village stopped giving milk?" asked Anna Maria.

"No, we hadn't heard," replied her younger sister Isabel.

"We have enough of our own here," interjected the head of the family, Raul. "Just recently, Father Ignacio said during the service that in the neighbouring village, two witches were communicating with demons and when they tried to catch them, they turned into black ravens and flew into the sky."

"Yes, these are terrible times," said Anna Maria. "It's good that the Church protects us from all kinds of devilish plots. Otherwise, I wouldn't know how to live."

Everyone present crossed themselves in fear.

"Let's have some tea," Isabel suggested, trying to lighten the mood.

The girls declined and went to their room, while the adults sat and talked for a long time, discussing the news and reminiscing about their childhood and their parents who had passed away a few years ago.

Years passed and the girls grew up to be diligent and hardworking, bringing joy to their parents. Their home was always a place of comfort and peace. The neighbours constantly praised them, using them as examples for their children. Every Sunday and on holidays, the girls attended church services conducted by the elderly Father Ignacio. He loved both of them and often asked to help tidy up the inside of the church, to which they always gladly agreed. It was a special honour to clean the house where God resides. Father Ignacio watched their efforts with affection and once said: "Each of us will be rewarded according to our deeds. For you, my children, the Kingdom of God is prepared for. I have never met souls purer than yours."

Eventually, Felicia began dating the tailor's son Jorge and soon they expressed their desire to get married. They decided to wed in the local church and Father Ignacio was happy to unite them in marriage. Laura was over the moon with happiness for her sister and proudly carried her veil during the church ceremony. In the evening, finding a moment of free time, the sisters sat together on a bench and talked.

"Jorge is a wonderful guy. I believe he will be a devoted husband to you," said Laura.

"Yes, I love him very much. I miss him whenever he's not with me. It's such a pleasant feeling," responded Felicia.

"I'm so happy for you. Please don't forget about me and remember, your children will have a loving and caring aunt."

The sisters laughed and hugged each other.

Before they parted Felicia whispered to her younger sister: "I want you to find your true love! I will pray to God for it every day!"

After Felicia left home, Laura felt lonely; she missed talking with her so much. A few years passed and, to help her parents, she got a job at a bakery. This helped distract from her sad thoughts and provided significant support to elderly parents.

Laura liked the smell of freshly baked bread and pastries. There was nothing like this scent. Sometimes Laura felt that she smelled like bread. Passers-by would come in involuntarily; it was impossible to walk past this bakery because of this slightly sweet aroma. Laura also enjoyed talking to customers, always finding a kind word for each of them. This set her apart from Don José's other assistant, Claudia, who had been working at the bakery for many years but wasn't as friendly as Laura.

The bakery owner, the old baker José, couldn't be happier with such a worker and always found a moment to praise her. The baker had no children. His wife had died long ago without leaving him any heirs. Now, looking at Laura, he tried to pass all his unspent paternal love to this girl. José taught her the secrets of baking. He explained how to knead sourdough and yeast dough. He showed how to determine the quality of flour. With special pleasure, the baker taught the intricacies of braiding various pastries from dough ropes. José did his work with such love that Laura felt he was putting a part of his soul into it. Maybe that's why their bread was so famous in the area.

Laura didn't immediately notice the young man who had recently started buying bread from them. Just an ordinary customer, like many others. Well, perhaps he was a bit more attractive than the others. Tall, dark-haired, with a pleasant smile. He already knew her name, but Laura couldn't bring herself to ask his. She considered it unseemly for a well-reared girl.

"Hello, Laura," she heard the familiar voice. "I'd like some of your fresh, crispy bread as usual."

The dark-haired young man stood at the counter, smiling.

"Good day," the girl replied. "Just bread, nothing else?"

"Well, not quite," the young man said, blushing.

"Pastries too?" Laura asked, not understanding.

"My name is Luis," he blurted out, glancing around. "Would you like to take a walk in the park with me this evening?"

It was clear how hard it was for him to say these words. He turned completely red and looked like he was about to sink into the ground.

Laura was taken aback. No one had ever asked her out on a date before.

"Well, I don't know," she stammered. "I have so much work to do…"

"I'll wait as long as it takes! Señor José won't mind if you leave early. He's known me since childhood."

"Really?" Laura was surprised. "He never mentioned your name to me."

"He's just afraid I'll steal his favourite worker," the young man said shyly and laughed.

Laura looked at him closely. She was starting to like him. Polite, modest, but not a pushover. He looked at her confidently and persistently with his coal-black eyes. She also liked his voice. It was low and slightly breathy. No longer a boy, but a young man.

"Well, alright. I'll run home after work and then come to the park."

"I'll wait for you by the waterfall! It's very beautiful there in the evening." "Ah, I see! I knew it," the bakery owner stood in the doorway, looking rather stern. "You finally got to my girl?"

Without the slightest embarrassment, he replied: "Señor José. If anyone knows, you know I would never hurt her. You and my father would twist me into a pretzel."

"Yes, I know, I know."

The stern mask fell from José's face in an instant. He approached the young man and playfully ruffled his hair.

"If I didn't know, you'd be out of here in a heartbeat."

"You can go home early today. Claudia will handle everything! Don't worry," he said to Laura.

In the evening, the young man and the girl met by the waterfall. The place was stunning at sunset. Laura noticed a boy standing with his back to her, thinking about something without noticing her.

"What are you thinking about?" she asked, approaching him.

Luis started in surprise and looked around guiltily. "Sorry, I didn't notice you coming. I like observing celestial bodies. There's so much mystery and unexplored things out there. These sprays reminded me of distant planets. Shall we take a walk along the river?"

He took her hand, and they walked beside the shore. The light reflected in the water among the lilies, making it seem like it was blooming with them. Swans swam gracefully on the river, creating an illusion of tranquility. Luis and Laura walked along the shore for a long time. The young man turned out to be a good conversationalist. He was interested in literally everything and was particularly fascinated by astronomy, though this was still dangerous. Heretics who went against the Church's teachings were openly persecuted, and the most fervent were thrown into dungeons.

Since then, they hadn't been apart for a single day. Señor José secretly rejoiced at the development of the relationship between Laura and Luis. The old man considered passing his business to them. Laura had become very dear to the baker, and he trusted her like no one else. He had known Luis since childhood. Their family was highly respected in the town. José had no relatives and old age was already knocking at his door. It was becoming harder and harder to manage his business.

There was one man Laura disliked so much that, after receiving payment for the bread, she tried to disappear from his sight as quickly as possible. His name was Don Pedro, and he was one of the most respected and pompous members of the city council. Laura often had to deliver bread to his home, as she did for many others.

That day, Don Pedro was alone in his mansion, so Laura tried to leave even faster once he paid her.

"Wait, don't rush off," he said. "I have a proposition for you. I've been watching you for a long time. I hope you could use some extra money. Your parents are so old now, they need medicine. You're so beautiful, so you could earn a little bit more."

Don Pedro locked the front door and turned back to her: "You're a grownup girl now, right? You understand what I'm talking about?"

Fear gripped Laura. She looked around and backed away. But there was no one to call for help. Meanwhile, Don Pedro approached, grabbed her chest and tried to kiss her. Laura covered her face with her hand and turned away. However, she couldn't break free, and he continued trying to kiss her. In a moment, Don Pedro pushed Laura onto the table, but she picked up a bronze candlestick and struck the attacker on the head with all her might. He immediately went limp, and his grip loosened. She unlatched the door and ran outside. Laura ran, tears streaming down her cheeks. She felt as if her whole body was covered in filth and that all the passers-by were looking at her with disdain. She could still smell the unpleasant odour of that disgusting man. A few blocks away, Laura stopped to catch her breath and compose herself. Señor José must not see her in this state.

"I will never tell Luis about what happened!" she thought. "It's such a shame..."

"So, you, esteemed Don Pedro, claim that this person," the judge pointed at Laura, who was sitting on the defendant's bench. "Had an intimate relationship with the devil?"

"Yes, Your Honour, I do claim that," Don Pedro said, bowing his head.

"Tell us, how did you come to know about this?" the judge crossed his arms on the table.

"That evening I was walking in the park and saw this girl in the depths of the trees. Her behaviour seemed suspicious to me, so I decided to follow her. I hid behind a tree and started watching. At some point, a demon emerged from the shadows of the trees, and she engaged in carnal pleasures with it. Then the demon turned into a large black raven and flew into the sky, while the girl turned into a hare and ran into the depths of the forest!" Don Pedro said with feigned fear.

"That's a lie! He's lying! It's slander!" Laura shouted, jumping up from the bench.

The judge signalled her to sit back down.

"Thank you, esteemed Don Pedro," said the judge. "We have no further questions. The court will adjourn for several days. Remove the defendant."

"This is not true! Your Honour, you can't judge me based on this man's testimony!" Laura tried to shout, but no one heard her anymore.

The guards grabbed her by the arms and led out of the courtroom.

"Laura, I'm here!" heard the unfortunate girl.

She saw Luis. His eyes were confused, and he looked scared. He didn't understand what was happening. His whole life had changed in one day.

"I am innocent!" Laura managed to shout before being led out the door.

The dungeon was dark and foul-smelling. Rats scurried and squealed in the corners. Laura shrank and pressed herself into a corner. She didn't understand what was happening. One day, people in black robes came to their shop and took her away. Señor José tried to intervene, but he was rudely pushed aside, unable to do anything. She had been sitting here for several days after the trial and no one had come to see her. How she wished she could send a note to Luis and explain everything! Of course, this was all Don Pedro's doing! He slandered her because she had rejected him. But how could someone be thrown into prison on such grounds?! Laura bit her lip. If she had told Luis about Don Pedro earlier, maybe she would be free now.

The massive door creaked open. The torchlight penetrated the darkness and Laura shielded her eyes with her hand. Two people in black approached, grabbed her by the arms, and dragged to the exit. The prisoner and her escorts navigated a maze of corridors and finally arrived in a large room. Looking around, she understood everything. It was a torture chamber. A rope with a noose hung from the ceiling, a rack was placed in the corner. On the table lay instruments whose purpose she could only guess at. In the centre of the room stood a chair with sharp spikes instead of a seat. Laura's heart sank.

"Bring her to me," she heard a voice from the darkness. Only then did Laura notice a man sitting on a large, throne-like chair.

The girl was brought before that man, and she recognised him. It was Bishop Antonio. Laura had seen him several times in her church during holidays. He could deliver beautiful sermons about loving one's neighbour, earthly sins and God's punishment. Now he was sitting here in this dreadful room. For a moment, the girl was even glad to see him. She thought she could explain everything to him and the reverend bishop would release her. After all, he often spoke about justice.

"Your Excellency," Laura whispered. "This is a horrible misunderstanding. I have been slandered."

"Are you trying to say that the esteemed Don Pedro, who has done so much good for our town, lied?" the bishop asked indignantly.

"But it is true, Reverend Father! Don Pedro tried to assault me, and I hit him with a candlestick because of it," the girl replied.

"How dare you slander a respected man, you wicked girl?!" the bishop shouted. "You are accused of consorting with the devil. Is it not because of you that our villages have bad harvests, and the cows give little milk? Do you confess that all this is due to your connection with the devil?"

"What connection? I have a fiancé, and I love him," Laura said fearfully.

"You must not understand where you are," the bishop fumed, signalling the men in black.

They approached and tore off the girl's clothes. Finding herself completely naked in front of the men, especially a priest, Laura cried and tried to cover herself with her hands. But they tied her wrists and hoisted her up to the ceiling. Losing her footing, the girl desperately kicked her legs, turning around her axis.

"I repeat my question," she heard. "Do you confess your connection with the devil?"

"No, I do not confess! It's a lie and slander!" Laura shouted from above.

The bishop nodded to one of the torturers. There was a whistle of the whip. The girl screamed in pain, but even more from helplessness and indignation.

"I repeat my question," said the bishop. "Do you confess your connection with the devil?"

"No, I do not confess," the girl whispered through tears.

The whip whistled again and again. Her body was seared with excruciating pain. She didn't remember how many times they asked her and how many times the whip lashed her body. The poor girl fainted from the unbearable pain. Laura regained consciousness on the floor when a bucket of cold water was poured over her.

"Look at that, she's a stubborn one!" she heard one of the torturers say. "We haven't had one like this in a long time."

"Don't worry, we know how to get what we need," another one smiled.

They lifted the unconscious girl's body and dragged her to the spiked chair. Placing her on it, they clamped her hands and feet in iron shackles. Sharp pain pierced her body as dozens of sharp spikes dug into her flesh.

"You," the bishop paused to savour the horror in the girl's eyes. "Do you confess your connection with the devil?"

"No," the girl groaned.

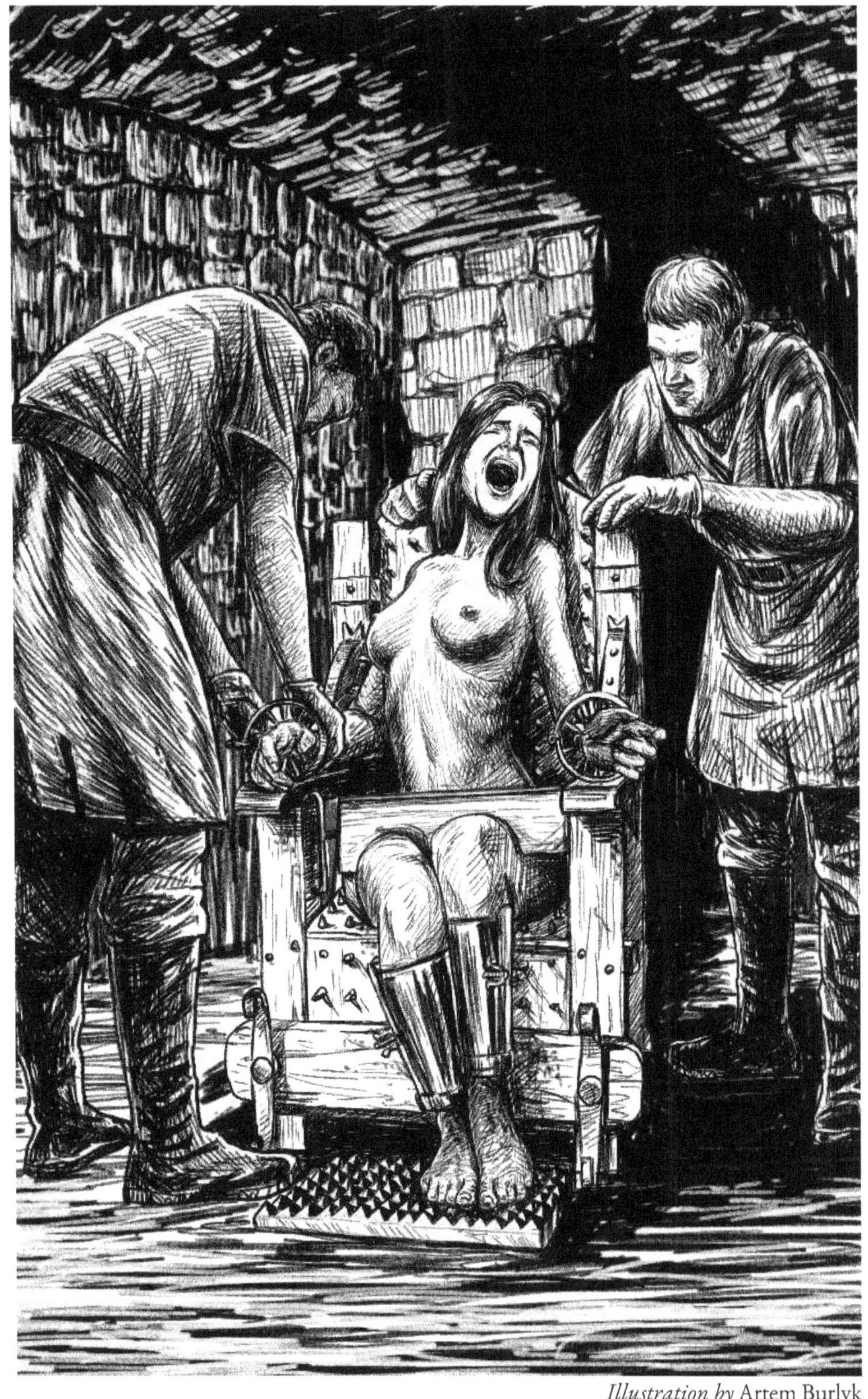

Illustration by Artem Burlyk

The bishop nodded to the men in black and they set to work. The torturers approached the victim from both sides, knelt and began to turn the screws of the clamps, which slowly but relentlessly tightened around her legs. Simultaneously, dozens of spikes penetrated her body, causing unbearable pain. Every movement inflicted excruciating agony. At one point, Laura thought she heard the crunch of breaking bones.

"God, if you exist in this world, save me," the girl groaned, unable to move.

"In this place, I am God!" said the bishop. "So I will save you. But only if you confess your connection with the devil. So, do you confess?"

"No," the girl whispered and fainted.

Laura regained consciousness from the shock of a bucket of icy water poured over her head. The water, running down her body, turned red. Looking at her blood the girl began to cry. She suddenly realised that being unconscious, not seeing all this and not feeling the pain, was the greatest blessing on earth. The torture continued for several more hours and only after extracting a "confession" was Bishop Antonio satisfied. Laura was dragged back to the dungeon and thrown to the floor. She lay there all night. The rats, sensing fresh blood, at first cautiously, then more boldly, began crawling over her and gnawing at her flesh. She lacked the strength to chase them away. She fell into darkness once more.

There was a knock, and the door creaked open. Several people in black stood on the threshold, holding torches.

"We bring you liberation and healing from all your suffering," one of them said, giving a sign to those standing behind him.

Two of them lifted the girl. She couldn't stand on her feet as her bones were broken. They then dragged her up the stairs. Laura, not understanding anything, looked at them with a cloudy, pain-filled gaze. She understood everything when the procession arrived at the town square. A huge crowd had gathered and, in the centre, stood a post surrounded by wooden logs.

The girl cried from the helplessness and pain that engulfed her entire body. Laura was brought to the post and tightly tied with ropes. She slowly raised her head and looked around. Hundreds of people were silently watching her, but she was looking for only one.

"Laura, I love you!" came a voice from the crowd.

Through her tear-blurred vision, she saw Luis and tried to say something, but could only move her lips. Her beloved stood among the crowd, his eyes full of tears. The city guards let no one approach the execution site. He bit his lips in despair and helplessness so hard that they bled.

"By the decision of the Holy Inquisition, Laura of the Lopez family has been found guilty of witchcraft. She has confessed to dealings with the devil and crimes against the residents of our town. The sacred court sentences her to purification by fire!" proclaimed the man in black, giving a sign to the people with torches.

They approached and began to light the logs from different sides.

The fire slowly grew, inching closer and closer to the girl's feet. The heat became unbearable and there was no air to breathe. Laura gazed into the faces of the people, hoping to find pity or understanding, but she saw nothing, but hatred and anger. The bonfire blazed stronger and stronger. The girl threw her head back and whispered: "Lord, if you exist in this world, accept my sinful soul and free me from earthly suffering!"

At that moment, she saw a raven soaring in the air, circling above the square and she thought about how much she wished to be in the bird's place. To fly, enjoying the air currents and the warmth of the sun, looking down at the earth and thinking about nothing.

Laura felt the flames begin to envelop her body, scorching her skin and filling the air with unbearable heat. She screamed, but it was not so much from physical pain as from despair and fear.

"Luis, I love you!" she tried to cry out, but her voice was barely audible.

She felt life slowly leaving her as the fire continued its relentless pursuit. Laura knew this was the end, but her soul refused to believe it. In the last moments of her life, she saw Luis's face and his eyes full of tears and despair. The fire rose higher, and Laura felt her consciousness begin to fade. The last image that flashed before her eyes was her beloved's face, the only bright star in the encroaching darkness and with this image, she went into eternity.

On a balcony overlooking the town square stood bishop Antonio and abbot Firenze. The abbot was the head of a men's monastery in a neighbouring province, and it was Bishop Antonio who had once appointed him to this position. Later, the monastery received a special status, placing the abbot under the direct authority of the Pope. Since then, they maintained close relations. The abbot remembered well to whom he owed his position.

They stood, leaning on the balcony railing and looked down at the girl writhing in agony.

"One less witch in the world," said the bishop.

"Did she take long to confess?" asked the abbot.

"No one resists for long with us," the bishop replied with a self-satisfied smile and discreetly placed his hand on the abbot's hand.

"After the evening prayer, I will be waiting for you in my quarters," said the bishop quietly, without turning his head.

Abbot Firenze slightly nodded in agreement and a lecherous smile appeared on his face.

Illustration by Artem Burlyk

Bianca

Bianca stood, pawing at the ground. Her rider's anxiety transmitted to her as he sat on her back, gazing at the enemy ranks lined up far below in the valley. This feeling was familiar to her, as it wasn't her first time in battle. But every time, the excitement made her heartbeat faster and her body tremble. Sensing that his faithful companion was nervous, the rider patted her neck and, leaning towards her ear, said: "It's all right, my dear. Calm down. We've been through so much together. Everything will be fine, Bianca."

The rider said this, being unsure that they would win today's battle. This time, the enemy was experienced and strong. His numerous victories spoke volumes. Their combat tactics were unpredictable and constantly changing. There was much to think about. Yes, their troops had also been well-trained, but now the enemy was formidable, and the man understood this.

It was sunny in the clearing. The horses grazed peacefully, lazily flicking their tails to ward off annoying insects. That morning, a mare had given birth to a small black foal and was tenderly watching it make its first attempts to stand on its legs. Her legs, as thin as sticks, were still very weak. The foal stumbled unsteadily and could not yet get her bearings after being separated from her mother. She had spent almost a year in that tight place. It was especially uncomfortable for her during the last couple of months, having to stay cramped with folded legs. But now she could see with her own eyes everything she had heard while in her mother's womb. She did not stray a step from her mother, occasionally nudging her belly to suckle some milk.

Time passed, spring turned into summer and the filly noticeably grew. Now she confidently ran through the meadows and slopes, but always within her mother's sight. The herd leader also kept a strict watch over her. He was always on guard, as wolves sometimes attacked the horses and they had to defend themselves. The smallest foals, the infirm and the old horses were easy prey for the predators. So the leader, a sturdy black stallion, ensured that the weakest stayed within the herd and never wandered off alone. He maintained discipline and strict order, aided by other horses who served as guards. In case of danger, they would signal the whole herd and the horses, bunching together, would flee from the threat.

After a year the filly turned into a slender young mare. Her black coat gleamed in the bright sun. The mane and tail streamed behind her as she ran, making it seem as if a mythical dragon was flying. Besides the horses, she made friends among other animals and birds that were plentiful in the area. She especially enjoyed racing with a black raven that visited her daily. Sometimes she felt like she was flying through the sky like a bird. They became so close that the raven would perch on her back, and she would leisurely carry him around.

Recently, she also noticed a young black wolf that came from the forest and watched her intently. At first, the filly would simply run away and hide among the other horses. But over time, she began to feel that he posed no threat to her. Moreover, she sensed that he wished to befriend her and run through the field in a race.

Illustration by Artem Burlyk

Time passed and the young horse lived an independent life. She had learned to find food in any weather. Last winter, snow fell, and she had to search for food breaking through the ice crust with her hoof.

This summer, the weather was wonderful. The filly loved to occasionally run up a high hill, near the edge of the forest. From there, the wonderful views left her breathless: on one side there was a valley, where her herd grazed, and on the other the endless sea. Each time she went to the hill, the leader snorted angrily, indicating his disapproval, but the filly didn't pay much attention. She knew he was worried about her and tried not to disappear in case of danger. In such occasion the mare could join the herd where she would always be protected.

Today, she was on the hill again, basking in the warm sun and nibbling on the juicy grass on the slope. Suddenly, she became alert and looked towards the sea where the sunlight reflected off the water's surface. In the middle of the bay, she saw a huge sailing ship. It was anchored close to the shore and two boats headed towards the land. Not tempting fate, the filly hurried down to the valley, where the herd leader awaited her impatiently.

The horses were peacefully grazing in the valley when suddenly, as if on command, they all raised their heads. A distant sound of hoof-beats reached their ears. The guards instantly took their positions on the flanks, while the rest of the horses huddled together. The leader nervously pawed at the ground, staring intently in the direction from which that noise was coming, ready to bolt at any moment. Then, riders appeared from both sides, galloping straight at the herd, gradually encircling them. The leader neighed loudly and led the horses, attempting to break through the group of riders.

The herd was now racing through the valley, with riders flanking and chasing them, shouting and throwing lassos, capturing one horse after another. The filly also tried to escape these terrifying riders. Suddenly, a lasso looped around her neck and an unseen force pulled her aside. She reared up, trying to free herself from the noose, but it only tightened around her neck. Then she saw the one responsible rider on a large bay horse pulling the rope.

Then, she and several other captured horses were taken to the seashore and transferred to the ship she had seen from the hillside. They were placed on the upper deck, firmly tied to the rail with ropes. The captain gave the command and the ship, raising its sails, slowly began to sail towards the horizon where the sky met the water. The horses nervously stamped in place and neighed loudly. Everything was new and strange to them: these people running around the deck, shouting incomprehensible things, the ship swaying rhythmically on the waves, the vast sea that was both frightening and alluring.

The filly watched as the shore of her homeland slowly receded and thought: "I will never see my mother again. These cruel beings have separated us forever. It's good they didn't catch her. Let her live in freedom. It is so sweet to be free and you only realise this when your freedom is taken away."

Then she asked herself: "I wonder, what about my father? Is he still free? I don't even know who he is."

These thoughts made the filly sadder. She closed her eyes and lowered head.

The horse sensed his approach before she heard it. The filly started and opened her eyes. Yes, it was him. Her captor. The one who had taken away her freedom. She neighed and nervously pawed at the deck. He stood next to her, silently watching. Then he stepped forward and extended his hand, intending to stroke her. This made her even more agitated, and she struggled, but the strong rope held her securely.

"Don't be afraid," the man said. "I won't harm you."

But the animal did not understand his words and continued to nervously prance in place.

"All right, all right, I'll go. Just don't be so nervous," the man said and slowly stepped back.

A few days later, she was taken to a farm where several other horses lived. Here she could run, but only within the confines of the fence, which greatly distressed her, as she had been born free and always roamed wherever she wanted. The man who had caught her came to the farm every day, but the mare wouldn't go near him and always tried to keep her distance.

He could watch her for hours and once said aloud: "I'll name you Bianca. You're so beautiful! It's impossible to take my eyes off you."

Weeks passed, followed by months. Bianca had already adapted to her new place. She had become more accustomed to the people who brought food and water and took care of the horses. There was only one person she still feared, the one who had taken away her freedom. He kept coming, always talking to her. In those moments, Bianca would snort angrily and paw at the ground. But eventually, her fear passed and one day she allowed him to come close and stroke her mane.

"Good girl! Don't be afraid of me," he whispered in her ear.

Bianca still snorted and shook her head, but she no longer ran from him. She also liked his voice. The slight rasp of his baritone had mesmerized her. With each passing day, she feared him less and less. He tried to visit her as often as possible and, to her surprise, she began to get nervous if he was late.

One morning, a groom and his assistant came to her and, after some fussing, put on a bridle and saddle. It felt strange and uncomfortable, but she spent several hours in them. Then these men returned and removed everything. This went on for several days. Bianca didn't understand why they were doing this until one day the man, who had brought her here, mounted her. Taken by surprise, Bianca reared up, trying to throw the rider off, but she couldn't, as he was an experienced rider. The struggle lasted a few minutes and Bianca relented under the confident hand of the horseman.

"It's all right, my girl, it's all right!" he soothed her, stroking her neck. "We are one now. I will never hurt you. I promise you."

Several years passed since then and her master never broke his promise. She never heard a harsh word from him. He always made sure she was well-fed and watered. Often spoiled her with treats, which she loved. In return, she was devoted to her owner and saved him from certain death several times, carrying him swiftly away from pursuers. Once, their squad fell into an enemy ambush. Many warriors were killed, and her master was seriously wounded. He managed to stay in the saddle, which saved his life. Bianca broke through enemy lines and brought the rider home, where he was lifted from the saddle and given first aid. He was treated for a long time and during this time, no one could approach her. She waited only for him, her master. The man who had once taken away her freedom.

Illustration by Artem Burlyk

Today was an unusual day and Bianca felt it. The enemy ranks could be seen in the valley below. They had lined up their soldiers in a semicircle and stood motionless in anticipation. Colourful banners fluttered above their heads and occasionally, the neighing of horses could be heard. Everyone was waiting for the signal to attack, but no one dared to start first. Then, a broken horn sounded, followed by the beating of drums. The cavalry pointed their lances forward and advanced toward the enemy lines. From a slow trot, the cavalry transitioned to a gallop and soon the spear-tipped avalanche was racing down the valley towards death. When they were almost upon the enemy lines, there was a slight stir. The soldiers took a few steps back and cannons, hidden from the attackers, replaced the infantry. A command rang out and the enemy ranks were engulfed in clouds of smoke. The next moment, fire mowed down the attackers, turning men and horses into a shapeless mass.

Then came a second volley, followed by a third. But neither Bianca nor her master heard it. They lay side by side on the ground as if to show that even in death, they remained together. The battle did not last long. The field was strewn with the dead and wounded. Blood flowed in streams down the valley and high in the sky, the ravens circled, waiting for their feast.

Nathaniel

"We know you're behind Roger's death. But we can't understand how you, a black man, could have had a hand in it," Nathaniel heard an unfamiliar voice.

He couldn't see the speaker because a canvas sack was pulled over his head. Nathaniel was sitting on a chair, with his hands and feet tightly bound to it.

"Especially since he was 'taken out' by a professional with a very specific signature," the same voice continued.

Nathaniel remained silent, understanding that no one and nothing could save him now. He also guessed that this silence was crucial for the life of someone he owed a lot to.

"Let it be over quickly," Nathaniel thought.

He wasn't afraid of death, as he had faced it many times in his life. Although his religious feelings were not too strong, he believed deep down that there was life after death, so approached it philosophically. The only thing he feared was torture by fire. Nathaniel had fought through the entire war from beginning to end, but he always felt a fear of open flames. So now, he prayed to God that it would all end quickly and without pain.

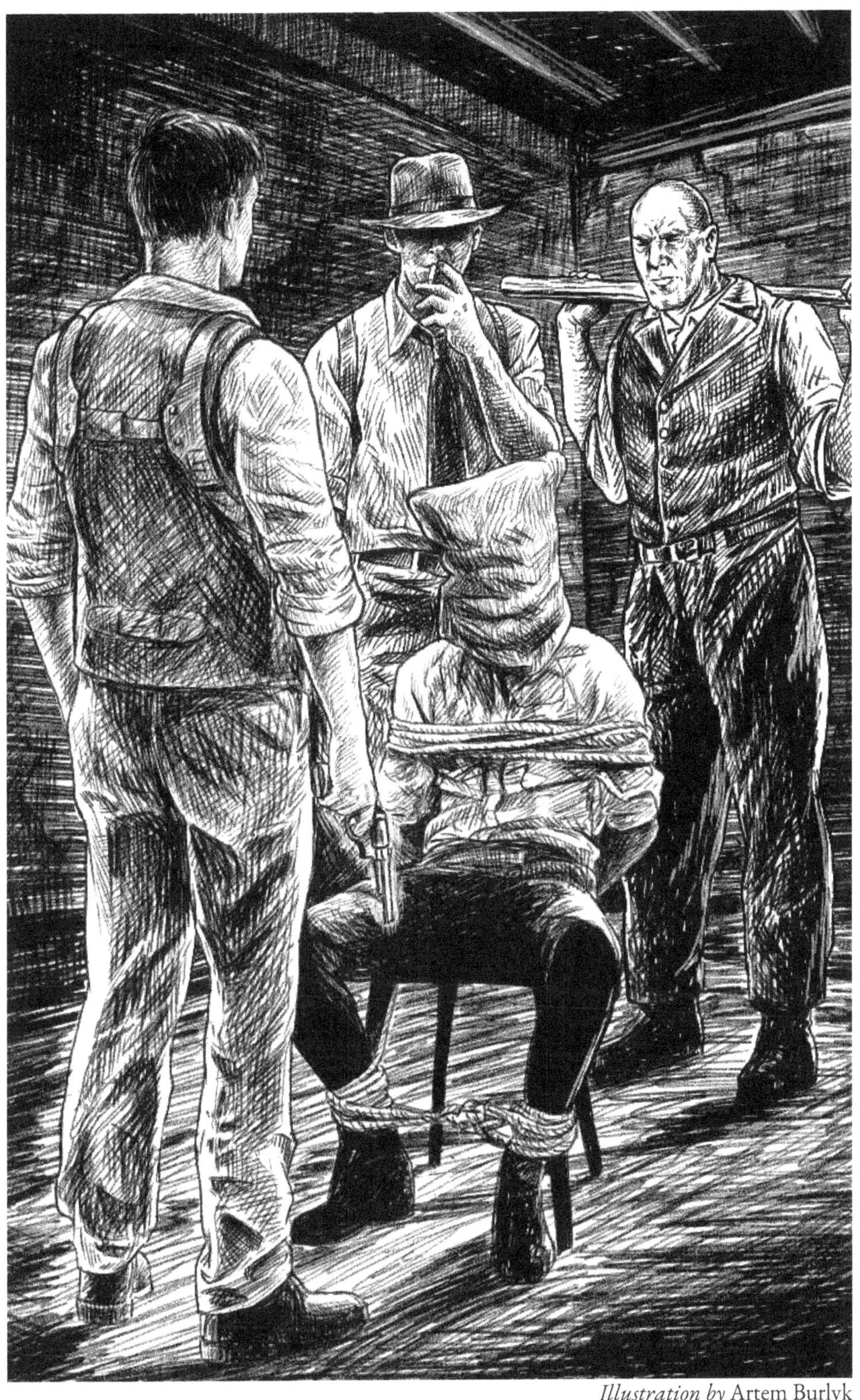

Illustration by Artem Burlyk

"Captain!" Nathaniel heard the voice of a guard soldier. "Someone is asking for you at the checkpoint."

"Who is it?" Nathaniel inquired.

"I don't know," the soldier replied. "He didn't give his name."

"All right, I'll be there soon," said the captain.

He put his wife's letters into a cardboard box, put on his cap and went outside.

In front of the military unit's gate stood a black man.

"Good day, was it you who asked for me?" Nathaniel addressed the stranger.

The man turned sharply, looking Nathaniel directly in the eyes and asked with hesitation: "Did you participate in the Battle of Five Forks in April 1865?"

"Yes," Nathaniel replied. "I was a soldier then. But what is this about?"

"Did you help a prisoner escape?" the stranger asked, still hesitant.

Nathaniel did not answer immediately. He looked intently at the man, thinking about something. He remembered that incident with the prisoner. It was lucky that amidst the chaos, no one noticed one of the captives slipping away, or the outcome could have been very different, and he might not be a captain today.

"Why are you asking me about this?" Nathaniel asked after a pause.

"My name is Harry, and I am that former prisoner. You bandaged my thigh," he said, gesturing to his left leg.

Nathaniel looked closely at Harry and something familiar flashed in his memory. Of course, many years had passed, so remembering the details of those days, especially that night, was very difficult. Nathaniel was not inclined to be open with a stranger. On the other hand, his curiosity was piqued. He had almost forgotten about that incident, but this meeting brought back memories.

"How did you get back to your own?" Nathaniel finally replied, indicating that he remembered Harry.

"I hobbled there in the morning with the help of your stick," Harry said, relaxing.

Then he added: "I've finally found you!"

A lot of time had passed since Harry's family moved to the North and finding Nathaniel after the war had only been possible now. It helped that there weren't many black men with that name in the victorious army.

"Why were you looking for me?" Nathaniel asked.

"It's a long story. Do you have time to meet after your duty?"

"Well, yes. I don't have a family and live in the barracks. So, come here at six in the evening today."

"Alright, I'll come!" Harry replied and, limping slightly, walked away.

They were sitting in a tavern, drinking beer. Harry felt uncomfortable and Nathaniel noticed it.

"Relax, no one's going to kick you out of here," he said in a calm voice.

"I've never been to places like this," Harry responded. "You know why."

"This is what we fought for. So that everyone has equal rights, and no one can infringe on your freedom," Nathaniel exclaimed.

"I still feel like a second-class citizen, even here in the north," Harry said with sadness in his voice.

"It will take a long time for people to forget this shameful period in our history. It's like the story of Moses, who led his people through the desert for forty years until the last of those who had seen slavery died. Alright, let's leave that to history. Tell me what brought you to me after all these years?"

Harry found it hard to start the conversation. He remembered the last time he spoke with Jonathan. Back then, they had their own plans and visions for the future. Everything changed with his son's death. His wife, Dolores, became silent and withdrawn. She was very afraid for their children, and this affected the overall atmosphere of the family.

"They killed my firstborn, Jonathan!" Harry finally exhaled.

"I know who did it but you understand that I have no chance of bringing the case to court. So I decided to take my family to the North, so my children could grow up as free people and have the same rights as all other citizens of our country. I have no one here except you. That's why I found you," Harry said and fell silent.

It was clear how hard these words were for him.

"I see," Nathaniel replied after a brief silence. "Where are you staying?"

Harry gave the address and said: "I've temporarily found work at the port. The work is hard, and the pay isn't enough to support the family, so my wife Dolores and I are willing to take any job. Our girls have grown up enough to take care of themselves. The older boys can also work part-time, but they still need to study. By the way, the first son born after I returned from the war, I named after you, Nathaniel. So you have a namesake in my family."

Nathaniel looked at Harry with surprise and smiled: "I'm very pleased. I'd be happy to meet him."

"Mama, Mama!" came a shout from outside.

Dolores looked out the window and saw the twins, Maria and Elizabeth, racing home.

She opened the door, and the sisters burst into the house at that moment.

"Mama, there's a man in a uniform asking for Dad," Maria blurted out, barely catching her breath.

"That's an officer," Elizabeth said, looking at her sister reproachfully.

"Well, so what if it's an officer?" Maria replied, tugging her sister's sleeve.

"Enough, don't argue," Dolores said.

She knew how much the girls loved to compete and she didn't want to witness their escalating argument: "Invite him in."

"That must be Harry's friend," Dolores thought.

Her husband had told her about the meeting and that he had invited his friend over.

Soon, a tall black man in a captain's uniform appeared at the doorstep. The girls peeked curiously from behind him.

"You must be Nathaniel?" Dolores asked.

"Yes, that's me and you must be Dolores?"

"Indeed, it's a pleasure to meet you," the woman smiled, extending her hand in greeting.

Nathaniel removed his cap and shook her hand.

"Please, come in and have a seat," Dolores invited him. "Harry will be here soon. He sometimes gets held up at work."

"Thank you," Nathaniel replied and sat in the offered chair.

"How are you settling in here? Harry told me your story. I'm very sorry," Nathaniel coughed, realising he had touched on a sensitive subject.

"Yes, it was very hard for us to accept our son's death," Dolores replied with pain in her voice. "That's why we decided to move north, so our other children could grow up free and never have to remember the horrors we went through. Also, I want to thank you for helping Harry escape captivity. He always spoke of you with kindness."

"Oh, we have guests!" a voice called out. Harry stood at the door, smiling.

"Come in, don't just stand there. We're about to have dinner," said Dolores.

The evening passed quickly in conversation. Nathaniel met the older sons who arrived later. He was particularly pleased to shake hands with his namesake.

Before leaving, Nathaniel said: "My former commander, General Willis, is now the state governor. I once carried him, wounded, off the battlefield. We don't see each other often, but whenever we do, he always asks if I need any help. He is a very good man and has always been strongly opposed to slavery. I'll talk to him about getting work for you and Dolores, as well as schooling for the children. I think he won't refuse me."

Nathaniel kept his word and soon, for the first time since their move, life in Harry's family began to improve. Harry himself was hired by a construction company, Dolores got a job at a sewing factory and the children started attending school. In time, the older sons began helping their father at work, becoming true helpers for the family.

"Nathaniel! I want you to leave the service and come work for me. I need loyal, reliable people," said Joe Willis, puffing on his cigar.

Cigars were his weakness. Even on the battlefield, he never let them out of his mouth.

"But sir, what can I do? I don't have the proper education. I only know how to fight and besides, I'm black," Nathaniel replied with frustration in his voice.

"Exactly, black!" Joe exclaimed. "Do you know how much effort I put into getting the amendment to the Constitution passed that would allow black people to vote? It was incredibly difficult. We had to use a lot of different levers to get that amendment ratified. Yes, for now, only men have the right to vote, but soon women will too. I am confident of that."

At the mention of women, Nathaniel's expression darkened. Joe noticed this.

"Yes, I know... I'm sorry for reminding you about Sophia. But we can't bring her back and we must build our country where everyone has equal rights so that such things never happen again. I'm running for office, and I need the support of the black community. That's why my team needs you. You're a war hero and you know first-hand what slavery and humiliation are. Your wife was killed just because she was black."

"What do you need me to do?" Nathaniel asked, his voice hoarse with emotion.

"I've already spoken with your superiors. You'll be discharged from service with all your benefits and social privileges intact. I'll provide you with housing.

You'll enter public service and work in my department. Initially, you'll help with my election campaign. At the same time, you'll attend college to obtain the necessary education. When we win, you can choose where to apply your knowledge and experience."

"What if we lose?" Nathaniel asked.

"We have a good chance of winning, but we must not overlook the fact that since the war ended, the residents of the South have gained strength and will now try to take as many seats in Congress and government as possible. The risk is great and that's why I need your help. But even if we lose, our fight won't end. It will be a precedent in our history that future generations will build upon."

"Alright, sir, I agree," Nathaniel replied after a brief pause. "How much time do I have to wrap up my affairs and hand over my position?"

"I think two weeks should be enough," Joe said extending his hand in farewell.

Nathaniel, like most black people of that time, was born into slavery and did not remember his parents. His childhood was spent among strangers who, when possible, substituted as a father or mother figure. Nathaniel was luckier than many of his peers: he was bought by Hugh Cooper, a prominent industrialist from the North. Hugh took the boy to his estate, where he lived almost as a member of the family. There, he became friends with Hugh's children, daughter Eleanor and son Jerry. In their family, slavery was condemned and their attitude toward black people was more than friendly. Hugh's wife, Elsa, had died a few years earlier from malaria and the children were raised by a black governess, Maria. Nathaniel was her first assistant, as there was always a lot of work in the estate. The boy was curious, and he was drawn to knowledge like a magnet. The master's children, who were taught by various teachers, noticed Nathaniel's interest in education and taught him to read and write. Hugh was very busy with his business, but when he saw his children teaching

Nathaniel, at once allowed him to study with them. From that moment on, the boy's life changed dramatically. He eagerly absorbed knowledge and made significant progress, much to the teachers' astonishment.

As years passed, the boy gradually turned into a sturdy youth and then into a young man.

Nathaniel remembered the events of that day very clearly. Hugh arrived with his friend, Major Joe Willis. They went into the living room and Hugh ordered that Nathaniel be summoned. He did not delay and entered the living room within a few minutes.

"Nathaniel," Hugh began. "I have good news for you, our state government has passed a law abolishing slavery. From now on, you are a free man and have the right to decide what to do next. Over the years, you have never disappointed me and have become a full-fledged member of our family, so frankly, I will be sad if you leave us."

Nathaniel was a bit taken aback by what he heard. The rush of blood to his face made him momentarily darker. He didn't know what to say. So now, he could go wherever he wanted and do whatever he pleased, and no one would command him? Nathaniel couldn't complain about the years spent on the estate, but he had never left it. Therefore, he didn't know what to do with the freedom he had suddenly received.

"But if you want, you can stay with us. There's always plenty of work to do, as you know," Hugh added, seeing how hard it was for the young man to process what he had heard.

"Well, if you want to dedicate yourself to serving in the army, I can help with that," Major Willis chimed in.

"Thank you, sir," Nathaniel finally managed to say. "Please allow me to stay with you. You have done so much good for me that I can't even imagine leaving this house."

"Well, alright," Hugh replied. "You will continue doing the same work, but now you will receive a salary. But remember you are now free to choose your path. Now go, we need to discuss some matters."

Nathaniel walked away, not feeling the ground beneath his feet. He didn't know what to do with the freedom that had suddenly fallen upon him. His head was spinning with excitement. The weather in December was quite cold, but he didn't feel the chill. It seemed that even the air now had a different, new scent.

"We can now get married peacefully and no one, you hear, no one will tell us what to do!" Nathaniel spoke with such emotion that Sophia almost held her breath, afraid to interrupt him.

Her heart was pounding so hard it felt like it might burst out of her chest.

"Where will we live?" she asked.

"I'll talk to the master. He will help us," Nathaniel said.

"But he is no longer your master," Sophia noted with a smile, leaning against his shoulder.

That evening, the lovers stood for a long time, watching the bright red sunset and dreaming of a happy future together.

Two months later, they got married and moved into a small house that Hugh kindly provided for them. Their new life began, full of hope and ambitious plans.

But in the spring, war broke out and all their plans fell apart. Nathaniel volunteered for the army and went to serve in a unit under Major Willis. The major was very glad to see Nathaniel among his soldiers. Little did he know that he would owe his life to this very man.

It was the third year of the war. Major Willis's unit was preparing to storm a fortified Confederate position. The numerical advantage was on the side of the Union troops, which instilled hope for success. However, the attacks were unsuccessful. The enemy fiercely defended their position, occasionally launching counterattacks using a new tactic of dispersed formation. In the first moments, the attackers were cut down by artillery shrapnel. The field was strewn with the bodies of the wounded and dead, but the major repeatedly rallied his soldiers to attack, leading them against the enemy.

During one of the attacks, a shell exploded near the major, throwing him several meters backward. Nathaniel ran to him, grabbed his jacket and turned him face up. The major was breathing heavily, his face covered in blood. Nathaniel took out a bandage and wrapped his head, then, lifting him onto his shoulders, carried his commander back into their lines. He dragged the unconscious Willis to the field hospital and handed him over to the medics. Then he returned to the front, but it was clear that continuing the attack was pointless. That day, despite favourable conditions, their army was defeated. They lost several thousand men, killed and wounded. The troops were ordered to retreat.

Nathaniel remembered the events of that well. His squad was ordered to scout the area. They advanced and unexpectedly encountered an enemy convoy. Their first attack was repelled and then the corporal ordered them to split up and strike from the flanks. This time they were lucky: several enemy soldiers, including their commander, were killed. The rest raised their hands and surrendered. Corporal Jennings ordered them to collect weapons and assist the wounded. Nathaniel saw a black soldier wounded in the leg and started bandaging him. The wound was not serious, but the poor fellow had lost a lot of blood. While applying the bandage, Nathaniel couldn't help but say: "Here we are, both black, yet fighting against each other. I fight for freedom! I want to be free, to live in my country and have the same rights as whites. So, tell me, what do you fight for?"

The prisoner looked down at his feet and remained silent, frowning. After bandaging the wounded, they were loaded onto wagons and, along with other prisoners, taken to the Union's central location. There, they were all placed in a barn that had miraculously survived the shelling.

Nathaniel thought a lot about that prisoner.

"How? How can you fight for your oppressors? What is this? Has slavery ingrained itself so deeply in them that they don't even consider the thought of being free?"

Illustration by Artem Burlyk

He stayed awake late into the night and, when everyone else was asleep, he quietly left the army tent and approached the barn. The night was dark, but the moonlight peeking through the clouds helped Nathaniel spot a small hole in the corner of the barn. Trying not to attract the attention of the guard assigned to watch the prisoners, he carefully slipped inside. The barn was dark and quiet. Everyone was sleeping on the floor. When his eyes adjusted to the darkness, he found the poor fellow by the bandage on his thigh. Nathaniel gently nudged his shoulder and, when he opened his eyes, Nathaniel gestured for the wounded man to follow him. He crawled through the hole and then helped the prisoner get out.

They walked silently and slowly, as the prisoner frequently had to stop due to his injured leg. Nathaniel looked around, found a sturdy stick, and handed it to the prisoner. They continued. Walking was much easier for the wounded man now. Soon, the moon emerged from behind the clouds, illuminating everything around them. Nathaniel stopped and, pointing towards the forest, said: "That's it, you go on alone from here. Your units are over there."

Then he added: "Remember what I told you yesterday. The war will soon be over. You no longer have the strength or resources to continue fighting us. It's up to each of us to decide the country in which we'll live: a country of slaves and masters or a free country. It's hard for you, southern black people to understand us. But remember, once you taste freedom, you'll never want to be a slave again and I'm ready to die for that. Alright, go, brother. God willing, we'll see each other after the war."

Nathaniel turned and quickly headed back.

"What's your name?" came a shout after him.

"Nathaniel, my name is Nathaniel," he yelled into the darkness.

When Nathaniel went off to war, Sophia promised to write to him every week. Since then the letters arrived regularly. Sometimes he received them with delays, as the army was constantly manoeuvring and finding a unit on the march wasn't always easy. When Nathaniel didn't receive a letter for a long time, he would take out the old ones and read them several times, as he carried them with him in a special pouch. All the letters began the same way: "Hello, my dear!" Then his wife wrote about everything that had happened during the week, about her feelings and how much she missed him. Sophia rarely asked about the war because she was very afraid of it and constantly tried to push away thoughts that something might happen to her husband.

The war was nearing its end, but he had never experienced such a long delay in receiving a letter. Every time the regimental mailman came, Nathaniel looked at him with hope, but upon seeing his expression, he understood that there was no letter for him.

"Nathaniel, you're being called to the headquarters," he heard the voice of a messenger who had ridden up on a horse.

"What happened?" Nathaniel asked, but the rider just shrugged and rode off.

Nathaniel immediately headed to the headquarters tent, located on the top of the hill. Before entering, he straightened his uniform.

"Private Walker reporting as ordered!" Nathaniel announced.

Waiting for him there was Lieutenant Colonel Willis, who had already recovered from his injury and two junior officers. They looked at Nathaniel strangely and he didn't like it. But remained silent, afraid to break the protocol.

"Nathaniel," Willis began slowly. "I received a letter from Hugh. Sophia is no longer with us. She was killed by some scoundrels because she tried to defend her rights. I'm very sorry. This is not the kind of country we are shedding blood for."

The ground seemed to slip away beneath Nathaniel's feet. He grabbed at the collar of his uniform, trying to unbutton it because he was starting to suffocate. The officers rushed to him and sat him down on a chair.

"Nathaniel, the war is practically over. Go home. Here is your permit to travel," Willis said, handing him a piece of paper folded in quarters.

Nathaniel took it, not understanding anything and, without saying goodbye, left the tent.

Many years passed. Nathaniel returned to the army and rose to the rank of captain, but he never started a family. Now he is being offered the chance to leave the service and start a new life. Well, he is ready to serve his country not only on the battlefield.

"Nathaniel," Governor Joe Willis paused and took a puff from his favourite cigar.

He remained faithful to his habits and smoked only 'Partagas'. He stood with his back to Nathaniel, looking out the window. Nathaniel sat in a chair, waiting. He knew the governor's habit of making long pauses during conversations and thus asked nothing. Joe Willis disliked idle chatter, so he always carefully considered every word before speaking. For this, he was respected by his allies and hated by his enemies. The governor was over seventy but was as sturdy as an oak. His sharp mind allowed him to engage in verbal battles with opponents much younger than himself. Joe Willis was one of the most authoritative and influential senators before he was elected governor. During his tenure as the state governor, he implemented many reforms and earned the respect not only of his party colleagues but even of his opponents.

Nathaniel was his right-hand man in all matters. During his time on the senator's and later governor's team, Nathaniel received a proper education and sufficient experience in the country's political life. He enjoyed immense respect among the black population not only in his state but throughout the country. Joe Willis owed much of his success to Nathaniel. They worked in tandem and never let each other down. But now Joe was grim and reluctant to continue the conversation.

"Nathaniel," the governor finally said. "You know that lately, it has become increasingly difficult for us to work. I am too old to fight my enemies. Those we defeated many years ago are now breathing down my neck. They are stronger than ever. There is discord in our party and the enemies will undoubtedly take advantage of this. Do you know Roger Harris?"

At the mention of this name, Nathaniel's face twisted into a painful grimace.

Since Harry found him, they had seen each other quite often. Over time, their relationship grew into a friendship and Nathaniel always gladly visited Harry's home. Not having children of his own, Nathaniel interacted with his friend's children as if they were his own. The birth of the first grandchild was an incredibly significant event for him, especially since he was the son of his namesake. But that day, Nathaniel didn't recognize Harry, as he was very distraught.

"What happened?" Nathaniel asked.

Harry was silent for a moment and then replied: "I read in the newspaper that Roger Harris is running for governor of our state."

"Well, yes, I know," Nathaniel responded. "So what about it?"

Harry slowly lifted his gaze to him and said angrily: "It's him! He was among those who killed Jonathan."

"Are you sure about this?" Nathaniel asked.

"If I weren't sure, I wouldn't be sitting here! I never thought that in my country, murderers would hold public office. Is this the country you fought for?" Harry asked reproachfully.

That time, Nathaniel found nothing to say in response to his friend and now this name resurfaced again.

"Yes, of course, I know that scoundrel," Nathaniel replied, clenching his fists. "He was involved in the murder of my friend's son many years ago."

"Is that so?" Joe was surprised. "I suspected that this guy had blood on his hands, but now I know for sure. It's a shame we can't bring him to trial.

He has very influential people backing him and a lot of time has passed since then. Also, we couldn't find your wife's killers either. They know how to cover their tracks."

Nathaniel grew even gloomier and bit his lip in anger.

"I have a very unusual request for you," Joe said, looking Nathaniel in the eyes as if doubting whether to voice it.

"You know, sir, that you can rely on me for anything," Nathaniel replied, noticing the doubt in Joe's eyes.

"I didn't tell you about this earlier because I didn't have the right," Joe continued. "But now I'm going to ask you to do something. Next Wednesday, the "Lusitania" is arriving at the port. You will rent a stagecoach and meet someone."

Joe took out a map of the port and, pointing to a spot on it, said: "You will wait here. Tie a blue ribbon to the charioteer's seat so that the arriving person will be sure it's the right coach. Do not speak during the meeting; he doesn't know our language well. Silently give him this package."

Joe handed Nathaniel a thick package sealed with wax.

"Then take him to this hotel," Joe handed Nathaniel a slip of paper with the address written on it. "You'll also need to take him back, but we'll discuss that later."

Illustration by Artem Burlyk

The following Wednesday, Nathaniel stood at the designated spot. He tied a blue ribbon to the driver's seat of the stagecoach. There were still a few hours before the steamship's arrival and, to kill time, Nathaniel decided to take a walk along the pier. He went to its edge, sat on a bundle of thick ropes, closed his eyes and let the sea breeze blow over his face.

"I wonder who this person is?" he thought. "Why is there so much secrecy surrounding his arrival?"

But he pushed these thoughts away because he was used to silently doing his job and not asking unnecessary questions. For some reason, he suddenly remembered Sophia. Many years had passed since his wife's death and, over time, her image had started to fade. But now, sitting at the edge of the pier, he imagined Sophia very clearly. His wife was wearing the same dress she had worn when she saw him off to war. Only she wasn't waving goodbye, but calling him to her. His thoughts were interrupted by a long horn blast, the multi-decked "Lusitania" was entering the port.

Nathaniel recognised the man immediately. A young man in a cap and suit separated himself from the crowd of arrivals and walked resolutely toward the coach. He carried a small bag and, despite the summer heat, he wore leather gloves. Nathaniel opened the coach door for the passenger and helped with the bag. When the man was seated, Nathaniel handed him the package and closed the door. Everything happened without a single word. They didn't even greet each other, only exchanged glances and that glance sent a shiver down Nathaniel's spine.

"Murdered candidate for governor! Mysterious killing! Revenge or electoral struggle?!" shouted the newspaper boys in unison.

Nathaniel called one over and bought a newspaper. On the front page was a photograph of Roger Harris with a brief description of what had happened. He had been found in his garden, where he usually went for walks with his loyal Doberman. But that evening, Harris had gone for a walk alone because the dog had unexpectedly died the day before. None of the servants had noticed anything suspicious. When it began to get dark, they started searching for their master and found him lying by a tree. A sharply pointed shuriken star was embedded in his left temple.

"So, are you going to stay silent?" continued the male voice. "Tell us how you're involved in Roger's murder and maybe you'll die without suffering."

Nathaniel's head hurt terribly; he was afraid to move it because of the pain. He was desperately thinking about how his captors had tracked him down. The captured remembered how the previous evening a stranger had stopped him on the street and asked for directions to a nightclub. When Nathaniel bent over the piece of paper with the address, a powerful blow to his head knocked him out. He regained consciousness here, sitting on a chair with his hands and feet tied.

"We are sure you know both the person who ordered and the one who committed the murder. It had to be organised so meticulously! First, they poisoned Dolly, as the dog was always with Roger and wouldn't let anyone near his master. So, on that fateful evening, Roger went for a walk without his dog. Distracted by grief over losing his beloved pet, he let his guard go and paid the price. A shuriken is a specific weapon and only a top-class master could throw it so accurately. This is not a simple murderer. We believe he isn't local. He's probably not even in the country anymore. So, will you help us find the mastermind?" the man's voice became firm and decisive.

Nathaniel remained silent. He had understood everything when he read the newspaper, but hadn't shared his suspicions with Joe Willis. Joe had appreciated his assistant's silence, trusting Nathaniel as he did himself. The image of Sophia appeared clearly in Nathaniel's mind again. She was calling him, waving her hand. For her sake, for Harry's son, for Joe – the man to whom he owed so much, he would remain silent. Nathaniel knew that no one would save him now. These people knew no mercy and left no witnesses.

The sack was suddenly pulled off his head and Nathaniel squinted as a lamp shone directly into his eyes. He couldn't make out the figure standing before him due to the bright light. The man held a revolver in his right hand. At least two others stood behind Nathaniel, which he deduced from the sounds coming from behind him.

"So, you're going to stay silent, you black bastard?" the man in front of him asked.

"Don't waste your time, somebody has been waiting for me for a long time," Nathaniel replied.

"Well, I figured it wouldn't be easy with you. This isn't the battlefield where things are much simpler. Well then, send my regards to your wife," the man said, raising the revolver and firing three shots into Nathaniel.

Passang

"Teacher," Tobjal's anxious voice echoed. "They are close, we need to leave."

Passang said nothing, continuing to sit on the floor with his eyes closed. In his mind, he was far from here, soaring above the snow-capped mountain peaks. He was gliding in the sky along with his friends – mythical dragons. The monk wasn't afraid, he was used to such flights. From above, a magnificent view of the mountains and the monastery, where he had spent almost his entire life, unfolded. The monastery clung to the edge of the mountain and its sharp roof seemed to be an extension of the mountain peaks. Passang circled over the monastery, carefully observing its contours as if realising he was seeing it for the last time. Suddenly, he saw a red sun rising from behind the mountains, filling the entire valley with its crimson rays, gradually climbing up to the monastery walls. The dragons began to nervously look around and flap their enormous wings sharply. They were shouting something to him, pointing their heads downward.

"Teacher," the student's voice rang out again. "We have little time."

Passang opened his eyes. His face was full of tranquillity.

"Take everything you have prepared and go. I will stay here and meet them. Save the books and ancient manuscripts and most importantly, save yourselves. You are the bearers of the knowledge that will help future generations understand the meaning of life and maintain a connection with our past."

The students silently bowed and left the temple, while Passang remained sitting on the floor, silently gazing at the statue of Buddha.

"Passang," his father's voice was solemn. "You have turned six years old. It is time to fulfilll the purpose for which you came into this world. Tomorrow morning, I will take you to the monastery, where you will become a novice. Our senior teachers have been waiting for you for a long time. They know that you are destined to become a great person, a healer of human bodies and souls. Tonight you will spend your last night in our home and tomorrow early in the morning we will set off. Go, you have time to talk with your mother, as well as with your brothers and sisters."

Passang silently bowed to his father and went outside. His heart fluttered at his father's words. He had always known he would have to leave his home, but the immediacy of this moment bewildered him so much that felt lost for a while. He would bid farewell to his parents, brothers, sisters, and his old lifestyle, as he embarked on a new adventure full of unknowns. These thoughts saddened Passang and, with his head down, he walked to the backyard where he usually played with the other children.

The journey to the mountain monastery was long and exhausting. Finally, the horses stopped and Passang peeked out of the carriage window. They were standing at the closed gates of the monastery. His father climbed down from his seat and said: "Well, here we are. Get down, son, it's time to say goodbye."

Passang jumped to the ground and looked around. There was no one around, just the grim walls of the monastery and the tall mountains surrounding it.

"No matter how hard it may be, there is no way back for you. This is now your home and your family. Serve honourably and fulfilll your destiny.

Goodbye," his father said, turning the carriage around and driving back down the road into the valley.

Passang picked up his bag and headed to the gates. Huge and black, they seemed to reach up to the sky. The boy took hold of a large bronze ring and timidly knocked. No one answered. He knocked again. This time, the gates opened slowly, and an old monk appeared in the doorway. The monk looked intently at the boy and then shut the gates in front of him. Passang was bewildered, this was not how he had imagined meeting the monastery's inhabitants. He stepped aside and sat down opposite the gates. Remembering his father's words, he understood there was no way back home. Passang had to become a novice in this monastery and so he waited.

The boy sat in front of the gates for three days. During this time, no one came out to him. Just as Passang was beginning to despair, the gates creaked open again. Two monks came out, bowed to him and gestured to come inside. And so, a new life began, in which he was destined to become a great teacher and healer of both human souls and bodies.

Life in the monastery was measured and orderly. The monks prepared food, gathered provisions, engaged in physical exercises and meditated. Over the years spent here, Passang read many sacred scriptures and became the favourite student of the monastery's mentor. Eventually, older companions who had arrived at the monastery before him started to seek Passang's advice and help. They did not know that Passang had been chosen for his mission long before his birth. This was known to only a few who eagerly awaited the arrival of the extraordinary boy. When Passang's father was informed of this, he received the news with respect and understanding. For their family, it was an honour to dedicate a child to serving their people and Passang did not disappoint his father. In all these years, his father visited only twice to see his son and each time, after talking with the abbot, he was convinced that the boy was in his rightful place. Thus, he could not help but rejoice in his son's success. A son who no longer belonged to him.

"Passang, tomorrow you will go with our brothers into the mountains. We need to gather medicinal herbs for tea. It will be a dangerous journey. Prepare warm clothes, food supplies and water," ordered the abbot.

"Alright, teacher," replied Passang. "How many of us will there be?"

"There will be five of you," said the abbot. "I hope that you all return. Last time, one of the brothers fell into the abyss, so I ask you to be extremely careful. You are approaching the moment when many earthly secrets will be revealed to you. Only the chosen ones can gather these herbs. You must know where they grow and how to collect them. Moreover, you need to see something with your own eyes."

"What do you mean?" asked Passang in surprise.

But the abbot raised his hand, signalling that the conversation was over.

By morning, all five monks were ready for the journey.

Tsering, the eldest and most experienced of the expedition members, said: "I hope the weather will favour us and we will reach the intermediate camp without any problems today. Save your strength, watch out for each other and be extremely careful. The road is full of dangers."

Tsering was one of the abbot's assistants and had a great affection for the young novice because of his diligence and curiosity.

He said to Passang: "This is your first time going with us, so always stay close to me. Watch me closely and do what I do."

They set off with the first rays of the sun rising over the valley and reached the intermediate camp, which the monks set up in a small cave on the mountainside by evening. The next morning, a new stage of the ascent began. The path went steep, and their progress slowed noticeably. They had to scramble over rocks, risking a fall into the abyss. Despite this, they managed to climb to a large plateau, where walking was much easier. A thick mist obscured the view, but Tsering confidently led his companions along a barely visible path familiar to him. Suddenly, the band of fog ended abruptly and everything around was bathed in bright sunlight. The mist stood behind them like a solid wall and the novice travellers found themselves in a sunlit green valley. Passang felt as if they had entered another dimension, filled with vibrant colours, unusual sounds and scents. Here, even time seemed to move differently. Sometimes it felt as if it had stopped altogether.

"Come, I'll show you something," Tsering said to Passang.

"The rest of you settle here and prepare some food. Tomorrow we will start gathering the herbs and, as soon as we finish, we will head back," Tsering addressed the rest of the group.

Passang followed Tsering and soon their eyes fell upon abandoned buildings.

Illustration by Artem Burlyk

"What is this?" Passang asked in surprise.

"This is the settlement of ancient people. Those who lived long before us," Tsering replied.

"But how tall were they if the doors here are twice our height?" Passang asked again.

"These were the people-gods. They possessed the knowledge that we partly use in our lives," Tsering said. "Come, I'll show you something else."

Tsering turned his back to Passang and gestured to him to follow. They approached one of the dwellings that had been well preserved and entered. Inside, they saw a pyramid-shaped room that seemed to be some kind of tomb. Tsering lit a torch and opened the door to a small chamber. Before them, seated cross-legged on a wooden platform, was a person in monk's robes. Passang flinched in surprise, but Tsering calmed him.

"This is our Lama Norbu. He has been here in a state of posthumous meditation[23] for twenty years."

"But he looks alive," Passang exclaimed.

"In life, he achieved the highest level of spiritual development and now continues his existence in a meditative state."

"But he's dead," Passang continued to be astonished.

"What is death, Passang? It is a transition to another state. Our lama is alive. His spirit is not here, but his body, as you can see, is incorruptible. Lama Norbu is one of our teachers. Those who have departed but continue to be with us in astral contact. They knew that you were to be born and knew your destiny. This is not your first life and not your last. The mentors awaited the end of your previous life and the readiness of your spirit to be reincarnated in a new body. All our lives move in the circle of Samsara until we reach Nirvana."

"I wonder, who was I in my past life?" Passang pondered.

---

[23] Tukdam — the practice of posthumous meditation. Buddhist teachings state that in this meditative state, the lama continues his posthumous existence, and his body becomes incorruptible.

"You will be surprised, but in one of them you were a woman," the monk laughed.

"A woman?" Passang exclaimed. "Wow! I would never have thought about this and who will I be in the next life?"

"This knowledge is hidden from us. The teachers can only observe the transition. You could be anything, a human, an animal or even a plant. No onc knows for sure and that is the essence of existence. However, it doesn't matter. You need to live in the present because the past is gone, and we have no control over the future," Tsering replied.

What he saw and heard deeply moved Passang. The young man already felt as if he was in another dimension and now he got this unexpected revelation.

"People – gods. What were they like and where did they go? What knowledge could they have passed on to us? Perhaps it is thanks to this knowledge that our lama was able to transition to another world, leaving behind an incorruptible body. He has been here for twenty years, and his soul is somewhere out there, in the astral plane or another body. What will my next incarnation be? What if I will be a woman again?"

That evening Passang had many questions, but he was tired and fell asleep in thoughts.

Early in the morning, everyone woke up, ate boiled rice and stewed vegetables for breakfast before gathering the herbs. These were special herbs that the monks used to make a healing tea. They drank it several times a day. It was said that thanks to this drink, the monks lived peacefully to old age, maintaining their sanity and remarkable strength.

When the herbs were gathered and packed into bags, Tsering said: "Let's rest a bit before the descent. The way back is always harder because descending is more difficult than climbing. Especially now that we are carrying a load."

Descending indeed turned out to be more challenging, but they managed to reach the intermediate camp before sunset, where the novices set up for the night before the final stage back to the monastery. In the morning they continued their journey and successfully reached the monastery by evening.

One of the monks' favourite pastimes was flying kites. This event required meticulous preparation. Few knew how to assemble the kites and how to control them. Even fewer were honoured with the opportunity to fly them. Passang remembered that day for the rest of his life. His friends, Darjan and Samdan, came running to the courtyard: "Passang, tomorrow we will fly the kites. The mentor just told us."

"Oh. So we will also rise to the sky," said Passang, as his heartbeat faster.

He waited for this moment for a long time and, finally, it had come.

In the morning, the three friends gathered at the monastery's exit. They were excitedly discussing something when Tsering approached them with his assistant, Ojin. Ojin carried a large bundle from which the ends of ropes dangled.

"Well, let's go," said Tsering and the procession moved towards the nearest mountain.

There, they unrolled the bundle and Ojin skilfully assembled two kites. They were colourful, with long tails. Ojin performed the first flight. He demonstrated to the others how to fly properly and how to control the kite. Tsering stood aside and observed. The friends took turns trying to control the kite without lifting off the ground and then, one by one, they soared into the sky.

Passang flew over the ground, breathless with excitement. Following him into the air was Samdan and they both shouted with joy and exhilaration. It felt like they could soar in the air like birds forever, but Tsering signalled them to return to the ground. It was truly an amazing day, the day Passang felt like a bird. The young monk thought he had flown before. This sensation was so familiar to him. By the end of the exercises, they returned to the monastery, so the kites were carefully packed away for the next time.

Five senior mentors sat in the room along with the abbot of the monastery. Passang stood before them.

"Your time has come," said the abbot. "You have been long enough in the monastery, studied many sacred books and now you are ready to fulfill the purpose for which you came into this life. Tomorrow, you will undergo the operation to open the third eye so that your abilities can fully unfold. For now, go and spend your day in peace and reflection."

The next day, Passang entered the room where everything was prepared for the operation. Besides the abbot, there were two old monks. They laid Passang on a wooden bed and began the operation. They carefully drilled a small hole in his forehead using special tools and closed it with a tampon soaked in special herbs. After this, Passang was taken to the basement and left in complete darkness for three days. On the fourth day, the same monks came for him. They blindfolded him and led him upstairs. After examining the wound on his forehead, they carefully removed the tampon and took off the blindfold. Passang opened his eyes and, terrified, jumped back. The monks standing before him were engulfed in a bright flame.

Illustration by Artem Burlyk

"You need to get used to your new abilities. What you are seeing now are our auras. Through them, you will be able to determine people's moods, their emotional states and their intentions. Most importantly, you will now be able to recognise and heal human illnesses," said one monk.

This marked the beginning of a new chapter in the life of the boy who had been taken to the monastery by his father many years earlier. By that time, Passang already knew much about the structure of the human body. Now, with even greater zeal, he began studying the works of various ancient physicians. The ability to see auras helped him accurately diagnose diseases and find the correct treatments. The fame of the young healer spread far and wide. Among those he healed were both simple peasants and noble dignitaries. For Passang, it made no difference who his patient was. His primary task was to help cure the person as he could see more than anyone else. Therefore, he never refused help to anyone.

"Passang, a government official has arrived. He wants to speak with you," the abbot said one day.

"Sure," Passang replied. "I'll be right there."

When Passang entered the room, a man of about forty-five years and average height rose to greet him.

He bowed and said: "Envoys from a neighbouring state are coming to visit us. We know they have long harboured plans to conquer our country. Could you secretly participate in the meeting to help us understand their true intentions?"

"Of course, I can," Passang replied, bowing to the guest. "When do I need to leave? There are many patients I need to see."

"You need to leave today," said the official. "But we can depart in the evening so that you can see as many of them as possible during the day."

"Alright," said Passang. "I will see those who need it the most and be ready by the evening."

The journey to the capital took two days. Passang had travelled this route with his father when he was still a child and thus remembered the road but only faintly. Nothing had changed since then. The same throngs of people in colourful attire and the same street noise. For the monk healer who had spent many years in the monastery's silence, the city's hustle and bustle was unfamiliar. Finally, the cart stopped at the gates of a house. A guard signalled, the gates opened, and they entered the courtyard.

"This is where our government meetings take place," said his companion. "Come, I will show you where we will meet the envoys."

They entered a spacious hall with a low table and two rows of pillows in the centre.

"You will hide behind those columns. They will be sitting with their backs to you, so they won't notice anything suspicious," said the official. "Now, I will give instructions, and you will be taken to a room where you can rest after the journey and eat. I know that monks are very restrained in their eating, so I asked our cook to prepare something you are accustomed to."

The official bowed and went outside.

Passang stood behind the columns, carefully observing the people seated with their backs to him. These were representatives from a neighbouring country that had always been hostile towards them. But now the neighbours were embroiled in a longstanding war with another state, so they unexpectedly sought help from Passang's country. The envoys were trying to persuade the government of the need to support them in the war and insisted on being allowed to station their troops on Passang's homeland territory. Passang understood perfectly well what was at stake. He could also see their auras. Crimson red, a colour seen only in wicked people, those trying to deceive.

There was a break in the negotiations and the guests were invited to lunch. When they left, Passang approached the table.

"Well, what do you say?" asked the official who had brought him here.

"They want to deceive you. Don't believe a word they say," Passang replied.

The officials began to confer while the guests were dining.

One of them, the oldest present, said: "If we allow them to station their troops here, it will mean that we support them in the war against those with whom we have always had friendly relations."

"On the other hand, if we don't allow it, they will attack us, and we don't have the strength to resist even a small detachment. They have always wanted to seize our country," remarked another official.

"I think this is a ploy to kill two birds with one stone without spreading their forces thinly. The neighbour's army is strong, but even to capture our defenceless country, they will need strength and time," added a third participant in the meeting.

"What do you think?" the oldest official asked Passang. "You have seen their mood; can you advise us?"

Passang stood, deep in thought and then said: "They will attack regardless. The decision has already been made. The fact that they sent envoys means nothing. They need to understand your mood and the internal situation of the country. You must give them an answer that will calm them down for now and prepare for war."

"We need to buy time and prepare for the attack. Therefore, we must strengthen our defensive fortifications on the mountain roads, evacuate as many defenceless people as possible to the mountains and stock up on drinking water and provisions. We may not be able to mount a strong resistance, but at least we will not surrender in shame," said the oldest official.

When the gates closed behind the envoys' carriage, Passang realised that war was closer than ever before. The auras of the people burned with anger and hatred.

"I must return to the monastery and prepare to receive the wounded," Passang told himself.

The next morning as he set out on his way back to the monastery, he looked at the city's streets from the window of his cart, aware that this measured and carefree life would soon end, and hard times were coming for his people.

The monastery courtyard was filled with the wounded. Monks worked day and night, providing them with assistance. There were not enough medicines and bandages, but the wounded kept arriving. Passang hardly slept. He cared for the injured and advised his fellow monks. By their auras, the healer could determine whether a wounded person would survive. If the aura dimmed, it was already impossible to help that person. Passang continued his tireless efforts, moving from one wounded person to another, his old heart ached with pain as he watched the ongoing slaughter. Despite the dire situation, he didn't abandon his duties. The monastery had become a sanctuary amidst the chaos and Passang knew that their work was more crucial than ever. The monks' dedication was unwavering, even as they faced the grim reality of war and the seemingly endless stream of those in need.

As Passang had predicted, hostilities began without a declaration of war just two weeks after the envoys of the neighbouring country had left. The enemy was strong, and the government simply did not have enough time or resources to prepare for the attack. Within a few days, the enemy managed to advance deep into the country, getting close to the capital. It was clear that resistance would be crushed within the next few days and the country would lose its independence. The only thing slowing down the enemy's advance were the difficult mountain roads and the ambushes set by soldiers and volunteers. Knowing all the trails and passes, they made it very difficult for the enemy. But the armies were unequal and within a few days, the occupiers invaded the capital. Those who could, fled to the mountains. Those who remained were mercilessly killed by enemy soldiers, who displayed horrifying cruelty.

Illustration by Artem Burlyk

Passang ensured that all the monks and novices left the monastery. They took everything they could carry. What they couldn't take, they burned or threw into the abyss. The wounded were evacuated and the dead were laid out in the backyard, as there was no one left to attend to them. Passang took one last walk around the monastery courtyard, gazing at its walls. His father had brought him here many years ago and now he must face his death here with dignity. Passang entered the temple, sat before the statue of the deity and immersed himself in meditation. He envisioned himself running across a vast field, a black dragon flying beside him. The dragon flapped its large wings, barely touching the ground. It flew so low that Passang felt they were flying together. A faint smile appeared on Passang's face.

The sound of soldiers' boots echoed from the stairs. The door burst open with a crack. Several soldiers rushed into the hall and froze. The monk sat with his back to them, motionless. His calmness momentarily confused the soldiers. An officer pushed through the crowd and approached Passang. He looked at his serene face and shouted: "Where are all the monks? Where have they gone?"

Passang slowly opened his eyes.

He knew the language the officer spoke, so he replied clearly: "They are where you will never find them. Our knowledge will never be yours. You can take our bodies, but our souls are immortal."

The officer cursed and drew his sword. Passang's vision shifted as the blade descended, finding himself once again running through the field with the black dragon. The peaceful smile remained on his face. With a swift motion, the enemy officer brought the sword down on the monk's head.

Netsumi

Netsumi often had dreams that seemed to dance on the edge of reality, slipping in and out of the waking world like shadows. Every dream, vivid and clear, foretold events yet to come. Each one playing out as if she were walking through a story she had not yet lived. From mundane moments to dramatic revelations, her dreams whispered secrets of the future. She had become quite adept at interpreting them, but today's dream was unlike the others. Last night, Netsumi was a butterfly. She flew over a land covered with trenches and craters from shells and bombs. The sun had just begun to rise over the ocean, its rays gliding over the waves, shimmering with all the colours of the rainbow. Suddenly, near a dugout, she saw two officers. One was kneeling with his uniform unbuttoned and before him stood a wooden box. The other stood behind him with a drawn samurai sword. Netsumi immediately felt that something dangerous was inside the box, so she fluttered down and perched on it. She hoped that by doing so, she could protect the man who seemed painfully familiar to her. The officer reached for the box and suddenly froze, seeing the butterfly land on it. He did not pull his hand back, keeping it extended until the butterfly flapped its wings and, taking off, settled on the edge of the parapet. The officer opened the box and took out a small knife. Then, whispering something, he stabbed himself in the left side, moved it to the right and yanked it upward. Without uttering a sound, he slowly slumped to the side. At that moment, his comrade swung the sword and brought it down on his dying friend's neck. The head separated from the body and hung by a thin flap of skin. The officer fell and a large pool of blood spread beneath him. The butterfly flapped its wings and, circling above the deceased, darted upward, toward the rising sun over the ocean. It flew to where a lone raven was soaring high in the sky, peering intently at the ground.

Illustration by Artem Burlyk

Netsumi stood by the coffins containing her parents and understood nothing. Just a few days ago, she had been a happy and beloved daughter and today she was a complete orphan. The little girl had not yet grasped that her mother would never braid her hair again and her father would never hug her. Netsumi was still too young to comprehend the full bitterness of the loss and realised that she was now alone in the world.

On that terrible day, Netsumi was playing with her friends in the park when the ground suddenly shook, and an earthquake struck. The children survived by being in an open area. Netsumi fell to the ground and screamed in fear. When it was over, she ran to her home, only to find a pile of ruins instead of the familiar house. The street was unrecognizable. Cries of people and groans of the wounded echoed from all sides, but where her house had stood, there was only silence. Her parents were buried under the rubble of their home.

"Come with me, little girl," Netsumi heard. "You'll stay with me for a while."

It was Ichiro-san, her father's colleague who sometimes visited their home and knew her well. He took Netsumi by the hand and led her away from the place where her childhood had ended.

"Mizuki," Ichiro-san called his maid. "Netsumi will be living with us. Please take care of her."

Mizuki understood what had happened from her master's look and, silently, took the girl's hand, guiding her inside.

Thus, Netsumi came to live in Ichiro-san's house. Besides the maid, there was an old gardener, Atsushi, who tended to the rather large garden behind the house.

Weeks and months dragged on in the unfamiliar home. Mizuki and Atsushi grew fond of the girl and did everything they could to distract her from heavy thoughts. Ichiro-san left for work very early and returned home late in the evening. His government job occupied all his time.

One evening, he came home and called for Netsumi: "Netsumi, dear girl, I am a very busy man and cannot give you the attention you deserve. You are a very beautiful and intelligent girl. Therefore, I want to enroll you in a maiko school[24]. There, you will receive a good education and learn many things. I will be coming often and you will have everything you need."

"As you say, Ichiro-san," Netsumi bowed. "I am deeply grateful for your care and the shelter you have provided me."

"You are already ten years old, and I think this will be a good choice for you," said Ichiro-san.

In the morning, after gathering her few belongings, Netsumi said goodbye to Mizuki and Atsushi and got into the car, which was still a marvel to the residents. This technological wonder had only recently appeared on the country's roads and was affordable only to very wealthy citizens, such as Ichiro-san. Netsumi rode in the car looking out the window. She saw the city gradually recovering from the earthquake's devastation. Spring birds sang along the road, trees and flowers were blooming. Netsumi was leaving the city of her childhood, the city she loved so much, and which had taken from her the most precious things.

After a while, the car stopped in front of tall black gates. The driver honked the horn.

Ichiro-san got out of the car and, turning to the girl, said: "We have arrived, Netsumi. This is your new home."

Netsumi turned around and looked at the imposing gates. The place where she was about to start her new life stood before her, both daunting and promising.

The girl took her belongings and stepped out of the car, looking around curiously. It was very beautiful here. Tall, ancient trees shaded the sun's rays. Everything was planted with flowers that, feeling the spring, were eager to

---

[24] Maiko — an apprentice geisha in Kyoto and Western Japan. Visually distinguished from a geisha by shorter kimono sleeves and a bright red under-collar.

bloom. In the distance, the ocean was visible, alluring with its mystery and grandeur.

At the sound of the horn, the gates opened. An older woman in a colourful kimono came out and greeted Ichiro-san. It was clear that they had known each other for a long time and that the woman knew the purpose of their visit.

"Netsumi, this is Mrs. Katsumi. She will be your caretaker at the school. I hope you will become an exemplary student," said Ichiro-san.

Netsumi silently bowed to the woman. Katsumi also silently gestured towards the door, and they went inside.

Ichiro-san stood outside for a bit longer, as if contemplating something, then waved to the driver, who started the engine. The car drove away, leaving Netsumi to start her new life in this beautiful and unfamiliar place.

Inside, the school was just as impressive as the garden outside. The halls were lined with intricate woodwork and national decor. Katsumi led Netsumi to a small room, simply furnished, but cosy.

"This will be your room," Katsumi said kindly. "Take your time to settle in. Dinner will be served in an hour and you will meet the other students then."

Netsumi nodded, placing her few belongings carefully on the tatami mat. She felt a mix of sadness for leaving her old life behind and excitement for the new experiences that awaited her.

A new phase began in Netsumi's life – one of becoming a well-rounded individual, a true priestess of love.

The girl was settled in a house where other trainees also lived. Initially, Netsumi kept to herself, but over time, she made friends with her peers, making it easier to grasp the complex art of the geisha. From morning until evening, the maiko engaged in dancing and playing the shamisen[25], singing, reciting poetry, reading books, and practicing calligraphy. As they grew older, the trainees were taught to understand the political and social life of the country, which was important for the men who would be their future clients.

---

[25] Shamisen — a traditional Japanese three-stringed instrument played with a plectrum.

Additionally, a professional geisha was required to master the refined etiquette honed over centuries, including the rituals of the traditional tea ceremony. The girls were taught aristocratic manners, how to conduct themselves in society, walk, sit, turn, engage in sophisticated conversation, dress stylishly, and laugh effortlessly. Despite the rigorous training and demanding schedule, Netsumi found joy in her new life. She poured her heart into every activity, especially the ikebana, where she could express her creativity and bring beauty to her surroundings. Her dedication did not go unnoticed, and her teachers often praised her progress. This encouragement fuelled her determination to excel and become a true geisha, embodying grace, elegance, and wisdom.

Ichiro-san, who had taken on the responsibility of supporting and helping Netsumi, visited quite often. Each time, he would have a private conversation with the headmistress, and they would talk for a long time. Then he would call Netsumi and inquire about her progress and needs. The girl never knew refusal, but she asked for things very rarely due to her modesty and shyness. Ichiro-san was frustrated by this and tried to bring her a gift each time, whether it was a new kimono or a bonsai in a clay pot.

This time, they were sitting in the tearoom.

"Tell me, Katsumi," Ichiro-san began. "When will she be ready?"

"The lotus flower has already bloomed, she recently turned seventeen. Does the master wish to pluck this flower?" Katsumi asked.

"Yes, I want to send her into adulthood. I want to be her first man," said Ichiro-san.

"Come next week," Katsumi said. "In the meantime, we will prepare her and then begin the ceremony. It lasts an entire week."

"Yes, I know," said Ichiro-san. "Who will prepare her?"

"I will personally take care of this. My assistant Nyoko will oversee the preparations," replied Katsumi. "She has been here the longest and knows the traditions well."

Ichiro-san nodded, satisfied with the arrangements. As they finished their tea, Katsumi called for Netsumi, who entered the room gracefully and bowed.

"Netsumi," the mistress began. "Ichiro-san has made an important decision regarding your future. You will start preparations next week. Nyoko will guide you through it."

Netsumi looked at Ichiro-san with a mixture of gratitude and apprehension. She knew that this moment would come but hadn't realised it would be so soon. The girl bowed deeply.

"Thank you, Ichiro-san," she said softly. "I will do my best to honour your trust in me."

Ichiro-san smiled gently at her: "I am confident you will, Netsumi. I look forward to seeing your progress."

With that, the meeting concluded and Netsumi returned to her studies. Her mind filled with thoughts of the upcoming ceremony and the new chapter of her life that was about to begin.

On the appointed day, Ichiro-san arrived at the school, where, as always, he was greeted by the headmistress. She invited him to the tearoom and brought a fragrant drink.

"Each evening, I will prepare the bed. The girl will be waiting for you. On the bed, I will leave three raw eggs. You must break them, drink the yolk and rub the whites between Netsumi's legs. This will help her relax and, in a week, you will be able to pluck this beautiful flower," said Katsumi. "Now, change your clothes and wait for me to call you."

After some time, the paper doors slid open with a slight rustle and Katsumi appeared in the doorway. She wore a green kimono adorned with bright flowers. The woman silently bowed to Ichiro-san, who was sitting on a mat, and then turned and went outside. Ichiro-san stood up and followed her in silence. They arrived at another building and, after a brief pause at the door, Katsumi opened it, letting the man inside. They approached a room with a paper lantern hanging above the entrance.

"Netsumi is waiting for you," said Katsumi, bowing and sliding the door open to let Ichiro-san into the room.

When the door closed behind him, Ichiro-san saw a low bed and Netsumi lying on it. There was no fear in her eyes, but rather, anticipation.

Ichiro-san approached the edge of the bed and bowed to her: "You have nothing to fear, my girl."

Netsumi did not reply but began breathing more rapidly. Ichiro-san squatted down and removed the satin cover that covered Netsumi. A stunning sight was revealed. Before him lay an incredibly beautiful young woman. Ichiro-san had often seen her as a small and awkward girl, but now Netsumi had blossomed. Her beautiful, lush hair was neatly styled into an intricate up-do. The makeup was flawless. She covered her breasts with her hands and her gaze showed excitement. The sight made the experienced Ichiro-san's head spin for a moment, but he quickly regained his composure.

Without saying a word, he took one of the eggs lying on the bed and crushed it in his hand. Carefully pouring the white into his palm, he swallowed the yolk. Then, with his free hand, he spread the girl's legs and began to rub the egg white between them. He repeated the same procedure with the other two eggs. Throughout the process, Netsumi did not make a sound. Only the rise and fall of her chest indicated that she was anxious.

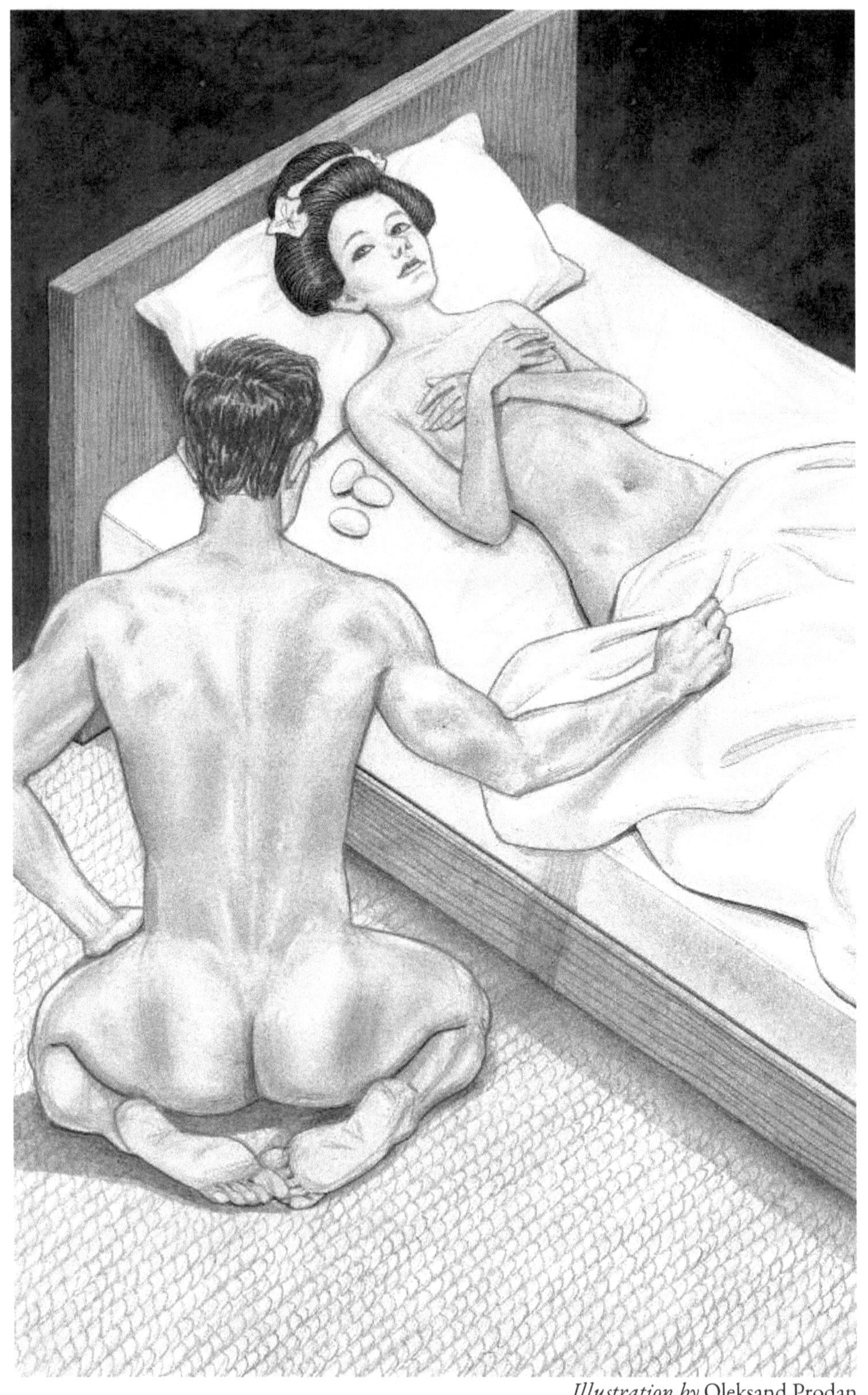

Illustration by Oleksand Prodan

"I will come back tomorrow," said her master. "For now, I will leave you alone."

He bowed and left the room. Ichiro-san visited her every evening for a week and, each time, Netsumi became less anxious. Finally, the moment came for which all this preparation had been made.

"I want you to remember this day for the rest of your life. Everything must happen impeccably on this bed, covered with a white sheet," he said, removing his kimono.

Despite his mature age, he had a fine physique and, for a moment, Netsumi even admired him, though she had never seen a naked man before. However, she did not dare to openly look at her master. Nervousness made her breathe rapidly. The feeling of something new, something previously unknown, overwhelmed her. Fortunately, he was experienced in matters of love and Netsumi did not have to feel any discomfort. He knew how to caress a woman and how to give her pleasure. She felt almost no pain when he entered her.

So she turned into a woman thanks to her master – a woman who was to be with him until her death. His lover, friend, and primary advisor.

When Netsumi's red collar was replaced with a white one with golden threads[26], Ichiro-san visited her again.

"I have rented a house for you nearby," he told her. "I want you to live separately from the others so that I can always see you. You will continue to work at this teahouse. Mrs. Katsumi is very pleased with you. You have great potential, and the clients enjoy your company very much."

"Thank you, my master," she said, bowing to him.

Later, the young geisha moved into a small house located nearby. It was well-kept and had a small backyard with trees and flowers. Over time, Netsumi made it comfortable and cosy for herself and her master. The house has been

---

[26] The replacement of the red collar with a white one with golden threads is a dedication ceremony when maiko apprentices become geishas.

transformed into a fragrant oasis, as no one could rival Netsumi in creating floral arrangements.

"Today we have two young cadets as guests," said hostess Katsumi. "Netsumi! You, along with Aiko, will serve them."

"Yes, madam," replied Netsumi and, nodding to Aiko, left the hall.

The young geishas walked down the corridor to the room where the guests waited. A light, melodious sound echoed as they walked from the small bells attached to their okobo[27]. Netsumi walked, unaware that this meeting would be fateful for her – a meeting that would change her life forever.

Netsumi slid open the paper doors and the girls entered. Before them, sitting on the tatami, were two young men in imperial academy cadets' uniforms.

"Still just boys," thought Netsumi as she sat down in front of them.

Aiko went to the corner of the room and began to prepare tea. Everyone was silent. When the tea was ready, Aiko brought the tray with the fragrant drink. Netsumi took a cup and offered it to one of the cadets, the one who seemed older. Then she offered a cup to the other and accidentally touched his hand. He blushed from the touch. Netsumi noticed this but said nothing.

"He is very shy, still just a boy, but already a warrior," she thought.

The evening passed unnoticed, allowing the participants to discuss many topics. The cadets were quite erudite, which pleasantly surprised Netsumi. The older one had already served in His Imperial Majesty's army and shared many interesting stories about his service and the customs in the military. The younger cadet initially stammered, but then spoke confidently and proved to be an excellent conversationalist, holding the attention of everyone present. It was clear that the boy came from an aristocratic family, making a military career his primary goal in life. The only thing that unsettled the cadet was

---

[27] Okobo — a platform shoes with small bells worn by geishas.

Netsumi's presence. He was afraid to lift his eyes and look at her and, every time he did, his face turned red.

"What a boy he still is," Netsumi thought, secretly smiling.

That evening flew by quickly in conversation. The cadets had to return to their barracks on time and they said their goodbyes.

"Netsumi," called Katsumi.

"That young cadet was asking about you. He wants to meet you again. I hope you understand that he will soon be going to the army, so there should be no serious relationship between you," the hostess of the teahouse added sternly.

"Don't worry, madam, everything will be fine," replied Netsumi.

"I told him when you will be working," said Katsumi. "So expect the guest."

On the appointed day, Netsumi walked down the corridor again, accompanied by the melodic chime of the bells. She slid the door and entered the room where Taro – the familiar cadet, sat on the tatami. The young man tried to remain calm, but Netsumi's experienced eye knew he was nervous. She bowed and went to the corner of the room to prepare tea. Then she brought the tray and placed it on the floor directly in front of Taro. She sat down beside him and poured tea into the cups.

"Thank you for coming, Taro-san," she said softly, handing him a cup.

Taro accepted the cup, his hands trembling slightly.

"Thank you for seeing me again, Netsumi-san. I couldn't stop thinking about our last meeting."

Netsumi smiled gently: "It is my pleasure, Taro-san. I hope our time together will bring you some peace before your journey to the army."

For some moment they sipped their tea in silence. The warmth of the drink calmed down Taro's nerves. Netsumi could see the determination and apprehension in his eyes.

"Mistress Katsumi told me that you were looking to meet me," she said while handing him another cup of tea.

He accepted it with a slight nod.

"Yes, I wanted to see you," Taro replied. "Ever since I met you, I can't think about anything else. All my thoughts are with you."

"Wow, quite the confession for such a young boy. Even an adult man doesn't always have the courage to say something like that," she said.

"I like the feeling that has arisen within me, but I don't know what to do with it. I will soon be going to the army. Our country is on the brink of war," responded Taro.

The young man said this with such a tone and feeling that Netsumi instantly forgot that the shy boy she first met a few weeks ago was sitting before her. This was a man, a warrior, filled with courage and determination to die for his country and his Emperor. Netsumi looked at him differently. Yes, she had been mistaken, he was no longer a boy. Something unfamiliar stirred within her, as if light, airy butterflies had begun a carefree flight inside her.

They spent the rest of the evening talking about various topics, Taro sharing stories of his training and dreams for the future, while Netsumi listened attentively, offering words of encouragement and support. Despite Katsumi's stern warning a bond formed between them that neither time nor distance could easily break it.

Toward the end of the meeting, Netsumi told him: "If you want to see me, come to my home. I don't live with the other girls. My master rents a house for me nearby."

She explained to him how to find her house and said: "When you see an ikebana with an orchid in the window, it means I am home and waiting for you."

"I wanted to give you something," he pulled out a small, intricately carved wooden charm and handed it to her. "This is a good luck charm. I hope it will keep you safe and remind you of our meetings."

Netsumi accepted the gift graciously: "Thank you, Taro. I will treasure it."
Netsumi escorted Taro to the doorstep and they said their goodbyes.

By returning home she looked around the room, checking if everything was in place for such an unusual guest. Her thoughts were tangled, so Netsumi decided to distract herself by playing the shamisen. She played with closed eyes, imagining her little yard, which she had transformed into a paradise, and the colourful butterflies that flocked to it from everywhere to taste the floral nectar. Netsumi envisioned the black raven that had started appearing a few months ago. At first, the bird did not allow her to approach, but later they became friends, and the raven began taking food directly from her hands. Netsumi talked to him as if he was a person and it seemed to her that the bird understood everything perfectly. It was a unique friendship, where both missed each other and were genuinely happy to meet again. Often, they would sit together in the gazebo and simply watch the sunset in silence. At such moments, Netsumi felt as if it wasn't a raven sitting next to her, but a person.

Illustration by Artem Burlyk

The shamisen's gentle music helped calm her mind. She found solace in the familiar tunes and the tranquillity of her surroundings. As she played, the thought of Taro lingered in her mind, mixing with the melodies. She wondered what the future held for him and how their paths had crossed so unexpectedly. With each note, she sent a silent prayer for his safety and well-being. As the sun began to set, casting a warm glow over her yard, Netsumi put down the shamisen and went to the garden. The sight of the blooming flowers and the gentle rustling of leaves brought a smile to her face.

A few weeks had passed since the meeting with Taro. Ichiro-san had gone to the capital for an extended period on business and Netsumi decided to place a new ikebana with an orchid in the window. She knew that the cadets had a day off tomorrow and her boy (as she had secretly started calling Taro) would come running for a visit. Netsumi was sure of it. All these days, she thought about Taro and the belief that their meeting was not ordinary never left her. Any memory of him made the butterflies inside her start their unstoppable flight.

She prepared a small arrangement of orchids and placed it in the window, signalling to Taro that she was home and waiting. The anticipation of seeing him again filled her with a mix of excitement and serenity, making her feel more alive than ever before.

Netsumi sensed rather than heard her guest's arrival. She approached the door and at that moment, there was a soft knock. She immediately opened it and saw him, her boy.

"Come in, please, have a seat. I'll make some tea for us."

The boy walked inside and sat down on the tatami mat. Taro devoured her with his eyes, clearly having missed her very much. After calming down a bit, he began to look around the room.

"Do you like it here?"

Taro was startled by the question, which greatly amused her.

"Yes, very much. It's so cosy. You know a lot about flowers, don't you?"

"I love creating ikebanas, as each arrangement conveys a mood. Through flowers, you can express your feelings. It's a true art and I learned it for a long time when I was still a maiko, an apprentice in our school. For example, this ikebana that you saw in my window. With it, I wanted to say that this home is happy to see you," she laughed.

Taro smiled, understanding the sentiment behind her words.

"Your ikebanas are beautiful, just like you."

Netsumi blushed slightly, touched by his compliment. She brought the tea tray and placed it between them, pouring tea into cups.

"Thank you, Taro," she said, handing him a cup. "Your words mean a lot to me."

As they sipped their tea, a comfortable silence settled between them. Netsumi felt a deep connection growing stronger with each moment spent together. The butterflies inside her seemed to dance with joy, mirroring the happiness she felt in Taro's presence. Then they chatted for a long time on various topics and, once again, the girl noted the boy was far ahead of his peers in terms of erudition. Taro could recite great poets, had knowledge of philosophy and other sciences. It was incredibly interesting and comfortable to be with him. The bond between them, initially formed out of curiosity and attraction, was blossoming into something much more profound and meaningful.

As evening approached, Netsumi moved closer and ran her hand over the young man's face and stared into his eyes.

"You are very young, and you've never been with a woman before. Come, I want to show you something," she whispered and, keeping his hand, led him to the bedroom.

They made passionate love for a long time. Despite her experience, Netsumi felt a difference between what she had felt before and what was happening now. She had never experienced such pleasure with other men. Taro was somewhat clumsy, but tireless and very gentle. At one point, Netsumi, exhausted, pulled him close to her chest and whispered: "Let's wait a little or I'll die."

Taro moved slightly away from the girl, who lay with her eyes closed, breathing heavily. He couldn't get enough of this beauty. The beauty of his first and only woman, though Taro didn't know it at the time. From happiness, the young man felt like he was in the heavens and barely understood where he was and what was happening to him. At that moment, the bed in Netsumi's house was the centre of the universe for him.

Netsumi looked at Taro with a sense of fulfillment and a newfound tenderness. The intensity of their connection was unlike anything she had ever experienced, and the same wonder was reflected in his eyes. They lay together, wrapped in each other's arms, basking in the afterglow of their shared intimacy.

"Taro," she said softly. "This moment will always be special to me."

He nodded, unable to find the words to express his feelings. Instead, he held her tighter, silently promising that this bond would not be broken. They drifted off to sleep, with the sounds of the evening blending into a gentle lullaby, anchoring them in a world where only they existed.

"Who is this man?" Ichiro-san asked sternly.

"He is a cadet at His Imperial Majesty's Academy," Netsumi replied, lowering her eyes.

Ichiro-san frowned and walked to the window. Yes, Netsumi was under his patronage, and he supported her. At the same time, she was a highly skilled and sought after geisha with many respectable clients. He was unhappy that another man had started appearing in the house he rented for her. He completely trusted her. Over the years, she had never let him down and had become not just a lover, but a loyal friend and primary advisor. Holding a high position in the government he often consulted her and she with her sharp mind and keen intuition, always provided advice that he heeded. He could not discuss such matters with his wife. In any situation, he would go to his lover, knowing that she would always help him. Netsumi was his solace, someone with whom he could relax both mentally and physically. But it was clear for him that he could not possess her as a thing. He decided that he would accept any decision she made with dignity, even if she wanted to leave him.

Netsumi, on her part, remembered how much he did for her and tried not to disappoint her patron in any way. The only thing she could not deny were the meetings with Taro. It was beyond her strength. With him, Netsumi felt like a little girl flying in the sky and this feeling was precious to her.

"I see. You must understand, Netsumi, that your actions reflect on me as well. I have always trusted you and valued our relationship. But this cadet... he cannot offer you what I have."

Netsumi nodded, tears welling up in her eyes.

"I understand. But Taro... he makes me feel alive in a way I haven't felt before. He is young and idealistic, and I... I cherish our time together."

He sighed deeply, placing a hand gently on her shoulder.

"I do not wish to stand in the way of your happiness, Netsumi. But I must upset you. I am being transferred to work in the capital as we are on the brink of a great war. I will not leave you here. You are coming with me. So you have two days to finish your business and say goodbye to him," he told her and left.

His words struck like a bolt of lightning from a clear sky. The sweet dream had ended just as it began.

Netsumi had not seen Taro in the two days before she left for the capital. She wrote him a note.

"My dear boy, the time has come for us to part ways. Do you remember when I told you about the sakura blossoms? Each year they fade only to bloom again the next. Love is the same: keep it in your heart and in time it will flourish once more. Forgive me for leaving without warning. My master received a promotion and moved to the capital. I must go with him. He has done much for me, for

which I am endlessly grateful. Do not look for me. Walk your path with honour. You are the best thing that has ever happened in my life. Yours, Netsumi."

After writing a note Netsumi met with Aiko and said: "I am leaving tomorrow. Do you remember that boy, one of the cadets we served back then?"

"Of course, he looked at you so intently that I was afraid he would burn a hole through you with his gaze. I think he didn't see anyone else besides you that day."

"Yes, that's him. He comes to see me every week, but I don't have time to meet him anymore. I am leaving early tomorrow morning. Can you give him this letter?"

Netsumi handed Aiko a rolled-up sheet of paper. Aiko took it and said: "Don't worry! I'll do everything as you ask. Good luck in your new place, I will miss you."

The girls hugged and cried.

Netsumi took Aiko by the shoulders and said: "Thank you so much. Don't be sad. Maybe we'll meet again someday."

Aiko nodded, wiping away her tears. Netsumi felt a pang of sorrow, knowing she was leaving behind a dear friend and the young love she had found. But she also knew that life had to move forward, and she needed to face whatever the future held.

Early the next morning, Netsumi packed her belongings and prepared to leave with Ichiro-san. As she glanced one last time at the house and the garden she had tended so lovingly, she hoped that Taro would understand her decision and find strength in their memories.

As the car pulled away, Netsumi's thoughts were with her boy and she silently prayed for their happiness and wellbeing.

"He is being sent to the army. I contacted the head of the academy. Do you want to send him a letter?" Ichiro-san asked Netsumi.

"Yes, sir, if possible," she replied anxiously.

Netsumi had been living for several months in the apartment Ichiro-san rented for her in the capital. The capital overwhelmed Netsumi. The huge buildings, the crowds of people, the noise, all of it was so unfamiliar. She missed her little house terribly, the place where she had left a piece of her heart forever.

"A courier will come tomorrow to pick up the letter. He will be able to deliver it before the young officer is sent to the army, so hurry," said Ichiro-san. "I have to go on business to the provinces."

Netsumi took out a sheet of paper and sat at the small table by the window. She looked at the big city but saw nothing. Her thoughts were only of him, her warrior. After a moment, she began to write: "*My dear boy! I know you will soon be going to the army. Since I left, I haven't forgotten about you for a single minute. All my thoughts were about you, my boy. I will pray for you every day and will always be invisible by your side. Kisses, your Netsumi.*"

The girl folded the letter in four and placed it on the table. She sat there, lost in thought until evening, recalling the happy moments she had spent together with Taro. Netsumi hoped that her letter would bring Taro some comfort and strength as he faced the unknown challenges ahead. With a heavy heart, she prepared for the night, knowing that her thoughts and prayers would follow Taro wherever he went.

A few weeks later the big war erupted. Terrible and relentless. Netsumi began to understand from the very beginning that the war could not be won, and she tried to convey this to Ichiro-san, who was involved in the country's defence. But her patron, despite listening to his lover's arguments, still hoped for victory. Their army was still strong, but the recent atomic bombing, which had wiped two cities off the face of the earth, had completely demoralised him. The following days were filled with uncertainty and fear. Netsumi watched as the capital, once bustling with life and hope, grew quieter and more sombre. People walked with their heads down, carrying the weight of defeat. She thought of Taro often, wondering if he had received her last letter and how he was coping with the horrors of war.

Ichiro-san's duties kept him busy, but the burden of their nation's surrender was a heavy one. Netsumi did her best to support him, offering comfort and solace in any way she could. Despite the bleakness of their situation, she held onto the belief that brighter days would come.

On the day the Emperor's surrender speech was broadcast, the air was thick with tension. Netsumi and Ichiro-san listened in silence as the Emperor spoke of the need to endure the unendurable and bear the unbearable. Tears streamed down Netsumi's face as the reality of their defeat settled in.

"We have lost!" Ichiro-san was exhausted and dejected.

Netsumi had never seen him like this.

"Sir! We have lost, but this is not the end," Netsumi replied. "After every dawn comes a sunset."

She moved closer to him on the tatami mat, hugging him and gently stroking his head.

"Thank you for everything," Ichiro-san said, holding her hand. "For all the years you have been with me. I can't even imagine what my life would have been like without you."

That evening they sat on the tatami together drinking tea and talking. The weight of the surrounding world pressed down on them. They clung to each other, finding solace in their shared grief and love. As they said their goodbyes, Netsumi couldn't shake the feeling that this chapter of their lives was ending and a new, uncertain future awaited them both. How could they have known that it was their last evening together?

Illustration by Artem Burlyk

Netsumi opened her eyes and stared unblinkingly at a spot on the ceiling. She understood everything. Taro had gone with honour, not allowing himself to be covered in shame. All these years, Netsumi had woken up thinking about him and praying. Now the day had come, when there was no one left to pray for. Netsumi belonged to an ancient samurai family. None of her relatives were alive anymore, but she knew the samurai code very well. Long time ago, Netsumi had acquired a small kaiken[28] with a handle made of walrus ivory. She had decided that if the moment ever came for her to leave this world, she would perform the jigai[29] ritual without hesitation.

Netsumi stood up and began her preparations. The young geisha styled her hair into an elaborate hairstyle, applied makeup, put on a ceremonial kimono and sat on the tatami mat. She placed the kaiken in front of her on a satin cloth and, closing her eyes, reflected. For a moment, Netsumi remembered her dream about the officer and the butterfly that prevented him from opening the box with the knife. In her mind's eye, she saw again the decapitated body lying at the bottom of the revetment, the huge pool of blood and the black raven circling high in the sky, looking down.

Netsumi took out the wooden charm from her pocket, looked at it thinking about something of her own. Then put it back and reached for the dagger. Overcoming a moment of hesitation, she drew the kaiken from its sheath and firmly ran it along her carotid artery. In her final moments, Netsumi imagined herself as the butterfly once more, soaring freely over fields and oceans, untethered by earthly concerns. She hoped her spirit would find Taro's and, together, they would continue their journey in another realm.

---

[28] Kaiken — a short dagger, carried in a pocket-like space (futokoro) or in the sleeve pouch (tamoto).
[29] Jigai — a ritual suicide for women similar to male seppuku, where the woman cuts her throat or stabs the knife into her heart.

Peter

Peter finished his cigarette, threw it on the ground and stomped it out. Several crushed cigarette butts already lay there. He was visibly nervous, but he wasn't about to back down from his plan. The thick shrubbery at the end of the alley reliably hid him from prying eyes. The dim light of the park lamps barely illuminated the path between the trees, but it was enough for him to see the person he was waiting for. The life he had led in recent years had taught him to navigate well at night and he felt confident as he peered into the darkness of the alley. If the information he received was correct, the murderer of his brother would soon appear, and he would avenge his death. Peter took out another cigarette but didn't have time to light it. At the other end of the alley, a figure appeared, slowly walking towards him, looking down at his feet. Peter's heart began to race. He knew this feeling well, the feeling of a hunter who had spotted his long-awaited prey. Years spent in the gang had taught him to always be cold-blooded and composed. He calmly put the cigarette packet into his left pocket and took a knife out of his right pocket. The figure slowly approached. Yes, it was the scumbag responsible for his brother's suicide. Peter silently moved towards him. The man was deep in thought and startled when a tall figure suddenly appeared before him.

"How's your conscience, Jürgen? I've been waiting for you here for a while. I want to pass on a message from your friend, my brother," said Peter as he swung the knife under Jürgen's heart.

Jürgen gasped as he fell on the ground.

"My brother was not like everyone else, and it was not his fault, so he was born that way. Johan was an honest, bright person and you killed him. So now you'll die too!"

Peter spat at his feet, before quickly disappearing into the darkness.

Illustration by Artem Burlyk

A branch snapped and broke underfoot, but Peter managed to grab onto another and hung in the air. Johan, who was standing on the ground, froze in fear.

"Jump!" he called out to his brother in a muffled voice. "We've had enough apples."

But at that moment, the neighbour's dog barked loudly and lights flickered on in the house.

"Run!" Johan shouted, no longer hiding. "Run or it'll be too late!"

Peter jumped down from the tree and both brothers dashed towards the fence. Behind them, old Michael's shouts and the dog's frantic barking filled the air.

"I tell you, it was your brats, Hans!" old Michael wouldn't calm down.

"Well, how do you know it was them?" Hans defended himself weakly.

He had just come back from the night shift and had no desire to deal with the night-time adventure. The only thing he wanted was to sleep. But old Michael insisted and there was no chance of getting any rest.

"Well, what can I tell you, neighbour? I'll talk to them. If it was them, I'll punish both. Alright?" Hans said wearily, hoping to end the conversation quickly.

"But who will fix my tree? They broke it, you know," old Michael continued to fume.

"Ok Michael, let me talk to them first and then we'll decide what to do. If it was them, we'll find a way to compensate you for your loss. Agreed?"

"Boys. I want to know was it you who raided old Michael's garden last night, broke his tree and fence?"

Their father spoke in a calm voice, but it was clear that it was difficult for him to keep this tranquil tone.

"Well, answer. Honestly."

"Forgive us, father," Peter said. "We won't do this again."

"What do we need to do to make him calm down?" Johan asked.

"Alright, boys. You're already thirteen years old. At your age, I was working in a factory, and I didn't have time for such nonsense. I worked for my country and my people. I don't want my sons to shame my name! It's time for you to take responsibility for your actions. Now you will go to old Michael and settle things with him yourselves. I don't want any more problems with the neighbours. Is that clear?"

Peter and Johan nodded silently and walked out towards the neighbour's house.

Johan broke the silence first: "Why did I listen to you? Couldn't we have done without those apples?"

"They were delicious," Peter said with a smile. "Why does he need so many for? He lives alone."

"Alone or not, it doesn't matter now, but we have to pay for them. Some apple thieves you are," Johan said, giving his brother a light slap.

Peter didn't resist. He was only a few minutes younger than his brother and, despite being taller and sturdier, he silently acknowledged Johan's leadership. Johan had a completely different character than his unpredictable brother. Calm and thoughtful, he always helped Peter with homework or gave useful advice and Peter always listened to him. However, when it came to standing up for his brother on the street, Peter would jump into a fight without hesitation.

The brothers approached old Michael's house and Peter pressed the doorbell. A minute later, the owner appeared at the gate.

"So, you've come, you rascals?" old Michael asked them sternly.

"Please forgive us. We won't do this again," Johan said, lowering his eyes.

"What am I supposed to do about the tree? I've been growing it for years," the old man said grumpily, seeing that the boys realised their mistake.

"Right then, come on in. I'll treat you to some tea with apple jam. From the apples I harvested last year," he added sarcastically.

That evening, they sat at the table for a long time, drinking tea with delicious apple jam. The old man turned out to be not as old as he appeared at first glance. The large, jagged scar on his forehead gave him an aged and formidable look. But his muscular arms and strong build indicated that he could rival many younger men. He told the boys a lot about his childhood, his military service, the war, and what he had to endure after the defeat, staying in a prisoner-of-war camp.

"Remember this. Always, in any situation, remain human. I was captured in the war when I was wounded and passed out. An enemy soldier saved my life. He didn't leave me to die in the forest but carried me on his back for several kilometres. He shared his food and water with me. Yes, I ended up in a prisoner-of-war camp and he went on with his troops. But I stayed alive and now sit before you. This act turned everything upside down in my mind. It was us who attacked them, yet instead of shooting me, he saved my life. So, if not for this incident, I wouldn't be treating you to tea today. By the way his name was the same as yours," old Michael pointed at Peter.

The boys listened with their mouths open and didn't interrupt. Sensing their interest, old Michael continued to share story after story. He had no relatives, and it was clear that he wanted to pass on his memories to them. That evening the brothers gained a loyal friend, someone they subsequently visited regularly. The old man was delighted to tell them his personal stories and offer valuable life advice. In return, the boys helped him around the house.

Illustration by Artem Burlyk

"So, what now? You finish school and then what? You go to work in a factory like your father? Don't you see that he works like a slave and doesn't even see the light of day? He lives to work. It's not like that with us. In one day, you can earn as much as your father does in a whole month," Gustav told Peter.

Although much older he liked the young and daring boy. Peter listened silently. Yes, with his character, he couldn't see himself working in a factory from bell to bell. Here was freedom, a life full of adventures and money, lots of money. By nature, he was an adventurer, ever since childhood, he constantly got into trouble, for which his father often scolded him. Now, grown up, he thought about how he should live his life. The influence of old Michael and the stories of his past instilled in Peter a sense of respect for resilience and human decency. However, the allure of Gustav's words pulled him in another direction, promising excitement and wealth that the mundane factory life couldn't offer. Peter found himself at a crossroads, contemplating the path that would shape his future.

He met these guys one evening when he was returning home from training. Boxing was his favourite sport and, for over a year, he attended a club where he trained with a renowned boxing champion. That evening, the guys tried to mess with him, thinking he'd be an easy target. But they quickly learned otherwise. A few days later, Gustav found Peter and decided to talk to him. Gustav was the leader of the local gang, and he needed bold and well-trained fighters.

"Understand this. The war is over, but people still have gold and jewels. Those who weren't fools made reserves for the future and that future has arrived," Gustav laughed.

Peter was doubtful. He felt guilty towards his parents and even more so towards his brother. He loved Johan with a devoted brotherly love and was ready to do anything for him.

"So, what would I need to do?" he finally asked Gustav.

"For now, nothing. I mainly need your agreement. I'll find you when I need you," Gustav said, extending his hand to Peter.

He shook it, turned around and went home.

Days and weeks of Peter's self-proclaimed boring life continued. He hated it so much. Boxing was the only activity that distracted him. There, he gave his all. Conversations with his brother also calmed a bit and gave him a boost of optimism. It was always interesting and easy with Johan, who was well-read and could talk on any topic. Peter admired his determination and perseverance, qualities he often lacked. The brothers frequently argued, but never fought and always stood up for each other in front of their parents.

That evening remained etched in Peter's memory for the rest of his life. They were sitting in the treehouse their father had built for them when they were little. The brothers had grown up, but the treehouse still stood on the sprawling tree in the backyard. Sometimes they retreated there to be alone and talk without interruption. They could talk for hours until their parents started looking for them.

"What are you planning to do after school?" Peter asked Johan.

"I'm going to apply to the institute's biology faculty. I like science because it represents the future. There's so much unknown. I want to make an important discovery, and you'll brag to everyone that your brother made it," Johan smiled.

"Yes, I'd be so happy. I think you'll succeed. You're so determined, unlike me."

"But you have qualities that I lack."

"What qualities? How has knowing how to fight ever helped anyone build a life?"

"You need to understand that the meaning of existence isn't about whether you can fight or not. That's important too, but the main thing is that you have ambitions and a desire to achieve something."

Peter fell silent. He didn't tell his brother about his conversation with Gustav, as he didn't want to disappoint Johan and decided to change the topic.

"Listen, why don't you have a girlfriend yet? Look at Greta from next door, she looks at you all the time. She's a real catch!"

Peter traced two curved lines in the air with his hands, mimicking her figure.

Johan remained silent, staring at the floor.

"Come on, confess. Are you that shy?" Peter laughed.

"Brother, I'm going to tell you something and you can decide how to take it," Johan began straightforwardly.

He never called Peter 'brother', always by his name. This caught Peter's attention. The tone in which it was said also unsettled him. He sat down opposite Johan and asked: "What do you want to tell me?"

"Well, you see," Johan hesitated and paused for a moment. "I don't know how to explain this to you, but I don't like girls."

Peter knew his brother well, so he immediately recalled moments when they went to the bathhouse and Johan seemed shy about undressing. At the time, Peter chalked it up to shyness. Then he remembered how Johan looked at a certain famous actor when they went to the movies. Once was enough for Peter to see the film, but Johan went back to see it several more times. Connecting these memories, Peter began to understand. He realised that Johan had been grappling with his feelings for a long time. Though surprised, he wanted to support his brother.

"Do you like boys?" Peter asked with fear in his voice, hoping deep down that he was wrong.

Johan silently nodded.

"Do you know what they did to people like you before the war?"

Johan nodded again.

"We have to keep this a secret."

"You really won't stop respecting me because of this?" Johan looked at him hopefully.

"What are you talking about? You were born this way. We are of the same flesh and blood. You're not to blame for anything. To me, you were and always will be my only friend and brother."

"But you understand that I can't keep this a secret all my life?"

"Johan, it's okay. Let things go as they go. I'm always on your side. You don't have to explain anything. You're my brother and I love you no matter what. I'll kill anyone who dares to hurt you," Peter replied, clenching his fists.

Johan looked at Peter with a mixture of relief and gratitude. Knowing he had his brother's unwavering support made the burden he had been carrying a little lighter. For Peter, the awareness that he could stand by his brother no matter what gave him a new sense of purpose and determination. They were in this together, facing whatever challenges the future might hold.

"Be at the corner of the market square, by the cathedral, at eight o'clock tonight. Let's see what you're made of," Gustav said.

It had been a little over a month since their first meeting and Peter had almost forgotten about that conversation. His heart pounded with excitement and anxiety.

"What do I have to do?"

"You'll stand lookout while we 'have a chat' with a greedy bastard who doesn't want to part with the gold he deceitfully got from people sent to the concentration camps," Gustav replied with a wicked smile.

Five minutes before the appointed time, Peter was already at the location. As the city hall clock struck eight, a tall sturdy guy appeared from nowhere beside Peter.

"Follow me," he said quietly.

Peter obeyed and followed the stranger. After a couple of blocks, they stopped.

"See that entrance?" the stranger asked Peter.

The boy nodded.

"When we go in, you'll stand by the entrance and keep an eye on the street. If the police show up, come into the building and let us know. Second floor, apartment number seven. Got it?" the stranger asked.

"Got it," Peter said, his voice hoarse with excitement.

Peter didn't have to wait long. Soon, a lone man with a suitcase appeared on the street. It was getting dark, but it was clear that he was in a hurry. As he entered the stranger followed him. Two more men ran towards the building from the other side. Peter recognised one of them, it was Gustav. After they disappeared inside, Peter approached the door and carefully watched the street. About twenty minutes later, the stranger emerged, saying nothing as he walked away. Gustav followed him out.

"It's done. You can go home now, I'll find you," he said to Peter before quickly heading down the street.

A few days later, Gustav found Peter.

"Here is your share," he said, placing a bundle of banknotes in Peter's hand.

Peter had never held so much money before and his mouth fell open in astonishment. Gustav noticed his reaction and added: "There'll be another job soon. So, don't get too comfortable."

He patted Peter on the shoulder and disappeared in the darkness.

After that, there was another job, then a second, a third... Peter got used to the life of a fortune seeker and dropped out of school. He had so much money that he didn't know what to do with it all. He gave some of it to his mother so she could buy food and clothes. When she asked where the money came from, he explained that he'd been working part-time at the port. Peter couldn't show her all the money, as not even the port's manager earned that much. However, despite his efforts to keep it a secret, word about his involvement with the gang spread among the neighbours and they began to avoid him. This did not go unnoticed by his father.

"Come here, son, sit down," his father said, pulling a chair to the table.

Peter sat down, staring at his hands, which were trembling slightly. He felt both respect and fear towards his father.

"Now tell me, what kind of part-time work are you doing at the port?" his father's voice had a steely edge to it.

Peter remained silent, continuing to stare at his incessantly trembling hands.

"So, what the neighbours told me is true?" his father's voice was calm, but the tone left no hope for a favourable end to the conversation.

"Answer!" his father hissed with anger. "What kind of mess have you gotten into, you son of a bitch?"

"Dad, forgive me! I just couldn't stand watching how hard you work to support all of us," Peter squeezed out.

"I'll give you one chance to fix everything you've done. I won't bring this up again."

"Alright, Dad. I'll fix everything," Peter promised and got up from the table.

"Gustav, I need to talk to you," Peter said.

The gang leader was far from stupid and had a good understanding of human psychology; otherwise, the gang wouldn't have lasted so long.

"Of course. We're all here for each other," Gustav said with a hint of irony in his voice, which Peter didn't notice.

"I want to step away from this. I have problems at home, and I don't want to put my parents and brother at risk," Peter said.

"Yes, I understand you, my friend," Gustav said, putting an arm around Peter's shoulders. "We're human and we all have loved ones."

Gustav's apparent understanding provided Peter with a glimmer of hope. The boy thought he might be able to extricate himself from this dangerous path. However, he couldn't shake the feeling that things wouldn't be as simple as they seemed.

"So, you'll let me go?" Peter asked hopefully.

"Of course, how can I keep you with us against your will?" Gustav replied and, once again, Peter didn't catch the falsehood in his voice.

"Just one more job and you're free, agreed?"

"What job?"

"It's nothing complicated. Don't worry, it'll be just like always," Gustav reassured him. "I'll find you".

"Alright," Peter agreed. "But this will be my last job."

"Of course, my friend," Gustav said, looking intently at Peter.

"They bring money to the factory once a month," Gustav said. "We know who brings it and when. You'll stand here."

He pointed to a spot on the map.

"At this point, all vehicles slow down because of a steep incline. When the car aligns with you, you come out of hiding and shoot the tires with a pistol. We'll handle the rest."

"A pistol?" Peter asked, surprised. "Where will I get a pistol?"

"I'll give it to you before the job," Gustav said. "You know how to shoot, right?"

"I've shot a rifle with my dad before."

"Well, this is much simpler. I'll show you everything," Gustav said, looking intently at his accomplice.

Peter nodded, though anxiety gnawed at him. He knew this job would be more dangerous than the previous ones. But he also knew that seeing it through was the only way to leave the gang and protect his family.

Illustration by Artem Burlyk

On the appointed day, Peter waited for Gustav in a secluded spot. He was visibly nervous, as he had never gone on a job with a weapon before. Gustav appeared out of nowhere, as he always did. Throughout his time in the gang, Peter had never gotten used to it.

"Hold it," Gustav handed Peter a pistol.

"Before you shoot, lower this," Gustav showed Peter a small lever on the side of the pistol.

"The bullet is already in the chamber. Lower the safety and pull the trigger. At close range, you don't even need to aim. Understood?" Gustav asked.

"Yes, alright," Peter replied, trying to steady his nerves.

"That's all you need to worry about – stopping the car. We'll handle the rest! There are 35 minutes left," Gustav said, glancing at his watch, then disappeared into an alley without saying goodbye.

Peter spotted the car from a distance. It was moving slowly, swaying on the bumps. As it approached the turn with the incline, the driver eased off the gas and shifted to a lower gear. At that moment, Peter stepped out from his hiding spot and aimed the pistol at the car's tire. He pulled the trigger, but there was no shot. He pulled it again and again. Each time, there was only a treacherous click instead of a shot. The car stopped and three men with pistols jumped out. Peter started to run and immediately heard a police whistle. He didn't get far before he was knocked down and pinned to the ground.

Peter's heart raced as he was held down, the weight of his mistakes pressing down on him as heavily as the officers' hands. He realised that his naive hope of a clean escape from the gang's life was shattered. As he was cuffed and hauled to his feet, the reality of his situation set in. He would have to face the consequences of his actions and the promise he made to his father now seemed more distant than ever.

"Hubert, please, let the boy go," Michael said gloomily. "I've known him since childhood. He's confused, but he's a good guy. Don't ruin his life! I'll talk to him and his parents. I'll convince them to leave and settle as far away from our city as possible."

"Michael! This is an armed attack on an armoured car. What are you talking about?" replied the police captain indignantly.

"Hmm, didn't you say the firing pin in the gun was sawed off? He didn't even fire a single shot. He was simply framed," Michael persisted.

"What if it hadn't been sawed off?" Hubert responded.

"Tell me, how did it happen that a police patrol was in this exact place at this exact time?" Michael asked.

"I don't even know. They were supposed to be elsewhere," the captain replied thoughtfully. "That worries me. Do you think someone in my unit is in contact with the gang?"

"I'm not excusing the boy. But you see, he was set up? Make it so that he is released and I'll ensure they leave here. Don't cripple the boy's life."

"Alright, Michael! After all, we spent so much time in the prisoner-of-war camp, and you saved my life more than once. I remember everything."

As the old man had promised, the family moved far north of the country. They were grateful to old Michael for getting Peter out of the police's clutches. The forced relocation was tough. The father needed to find a job first. At the same time, he was busy looking for housing for the whole family. Johan had to leave school. The entire family routine was disrupted, and Peter was to blame. He understood this and tried his best to make amends. They wouldn't have been able to live in their old place anyway. All the neighbours in the area had turned against them. The police visited every other day. Their life had turned into a twenty-four-hour nightmare. The parents hoped that such things wouldn't happen in their new place and that they could start a new life. The family settled in a decent area of this ancient city. Soon the father found a job. Johan managed to transfer to a new school. It was hard for him because he had planned to continue his studies at an institute. Changing schools a year before enrolment had seriously affected his academic performance. Peter wasn't too concerned about school, but he still planned to finish it since he was determined not to return to his old life. Shortly after the move, he had a very serious conversation with his brother.

"Do you see what your actions have led to? You do not pity our parents or me! I had to change schools in the middle of the school year. Father left his job and all because you got involved with those scumbags. You will either get killed or end up in jail! Do you understand that?" Johan yelled at him.

Peter remained silent. He fully understood that he was the cause of the family's problems. Drawn to the easy life, he nevertheless promised to Johan that he would leave the past behind and straighten out his life.

"How's it going, Peter?" asked a stranger who approached him as he was returning home from work.

"What's it to you?" Peter snapped and tried to walk around the stranger.

"Gustav sends his regards," the boy smiled.

Peter felt as if cold water had been poured over him. He looked around warily.

"How did you find me?"

"We don't abandon our own."

"That much I've realised," Peter retorted angrily. "You wanted to set me up back then. Bastards!"

"Watch your words, buddy. We don't let our own go. You're either with us, or ...," he grinned menacingly.

"I promised my parents and brother that I would leave my past behind for good. Stay out of my sight if you want to stay healthy," Peter replied, pushing the stranger aside with his shoulder and walking home.

This encounter seriously unsettled Peter. He had recently started working at a factory and the job was depressing him. He reminisced about his past life, where he could earn in one evening what he now made in one or even two months. This steady and monotonous life bored him. He missed the adrenaline. Although he tried not to think about the past and pushed away any thoughts of big money and the easy life, the past refused to let him go.

One day, he had a big argument at work over the unfair treatment of workers and the low pay. Peter was walking home tired when two men blocked his path. One of them was an old acquaintance.

"Having trouble at work?" he asked with a smile.

"I see you're aware of all my problems," Peter clenched his fists.

"Calm down, don't get so worked up. We're here to help you," the stranger replied. "We've got a good job coming up. We need you. Decide now."

"Alright, to hell with it! What do I need to do?" Peter gave in.

Consequently, Peter began his double life. To his parents and brother, he worked a legitimate job, but he became an active member of the city gang. He rarely slept at home, explaining his absences with business trips. He was drawn into a life full of dangers and adventures. However, now he could help his parents with money. He didn't forget about his brother either. Johan was studying at the institute and making great progress. Peter was very proud of him, and everyone knew how much he loved and respected his brother.

That day, he was sitting with his new friends playing cards. Suddenly, the youngest and most audacious member of the gang, Thomas, burst into the room. Breathless, he stopped in the middle of the room and looked suspiciously at Peter. All the players turned to him in unison.

"Why are you so scared?" Peter asked him cautiously.

"Your brother," the boy could only say.

"What about my brother?" Peter said grievously, getting up from his chair. "Answer, or I'll kill you right now."

"Johan fell to his death," Thomas muttered.

"Fell? What are you talking about?!" Peter shouted.

"He jumped off the fortress wall into the abyss. It's all because of Jürgen. That's what my friends at the institute told me," Thomas replied guiltily, lowering his eyes.

He felt uncomfortable revealing the cause of Johan's suicide in front of everyone.

The ground seemed to shake under Peter.

He grabbed the edge of the table and said: "Tell me everything, I have nothing to hide from all of you."

Thomas, in detail, explained how Johan had confessed his feelings to Jürgen. How Jürgen had laughed at him and later, with his friends, glued a pink heart on his door. Soon, everyone at the institute knew about Johan's secret. Peter's brother couldn't cope with his feelings and the shame that had befallen him, so he decided to take his own life.

"I'll kill him," Peter said quietly and left the room.

No one stopped or called after him. Everyone knew what Johan meant to him.

A bullet struck the tree Peter was hiding behind.

"No, I won't give up that easily," he thought and dashed towards the river.

More bullets whizzed overhead. It had only been a few days since Peter had killed Jürgen and the police were already on his trail, closing in on him. Peter was running towards the river, heading to the old fortress. But it was clear that he wouldn't be able to escape. There were too many police officers, now advancing on him without hiding. The bullets in his revolver were spent and Peter angrily threw the weapon to the ground.

"The fortress," he thought and instinctively ran towards its walls.

He hid behind the gate and looked around. Stone stairs led upwards, and Peter ran to the wall of the fortress. He had been here many times alone, watching the sunset. But that was so long ago and now no one would give a broken penny for his life. Peter reached the wall and froze. The view from above was incredibly beautiful: the autumn forest, with flocks of birds above it. Close to the wall, a black raven was circling in the sky, almost without flapping its wings, gliding on the air currents.

"How I wish I could become that raven right now," Peter thought, and at the next moment, a gunshot rang out.

Peter turned towards the sound, slowly took a step forward, and, leaning over, fell from the high wall into the abyss.

Svitlana

Svitlana slowly regained consciousness. At first, she saw the chandelier on the ceiling, then the ceiling itself.

"What happened?" she asked herself and then a sharp pain shot through the back of her head.

The pain made her bite her lip and groan. The smell of burnt coffee lingered in the kitchen. Svitlana slowly turned onto her side and propped herself up on one arm. Her gaze fell on the phone lying on the floor. She picked it up and turned the screen towards herself. It was completely cracked.

"Yaroslav!" she screamed. "Son!"

Svitlana frantically unlocked the phone and read her son's last message.

"No. He's alright," she thought, trying to convince herself as she held her breath and pressed the call button.

"Hello," a harsh, unfamiliar voice answered.

"Who are you? Where is Yaroslav?" Svitlana asked.

"Who are you, woman?" the same voice replied.

"I'm Yaroslav's mother. Why do you have his phone?"

There was a moment of silence. Svitlana heard some noises, snippets of phrases, and indistinct sounds.

Suddenly, the phone came alive again and a different voice asked: "Are you the mother of this soldier?"

"Yes, I'm his mother. What happened? Why do you have his phone?!" she screamed desperately.

"Your son died a hero. He blew himself up with a grenade along with our fighters. We will make sure his body is returned to you," the man replied and ended the call.

Svitlana, collapsing onto the floor in exhaustion, wailed out loud.

"What, Svitlana, sitting outside again?" asked Iryna, the neighbour.

The girl silently nodded and hugged her school backpack.

"Ah," sighed the neighbour and headed towards the entrance of the building.

She knew why the girl often sat alone on the street. A suitor would come to her mother and to keep the child from interfering with their time together, she was sent outside. Svitlana sat and looked at the bedroom window, waiting for the light to come on. That would mean she could go back home. She was born out of wedlock and children like her were called bastards. She had never seen her father. He and her mother separated when Svitlana was about a year old and, since then, her mother had raised her alone. No one helped the woman with the child, so it was tough, especially since she also had to work. Moreover, Svitlana's presence hindered her mother's attempts to arrange her personal life. Men came and went, but the bitterness of feeling unwanted as a woman with a child never left. The men varied. Some tried to ignore her daughter, others treated her kindly as a child, but this last one was special. Svitlana saw the way her mother looked at him. His arrival marked a turning point in the girl's life. When he came over, there was no room for her in the apartment. When he didn't show up for a long time, her mother became nervous, cried, and took out her frustration on the child.

"Why did I ever give birth to you?! You've ruined my whole life," the girl often heard from her mother.

This nasty man had stayed in her mother's life for a long time. Over the years, Svitlana had grown into a slender young girl, and he began to give her lustful looks.

"Grow up a little more and I'll take care of you," he once whispered in her ear when her mother was in the bedroom and couldn't hear them.

These words made Svitlana feel so disgusted that she ran outside. She felt as if someone had poured a bucket of filth over her. That evening, she wandered the streets for a long time, not daring to go back home. Although she had grown up with the street boys, she wanted to be alone at moments like these, so no one would know what was troubling her. Since childhood, she has been accustomed to locking herself in her room and meditating where no one could disturb her. She would immerse herself in her fantasy world, where she felt comfortable and loved. The girl didn't know where this ability came from and kept it a secret from everyone. Only her friends – the black ravens – with whom she flew during her meditations, knew about it.

Svitlana loved animals very much. She felt sorry for stray animals, but her mother categorically forbade her from bringing them home. One spring day, she found a young raven that had fallen from its nest. It was still very weak and couldn't fly. A bit longer it would have become easy prey for stray cats or dogs. Svitlana brought it home and hid it on the balcony, not telling her mother a word. From then on, she had a little friend to care for. She made a small house out of cardboard for him, where he waited for her to come back from school. In the first few days, he didn't eat anything and the girl worried that her friend wouldn't survive. But with each passing day, he became livelier. At first, he started eating worms that Svitlana dug up for him in the park near the pond. Then his menu expanded, and he began eating the food that Svitlana's mother cooked. But she couldn't keep him a secret from her mother for long. Hosha (as she named the young raven) was becoming louder.

"Where did he come from?" her mother asked, surprised.

"He fell from his nest and the cats almost ate him!" Svitlana pleaded her voice full of entreaty.

To the girl's surprise, her mother said nothing. She shrugged and went off to get ready for work.

The young raven grew up to be very smart and amusing. He became a great joy in Svitlana's life. She often took him outside, where he was a hero to the local children. She taught him to fly and clearly remembered the day he first took to the sky, awkwardly flapping his wings. Eventually, he began to fly away for long periods to circle in the sky with other ravens like himself. But he always returned to the balcony, where Svitlana waited for him. One evening, he didn't return, and she went to bed upset. But in the morning, he met her on the way to school. The raven was not alone but had a companion. They circled above her all the way to school and accompanied home after classes. This continued until the cold weather set in and the pair flew away, never to return. Svitlana searched the sky for her friend every day and, not finding him, went home sad.

To help her mother, she started working part-time at a bakery. She liked watching the process of making dough and how it turned into bread and various pastries. The only thing that bothered her was the open flame. She always feared getting burned. Aware of that fear, the bakery workers often teased her. But Svitlana ignored them even though the fear was deeply ingrained. She didn't know its cause or how to overcome it. Working at the bakery gave her a chance to earn some money and, at the same time, avoid being at home, where her life was becoming increasingly unbearable. At work, she could forget her problems for a while. But the time flew by quickly and, after her shift ended, she reluctantly went home.

"Bitch!" her mother slapped Svitlana sharply. "How can you say such things about him? Do you want to break us up? Do you want me to be alone for the rest of my life? Oh God, why did I ever give birth to you?!"

Her mother screamed and wailed, while Svitlana stood clutching her cheek, red from the slap and cried. She cried from the overwhelming injustice that was tearing her apart inside. Svitlana had only wanted to tell her mother that her suitor had started paying unwelcome attention to her. Just last evening, he had tried to corner her in the hallway. She still remembered those filthy hands on her chest. Tears of hurt and indignation streamed down her cheeks and her body trembled like an autumn leaf. There was no one else she could complain to or ask for protection. Perhaps if her father had been around, this wouldn't have happened. But he wasn't there, so she turned to the only person she had in the world, her mother, and immediately regretted it. From then on, she thought only of one thing – how to leave this hateful house.

The phone rang in the apartment. Svitlana flinched at the sound, the phone had been installed recently and she was still not used to its ringing.

"Hello," Svitlana answered. "Speak, I'm listening."

There was silence on the other end, but she could hear someone breathing.

"Svitlana, is that you? This is your father! I'd like to see you," a voice finally said.

Svitlana froze, bewildered, the receiver still in her hand. She had never heard his voice before and couldn't fully believe it might be her father.

"Svitlana why are you silent?" he asked when she didn't respond.

"So many years have passed, and you only now want to see me?" Svitlana replied with bitterness and resentment in her voice.

"Svitlana, it's not like that. Your mother didn't allow me to see you," her father said.

"Don't lie! If you had wanted to, you would have found a way. Back then, when I needed help, not now," Svitlana shouted and hung up.

Later, she cursed herself for it many times. If she had listened to him, perhaps her entire life would have turned out differently and maybe her father would still be alive.

"Mom, why have you never told me about Dad?" Svitlana asked. "Why did you two separate? How is it that I have never seen him?"

"Your father is a scoundrel and a bastard!" her mother replied angrily. "Never ask or remind me about him."

So Svitlana didn't say a word to her mother about that phone call. A strange feeling took root in her and she thought about her father often. On a subconscious level, she felt a pull toward the person responsible for her birth, even though she had never seen him in her life.

Sometime later, her mother informed her that her father was no longer alive. He had been killed by a drug addict who needed money for a fix. How her mother found out about this, Svitlana never understood. Her mother said nothing more, but it was clear that she was deeply affected by his death.

Secretly from her mother, Svitlana prepared for the entrance exams to the institute. She knew her mother wouldn't support her wish to get an education, so she dedicated most of her free time to preparing for the exams. But when she saw her name on the list of accepted students, she happily shared this news with her mother.

"And what now? Do I have to support you for a few more years?" her mother's reaction was swift and harsh.

Once again, Svitlana regretted sharing her deepest aspirations with her.

The days and years of studying at the institute passed. She enjoyed studying and learning came easily to her. Simultaneously with her studies, Svitlana worked to help her mother and be as independent from her as possible. Her mother no longer reproached her as often as before, but sometimes they had serious arguments, so Svitlana started considering renting a separate apartment. To resolve this issue, she transferred to a part-time program at the university and found a full-time job.

Near the end of her last course, she overheard her institute friends talking about their fathers. It made her very sad that she couldn't say anything about her own father. She didn't even know where he was buried and had never visited his grave. After defending her diploma, she found out from her mother which cemetery her father was buried in, and, the next morning, she set out to find his grave.

"I'm looking for my father's grave," Svitlana said to the cemetery caretaker.

She gave his name and surname. The caretaker looked at her carefully and, waving his hand, led her along.

After a few rows, he stopped and, pointing to a grave, said: "Here he is buried."

A man she had never seen, but who resembled her so much stared back at her from the photograph on the grave. The grave was well maintained with some dried flowers still present.

"I see someone takes care of the grave," Svitlana remarked.

"Yes, his mother visited recently and brought flowers," said the caretaker, looking at Svitlana attentively.

Suddenly, she thought a thunderclap had sounded from a clear sky.

"So, my grandmother is alive?!" she shouted.

He paused and then said: "Yes, she's alive. His brother, your uncle, is alive too."

Svitlana didn't remember how she got home. Everything was like a blur. Not long ago, besides her mother, she had no one and today she found out she had relatives on her father's side.

"Mom, I need to talk to you seriously."

The tone of her voice did not please her mother. She had never heard her daughter speak to her like that.

"Where is father from? Which village? Don't tell me you don't know," Svitlana stood in the kitchen, her expression indicating she wouldn't leave without an answer.

Her mother, who always felt somewhat superior to her daughter, suddenly slumped her shoulders, lowered her head, and sat down on a chair.

"I don't know exactly where he's from," her mother replied. "I can only tell you the approximate area. There are several villages located there."

She named them, watching her daughter closely: "Why do you need this?"

"I want to meet my relatives," Svitlana replied coldly and, slamming the door, walked out.

By that time, she already worked for a financial company, lived separately from her mother, had a car, and was completely independent. A few days later, early morning, she drove to the area her mother had indicated. Her search yielded no results in the first two villages, but she was told that she might find who she was looking for in the third village. She went straight to the local grocery store and asked the shopkeeper if she knew anyone with her father's surname.

"Grandma Klava, you mean?" answered the woman and, without much thought, detailed how to get to the address.

Svitlana drove, her heart pounding wildly, ready to leap out of her chest at any moment. Could she really be about to see her grandmother? She arrived at the house, turned off the engine, and walked to the yard. Looking around, she climbed the steps and knocked. The door opened immediately and an elderly woman with a bowl in her hand appeared on the threshold. It was clear she had been cooking in the kitchen.

"Grandma Klava?" the girl asked hopefully. "I'm Svitlana!"

Illustration by Oleksand Prodan

The bowl clattered to the floor.

"Svitlana, my girl, you've come. We've been waiting for you for so long," the woman said with tears in her eyes and hugged her.

Svitlana hugged her back and they both began to cry.

"Well, why are we standing here?" Grandma Klava said, wiping her tears with her hand. "Come inside."

They went into the living room and Svitlana looked around. Photographs of unfamiliar people hung on the walls, but she recognised one: it was the same as the one on her father's tombstone.

"He suffered so much from not being able to see you," Grandma said. "Your mother did everything to keep you apart."

"So why are we waiting?" she continued. "Let's go to your uncle. He lives nearby."

"Why walk?" Svitlana replied. "I have a car. It'll be faster."

They got into the car and drove down the street. Svitlana still couldn't believe she had found her grandmother. She was in an emotional state unfamiliar to her. Everything felt like a fog and she moved automatically. These emotions overwhelmed her, making it hard to concentrate.

"Look over there," Grandma pointed to a man walking down the street. "That's your father's best friend. Stop by him."

Svitlana slowed down near the man and opened the window on her grandmother's side.

"Where are you hurrying off to, Petro?" Grandma Klava asked him.

"Lyuba sent me to the store," he replied reluctantly.

He approached the car and leaned towards the window.

"Wow, who's this beauty we have here?" he asked, intrigued, nodding towards Svitlana.

"Take a good look," Grandma responded with a mysterious smile.

He looked closely at Svitlana, then at Grandma in surprise, then back at the girl.

Turning to Grandma Klava, he asked: "Grisha's girl?"

She nodded silently.

"Well, come here, beauty," he walked around the car and, pulling Svitlana out from behind the wheel, gave her a tight hug.

Svitlana didn't know what to do. She hadn't yet recovered from meeting her grandmother and now this man was hugging her. That evening, she was on cloud nine, overwhelmed with happiness that hit her like a mountain avalanche. She had found her grandmother, uncle, cousins, and a host of other relatives. In one day, she discovered a family, big and loving, that knew about her and cared for her. It was the happiest day of her life. A day that changed her life forever.

"We did look for you," said Grandma, adding with a touch of bitterness.

"But if it hadn't been for your mother..." she shook her head.

Svitlana silently lowered her eyes. That evening she didn't want her new family to know about the complicated relationship with her mother. A mother who crippled a girl's soul with a brutal attitude and planted many psychological complexes from which she suffered all her life.

Svitlana didn't have much luck with men. They appeared and disappeared almost without a trace. She never had serious feelings for any of them, as she had grown up with men constantly changing in their home, subconsciously believing that was how it should be. Her mother's constant negative remarks about men also planted a prejudiced attitude in her. She simply used men, never considering the idea of a shared life. They, in turn, were wary of her sharp character. Not everyone dared to approach her. Those who did and were rejected said she was as wild and untamed as a young mare. Svitlana was a self-sufficient and independent woman who was used to solving her problems on her own.

With Oleksiy, however, things turned out completely differently. That evening, she was standing at a bus stop. It was chilly and it was raining heavily.

Her car was in for repairs, so she had to take the bus home late after work. The bus was delayed and she was quite wet in the rain when a yellow truck with the words "Emergency Service" stopped in front of her. A young man shouted to her through the window: "Get in, I'll give you a ride! The bus won't be coming and you're going to get completely soaked out here."

Svitlana hesitated for a moment but then climbed into the cab.

"Where are you going to"? the driver asked.

Svitlana gave the address and wrapped herself tightly in her jacket. She was very tired and cold.

The driver chatted the whole way, occasionally asking her questions to which she responded absentmindedly. She didn't even get a good look at him. The only thing she remembered was his voice. It was pleasant and soothing, exuding warmth and confidence. He dropped her off at the mentioned address and she thanked him before heading home, jumping over puddles.

"Good afternoon!" Svitlana heard a voice and turned around.

A young smiling man stood before her with a bouquet of peonies.

"Hello," Svitlana replied, frowning.

She didn't like these random street encounters.

"Don't you remember me? I gave you a ride home once when it was raining. Remember?" he continued, still smiling.

Only then did Svitlana recall him. His voice was unmistakable.

She smiled and said: "Ah, it's you! I'm grateful for that evening. If it weren't for you, I don't know when I would have gotten home."

"These are for you," he said, handing her the flowers. "My name is Oleksiy."

"Thank you so much. I'm Svitlana," she replied, taking the bouquet. "How did you know these are my favourite flowers?"

"You don't remember our conversation in the cabin?" Oleksiy asked, surprised.

Svitlana could only shake her head in confusion.

"Well, alright. What are you doing this evening? I'd like to invite you for a walk!" Oleksiy proposed with a determined voice that left no room for refusal.

Surprisingly, even to herself, Svitlana agreed and that evening they walked in the city park. This was how they began seeing each other and with each meeting, their relationship grew deeper. Oleksiy somehow seamlessly entered her life and sometimes it felt to her that he had always been there. Everything was different with him. In his presence, her usual hardness vanished. She transformed into a little girl who wanted just one thing: for him to hold her gently and whisper sweet things in her ear.

Even their first intimate moment was different. He approached it seriously.

"I don't want it to be ordinary. It should be amazing, unforgettable, and on pristine white sheets," Oleksiy whispered to her.

It truly was. Svitlana felt as if she were in a fairy tale. As if all of this were happening to someone else. One time, she lay on the bed, looking at Oleksiy, who stood before her completely naked, and thought that this had happened to her before. She was certain of it.

Eventually, she moved into his apartment, and they started living together.

"I want to introduce you to my parents. Tomorrow we're going to their village," Oleksiy said.

Svitlana grew nervous at his words and, hoping he might change his mind, said: "Maybe it's too soon?"

"It's not too soon at all. I've already told them about you. They're expecting us," Oleksiy replied.

The next day, they went to his parent's house and Svitlana realised she had found another family. Oleksiy's parents welcomed them warmly. Although his mother, Nastya, was quite reserved, Svitlana saw a kindred spirit in her. Oleksiy's father, Petro, was so delighted that he earned a few reproachful glances from his wife for his overly exuberant behaviour. Svitlana, who had

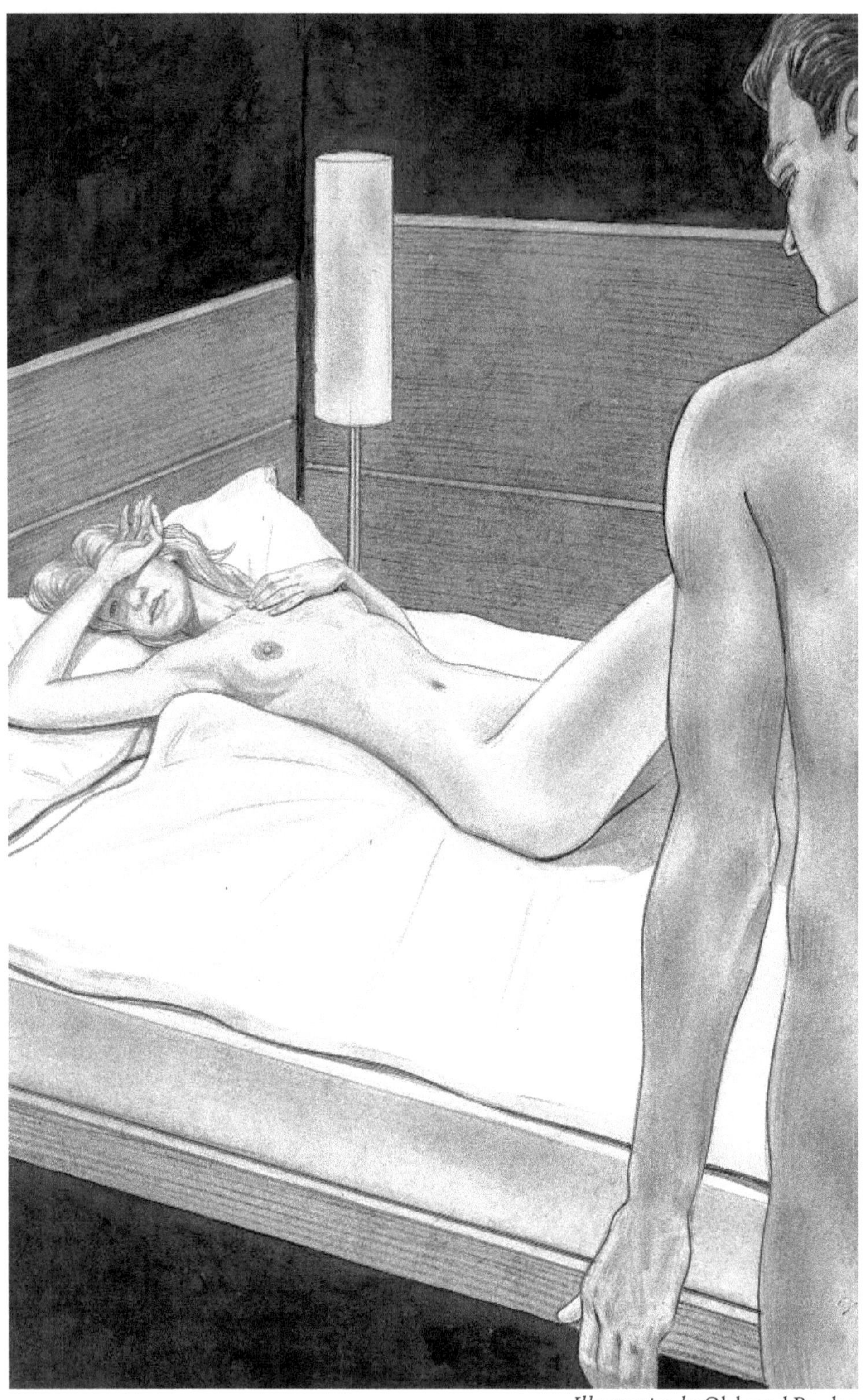

Illustration by Oleksand Prodan

grown up without a father, watched the relationship between Oleksiy's parents with interest and was happy for him.

Six months later, they got married and, a year after that, they had a baby boy named Yaroslav. The boy was calm and curious. As he grew older, Oleksiy's parents often took him to their place. They adored him and the child always eagerly went to visit them. On those days, Svitlana and Oleksiy had time to themselves, enjoying little honeymoons. With Oleksiy, Svitlana blossomed as a woman. They could passionately make love from morning till late evening. A torrent of tenderness flowed from her like an avalanche. She discovered abilities in herself that she hadn't known existed.

"Where did you learn all this?" Oleksiy asked in astonishment.

But Svitlana would just shrug, giving herself fully to her beloved husband. It's worth mentioning that Oleksiy was a skilled lover and knew how to please her. She had never experienced such intense pleasure with anyone else.

"What are you doing to me?" Svitlana whispered to him, nearly fainting from pleasure.

Then they lay entwined until morning, breathing in each other's scent and listening to the beating of their hearts.

That morning, nothing foretold disaster. They lay in each other's arms when the siren at the mine wailed. A minute later, the phone in the apartment rang. Oleksiy jumped to it, picked up the receiver, and after a moment, said: "Alright, I'm on my way!"

"What happened?" Svitlana asked in fear.

"An accident at the mine!" Oleksiy replied, quickly getting dressed.

Svitlana didn't say anything, she just hugged and kissed him silently. She could never get used to his sudden calls and each time her heart broke into pieces when he left.

Later that day, there was another call, this time at the door, but it was closer to evening. She already knew who was standing on the other side of the door. Svitlana slowly turned the key in the lock and opened the door. It was Anton Ivanovich, the head of the emergency service and Oleksiy's best friend. He stood before her, silent, his eyes full of tears. Svitlana turned, took a step into the apartment, and fainted.

They were buried in closed coffins, so nobody knew if there was anyone inside. When the rescue team descended into the mine shaft, there was a methane explosion. It was so powerful that there was no one left to save. Neither the miners nor the rescuers ever came back up.

Svitlana stood in a black headscarf, silent. She held the hand of ten-year-old Yaroslav, who watched the funeral procession and cried silently. The fairy tale that seemed like it would last forever ended in an instant. The colours around her faded and the sounds disappeared. Svitlana didn't know what to do. She had become so accustomed to the thought that Oleksiy would always be by her side. Now, she was at a loss. She had a small child to raise but felt like a bird with a broken wing.

"Svitlana," her father-in-law's voice was strained. "We are your family. You can always count on us. Don't worry about Yaroslav. If I have strength, he will be cared for."

Svitlana hugged Petro and burst into tears. Her mother had been living abroad for many years. She hadn't received as much help and support from her as she did from her in-laws. Over the years, they had become her family.

"Thank you so much. I don't know what I would do without you," Svitlana replied, somewhat calmer.

A few years later, Svitlana faced another blow. Her mother-in-law fell ill and became bedridden. Petro stayed by her side constantly. He seemed to age and wither almost overnight. The sparkle and enthusiasm vanished from his eyes. Then came the call from the neighbours – Nastya had passed away. Svitlana and Yaroslav went to the village. When they entered the house, they were met with a heart-breaking sight. Nastya lay on the bed and Petro sat beside her, holding her hand, no longer breathing. This devastated Svitlana so much that she couldn't even attend the funeral of Oleksiy's parents. She felt as if she had known them her entire life and had lost something most precious, important, and necessary.

Years passed and Svitlana worked and raised her son, never forgetting Oleksiy for a moment. She hadn't seen his body, so every time someone knocked on the door, she would startle. She imagined it was Oleksiy coming home, ready to hug her and say, looking into her eyes: "Well, I'm home. How have you been without me?"

But every time, disappointment awaited her behind the door.

Yaroslav was her only solace. He grew and became more like his father. His grandfather had made great efforts to ensure he became a true man. Svitlana saw the joy Yaroslav had in visiting his grandparents. His grandfather was a living encyclopaedia and Yaroslav would excitedly recount everything he heard from him to Svitlana. The grandfather also instilled in his grandchild a love for music, which helped him choose his profession. After finishing school, he enrolled in a music college to study piano and made significant progress. He was even offered an internship abroad.

Then the revolution began, and Yaroslav went to the capital with his friends. Svitlana knew she couldn't hold him back, so before he left, she just asked: "Be careful, my son. I have only you."

Yaroslav hugged her and promised: "Mom, everything will be fine. You understand me, right?"

Svitlana looked into his eyes and saw Oleksiy in them he had become so much like his father.

"I will pray for you, my son!" she replied and cried.

The events in the capital dragged on. The authorities did not anticipate the people's determination for justice and the people did not expect the authorities to start shooting at them. When the first casualties appeared,

Svitlana was beside herself. She went mad with worry when Yaroslav didn't answer her calls. From time to time, he came back to catch up on his studies, but it was clear that all his thoughts were there, on the Maidan[1], among his new comrades. Then the war came. At first hidden and unclear, then open and cynical. The attack came from those they never expected it from

"Mom, I'm joining the army. I can't sit idle while the enemy has invaded our land. Don't worry, I'll spend the first six months at the military training ground. It's safe there," Yaroslav assured her excitedly.

"Son, I can't hold you back. Your father and grandfather would be proud of you. I only ask one thing, be careful and remember that I only have you left," Svitlana replied with tears in her eyes.

Months passed and the war intensified with renewed force. The enemy was experienced, strong, well-prepared, and incredibly ruthless. They were opposed by untrained, poorly armed fighters. But soon, the attackers realised they underestimated the defenders. The enemy's losses were horrific, but they paid no attention, sending wave after wave of new troops.

Recently, Svitlana began having a strange dream. She saw Yaroslav standing on the fortress rampart, gazing into the distance. He faced her, but he couldn't see her. Then, from above, a bright beam of light broke through the clouds, shining directly on Yaroslav. He pushed off from the wall and spread his arms like those of a bird. He soared to the heavens, gliding along the beam as if it were a pathway. She stood below, calling out to him, but he couldn't hear her. This dream left her restless, filling her with a sense of foreboding.

That night, she barely slept. Waking up exhausted, she went to the kitchen to make coffee. Svitlana took out the cezve[2], added coffee, poured water, and placed it on the stove. At that moment, her phone beeped with a message. She immediately unlocked it.

---

[1] Maidan — the Independence Square in Kyiv.
[2] Cezve — a small, long-handled pot with a pouring lip designed specifically to make Turkish coffee. It is traditionally made of brass or copper, occasionally also silver or gold.

"It's from Yaroslav," thought with hope and opened the SMS.

"My dear mother, I love you very much! Forgive me for everything," it said.

The ground shook beneath her feet. The phone slipped from her hands and fell to the floor. Then Svitlana collapsed as well. A moment later the coffee boiled over, extinguishing the flame as it spilled from the cezve.

Illustration by Artem Burlyk

She stood at the cemetery, staring at the photo of her only son. She had never seen him like this before. Having matured, her son, in his military uniform, looked like an experienced warrior, despite just turning twenty. The person who informed her of Yaroslav's death had kept their promise. The body was handed over to the military, who then contacted her. The identification process was gruelling during which Svitlana fainted again. The unit's command took care of the funeral arrangements, and she later had the monument made herself, using a photograph sent to her by his comrades.

Svitlana sat by his grave, lost in her thoughts. Grey-haired and haggard, she no longer resembled the young woman who loved and enjoyed life just a few years ago. The death of her husband, the passing of his parents, and now the loss of her son had completely broken her. She was there, contemplating whether life was worth living at all.

Suddenly, she felt a wave of energy wash over her from above, as if someone had placed their hands on her and breathed new life into her. Bewildered, Svitlana lifted her head and looked around. There she saw an old friend, a huge black raven, descending from the sky. It perched on the monument and looked intently into her eyes.

Epilogue

"I asked the Guardians to bring you to me because I need your help," the voice of the Creator echoed from everywhere.

"I am listening. What kind of help do you need? Can I really assist you with something?" he responded.

"There is a soul left behind, currently on its final transition. It is connected to you, so only you can help her. She is struggling greatly right now, and we must send support. It's too early for her to come to us as she hasn't fully completed the mission," the Creator replied.

"What must I do?"

"Send her your love and strength."

"But how?"

"Do not question it. You know and can do everything. Come closer and close your eyes," the Creator commanded.

He approached the edge and closed his eyes. In his mind's eye, he saw an image of a cemetery and a woman sitting before a grave.

"That's my mother," he exclaimed, recognising her.

"She is one of the most perfect and enlightened souls I have ever encountered. She is now at the final and most challenging stage of her journey.

Therefore, she needs help more than ever. Only you can assist her," responded the Creator.

"Alright, tell me what to do," his voice filled with emotion.

"Send her your love, that burns brightly within you. She will sense and accept it. I will also send our helper to make sure she does not feel alone," the Creator replied. "She is waiting. Do not delay."

Suddenly, he felt an immense, radiant energy within him, surging and wanting to burst. It was like volcanic lava, with endless streams. He realised that this energy belonged to him and he could control it.

"Yes, now you can wield it," the Creator said, reading his thoughts. "Begin, for time is passing."

He envisioned the power from deep within him, a warm glowing light flowed out. Slowly, he moved his hands, directing the fiery dragon downwards, towards the woman sombrely sitting by the grave. Instantly, he saw the stream engulf her and he felt the healing energy penetrate her being. The figure of the woman below trembled as a bright light ignited within her. This light was his love, pure and powerful, reaching out to comfort her. As the energy flowed, he saw a large black raven descend from the sky, landing on the gravestone and looking into his mother's eyes.

The woman suddenly felt a warmth envelop her, as if someone invisible breathed life into her. She looked up and the sight of the raven brought a sense of calm and reassurance. Somehow, it was clear to her that she was not alone and that love and support surrounded her. Tears flowed, but they were no longer just of sorrow, but also of comfort and hope.

"Thank you," she whispered, feeling a connection that transcended the physical world.

She knew her son was with her, in spirit, guiding her through her darkest times.

"You did everything right," he heard the Creator's voice. "Now we can be at ease for this woman. She has enough strength to complete her mission.

Illustration by Oleksand Prodan

Our helper will always be with her, and she will not feel alone. You can return to your place and the Guardians will guide you."

"Will I ever meet her again?" he asked, turning back.

"Of course and not just you. But for now, don't think about it. She must first complete her journey, just as you did. In the meantime, we will wait. She will bring invaluable experience to the Treasury of Memories. Thank you for your help. Now go, do not delay. She has been waiting for you here for a very long time. For your faithfulness, eternal joy is yours. This is a place where love knows no end. Enjoy Eternity, my son!" the Creator replied.

The Wolf

Ulf

The hut's door suddenly opened, and panting Ulf stood at the threshold. Behind him, a wolf nervously paced.

"They've tracked us down," he said to Helga, alarmed. "It's the konung's[1] drakkar,[2] and about thirty warriors are there. Take our son and go to the mountains."

Helga quickly stood up and, glancing at Ulf, began to gather the necessary items.

"Kara and I will try to lead them in another direction," he said, helping his wife pack their modest belongings and food supplies onto a spread-out bear pelt.

"Wait for me until tomorrow evening," he continued. "If I don't show up, get in the boat we hid in the fjord and sail to where your people live. You know how to handle the sails."

Helga looked at Ulf, distressed. She would rather stand and fight the enemy with him, but she had to save their young son.

---

[1] Konung — a highest representative of the noble lineage among the Scandinavians in the early Middle Ages.

[2] Drakkar — from Old Norse Dreki — dragon. A wooden Viking ship, long and narrow, with a high prow and stern. Large drakkars could carry up to 100 – 150 warriors.

"We will wait for you. Be careful! There are so many of them," she said with a catch in her voice.

For the first time, Ulf saw tears in her eyes.

"Everything will be fine, my love. The main thing is to protect our son. Kara, follow me," he replied, and they left the hut.

Ulf escorted them to the path that led to the mountains. They embraced silently and went in different directions. She headed high into the mountains, carrying their son, while he and the she-wolf ran down, towards the shore, where the konung's drakkar had recently landed.

Illustration by Artem Burlyk

The drakkar glided across the water's surface almost silently. The sea was calm, and only the rhythmic splashes of oars disturbed the quiet. A grim Viking stood at the ship's prow, peering into the fog. He was draped in a wolf's pelt, with the wolf's head covering his own, making it seem like they were both gazing into the distance. Finally, the rocky outlines of the shore began to emerge from the mist. He gripped the ship's side and strained to spot a landing place. Soon, the drakkar struck the sandy bottom, and the man leaped ashore. The rest of the warriors began to jump off after him. Together, they lifted the ship and dragged it onto the beach. Then, a second drakkar arrived, followed by two more. They were also placed next to the first.

"Bjorn," the leader said to one of the warriors. "Take ten men and stay here to guard our ships."

Bjorn silently nodded and set about his task.

"The rest, follow me!"

The unit began slowly climbing the steep bank, trying not to make too much noise. From a distance, it looked like a giant serpent writhing as it crawled from the sea onto land in search of its next prey. The warriors emerged onto a plain and formed a semicircle at the edge of a wheat field. A small town with a sharp-topped church steeple was visible at the other end of the field. Seeing the shepherd boys running across the field, the leader realised that the element of surprise was lost, but this did not bother him much. On the contrary, he relished the terror and panic that his warriors brought. He waved his hand, and the lined-up ranks of warriors moved forward. Within a minute, the sound of bells reached their ears. The local church bells rang the alarm, warning the townspeople of danger. The warriors simultaneously broke into a run from their slow march, and a noisy avalanche surged toward the town, which had been peacefully sleeping just moments before.

The looting had been going on for several hours. The residents couldn't offer any resistance. Who could stand against such strong and experienced fighters? Cries of people being beaten echoed from everywhere. In some places, fires had started – the houses of those who had tried to resist the attackers were set ablaze. The leader and a few warriors approached the church. It was locked from the inside. Looking around, he ordered a log to be brought, which they used to break down the door. Inside the church, a few people had gathered. Among them stood a priest, holding a cross in his hands.

"You," the leader pointed at the priest. "Show us where you've hidden the valuables."

"In the name of our Lord God, stop this violence..." the priest began.

"Shut up!" the leader shouted, striking the priest on the head with his shield.

The priest fell lifeless to the floor. The women present screamed in horror and huddled together even more.

"Take them out of here," he ordered his warriors, and they pushed the people outside.

When no one was left in the church, he called two comrades, and they went to the altar. There, they found various church utensils used for services, a golden cross and a large book.

"Gather all this in a cloth and check all the rooms. There might be more valuable items," the leader said and went outside.

Looking around, he was satisfied. The job was done. Several wagons loaded with loot and prisoners stood in the centre of the town. Among them were young girls and children. Nodding approvingly, he ordered the warriors to move back to the sea, where their faithful drakkars awaited. Suddenly, his attention was drawn to a hut standing alone off to the side. The leader sensed that none of his warriors had been there. While the unit slowly moved out of the town, he decided to check the hut. The door was locked, but that didn't stop him. Kicking it open, he stepped inside but barely took a few steps before someone jumped on his back, hitting him with all their might. The leader spun around, trying to throw off the attacker. Finally, he managed to grab the attacker and throw him to the ground with all his strength. The leader reached for his sword, but it wasn't necessary. Lying unconscious on the floor was a girl of incredible beauty.

For a moment, he stood silently, admiring her. He had never seen such a beauty before. Her long red hair, delicate facial features, slender waist and shapely legs were mesmerizing. Suddenly, the girl moaned and stirred. The leader was startled, having momentarily forgotten why he was there.

Looking around, he found a rope. Tightly binding her hands and feet, he slung her over his shoulder and left the hut.

The loot loading was in full swing when he descended from the coastal hill, carrying the captive on his shoulders.

"Ulf, I see you didn't waste any time," his close friend Bjorn shouted.

"Indeed, I got quite a trophy. She almost killed me," Ulf replied with a laugh.

"Well, judging by how carefully you're carrying her, it's clear the trophy is valuable," Bjorn smiled.

"All right, help me load this valuable cargo," Ulf said to his friend, who helped lift the girl onto the ship.

Along the way, the captive regained consciousness and cowered in a corner where the loot was piled. Ulf tried to approach her, but she hissed at him so much that he decided not to push his luck and wait until they arrived at their home harbour.

On the shore, women and children waved cheerfully at the arriving drakkars, looking for their husbands and fathers among the warriors. Not far away stood the tribal elders, led by konung Gunnar. Everyone awaited the warriors returning from their raid, bringing back the captured spoils and prisoners.

Ulf jumped onto the pier and approached the konung.

"The raid was successful. We brought back rich spoils," he said.

"Praise the gods!" replied the konung, shaking the leader's hand.

Ulf watched closely as the goods were unloaded. When everything was on shore, he approached his captive, who hadn't made a sound the entire journey and said: "I'm going to untie your legs now, and you will follow me."

He bent down to untie the knot on her legs, but she clenched them and kicked him hard in the chest. Taken by surprise, Ulf rolled across the deck. Furious, he sprang up and lunged at the girl, knocking her out with a punch.

"What a fury I've got," he said, rubbing his bruised chest. Then he slung unconscious girl over his shoulder and carried her to his hut.

A sunbeam slid across the sand and illuminated his face. The fierce leader lay on a wolf's pelt under an overturned boat on the fjord's shore. He had been sleeping there for a week and didn't want to get up. Not because he was tired or hadn't slept enough. Ever since he had brought the captive home, there seemed no more room for him. Ulf untied her and immediately regretted it. He had never encountered such a woman before. The girl fought so fiercely that the Viking was afraid to step inside his own home. Whenever he saw her, he lost all his strength. Ulf didn't understand what was happening to him and how he could fear anyone. He, a warrior preparing to become a berserker[3], was powerless against a girl and his own captive at that. The villagers had started to mock him, and to avoid seeing anyone, he secluded himself on the shore, setting up a temporary shelter under the boat.

"Yes, I'll go to Hrevna," Ulf thought. "Maybe she can help me somehow."

---

[3] Berserker — a warrior who dedicated himself to the god Odin* in Old Norse society. Before a battle, berserkers would work themselves into a frenzy. In battle, they were noted for their ferocious strength, quick reactions, and insensitivity to pain.
Odin — a widely revered god in Germanic paganism. Odin, the All-father, was the primary god and chief deity of Norse mythology. His influence touched many parts of life and death in the Viking world.

Hrevna was the local healer who treated people with herbs and incantations. Ulf didn't know how old she was, but he remembered her from his early childhood and had always been wary of her. People said she was a witch, befriended spirits, and could foresee the future. But today, the fearless Viking decided to seek her advice and help.

"Greetings, Hrevna!" Ulf greeted gloomily. "I need your help."

"Hello, Ulf! So, you can't handle your Valkyrie[4]?" the healer replied with a smile.

He silently nodded his head.

"It's already shameful to walk through the village. Even the children laugh at me. You should come to my home and talk to her. She won't fight with you. As for me, I feel utterly helpless. I can't do anything with her. I can't even enter my own home. I don't understand what's happening to me: I think about her constantly. Sometimes, out of anger, I want to kill her, but then I realise that I simply don't have the strength to do it, and I'm ashamed to admit this to myself."

Hrevna smiled mysteriously.

"It's such a blessing that you're feeling all of this! You were raised for war, not for love. That's why these feelings were unknown to you before. I will help you. Wait for me here!" the healer said, heading towards the exit.

She returned after a few hours.

"Go home! Don't be afraid," the old healer said softly. "Don't ask me anything more!"

Ulf stood up and left the hut. He walked, thinking about what the old healer had told him, and hesitated as he approached his home.

"So, Ulf? Still running away from your wild girl?" a voice called from behind.

____

[4] Valkyries — in Scandinavian mythology, warrior maidens who participate in the distribution of victories and deaths in battles as Odin's assistants.

He turned and saw Bruni, the konung's son, along with two other warriors, Ugi and Beinir. They stood there, smirking contemptuously.

"Come on, we'll help you tame this wild mare. We're already ashamed of our comrade," Bruni said, and they laughed.

"We'll show you how it's done, and you can watch it from the sidelines," added Ugi.

"Just try it. I'll behead anyone who comes near her," Ulf said angrily, drawing his sword.

"Well, you asked for it!" Bruni shouted arrogantly, and they attacked Ulf from different sides. A desperate and uneven fight ensued. However, Ulf was one of the best fighters in the tribe, and soon, two of the warriors lay lifeless on the ground. The fight continued between Bruni and Ulf. Throwing aside their swords, they grappled and rolled on the ground, each trying to choke the other. At one point, Bruni ended up on top and began strangling Ulf with both hands. Ulf fought back with all his strength, but Bruni did not loosen his grip. Suddenly, Bruni froze; his eyes widened, hands weakened, and blood trickled from the mouth. Ulf, not understanding what had happened, pushed off the limp body of his opponent and, swaying noticeably, stood up.

Illustration by Artem Burlyk

"The konung will not forgive you for his son's death," he suddenly heard from behind him.

He turned and saw his captive calmly wiping the knife on some grass.

"You killed him?!" Ulf asked, breathing heavily.

It was more a statement than a question.

"Of course," the girl replied calmly. "Otherwise, he would have killed you."

"Wait! Do you speak our language?" Ulf asked, still not comprehending.

"My name is Helga. I was not even ten years old when I was kidnapped by your tribesmen who live north of here. I spent eight long years in their captivity. Last year, our king ransomed me along with other captives. That's why I know everything: your language, culture, customs. I even adopted your gods, for which I was not welcomed back home. But we can discuss all this later. So, what are we going to do?" she asked, emphasizing the word "we" with a smile.

Ulf was stunned by this striking change in his captive. Not long ago, she was considered his property; now, he feels dependent on her. The brief moment of confusion passed, and Ulf began to think quickly.

"We need to cover up the traces of the fight and hide the bodies! By the time they find them, we'll be far away!"

He dragged all three bodies into the nearest bushes and covered the bloodstains with sand.

"Now, we need to gather the essentials. Let's go," Ulf said and headed towards the hut.

The captive silently followed him. He entered the hut and stopped in bewilderment. Inside, his home was unrecognizable. During her days of captivity, the girl had managed to tidy up the place. Now, the hut's owner didn't know where anything was.

"Now I understand how you got my knife!" he said gloomily. "Alright! You gather what we need."

Without saying a word, the captive spread a large piece of cloth on the floor and efficiently began packing things into it. Ulf silently watched her. He undeniably liked this woman. There was no trace of confusion in her. Helga's movements were decisive yet graceful, and her flexible posture captivated him. He watched her, unable to tear his gaze away.

"That's it. I don't think we need anything else. Now we must go," she said, standing up straight.

Her words jolted Ulf, but he quickly recovered. Hoisting the sizable bundle of belongings onto his shoulder, he said: "Let's go! I have a boat with sails. There are also prepared supplies. It's getting dark, and we must leave the fjord unnoticed."

They left the hut and followed the path leading down to the water. After a few meters, Ulf glanced back at his home, where he had lived as a hermit on the edge of the village. That village had, in an instant, become foreign to him. Now, there was no way back. He walked into the unknown, following the woman who had changed his life entirely.

The fugitives sailed through the night, and at sunrise, they saw land appearing on the horizon. Ulf adjusted the sails to catch the morning breeze and leaned on the rudder. As if sensing its imminent arrival, the boat glided smoothly over the water towards the coast. Soon, it reached the shore, and Ulf jumped into the water. Then he helped his companion onto the land, carefully carrying her and setting down on the sand. Tying the boat to a nearby rock, he said: "We need to scout the area. Will you stay here or come with me?"

"I'm going with you. What if someone attacks you? Who will protect you?" Helga said with a smile, looking mysteriously into the Viking's eyes.

He snorted angrily and, lowering his gaze, muttered: "Thank you for helping me back then, but I could have handled it myself."

His pride wouldn't allow Ulf to acknowledge a woman's superiority. As a ruthless warrior, it was unusual for him to follow a woman. However, deep inside, he began to understand nothing was wrong with it. On the contrary, he felt that a woman's intuition and life experience could help him make the right decisions.

"Of course, you could have handled it. I don't doubt that," the girl said with a smile.

Then, with a serious look, repeated: "I'm going with you."

The seasoned warrior's heart beat faster at her words, and he was short of breath. All he could do was nod in response. They slowly climbed the steep, rocky shore, and soon, an incredible view opened up before them. A mountain stream descended from a massive mountain, with a multicoloured rainbow shimmering in its spray. A dense forest spread at the mountain's base, inviting with its mystery.

"I think it would be hard to find a better place to live," Ulf said.

"Yes, I like it here," Helga replied with enthusiasm in her voice.

"Look around while I hide the boat and bring our things."

Helga silently nodded to him, and he set off back towards the sea. When he returned, Ulf began constructing a temporary shelter to provide refuge in case of bad weather. Helga started preparing dinner, skillfully slicing dried meat, bread, and vegetables. At some point, he marveled at how adept she was with the knife — his knife, which she had taken for herself and with which she had saved his life.

"She could have easily killed me, like Bruni," Ulf thought, shuddering at the idea.

For a Viking, being killed by a woman was a great shame.

"The road to Valhalla[5] would have been closed to me," the warrior continued to think with a sinking heart.

---

[5] Valhalla — in Scandinavian mythology, the heavenly hall where warriors who died on the battlefield go. There, they continue their previous heroic lives.

Meanwhile, Helga finished her preparations and called him to dinner. She straightened up and began wiping the knife with a piece of cloth. Ulf approached Helga, took the knife from her hands, and placed it in the sheath that hung from her belt. After doing so, he stepped back and looked at her intently. Helga placed her hand on the knife's handle and looked up at him. Ulf waited with bated breath for the decision of his former captive. At that moment, it seemed to him that time had stopped. Helga slowly removed her hand from the handle and smiled at him. Ulf sighed with relief, stepped towards her, and embraced her tightly. For a while, they stood motionless, listening to their accelerated heartbeats[6]. Then Helga raised her head and said: "Now I am yours, and you are mine."

That night, they made love so passionately that they fell into an exhausted sleep only by dawn, wrapped in a bear skin. When the first rays of the sun fell on them, Ulf gently lifted the edge of the skin and looked closely at Helga, who was peacefully sleeping. The Viking lifted a strand of her red hair, and in the sunlight, it seemed to be ablaze with fire. He was captivated by the sight. Ulf felt an unfamiliar sensation spreading inside him, filling his body with warmth and peace.

Long months of their forced exile stretched ahead. During this time, Ulf built a cosy yet sturdy dwelling. With winter approaching, they needed to prepare thoroughly for the cold months. Helga cautiously approached this task, stocking up on dried berries and mushrooms from the nearby forest. Ulf regularly went hunting and fishing — fortunately, there was plenty of game in the surrounding area and fish in the sea. One spring day, Ulf went hunting as usual, and Helga stayed behind to manage the household. She always found something to keep herself busy. She knew how to tan animal hides and sew

---

[6] Old Norse tradition of courtship. A young man who intends to propose to a girl must place a knife in the sheath hanging at her waist. If the girl takes the knife out and throws it at his feet, it signifies refusal. If she leaves the knife in the sheath, it signifies her acceptance.

clothes from them. She also enjoyed making unique decorations for clothing, a skill her mother had taught her before being captured during a raid by a rival tribe. Ulf was an excellent hunter, so Helga never lacked materials for her sewing.

However, that day, Ulf returned earlier than usual. Helga heard his shouts from afar and ran out of the hut, leaving her sewing. She saw Ulf approaching quickly, carrying a large grey beast over his shoulders, blood dripping from it. Confused, she took his weapons and let him inside. Ulf slowly knelt and carefully laid the animal on the floor.

"It's a she-wolf," said Ulf". I found her at the forest's edge. She's seriously injured, and her mate is dead. They must have fought with a bear that just woke up from hibernation. There are tracks everywhere."

"What are we going to do with her?" Helga asked.

"We'll heal and keep her with us! I couldn't leave her to die out there."

Helga looked at him closely, impressed by his actions.

"You're not as heartless and ruthless as I thought a few months ago," she thought.

"Heat some water; we need to clean her wounds. I'll prepare some herbal poultices!"

Ulf immediately started a fire and, once it was going, ran to the mountain stream to fill a copper kettle with water. When the water was warm, Helga carefully cleaned the wolf's torn wounds and applied poultices made from finely ground medicinal herbs she had gathered on the mountain slope. The predator had lost a lot of blood and was very weak. She could only muster the strength to open her eyes and whimper softly.

A few weeks passed. Helga's careful hands did their job. The she-wolf revived and began to stand on her feet. Despite her weakness, she could already eat independently and go outside.

"What shall we call her?" Helga asked one day.

"We'll call her Kara," Ulf answered after a brief pause.

"Good, I like that name," Helga said, hugging him tightly.

Helga felt at ease with him. The years spent in captivity had taught her to be tough. She learned to protect herself, and few dared to approach her. But with Ulf, she felt like a small, defenceless girl. She only wanted to curl up in a ball while he patted her back and whispered sweet things in her ear. The feelings growing inside her intensified daily. Meanwhile the life forming within her, along with her feelings, was making itself known more decisively. However, Helga had not yet dared to tell her beloved.

One day, noticing Helga's odd behaviour, Ulf asked her: "Is everything alright with you? You seem strange. I can't understand what's happening to you. Are you ill?"

"I am ill, indeed," Helga snuggled up to him.

"With what?" he asked, concerned.

"Not what, but who," Helga laughed.

She leaned back slightly from Ulf, looked into his eyes, and said: "I'm sick with you."

"I don't understand anything," he replied. "Can you explain more clearly what's happening to you? What hurts?"

Helga smiled mysteriously and said: "By the time the cold comes, you will become a father! We're going to have a little member of our family. What do you want, a boy or a girl?"

Ulf stood motionless for a moment, not even blinking. Of course, he knew how children were born, but he couldn't grasp the fact that he, a fierce warrior, was going to have a child.

"So, it turns out that...," Ulf began slowly. "You, I mean we, are going to have a baby?"

"Well, yes, imagine that," Helga said, almost nervously, due to his slowness in understanding.

"So, I'm going to have a son!" Ulf shouted joyfully and, grabbing his beloved in his arms, spun her around in the air.

"Yes, yes, you're going to have a son!" Helga shouted back to him. "But put me down. I'm getting dizzy."

He carefully set her down and said: "We need to prepare for the baby's arrival. Also, we need to stock up on more food for the winter, insulate the hut, and gather more firewood."

Ulf paced back and forth in the hut, thinking out loud about what needed to be done. Helga watched him with a smile, marvelling at the changes in this man: the one who had once taken her freedom but had given her the most precious feeling on earth.

One morning, Ulf woke up and noticed Helga standing in the doorway, staring intently at something. He approached, embraced her, and asked: "Is something bothering you?"

"Look," Helga nodded towards the nearest tree. "They've been here more than once, watching us."

Ulf turned his head and saw two ravens perched on a branch, observing them closely.

"Those must be Huginn and Muninn,[7]" Ulf said. "Odin's messengers. They fly around the world and tell him everything that's happening."

"I think they've already told him that there will be three of us soon," Helga smiled and snuggled closer to Ulf.

---

[7] Huginn and Muninn — a pair of ravens in Scandinavian mythology who serve the god Odin and report to him everything that happens. Huginn means "The one who thinks", and Muninn accordingly "The one who remembers."

Illustration by Artem Burlyk

As Helga had predicted, just before the cold weather set in, she gave birth to a beautiful baby boy, whom they named Vidar, in honour of Odin's son. During those days, Ulf was hardly recognizable. He ran around frantically, not knowing what to do first. Fatherly instincts, which he had never known he possessed, awakened within him. His face softened with such tenderness when he held his son in his arms that Helga felt genuine joy for the man her once fearsome captor had become.

The harsh, cold months passed, and spring arrived. For the young couple, its arrival signified a new beginning after a long period of stillness. Watching nature awaken from its winter slumber, they both felt a sense of joy and hope for a better future.

"We can't live here alone for long," Helga said one day. "Sooner or later, we'll have to join other people. Vidar is growing up and needs to be among children, not animals. Of course, Kara is a good nanny, but she's a wolf. A child needs human interaction."

They both looked at the corner where Kara lay on the floor. Vidar was crawling all over her, tugging at her fur, trying to open her mouth and pulling her ears. The she-wolf tolerated it all, occasionally growling when the child became too much for her.

"Yes, I understand," Ulf replied. "But where can we go? We can't return to my people. The konung will never forgive me for Bruni's death. We can't expect kindness from your king either. After what we've done there, I doubt we can expect a warm welcome."

"We could try to sail far away, to a place where no one knows us and cannot find us," Helga suggested.

"I know of a place we can sail to," Ulf said. "I've never been there, but I've heard from my kinsmen that that land is very rich and its people are hardworking. They are also strong and freedom-loving warriors who keep neighbouring tribes in fear. My kinsmen have settled there quite well, and only a few want to return. We call that place The Land of Wolves."

"Alright, as you say. You know I'll always be with you wherever you go."

Ulf pulled Helga close, running his hand through her hair, and said: "Where would I be without you? Rather, without you both."

They laughed as they watched Vidar climb onto the she-wolf's back and try to bite her ear with his newly sprouted teeth.

The summer that followed delighted the fugitives with its fine weather. The habitual rains and fogs of these places gave way to sunny days. As usual, Helga busied herself with gathering mushrooms and berries, and making clothes and shoes. The child was growing and could already stand on his own. Kara never left his side, except when she went hunting with Ulf. She had become his loyal and indispensable helper, aiding in tracking game and guarding against the dangerous predators that roamed the area. Ulf was an excellent archer, though he relied more on his sword in battle. Since they had settled in this land, Ulf had never seen any signs of human life. He had travelled far into the mountains and circled the entire forest but never came across human tracks. But today, Kara was behaving strangely. She was nervous, and her behaviour suggested that she sensed something unusual.

Ulf knelt before her, took her head in his hands, and said: "What's wrong, my good girl? What's bothering you?"

Kara freed herself from his hands and dashed off toward the forest's edge, turning back occasionally as if urging him to follow. Ulf ran after her, cautiously looking around. He understood that the wolf's behaviour was triggered by something unusual and was ready for anything. Catching up with her at the forest edge, he noticed Kara circling a spot, sniffing around. On the ground he saw the remnants of a bonfire and gnawed bones. Ulf looked around and began studying the tracks left b y the uninvited guests.

"There were five of them," he thought. "They went toward the sea. So they must have come from there too."

These thoughts brought an unpleasant tightness to his chest. It had been nearly two years since they had settled here, and until now, no one had disturbed them. Ulf understood that, by all laws, he had to answer for the killing of the three warriors from his tribe. Under different circumstances, he wouldn't hide and would face the elders' judgment, but now he had to think not only of himself. Therefore, he couldn't recklessly risk his life.

That day, Ulf shot a hare that Kara had driven toward him. Strapping the catch to his belt, he slowly trudged toward the hut where his beloved wife awaited him. She had transformed from a captive into the most important person in his life, giving him such a wonderful son. Remembering the child, he smiled and headed more briskly toward the foot of the mountain where his family lived.

Several weeks passed, and Ulf almost forgot about the incident with the discovered tracks. Today, he decided to go fishing and, as usual, took Kara with him. The she-wolf ran ahead, sniffing the ground. She reached the cliff where the descent to the sea began and froze. Suddenly, she bared her teeth, and the fur on her back stood on end. Ulf cautiously approached the cliff and looked down. What he saw made his heart pound so fiercely it seemed the people disembarking from the vessel onto the shore might hear it. Yes, they were Ulf's tribesmen. He recognised the konung's longship by the sail's colour and the dragon's head at the prow.

"Helga!" the thought shot through his mind.

"I need to save her and the child. Kara, follow me!" Ulf commanded and dashed toward the hut.

Illustration by Artem Burlyk

Ulf turned once more to make sure that Helga had disappeared from sight. High up in the mountains, he had set up a small cave in case they had to leave their home unexpectedly. There was always a supply of food and water there. Also, it was difficult for strangers to find a cave on the mountainside. Now Helga was heading there, and he needed to lead the pursuers as far away in the opposite direction as possible. He ran towards the forest and hid in the bushes. The she-wolf lay down beside him. The newcomers had to pass very close by, as this was the shortest path to their hut. After a few minutes, Kara growled. In the distance, a squad of twenty-five to thirty warriors appeared. They were walking at a slow pace, constantly looking around. When the squad passed by them, Ulf drew his bowstring and, carefully aiming, released it. The warrior at the rear flailed his arms and silently fell into the grass. This gave Ulf a time advantage, and immediately, two more newcomers lay lifeless on the ground. The rest of the squad turned at the noise. A familiar call to Ulf echoed, and the warriors instantly shifted into battle formation, covering themselves with shields. Ulf released two more arrows, but they struck the shields and caused no harm.

"Kara, follow me!" Ulf shouted and ran, luring the newcomers after him.

He ran, hearing the shouts of the pursuers behind him. Near a huge boulder, Ulf set up an ambush, and two more former tribesmen fell to the ground, pierced by arrows. However, there were still many of them, and splitting into two groups, they started to encircle him from both sides. He knew this tactic and already understood that he would not get out alive. He only wanted to buy time for Helga to hide in a safe place.

"Well, my beauty," he patted Kara on the neck. "Shall we give them one last fight?"

Ulf waited until the pursuers were close enough and released several arrows in their direction. Two more warriors fell motionless to the ground. There were no more arrows, and Ulf, discarding his bow, drew his sword and charged at the enemy. They fought desperately and fiercely. Kara managed to maul one of them but fell, killed by a sword. Ulf fought with desperate fury. All wounded, he threw himself at the enemy again and again. Several more warriors fell under his blows, but the forces were unequal. Ulf fell, pierced by a spear, never releasing his sword from his hand[8].

"To Valhalla!" he wheezed, looking with a clouded gaze at the boundless sky where a pair of black ravens circled.

------

[8] For a Viking, it was a special honour to fall in battle but not release the weapon from his hands. In this case, according to legend, the warrior would enter the realm of the god Odin Valhalla.

The Oak Tree

The smell of burning was growing stronger and stronger. The wind blowing towards the oak tree carried this smell from afar. Still sturdy, yet already quite old, branches swayed back and forth, scaring the birds and animals that had taken refuge from the wind deep within its crown. It was ready to die. The oak tree had seen much over the five centuries it had lived on this land. Every year, birds nest in its branches, and watching them take their first flight from their parental nest was fascinating. Every spring, small and helpless squirrels appeared in its hollow, eventually crawling out and starting to climb the trunk and branches. The squirrel family gathered its acorns and hid them in the hollow and nearby. Just as it had once been buried in the ground by a squirrel unknown to it. It shed its covering of leaves every autumn and remained bare until early spring, when the buds began to swell with the onset of warmth, and green leaves appeared. Life thrived on it all summer and into late autumn, only to fall silent again for the long winter months. Such was the cycle of life over the long five centuries. And soon, all of this would come to an end. The fire that had engulfed the trees at the forest's edge was already visible, and the smoke began to gradually penetrate deep into the crown, where the forest dwellers sat, hiding in fear.

"Yes, it's time to slowly make my way to where the sun shines. To where it's warm, where life bustles and thrives," thought the sprout as it began to slowly but steadily seek an exit from the acorn in which it had been since last autumn.

Gradually, it began to gain strength, and soon, the acorn split into two equal parts. The crack on its surface grew larger every day. When nothing held it back, it crawled out of its temporary shelter and directed its growth upwards.

Weeks passed, and a barely noticeable thin sprout appeared on the earth's surface among the grass and old leaves. Every day, it grew taller, and soon, small green leaves appeared at its tip. At first, there were two, and when swaying, they resembled butterfly wings. Then, more leaves appeared, and they began to look like a flock of butterflies trying to lift off the ground, flapping their wings in unison. From the side, it seemed as if the sprout itself was striving to fly upwards, trying to break away from the earth with its leaf-wings.

In half a year, it had stretched out enough and had grown stronger. Gradually, it began to feel the power that strengthened within it daily, but soon summer ended, and autumn came. The young oak had to part with its foliage for the first time. The ground around it was covered with the leaves of its older neighbours, who had sheltered it from the bad weather since it appeared on this land. There were so many leaves that the entire ground was covered with a thick, multicoloured carpet by the time the cold arrived.

His first winter was very frosty and windy. He often thought he wouldn't survive it. It seemed to him that his thin trunk would freeze, and the life inside him would be stilled forever. But when spring came, the forest buzzed with life again. Animals began emerging from their burrows, running on the ground and climbing trees in search of food. Birds started building nests in the branches. From the swollen buds, green leaves gradually appeared. Amid this general revival of life, the young oak felt himself filling with vitality again. He reached upwards once more, towards where the sun was hidden behind the crowns of the older trees. The branches were already covered with countless leaves, spreading in all directions. They rustled and whispered in the wind that wandered through the forest. It seemed as though the young oak was speaking in his language with his older neighbours, the mature trees that grew around him.

Years flew, followed by decades. Now, he was a mature and sturdy oak tree, having secured a worthy place among his kin in the forest. Not as strong as some, but no longer hiding in their shadow, he felt himself a full-fledged member of the forest brotherhood. His roots spread further and further, intertwining with the roots of other trees. This was how communication happened with his forest brothers, who would warn about weather changes or approaching danger. He never felt lonely. Since his branches had strengthened, a pair of ravens had settled in them, year after year raising their chicks. It was fascinating to watch the young ravens make their first tentative flights, standing and swaying in the wind on the branches. He wanted to gently nudge them so they would rise above the ground and finally experience the joy of flight. However, there was no need for this, as the father raven was always nearby, watching over his children and helping them take their first step into the airborne road. This continued for many years. As one pair of ravens moved out, another moved in. He had grown accustomed to his branches becoming a reliable shelter for birds and animals.

Illustration by Artem Burlyk

A rather deep hollow formed in its trunk when the oak lived for over a hundred years. A squirrel took advantage of this, making a cosy home inside. Every spring, the oak delighted in the warmth that appeared within it with the birth of squirrel kits. During these days, the mother squirrel practically never left the hollow, feeding the babies with milk. She occasionally ventured out to find food and replenish her lost strength. Over time, the kits' eyes began to open, and their tiny bodies became covered with fuzz that vaguely resembled their mother's fur. After a few months, the little ones slowly crawled out of the hollow. Initially, they did so cautiously, peering out where the sunlight and forest sounds penetrated the hollow, but each day, they became bolder. Soon, their mother could no longer keep track of her growing family, who were visibly maturing. Every day was spent jumping and running along the branches. The kits did not dare to leave their cosy home when it rained heavily and thundered. They would sit at the bottom of the hollow, huddled together, trembling with fear. But when the storm passed, they crawled out again. They liked the forest after the rain when the air was so clean it made them dizzy. Raindrops slowly fell from the leaves as if inviting them to play. The squirrel kits increasingly explored the world around them, and their mother tried to stay close. Along with exciting discoveries in the forest, dangers also lurked for her children. After a while, the squirrel kits, now stronger and more accustomed to the world, began to leave the parental hollow in search of an independent life.

He joyfully watched this life cycle, feeling like its centre for many years. Recently, butterflies migrating far to the south had liked him. They covered his trunk every summer, creating a colourful, moving blanket. From the side, it seemed as if he came to life. Just a little more, it looked like he would shake the earth from his roots and walk, swaying, through the forest. He waited for this moment all year and was very saddened when, at an inaudible signal, the butterflies would flutter into the air, circle above him, and set off on their long journey.

This little girl started visiting him a few years ago. She was very young then. The girl would sit at his base and remain silent for a while with her eyes closed. Then, she would stand up and hug him. He felt her heartbeat, and it made him happy. In those moments, he longed to embrace her with his branch-arms so she would feel calm and protected. When she started talking to him, he understood every word and regretted being unable to respond. The girl was coming to the forest very often. Sometimes, the oak thought he was her only friend, as she shared her most intimate thoughts with him. Even today, now grown up, she had come to see him again. The young woman hugged the trunk with her arms. He listened to her heart racing and waited silently for her to speak.

"Sorry I haven't come for so long," the girl said, continuing to hug the oak. "But I don't know what to do with my feelings. I think I'm in love with him. All my thoughts are only about him."

She then fell silent as if pondering something.

After a minute, the young girl moved away from him and sat on the ground, pressing her back tightly against the trunk. She looked up towards where the branches floated in the sky. After a moment of silence, she said: "You know, I like the feeling I have right now! It's like a flock of butterflies fluttering inside me whenever I think of him!"

He then remembered the butterflies that visited him every year and smiled inwardly.

After sitting a bit longer, the girl stood up and said goodbye: "Alright, that's it. I'll run home. Don't miss me too much."

One day, his young friend came not alone. She was with a boy, and the couple happily chatted about something. When they approached, the girl turned to the boy and mysteriously said: "Now, I'm going to share my biggest secret with you. Are you ready to hear it?"

"You brought me to the forest to reveal your secret? I'm already getting scared. Are you a forest fairy?" the boy laughed.

"Well, in a way, you might be right," the girl replied. "Turn around."

The boy turned around but looked at her in surprise, seeing no one.

"This is my oldest and most faithful friend," the girl said, pointing to the oak.

"He's enormous and must be several centuries old," the boy said, gazing at the mighty, sprawling crown of the oak.

"Come here," the girl called. "We need to feel his breath!"

They approached the oak and hugged it, pressing their bodies tightly against the trunk. Nothing brought the oak as much joy and satisfaction as the beating of two loving hearts. These two young people reminded the oak of an incident that had happened many years ago. Late in the autumn, just before the cold set in, a wounded wolf appeared at the base of the old tree. It was a strong and mature wolf, barely able to reach the oak and collapse among its roots, which had emerged from the ground. The roots sheltered him from the wind and bad weather. The wolf was bleeding and breathing heavily. Following him came a she-wolf, who lay beside him, trying to warm her beloved with the heat of her body. She licked his wounds and didn't leave his side for a minute, but one morning, the oak no longer felt the wolf's heartbeat. The she-wolf didn't abandon her companion, continuing to cover him with her body, hoping he would come back to life. But her hopes were in vain. Life had left the wolf's body forever. The cold intensified, but the she-wolf stayed. A few days later, the oak no longer felt her heartbeat either. Then, snow fell, covering their bodies with a thick, fluffy blanket.

Illustration by Artem Burlyk

Only this happened many years ago. So long that he had already lost track of the years and decades. Now, he understood that soon, his life would come to an end. The forest inhabitants were fleeing from where death was approaching. He was comforted by the thought that the raven chicks had already flown away and the squirrel kits had become independent enough to escape danger. The wind was strengthening, and the flames from the neighbouring trees gradually started to leap onto his branches. Soon, the merciless fire began greedily licking his trunk. The old oak was ready for death and awaited its approach.

Severyn

Severyn stood by the wagons that formed a defensive line and smoked his pipe. He gazed into the night distance. There, in the enemy camp, fires were burning. The enemy would launch an attack tomorrow morning, which would be the decisive day. The commander already knew that this would be his last battle, yet he remained surprisingly calm. He had often gone into hertz[9] combat, and facing death was familiar to him.

"Do not fear death! Seek it out, and it will hide from you," these words of old Vovkulaka[10] he recalled before every battle.

He always remembered his old comrade's lessons, even though it was long ago. Now, the moon shone brightly above him, and the stars formed strange constellations in the night sky. He could hear the voices of people and the neighing of horses in the enemy camp.

"Otaman[11], everything is ready!" the voice of his loyal comrade, Hrytsko Netreba, rang out.

---

[9] Hertz combat — a group of daredevils and brave men among the Zaporizhian Cossacks would step out before a battle and approach the enemy closer than the range of a musket shot. They would mock and taunt the enemy with insults or gestures, driving them to a frenzy, causing tension and nervousness. In doing so, they often exposed themselves to musket and cannon fire, which sometimes led to the death of the brave men.

[10] Vovkulaka — wolverine.

[11] Otaman — the commander in Zaporizhian Cossacks formations.

Severyn started, turned silently, and looked at the breathless Cossack.

"The boys have dammed the river. We can start the crossing as soon as the water level falls," Hrytsko continued.

"Good, brother! We have a few hours until morning. So, we must have enough time to ferry our troops along with provisions, supplies, and artillery. First of all, send the wounded. Set off without waiting for orders as soon as the river recedes. We need time to set up trenches on the other side so there is a place to retreat. Make sure to leave a guard with explosives on the dam. I'll signal when it needs to be blown up," Severyn told his comrade.

He nodded silently and disappeared into the darkness. The commander returned to his thoughts. The bloodied army was cornered by the enemy against the river. For several days, the enemy had tried to break through the defence, but the defenders held their ground and gave a worthy response. The day before yesterday, reinforcements arrived for the enemy, and it became known that they were planning a new attack in the morning. This time, there was no chance of holding out. At the council, it was decided to dam the river so the water level would drop and the remnants of the army could be led out of the trap. Everything had to be done quickly and unnoticed by the enemy. Only volunteers who would face certain death would stay with the commander, but that would be tomorrow. Now, he smoked his pipe and thought about his wife, his parents, and his son Vasylko, who had been captured by the enemy many years ago.

Kateryna was breathing heavily. Tears streamed down her cheeks, but she was happy because she finally heard the voice of her firstborn. The childbirth had been difficult, and it seemed she wouldn't survive it, but the old midwife Paraska skillfully did her job and now held her son wrapped in a blanket.

"Hold your Cossack," she said to the woman, placing the child beside her.

"I've never seen such a giant before. A great warrior will grow from him. You will be proud of your son. See how his eyes are darting around? He probably wants to scold us for not feeding him."

Kateryna placed the baby to her breast, and he, catching the mother's nipple, sucked greedily. The mother sighed with relief and looked more closely at her son, who was drawing the nourishing milk from her. With each of his gulps, she felt better. A warm weariness spread throughout her body.

"I will name him Severyn," Kateryna told the midwife. "Mykyta and I decided on it. It's a pity he wasn't here, but he will return soon and rejoice at his son."

The child grew quickly. Like many of his peers, he was restless and curious. One moment, he was in the kitchen with his mother making dumplings; the next, he was in the pasture with his grandfather herding cows, and then he was learning to shoot a bow with his father. He succeeded in everything and found everything interesting. Sometimes, Severyn felt that he wouldn't have enough time in his life to master everything and eagerly sought new knowledge.

When Severyn turned eight, his father took him to the Sich[12] school. This was a real challenge because boys faced strict teachers on their own. The head teacher was Hieromonk[13] Nikodim, who devoted all his time and knowledge to the students. He was the most experienced of the teachers, having lived for several years in distant countries studying foreign languages and various sciences. At the school, the children studied the law of God, writing, arithmetic, languages, geometry, geography, astronomy, music, and other sciences. There was a special emphasis on military-physical education, where the boys were prepared for future military service. Of all the subjects, Severyn liked poetics[14]

---

[12] Sich — the Zaporozhian Sich was a semi-autonomous polity and pro-state of Cossacks that existed in Ukraine between the 16th and 18th centuries.

[13] A Hieromonk, also called a priest-monk, is a monk who serves as a priest in the Eastern Orthodox Church.

[14] Poetics — the study of poetry and the art of writing poems.

the most. He quickly and effortlessly composed short poems on any topic. His witty verses were very popular with his friends, who often asked him to write something humorous about other students or teachers.

"Petro walked through the village,

his chicken saw him,

if it weren't for my stick,

she would have eaten him,"

Severyn teased his friend, who once shared how he got scared of a chicken in his childhood.

The friend didn't get offended; instead, he laughed with the others.

The young student was interested in all the subjects taught at the school but had a special affinity for astronomy. Before sleeping, the boy loved looking at the endless night sky and observing celestial bodies.

"Where is the edge of the sky?", "I wonder where God lives?", "Is there life on other planets?" Severyn asked himself and then his mentor Nikodim.

The old monk gladly shared everything he knew about the planetary system with his curious student.

"No one knows if there is an edge to the world," he replied to the boy. "Only Almighty God knows everything. The Holy Church considers Earth to be the centre of the universe. As a clergyman, I should not doubt this, but I have read some works by Western scholars who have proven this is untrue. I completely agree with their conclusions. Our Earth, along with other planets, revolves around the Sun. We can track this on specific days of the year, during the equinoxes or the longest night or day. Our ancestors were not fools and understood this very well because they lived in harmony with the universe. It's a pity that modern progressive scientists do not have support and instead face persecution for their beliefs."

When school was out, Severyn returned to his village, where his mother, younger sisters, and grandparents eagerly awaited him. These days were like actual holidays for the family. The sisters would run to the neighbours' children, proudly announcing the return of their brother, the future otaman. The grandparents were so excited as if a foreign delegation was coming. Only the mother was usually calm. She knew exactly what her firstborn loved most, so she would go to the kitchen to prepare his favorite dish—zatirka.

For this, the dough was prepared in advance. The flour was then sifted, and the dough was rubbed with a wooden paddle[15] until small balls the size of beans were formed. These balls were then added to the meat broth and cooked until ready. The finished dish was seasoned with butter or lard. The aroma of this zatirka spread throughout the house, tempting its inhabitants.

The father always arrived last. He saw his son more often because he was also in service and regularly visited the Sich school to check his progress. Each time, he was reassured that Severyn was in the right place.

The teachers spoke highly of the boy and predicted his great future. This time, too, his father rode up to the house and, jumping off his horse, shouted: "Hey, son, come show yourself to me!"

Severyn stepped outside, and his father embraced him. After that, Mykyta stepped over the threshold, crossed himself in front of the icons in the corner of the house, greeted his parents and wife, grabbed his daughters together, and lifted them: "Oh, my beauties! I brought you some candy from the fair."

After placing the girls on the floor, he took two rooster-shaped lollipops from his bag and gave them to the little ones.

"Son, will there be a war this year?" asked the grandfather.

"I don't know, Dad. We are always ready for it," he replied. "Our company is growing every day. We must be ready for a long campaign as bad news reaches us. So, we will act preemptively and not wait for the enemy to come to our home."

---

[15] Wooden paddle — a wooden spatula used for stirring, commonly used in cooking. It is traditionally used when making jam and preserves.

"That's right," the grandfather said approvingly. "Once, our ancestors deliberately warned the enemies about their march so they would be afraid. Those were glorious times."

"Yes, Dad, exactly," the son replied. "It's enough to fend off enemy attacks. Let them fear us. We are now stronger than ever. Only our allies should not let us down, though I do not trust them very much."

"Have you talked enough?" Kateryna asked the men. "Let's go to the table. We have such a celebration today."

After a shared prayer, the family sat down at the table and began to have lunch. Severyn watched his relatives with interest, whom he hadn't seen for several months. The quite elderly grandfather and grandmother sat next to each other like two doves, quietly observing the large family at the table. His father and mother couldn't hide their joy from the reunion, looking at each other with tenderness and love. Only the sisters couldn't sit still. Marichka and Sofiyka, who were close in age and looked very much alike, proudly glanced at their brother, barely restraining themselves from running to their friends to share the news. Severyn, who had just turned seventeen, watched his sisters with curiosity. Since he had last seen them, they had grown significantly and become more beautiful.

"A little more, and I'll have to start chasing away their suitors," the boy smiled.

Lunch ended. The grandparents went to rest as they could no longer handle the summer heat as easily as they used to. His father went to the village elder to handle some matters. The sisters disappeared as if they had never been there. Only Severyn stayed to help his mother clear the table.

"Mom, I'm going to take a walk around the village. Maybe I'll see some friends," he said later.

"Alright, son. Okhrym often asked about you, and so did a few others," his mother replied with a mysterious smile.

Severyn walked along the village street, curiously examining the places where his childhood had passed. There was the pond with willows that had grown even larger, spreading their flexible branches over the water. The church on the hill, near which sheep and goats grazed. The freshly whitewashed cottages, surrounded by flowers, delighted his eyes and brought back pleasant childhood memories.

"Oh, our future otaman is coming!" suddenly rang out a clear girl's voice.

Severyn started in surprise and turned around. A few girls stood by the fence, looking at him mischievously.

"No, he's probably going to be a whole hetman[16]!" replied another, and the girls burst into loud laughter.

"Oksana, is that you? You've grown so much, I didn't recognise you," the boy addressed the girl who had spoken first, not at all upset.

Severyn approached the group and greeted them: "Good day, beauties. Who are you waiting for?"

"We're waiting for you," Oksana replied. "Your little sisters told the whole village yesterday that their brother was coming home."

Severyn waved his hand: "They are so restless."

"What are you doing this evening? Maybe we can gather at the edge of the village? I think we have a lot to talk about. I'm going to visit Okhrym, so we'll come together. Agreed?"

"Well, alright! Don't be late," Oksana replied, and the girls laughed again.

That evening, Severyn remembered for the rest of his life. He walked Oksana home and couldn't stop talking with her. The girl didn't interrupt him, listening intently to everything he told her. She liked the boy more and more. Sometimes, she thought she had known him her whole life. She didn't want that evening to end, but they had already reached Oksana's house, and with regret in her voice, she said: "Well, here we are. It's time to say goodbye."

"I will come to see you tomorrow," Severyn replied politely, in a tone that brooked no refusal.

---

[16] Hetman — the title of supreme military and political leader of the Zaporozhian Cossacks.

The girl looked at him carefully once more. She undoubtedly liked this young man.

"Alright," Oksana answered, blushing. "Good night to you, Cossack!"

They met the next day and didn't part until Severyn's departure.

"I will wait for you," Oksana said with tears in her eyes, pressing against his shoulder.

"Everything will be fine! I'll come back as soon as I can. It won't be as long as last time. So wait for me, my darling," Severyn said and hugged her.

The boy returned to the Sich school, hoping to return to Oksana as soon as possible. This opportunity came unexpectedly quickly. A great war began, and Severyn came home to say goodbye to his family.

"Mom, I'm going on a campaign as a djura[17]! It's a great honour for me. Dad supports my decision. We'll be in the same regiment, just in different companies. My mentor will be the old sorcerer Vovkulaka."

"Alright, son. I bless you, my child," his mother said, crossing her son.

"I'm going to say goodbye to Oksana, okay?" Severyn shouted and ran out into the street.

"Yes, go. She's waiting for you," his mother said to herself, wiping away the tears streaming down her cheeks.

Severyn walked through the village, his heart pounding like never before.

"How will Oksana take my decision? Will she wait for me?"

Various thoughts swirled in his head.

He saw her immediately. Oksana stood on the porch, looking at him.

"I knew you would come. I dreamed of you last night," Oksana said to Severyn instead of greeting him.

"I came as I promised."

Oksana looked into the boy's eyes: "You came to say goodbye!?"

---

[17] Djura — in Ukraine in the 16th – 18th centuries, this term referred to a young weapon bearer or apprentice to the Cossack elders or senior Cossacks.

"Yes, I'm going on a campaign with our comrades. Will you wait for me?" Severyn couldn't hide his anxiety.

"I will wait as long as it takes and pray for you every day," the girl said, tightly hugging the boy.

Six months had passed since the start of the military campaign. The young djura was no longer as inexperienced as he had been at the beginning. He had become an excellent squire. For the old Vovkulaka, finding anyone better than Severyn was hard. In the campaign, they complemented each other. The old wisdom, combined with the young man's temperament and eagerness to learn, formed a perfect tandem. The old Cossack tried to impart all his knowledge and skills to the boy, and Severyn eagerly absorbed everything he had heard from his mentor.

"Tell me, is it true that you can turn into a wolf?" Severyn asked his old friend.

"Yes, I can," replied the old sorcerer. "And you will be able to as well, if you realise something.

"What exactly?" the boy asked, intrigued.

"This is a very old knowledge passed down to us from the ancient mages. With its help, you can transform into anyone. Be it a wolf, a raven or even a butterfly. You must transfer your consciousness to someone else. Then, you will see the world through the eyes of the being you inhabit. Want to scout the enemy camp? Transform into a wolf and run among their ranks. Want to see the land from above? Fly as a bird," the old warrior replied calmly and thoughtfully.

"I would like to learn this," Severyn blurted out.

"Everything in its own time. Not everyone is meant to master this knowledge. Stay close to me and learn from what I do! In time, we will decide if it's worth revealing this to you," said Vovkulaka, looking intently at his young companion.

The boy couldn't contain his curiosity.

"They say you can put a mana[18] on people?" he asked the sorcerer impatiently.

"Well, if they say so, then it must be true," the old Cossack replied with a smile.

Then he added: "Sit across from me and listen!"

Severyn settled comfortably on a sheepskin and prepared to listen. Vovkulaka slowly took out his pouch[19] and began to fill his pipe with tobacco. Once he had lit it, he began to speak: "Long ago, powerful warriors came to our land from distant places. They called it The Land of Wolves. These were strong and daring people. They liked it here so much that they decided to settle on our land, adopting our traditions, culture, and language. In turn, we learned the art of combat, seafaring, and much more from them."

The more the Cossack spoke, the deeper Severyn sank into an unknown state. He imagined himself sailing a large boat with a sizable group of warriors. Then, a woman appeared, reaching out to him and shouting something. He tried to touch her but couldn't because his hands had turned into tree branches. Suddenly, he found himself at the edge of a large cliff with a great beast. After standing there for a moment, he ran and jumped into the abyss. The boy felt the natural sensation of falling into the chasm and screamed in fear. Severyn opened his eyes and looked bewilderedly at Vovkulaka, who was smiling as he smoked his pipe.

"What was that?" he asked the sorcerer fearfully.

"You travelled to other worlds," Vovkulaka replied. "To places where your soul once was or will be."

"Can you, in these visions, go to places you've never been?"

---

[18] Mana — casting spells, enchanting or bewitching. The ability of sorcerers to perform a form of hypnosis.
[19] Pouch — a small bag with a drawstring used for storing tobacco, valuables, etc.

Illustration by Artem Burlyk

"Yes, and I believe you have the ability to do so. I can tell you one thing: you will be a great warrior, but your son will betray you. You will try to sentence him to death, but you will not kill him. Now go. I need to be alone," said the old man, closing his eyes.

The conversation with the old Cossack was etched into Severyn's memory forever: he remembered it until his dying day. After three years as a djura, he passed his final test and was accepted into the brotherhood. He honourably completed all the tasks, including the hardest one — navigating the river rapids by boat. For his love of sword fighting and skill with cold weapons, he earned the nickname Porubai (The Chopper).

The military campaign soon ended, and many returned home. During this time, his grandparents died, leaving his mother to manage the household alone. His sisters were growing up and were her main helpers at home. Severyn rode home, thinking about the one who promised to wait for him. Since his departure, he constantly remembered Oksana and every time his heart raced wildly.

"Did she wait for me? Has she forgotten me?" these thoughts gave him no peace, day or night.

Sensing her son's return, the mother had prepared his favorite lunch dish. The meal passed quickly with conversations. The absence of his father and grandparents left empty, sorrowful places at the table. His father was delayed with business and was to arrive later. Looking closely at her son, Kateryna smiled and said: "Go on, I see you can't sit still with us. Go to make the girl happy."

He ran, not feeling the ground beneath his feet. Severyn stopped by the fence of Oksana's house and glanced around. Finally, he gathered his courage and stepped into the yard. At that moment, Oksana appeared in the doorway: "I knew you would come. I felt it in my heart. I dreamed of you all night, just like last time."

They embraced and stood motionless for a few minutes.

"I dreamed of this day. I'm sorry I made you wait so long," Severyn finally said.

"I waited for you and prayed every day for your safe return home," she whispered in response.

A few months later, during Maslyana[20], the young couple married and settled in Severyn's home. His mother was delighted with her daughter-in-law, having known her since childhood. His sisters welcomed Oksana as an older sister and were very happy that their brother had such a wonderful wife. The expansion of the family also pleased his father, who was often away due to his service. There was plenty of work for everyone on the large estate. A year later, the family grew again. Oksana gave birth to a son, whom they named Vasylko.

Years passed. Sisters Marichka and Sofiyka got married and moved to nearby villages. The women mainly managed the household, as Severyn and his father were often away from home for long periods. Before long, Kateryna fell ill and passed away after several months. The sad news struck Mykyta hard, and he decided to leave his service and return home for good. Moreover, his old wounds were increasingly causing him trouble. At home, his daughter-in-law took care of him like a father. Together, they continued to run the sizeable household. Vasylko especially delighted the old man, who eagerly shared his experience and knowledge with his grandson. Granddad would carve a flute and teach him how to play it, or make a bow and arrows and show him how to shoot.

"Aim not with your eye, but with your heart," he would tell the small boy. "Let go of any thoughts. Relax and release everything that hinders you. Then the arrow will hit the target precisely."

Everything the old Cossack knew was gradually passed on to the grandson. They were two friends who couldn't live without each other. Vasylko's father

---

[20] Maslyana, also known as Butter Lady or Butter Week, is an Eastern Slavic religious and folk holiday that has retained elements of Slavic pagan mythology in its ritual.

taught him how to ride. The grandfather was too old for such exercises. When Severyn came home, they organised horse races. At first, Vasylko was afraid to sit alone on the large, fast horse, but over time, he learned to control it and could gallop like his father. Severyn's nickname was well-deserved. He wielded his saber so skillfully that anyone on the receiving end of his strikes was bound to be in trouble. This art was once taught to him by the old characternyk[21] Vovkulaka, who had since died and was buried in the communal cemetery.

"The saber is an extension of your arm. Feel its cold and strength. It is your only hope and helper," he would instruct his young friend.

In his turn, Severyn did not disappoint his comrade, becoming one of the best fencers in the community. Now, he aimed to pass on these skills to his son. To this end, he bought a small saber at the fair, as his own was too heavy for the boy. They practised slicing pumpkins mounted on poles while riding on horseback. Vasylko couldn't match his father's skill yet, but he tried to do everything as adeptly as possible to not disappoint his teacher. Grandfather Mykyta watched these contests with pleasure, encouraging and supporting his grandson in every way.

"Yes, son, yes! Cut them down!" he would shout excitedly to the boy, recalling the times when he fought enemies to the death.

Vasylko admired how his father did it. Severyn would gallop on his horse and, with a shout of "Assa!", sliced the pumpkin into several pieces. Vasylko kept his eyes on his father's saber but couldn't fully follow its movement. In his father's hands, it looked like a flash of lightning.

"This is how we deal with our enemies and those who betray the faith of our fathers and grandfathers, son," Severyn often told Vasylko, recalling the words of the old characternyk.

---

[21] Characternyk — a Zaporozhian Cossack credited with possessing magical powers, a sorcerer.

Severyn couldn't believe that his son would ever betray him, so he did everything possible to prevent this. He tried to raise the boy faithful to the traditions and beliefs of their ancestors.

Severyn was at the Sich on that fateful day when a breathless Hrytsko Samokhvat ran up to him.

"Severyn! Your village was raided, and I think…" his comrade stammered.

"What? What? Speak!" shouted Severyn.

"I think no one from your family survived," replied Hrytsko, hanging his head.

Severyn rode his horse through the steppe, trying to push away terrible thoughts. He saw smoke rising over the village from afar, and his heart tightened. He gripped the reins tighter and urged his horse, which was already running at full speed.

A small group of people stood silently by the ruins. Severyn jumped off his horse and rushed towards the crowd. When people saw him, they parted to let him through. Near the burnt house lay his father and Oksana. Dropping to his knees between them, he placed a hand on each and bowed his head. Tears rolled down his cheeks. He could not comprehend the terrible loss.

"Oksana was in the field when they attacked the village. She killed one of the attackers with a scythe, but there were too many of them. We brought her here so you could bury her. They shot your father right here, near the house. He tried to protect his grandson, but he didn't make it in time," said the old neighbour Levko.

"Where is Vasylko?" Severyn asked, lifting his head.

"They took him with them, along with many others," the neighbour replied after a brief pause.

Severyn groaned in anger and clenched his fists. Despair and helplessness took his breath away. Slowly, he realised that he had lost everything most dear to him. He rose from the ground and hoarsely said to the villagers: "Help me bury them properly. There is nothing more for me to do here!"

A few months passed after that most terrible day of his life. Severyn finally settled at the Sich, where he was soon elected as a kurin's[22] otaman. The thirst for revenge never left him for a moment. So, when the community gathered for a campaign against the enemy, he became noticeably agitated and began preparing his kurin for the campaign.

"Alright, brothers! Prepare your weapons and supplies and load everything onto our chaikas[23]. Mount the falconets[24] on the bow. Attach an empty boat to each chaika. We can store some of the provisions, clothing and gunpowder there. We set off in three days. So, we have time for preparations."

---

[22] Kurin — a military unit of Zaporozhian Sich. Each consisted of a few hundred Cossacks with their land, treasury and flag.

[23] Chaika — a deckless rowing-sailing boat used by the Cossacks in the 16th – 18th centuries. It could hold up to 50-70 people and was armed with falconets.

[24] Falconet — a light cannon with a calibre of 30 mm.

Illustration by Artem Burlyk

The Cossack flotilla was approaching the enemy shore. The sea was calm, with a light mist. The oars quietly splashed in the water. Severyn stood at the bow of the chaika, gazing into the night sky. The moon shone brightly, and the sky was dotted with stars forming various constellations. Suddenly, he felt as if this had all happened to him before. He shook his head, but the feeling didn't go away. The otaman clearly realised that he had done this before: the sea, the boat's bow, the splashing of the oars, and the approach to the enemy shore.

A shout from one of the Cossacks brought him back to reality: "Lights! We're getting closer."

Indeed, in the distance, the lights of a fortress appeared in the night sky. A strong stone structure protected the enemy from the sea. In the town itself was the largest slave market, where captives were sold into slavery. The thought of this made Severyn grind his teeth. It was unlikely he would find his Vasylko there, but he would avenge the death of his father and wife and free other captives. Knowing the enemy's language, which he had learned in the Sich school, he gathered a few daredevils who also knew it. Some had been in enemy captivity and managed to escape; some learned it in school, like Severyn, and some traded with them in the past. So, the group dressed in enemy clothing and set off in two boats toward the gate, where the guards were stationed. The rest of the flotilla, led by the kish's otaman[25], sailed as close to the shore as possible and lay in wait. Everyone kept silent, awaiting the signal.

"Praise be to Allah! Open the gate. We are exhausted after a long journey," Severyn said to the guard standing on the fortress wall.

"Who are you, and where are you from?" the guard asked in surprise. "It's late, and we have orders not to let anyone in until dawn."

"You devil! You dare not let in the envoy of the vizier[26] himself, delayed by a storm on the road? Will you make me wait here until morning, sitting on

---

[25] Kish's otaman — a chief officer of the Kish (central body of government) of the Zaporozhian Sich in the 16th-18th centuries.
[26] Vizier — a high-ranking political advisor or military minister in the Near East, especially in the Ottoman Empire.

the ground by the gate? Tomorrow, I will learn your name, and soon, you will hang on the gallows with crows pecking at your eyes!" Severyn shouted angrily.

Silence reigned on the wall for a moment. Soon, there was a clatter behind the gate, which slowly opened. A guard with a torch appeared in the gate's opening.

"Where are you? Come in quickly," he said.

Severyn and his comrades slowly moved towards the gate.

"You have few guards at the entrance. Where are the rest of them?" Severyn asked sternly.

"There are four of us here, and the others are resting," the guard said, pointing to a small hut near the gate.

"Alright, you three, go to the wall. Check how the Khan's[27] guards are doing their duty," Severyn ordered with a wave of his hand. "We will check on the others."

As they approached the hut, from which light was seeping, the guard grew suspicious and stopped.

"You are not the vizier's envoy. Who are you?" he shouted, reaching for his saber, but at that moment, his throat was slit, and he fell lifeless to the ground.

Severyn gave a signal, and the Cossacks immediately dealt with the guards on the wall.

"Forward!" Severyn burst into the hut and saw several warriors drinking tea on a carpet. They looked at the strangers in bewilderment, confused by their sudden appearance. The Cossacks didn't wait for their questions and, without hesitation, cut down the guards. Once the sentries were dealt with, Severyn whistled to the Cossacks waiting on the fortress wall. They lit a torch and gave the agreed signal to the comrades hidden at sea. In an instant, hundreds of oars hit the water, and the chaikas surged ahead toward the shore. The fortress gate was already open as they began to dock at the pier. The Cossacks moved silently into the fortress.

---

[27] Khan — the highest noble title in the Ottoman Empire.

Severyn waited for them there and, as soon as everyone had gathered, commanded: "Burn them, brothers!"

The sun began to appear behind the fortress walls, slowly illuminating the city that was still burning. The entire square and streets were littered with enemy bodies. The military garrison had been slaughtered, and the city residents had hidden in their homes or fled to the mountains. The Cossacks gathered loot, took it to the shore, and loaded it onto boats. Severyn, along with several comrades, reached the square. There, behind a sturdy fence, sat about two hundred captives. They looked at their night guests with fear and hope.

"Do not be afraid. We will free you," Severyn said to them. "Has anyone seen a blonde boy named Vasylko?"

"We haven't been here long. Those who were here earlier have already been sold and taken overseas," answered a young woman. "I do not recall such a boy."

Severyn motioned to the Cossacks standing beside him. They broke the lock on the gate and opened it.

"Alright, now you are all free, and we will take you home. Head to the dock and board the chaikas. We have a long and difficult journey ahead," Severyn said as he looked around the square.

Heavy thoughts overcame him. He didn't even notice when he found himself on a narrow street. Coming to his senses, he turned back and suddenly heard: "Are you looking for your son?"

Severyn turned sharply and grabbed his saber. A young gypsy woman was standing by a covered wagon, staring intently at Severyn.

"Don't look here. He is already far across the sea," the woman said without waiting for a response.

"Did you see him?!" Severyn shouted at her.

"Yes, I saw him. All I can tell you is this: one day, you will meet your son, but do not kill him. He is your blood," the woman said and disappeared as suddenly as she had appeared.

Severyn stood for a moment, not understanding anything, then shook his head, looked around, and went to his warriors, who were already preparing their boats to sail.

The campaign was successful. Captives were freed, and the city—hub of the slave trade—was burned. Great loot, along with several prisoners, was transported onto the chaikas. The fleet slowly moved out into the open sea. Severyn stood and gazed at the black smoke rising high into the sky over the burnt fortress. Just a few months ago, he had watched the same smoke over his village. These memories pained his heart, and the commander sat down at the bottom of the chaika.

"She said I shouldn't kill him. Vovkulaka also told me this. It's some kind of witchcraft," he thought, listening to the mast creak as the sails caught the wind.

Severyn didn't notice when he fell into a dream. He dreamed of a field covered with rye. He was walking towards Oksana, who was leading Vasylko by the hand. Severyn felt he was about to embrace them both, but with each step he took, they only moved further away. Some invisible force prevented him from approaching them. Suddenly, heavy black clouds covered the sky and began to rain. Lightning struck from the sky, and his wife and son disappeared into the darkness. Severyn shuddered and opened his eyes. A storm was starting at sea. Thunder rumbled in the sky, and lightning flashed from time to time. The chaikas desperately fought against the waves and finally reached the mouth of the river, where it was calm. The sea campaign was over. They just had to sail up the river to the Sich, which had recently become Severyn's home.

Years passed, alternating between times of peace and war. A few years after taking the enemy fortress, the brotherhood embarked on a campaign across the sea and burned the suburbs of the enemy capital along with the

Sultan's[28] fleet. There, too, Severyn searched for his Vasylko but did not find him. He returned once again in a gloomy mood. Heavy thoughts gave him no peace, day or night. A year ago, he was elected a military commander at the military council and now had additional responsibilities to the brotherhood.

Severyn, in particular, was responsible for border security and food supply. He and a few comrades travelled to the most remote outpost to check the distant borders. After a few days, they stopped in the middle of the steppe covered with wavy feather grass. The Cossacks built a campfire and began to prepare kulish[29]. Severyn took out his favourite pipe, filled it with a mixture[30] and lit it. The pleasant tobacco smoke spread across the steppe. Here and there stood stone statues, silently observing the unexpected guests.

"Do you see how many there are?" asked his friend Stepan Chayka.

"They have been standing here for hundreds of years. How much have they seen? Who built and erected them? No one knows. We must preserve this heritage for our children and grandchildren," Severyn replied, suddenly falling silent.

Knowing his friend's pain, Stepan placed a hand on Severyn's shoulder: "Come, brother, let's eat the kulish. The lads have finished cooking."

Severyn silently nodded and gloomily walked to the campfire where the Cossacks were seated.

---

[28] Sultan — the term is distinct from king, though both refer to a sovereign ruler. The use of "Sultan" is restricted to Muslim countries, where the title carries religious significance.
[29] Kulish — simple thick soup popular among peasants and Cossacks in old times.
[30] Mixture — Cossacks smoked pipes that added a mixture of tobacco with various herbs, such as thyme, wormwood, mint, oregano, holly, etc.

Illustration by Artem Burlyk

The council of elders was in full swing. Yesterday, envoys arrived from the king of the neighbouring state with a request for help. For such occasions, Severyn took out a large pipe made of white clay, leisurely lit, and passed it around. The Cossacks smoked in turn, sending fragrant smoke up to the ceiling. In the corner, at a separate table, the royal envoys sat, waiting for the council's decision. The first to speak was the Kish otaman Roman Kulyk: "As you all know, dear brotherhood, envoys from King Stanislav have arrived with a request to join the fight against the enemy invasion. The king's army is besieged in a fortress a few days' march from the Sich. The food supplies are gradually running out, soon leading to starvation. I appeal to you, dear comrades, to consider this issue and give your answer right now, as the envoys must return home today."

"Isn't this the same king from whom our freedoms suffered so much oppression?" sarcastically asked one of the oldest Cossacks, Mykhailo Kishka.

"Yes, the very same," confirmed the military artilleryman Stetsko Hlukhyi. "Not only did we suffer oppression, but the peasants did too."

A cloud of discontent hung over the tables where the council of elders sat. Here and there, threatening shouts were heard, growing into a continuous clamour. The royal envoys sat, silently drawing in their heads, not moving. When everyone had spoken and the noise began to subside, Severyn stood up and addressed those present: "I hope no one can accuse me of sympathy for our neighbours and their king. I have fought against them more than once and know their worth and promises. Now, they are in a difficult situation. In a couple of weeks, the fortress will fall. The Sultan's army is quite powerful, although it has suffered some losses."

After a short pause, Severyn continued:" I want to ask you, dear brotherhood, the following. Where will the Sultan's army go after the fortress is taken? Will it not come to visit us? To our lands. Do you think they have forgotten about the burned fleet and the suburbs of their capital? I do not think so. The Sultan is vengeful and has a good memory. Moreover, we have our own scores to settle with them."

At Severyn's words, he gripped the hilt of his ordynka[31] so tightly that his fingers turned white: "So, I believe we must assist our neighbours with certain demands for us and our peasantry. It is time to overcome our common enemy, who will crush us individually like puppies. Especially since we haven't gone on campaigns for quite a while. It's time to stretch our muscles and gain military glory."

That was the decision. The king's envoys were sent back with the promise of assistance. Certain demands were also made, which the king agreed to fulfil after achieving victory over the enemy. The Sich turned into a beehive. The brotherhood was preparing for a long campaign. Messengers were sent to all the palankas[32] with orders for all able-bodied Cossacks to come to the Sich. Only the distant borders and major cities were left guarded.

A week later, the army set out westward, where the besieged royal army awaited them. After marching for several days, the Cossacks set up camp facing the enemy camp on the river's opposite bank. After a military council, it was decided to attack the enemy in the morning before the enemy learned of the reinforcements.

Scouts were dispatched to the fortress to inform the besieged about the attack plans and coordinate the timing of the assault. The artillerymen began setting up positions for the cannons to support the assault with fire. The infantry prepared rafts to cross to the other bank. Everything was done in complete silence so that the enemy would suspect nothing. Soon, the scouts returned and confirmed the attack time. They also reported that discipline was low and morale was declining in the enemy camp. The sultan's army was resting and guards were posted very irresponsibly. With the cavalry, Severyn

---

[31] Ordynka — a Cossack saber with a massive guard and a wide blade. Borrowed from the East. Other types of sabers used included karabela, chechuga, shamshir and kilij.
[32] Palanka — an administrative-territorial unit of the Zaporozhian Sich.

moved downstream to cross to the opposite bank and be the first to strike the enemy camp, thus ignaled the attack.

Several hours passed. The moon shone brightly in the sky. Severyn's detachment had already crossed and was forming into battle order. He commanded when everything was ready, and the Cossack line slowly moved forward. After a while, the riders saw the enemy tents and fires along the camp's perimeter. Unsuspecting guards walked leisurely among them.

Severyn drew his saber from its sheath and shouted: "Forward! Cut them down, brothers!"

Illustration by Artem Burlyk

The Cossack line trembled and charged towards the camp. The guards reacted too late and sounded the alarm. Enemy soldiers began to run out of the tents, becoming easy prey for the Cossacks. Severyn cut down enemies left and right. At one point, in the firelight, he saw a young janissary[33] running towards him, shouting something. The otaman jumped at him and, with a shout of "Assa!", skillfully struck with his saber. The janissary tried to defend himself with his yataghan, but there was no chance to withstand Severyn's blow and he fell, struck by the Cossack saber.

Hearing the enemy trumpets, the Cossack artillerymen fired a volley at the enemy positions. The assault by the fortress defenders and the Cossack army began simultaneously. By morning, it was all over. The Sultan's army was defeated and fleeing. A few days later, a humiliating peace treaty for the Sultan was signed. The combined army celebrated the victory and gathered captured trophies. The next day, the Cossack army set out for the Sich. They had kept their promise. Now it was the king's turn to fulfill the Cossack demands.

After returning from the campaign, the Cossacks went about their daily affairs. The victory had not come easily. Many brothers had fallen under the fortress walls. At the same time, others needed to recover and heal their wounds. Winter lay ahead, which the warriors had to endure. Many of them went home, so only a small garrison of permanent residents remained at the Sich.

The cold winter months dragged on, and life began to return to the land. The river was slowly freeing itself from the ice that had bound it for long, frosty months. Buds were swelling on the trees. Birds began their spring songs. Severyn sat on a wooden log, engaged in his favourite activity — sharpening his ordynka. From the last campaign, it still had a few notches, and he was slowly fixing them. It had been half a year since the night battle at the fortress,

---

[33] The Janissaries — the regular infantry Corps established by the Turkish Sultan Murad I in 1365. This military force comprised boys aged 8 to 16, taken as a tax or captured during military campaigns. Thus, many Janissaries were Christians later raised in strict Islamic traditions.

and he kept recalling it, unable to understand why his thoughts constantly returned to that night. Finding no answer, Severyn sheathed his saber and went to the military scribe to learn about any news.

Dmytro Babiy, who held this position, was delighted to see his friend.

"Come in, sit down," he invited Severyn. "How's your health?"

"All is well, thanks to God," Severyn replied. "Any news? What's happening around? The winter was long and frosty, and we were cut off from the world because of it."

"There is news, but I doubt they'll please us," the scribe replied gloomily.

"Just say it; don't beat around the bush," Severyn tensed.

"This winter, King Stanislav died — the same one who promised to support our freedoms. The new king is Janusz, who has always been hostile to us. Now, he is gaining strength to reclaim his power over our lands. So, I think we need to gather the army again to defend our rights. Because it seems to me there will be a great war," Dmytro added grimly.

"Well then, we must immediately convene a great council and decide what to do next," replied Severyn as he rose from the table. "There's no point in sitting and waiting. We need to act preemptively, as our princes did in the past."

As the military scribe predicted, the neighbouring kingdom soon went to war against the Cossack lands to reclaim lost power. The kish's otaman suddenly fell ill and remained at the Sich, so command of the campaign was entrusted to Severyn, who had recently been elected as military otaman. However, the Cossack army did not have time to gather together and was defeated in the first battle. They had to retreat to save the remaining forces. The enemy pressed on, giving no rest. The Cossacks found themselves pinned against the river with no way to cross. It was decided to set up camp and build defensive fortifications. They arranged the wagons in several rows in a semicircle and placed artillery on them. In front, they dug a trench to prevent a cavalry attack. The horses, ammunition and wounded were sent closer to the river. The Cossacks held out for several days, but their provisions ran out, and they had less and less gunpowder for their muskets and cannons. Severyn understood that they could not hold out for long, so at the military council, they decided to secretly dam the river upstream to quietly leave the camp and lead the army out of the siege. All night, the Cossacks kept the campfires burning and pretended people were in the camp. Once the army had crossed to the other side, Severyn ordered a detachment of volunteers, who had volunteered to cover the army's retreat, to dig fortifications on the opposite bank of the river and set up cannons.

In the morning, the drums sounded — the enemy launched an attack. Bursting into the camp and finding no one there, the enemy soldiers were initially confused, then rushed to the river. There, at the crossing, their formation broke. Infantry and cavalry became mixed. At that moment, Severyn gave the command to the artillerymen. The next moment, a canister shot mowed down the front line of the attackers. The screams of dying men and horses echoed everywhere. Blood flowed down the shallow riverbed instead of water, but this did not stop the enemy. They surged forward relentlessly in a massive wave. Several more cannon volleys were fired, and Severyn gave the command to attack when there was no more ammunition. Three hundred daredevils charged down, cutting down the enemy mercilessly. After a few hours of fighting, the riverbed turned into one large grave. The enemy kept throwing new forces into the battle. Realising that it was impossible to hold out, Severyn gave the command to blow up the dam, which had been rigged with explosives. He and a few Cossacks fought, surrounded by hundreds of enemies. The distant explosion went almost unheard. Within minutes, a large, turbulent wave of water washed away everyone remaining in the riverbed. The water carried away both the living and the dead, sweeping them into the distant sea. High in the sky, a flock of ravens circled, never receiving their bloody feast.

Aponi*

The road suddenly ascended, halting the small caravan. The horses, burdened with looted goods, neighed softly and pawed the ground, refusing to go uphill. The riders dismounted, pulling them along while shouting and whipping them. Captive women huddled together, refusing to move. One of them, her hands tightly bound with leather straps, was being dragged by an enemy rider. She glared at her captors with hatred, but nothing escaped her lips. The woman's mind was racing for her home, which had recently been destroyed, and husband, killed alongside other tribesmen. Now, all her thoughts were of revenge for their deaths. The rider holding her by the strap frequently glanced back, leering lustfully. She knew what awaited her and the other women that evening, yet she remained remarkably composed. A sharp bone knife, securely hidden in leather moccasins, was her last hope, offering a sense of calm. Her childhood had been spent under grandfather's watchful eye, learning many tricks. He had often stressed that a knife should always be within reach, for the time might come when it would be one's last and truest friend. Now, Aponi fixed her gaze on the rider with war face paint and horns on his head, barely containing her desire to kill him. She would avenge

---

* Aponi – butterfly

her fallen kinsmen, and this revenge would be terrible. Nothing and no one could stop her from carrying out that intent.

"Aponi, where are you?" the girl heard as she played with butterflies in a sunny glade. Nizhoni[34], her mother, walked toward her daughter, shading her eyes with the hand to see better in the bright sunlight.

"Look how many there are!" the girl exclaimed emotionally, waving away the butterflies circling around and trying to land on her head.

"I also loved playing with butterflies when I was little. I always thought they were the dancing souls of our deceased ancestors," her mother replied.

"Mother, I think so too. Grandpa told me so many legends that I'm sure they are indeed their souls," the girl said excitedly. "I just adore Grandpa. It's so interesting with him."

"Yes, I also loved listening to these legends when I was a child. He heard them from his grandfather, who in turn heard them from his. This is how the history of our people is preserved and passed down from generation to generation," her mother said after a short pause. "Well, you've had your fun, but now let's go home. Father will be back from hunting soon, so we need to prepare a delicious dinner. Tomorrow, we have a lot of work: I will teach you how to tan bison hides, which our hunters are bringing today. Also, we will continue making the jewellery you love so much."

---

[34] Nizhoni — beautiful.

Illustration by Artem Burlyk

Aponi reluctantly tore herself away from her play but happily dreamed of how she would learn everything her mother knew and one day pass on this knowledge to her own children. The mother took her daughter's hand, and they walked toward the village, which was located on the bank of a turbulent river. As they walked home, Nizhoni looked at her daughter again, her eyes filled with tenderness and calm. She felt certain that Aponi would grow up to be a strong and wise woman who would honour the traditions of her people. Soon, they reached the slope of a hill from which their settlement was visible. Several dozen tipi[35] huts formed a circle, in the centre of which stood a tall wooden totem with the image of a wolf. Women were engaged in their daily tasks, while children ran around the homes shouting and laughing. The tribe was living its usual life, awaiting the hunters who had set out on a hunt a few days earlier.

Kwahu[36] was riding leisurely at the head of a large group of horsemen. It was evident that the hunt had been successful. The horses were pulling a heavy load tied to long poles[37]. The warriors looked tired but satisfied. The thrill of the hunt still lingered with them, and they were still mentally out there on the endless prairie. They chatted with each other, joked and looked forward to soon being reunited with their families. Only Kwahu rode silently, not responding to his comrades' jokes. He was thinking about what he had seen in the prairie, which troubled him. The danger was close. Its presence was felt everywhere. This could not be ignored.

"I need to consult with the chief and urgently convene a tribal council to decide on our next steps," Kwahu thought. "We must protect our loved ones at all costs."

---

[35] Tipi hut — a tent made of tall poles covered with skins.
[36] Kwahu — eagle.
[37] For transporting goods, Native Americans used long poles attached to horses and dragged them.

Then he remembered his daughter Aponi and smiled. The girl was growing up and becoming a real helper to her father. With such a combative spirit, she should have been born a boy. However, he was grateful to his beloved squaw[38] Nizhoni, for giving him such a restless wonder. In his absence, the girl's upbringing was overseen by Nizhoni's father, the old and experienced warrior Keruk[39], who had been the head of the tribe for many years. He was rightfully respected by warriors, women, and children alike. The latter adored the chief because finding a better storyteller of ancient legends was impossible. In their free time, the children would gather around him and listen with bated breath to stories about their ancestors. No matter the task in the tribe, it did not proceed without Keruk's involvement. Whether moving and choosing a place to live, cultivating fields and planting corn, gathering edible roots and mushrooms, fishing and hunting, preparing for winter, and organising celebrations. Every time, people would go to him for advice and help. Perhaps because of this, the tribe had not known sorrow and suffering for many years. Now, dressed in ceremonial attire made of eagle feathers, the chief led a crowd of tribesmen to the edge of the village to meet the returning hunters.

Kwahu rode up to the crowd, dismounted, approached the chief, and greeted him, placing his hand on his chest: "Greetings, father! The hunt was successful; we hunted several buffalos, and now our tribe will have enough food for a long time."

"Greetings, my son," replied Keruk. "We have all been waiting for you. You have done your duty. Now, the women will handle the spoils, and you need to eat and rest."

He waved his hand, and the women, with the help of the warriors, began to deal with the load.

---

[38] Squaw— wife.
[39] Keruk — bear.

Aponi ran up to Kwahu and hugged him, followed by Nizhoni, who embraced them both.

"We prayed to the spirits daily to keep you safe," she told her husband.

"I missed you all so much! How have you been, my dear ones?" Kwahu responded, looking into his wife's eyes.

The woman did not reply; she just buried herself in his long hair that flowed from his shoulders.

"Was everything alright during the hunt, my son?" asked Keruk. "I can see that something is troubling you."

He stood aside, admiring how his daughter and granddaughter clung to Kwahu.

"We need to talk, father," Kwahu said in a tone that immediately made his wife and daughter understand they needed to leave the men alone.

Nizhoni took her daughter's hand and said: "Perhaps you should eat first and then discuss your matters?"

The chief raised his hand and said: "Go and take care of your tasks, woman. Your husband will come to you soon."

When they were alone, Keruk asked: "Did you see them?"

Kwahu was always amazed at the chief's ability to sense and predict events. So this time, he didn't even ask for clarification about whom the chief was asking. He knew exactly what Keruk meant.

"No, I didn't see them, but they are there. They left many tracks. It seems they did it on purpose, to let us know they are around and to scare us," Kwahu said with concern.

"We have lived in peace and quiet for so many years. After the war tomahawk was buried, they never appeared on our territory," the chief said sadly.

In the largest tipi, located in the centre of the settlement, sat the tribal chief Keruk, Wekesa[40] – the old and wise cassique[41], and several other warriors. This dwelling was used for rituals and communal prayers. It was noticeably different from the rest of the homes, as it was dug into the ground and had wooden walls. On those walls were depictions of wolves along with other exotic animals. A fire was burning inside, and the attendees silently watched the flames licking the logs. Everyone was waiting for the chief to speak. Keruk sat quietly for a while, smoking his pipe and releasing thin streams of tobacco smoke from his mouth.

Then he straightened up, handed the pipe to the warrior sitting next to him, and said: "You all know why I have gathered you here. Many years have passed since the great war with the Horned Ones ended. They promised never to appear on our land again and have kept their promise until now. But our warriors have brought bad news from the hunt. The Horned Ones have once again violated our borders. It was done in such a way as to make it clear that they no longer adhere to the peace agreement. So it is imperative to prevent a new war because, in the event of defeat, we will once again have to seek a new place to live."

"Why should we leave our lands for someone else's desire?" I was a teenager when that war ended, and I remember well how hard it was for us to leave our settled lands," said Jakee[42], the youngest of those present.

The old cassique looked at Jakee disapprovingly and shook his head. Wekesa liked this young man, whom he had known since birth, but his hotheadedness always caused trouble. The young warrior spoke first, although he should have waited for the eldest present to speak. Seeing the reproachful look, Jakee, feeling embarrassed, lowered his head.

---

[40] Wekesa — wise man.
[41] Cassique — a chief priest of the tribe, shaman.
[42] Jakee — moon.

"Yes, that war cost us many lives, and we had to yield to the enemy for the sake of preserving our tribe. At that time, we did not have the strength for victory, so making peace was the only right decision for our future. Thus, we have lived in peace for a long time," replied Keruk.

"However, these years have not been wasted for us! We have grown stronger and larger thanks to avoiding a devastating defeat back then! But they have also made good use of their time! Our warriors say they are very numerous. What do you say to this, wise cassique?" said the tall and sturdy Tokela[43], addressing Wekesa.

"I believe that war with the Horned Ones is inevitable. Our ancestors always fought with them. They cannot be trusted because treachery and hostility towards us are in their blood," said the old Wekesa. "But we must prevent this war because our allied tribes are currently suffering from an unknown disease and are unlikely to be able to help us."

"You say they are many?" the chief asked Kwahu.

"Yes, judging by the tracks we saw, they are numerous and have plenty of horses," replied Kwahu.

These words darkened the chief's expression. The presence of horses always gave an advantage on the battlefield, and ignoring this would be extremely dangerous.

"Kwahu," the chief said after a short silence. "Take a few warriors with you and go to the Horned Ones. Tell them I want to negotiate with their chief. At the same time, see how many there are and gauge the mood within the enemy tribe. Set out early in the morning. We will await your return."

Keruk stood up, signalling to those present that the council was over. Kwahu bowed and was the first to head to the exit. The warriors began to file out one by one. The chief, now alone, sat down on a deer skin spread on the floor and fell into deep thought.

---

[43] Tokela — fox.

Aponi was sitting by the river, silently watching the water flow around the rocks and rush downstream with a roar. The girl liked sitting there alone. From the moment she could walk, she had been fascinated by everything related to nature, the animal world and the history of her tribe. Fortunately, her grandfather seemed to know the answers to all her questions. Now, Aponi sat by the water, listening to its murmur, feeling as if the river was talking to her.

"I should visit Grandpa," thought Aponi. "I haven't listened to his legends and stories in a long time."

The girl stood up and headed to the main tipi, where the warriors were dispersing after the council. She carefully lifted the flap at the entrance and peeked inside. Keruk was sitting on the floor, staring motionlessly at the dying fire. His thoughts were far away when his granddaughter called to him.

"Grandpa. How are you feeling? Are you alright?" she asked Keruk.

"Yes, my little one. I am well. We haven't talked in a long time," replied the chief, awakening from his thoughts.

"You haven't told me any legends in a while."

"Alright then," Keruk agreed, standing up. "Let's go for a walk; it's not a place for children here, only for the chosen ones."

He took Aponi's hand, and they walked to the edge of the village. There, on the slope of a hill, they could enjoy a beautiful view of the tall mountains rising in the distance.

"What do you want to hear about?" asked Keruk.

"Grandpa, why is there a wolf depicted on our totem?"

Illustration by Artem Burlyk

Grandpa looked closely at the girl and began after a short silence: "Well, listen. This happened a long time ago. Our ancestors lived far beyond the mountains then. Nothing troubled them; people lived in peace and harmony with nature and the forest spirits. Men engaged in fishing and hunting, women took care of household chores and looked after the children, while the smallest ones played from morning until late evening. One day, a black wolf came out of the forest with a little blue-eyed, fair-faced girl. Our ancestors had never seen white-skinned people before and were surprised by her. They took the girl in and raised her as a family member. Over time, she grew up, became the chief's wife and bore him many children from whom our lineage descended. In honour of the wolf who saved the girl from death and brought her to us, we began to be called the Children of the Wolf. Since then, the wolf has been a symbol of the tribe, and its image has appeared on our totem."

"Grandpa, my mother also has fair skin and blue eyes. So, does that mean she is a direct descendant of that girl?" Aponi asked after thinking for a bit.

Keruk squinted, looked at the inquisitive girl and said: "I was still quite a young warrior back then. One day, we went hunting and came across a plundered settlement of white people. They were all killed by the horned ones. Under an overturned wagon, I found a little girl who, having hidden from the attackers, was trembling in fear. I brought her home and gave her to your grandmother. That's how your mother came to be with us and became our beloved daughter."

Keruk patted the girl on the head and added: "Now go to your mother. I need to be alone with my thoughts."

"Thank you, Grandpa, for such a wonderful story," said the girl.

She got up and headed home along the narrow path. Aponi thought about what her grandfather had told her. In her imagination, she saw the black wolf with the little blue-eyed girl, her mother hiding from the attackers and the terrible and ruthless horned ones, notorious for their cruelty. That tribe got their name because they wore animal horns to instil fear in their enemies. The horned ones did not live in peace with neighbouring tribes and were extremely unreliable in any dealings. The Wolf's Children had already suffered more than once from their treachery and cruelty. Now, they had appeared again in their lands. Aponi understood that danger was approaching but didn't know how to prevent it. With these thoughts, she reached her tipi, where Nizhoni awaited her.

"Finally," said her mother when Aponi arrived. "I was just about to go look for you. We have a lot of work to do. Your father brought buffalo hides; we must tan them to make clothes. You'll help me with this. First, go and collect some oak bark for the decoction."

Aponi took a knife and a woven basket and went to the forest across the river. There, she felt in harmony with nature. She breathed in the forest air, listened to the rustling leaves above and talked to the trees. Her grandfather had taught her this. He often said: "We are all children of Mother Nature. People, animals and trees all have souls. So, never harm them intentionally or without reason. Want to hear the answers to your questions? Listen to the wind and talk to the trees. Learn to recognise the signs you receive in response."

Among the many forest trees, Aponi had chosen her tree. It was an ancient oak emanating forest magic. The girl loved to come to it when she wanted to be alone, hugging the sturdy trunk with her little arms, inhaling the tangy oak scent. In such moments, it seemed to Aponi that she was merging with the tree itself, becoming an inseparable part of it. Then, she would soar in her daydreams to her secret kingdom. Today, too, she came to her friend, hugged it, and, after standing silently for a few minutes, she stepped back from the tree and said: "I'll take a little bit of your bark, okay? My mother asked me to bring it for a decoction to soak the buffalo hides."

The girl carefully began to cut the old bark, which had already started to peel off. After collecting enough, she lifted the basket, patted the trunk and said: "Thank you very much! Now I have to go home because there is much work to do. Don't be sad without me."

At home, Aponi gave the bark to her mother, who threw it into a large pot with boiling water. When the decoction was ready, they removed the pot and let it cool. Then, they placed the buffalo hide in it and left it until the next day.

"While the hide is soaking to the desired condition, we will make some decorations," said Nizhoni.

"What kind of decorations?" asked Aponi.

"Today, I will teach you how to make a dreamcatcher. It is a very powerful talisman that will protect you while you sleep, but you must be careful with it. During its creation, you need to think only about good things. Imagine that you are weaving your good thoughts into it."

They sat on the floor, and the mother began to show her daughter how to make the talisman. She had already prepared willow branches, deer sinew, colourful threads and stones. The most important element was bird feathers: owl feathers for women's decorations and eagle feathers for men's. Nizhoni was a true craftswoman. She explained to Aponi which threads and stones to use for different purposes. The girl eagerly learned this art. They didn't notice the sun hiding behind the horizon as they worked.

"That's enough for today," said her mother. "We'll finish tomorrow, but now it's time to sleep."

All night, Aponi had strange dreams. She had never seen anything like it before. In the dream, the girl was riding on the back of a black wolf while a great eagle soared high in the sky, watching her from above the clouds. An old oak tree walked through the forest, shaking the soil off its roots. There was also a young man who stayed close by, but Aponi could not clearly make him out. When she woke up, Aponi immediately told her mother about the dream.

"That's very good," Nizhoni rejoiced. "It means you were making your talisman with the right thoughts. From now on, it will catch only good dreams and drive the bad ones away from you. Now we need to finish the work, and then you'll take the talisman to the cassique. He will say a special prayer to the gods over it."

So it was done. Aponi took the finished talisman to Wikesa, who carefully examined her work, nodded approvingly and performed a special ritual.

"Now, it must always hang above your head! The dreamcatcher will protect you from evil spirits and offer good advice while you sleep."

From then on, the talisman resided in Aponi's tipi, and she never parted with it.

"Kwahu is returning! Kwahu is returning!" shouted the children from outside. They were the first to notice the small group of warriors heading towards the village.

Keruk went outside and walked to meet the group. Kwahu rode up to him, jumped off his horse and, bowing, said: "I met with them and conveyed your request. Their chief, Lone Coyote, will arrive tomorrow morning for negotiations. So we need to be ready."

"Thank you, my son," replied Keruk. "Go rest now. We have a tough day ahead tomorrow."

Just as the sun peeked over the mountains in the morning, a small group of horsemen rode into the village. These were the horned ones, headed by their chief, Lone Coyote. The entire village, led by Keruk, Wikesa and other warriors, went out to meet them. Lone Coyote dismounted, approached Keruk, and greeted him: "Greetings, chief! I am glad to see you again. It has been a long time since the war tomahawk was buried."

"Greetings to you as well. Yes, much water has flowed since then. I thought I would never have to meet you again," replied Keruk.

"Everything changes; life does not stand still. I wouldn't be standing before you now if it weren't for the events that have occurred recently," said Lone Coyote.

"Very well. It is not good to keep guests outside. I invite you and your warriors to the tribal council," said Keruk, turning and gesturing for the guests to follow him.

They went to the main tipi and sat in a circle. On one side were Keruk and his warriors, and on the other were Lone Coyote and his men. Keruk lit a pipe, took a few puffs and passed it to the warrior beside him. When the pipe had made its way around the circle to everyone present, he addressed Lone Coyote: "Now, tell us what made you break your promise not to enter our lands. You have upheld the peace agreement for many years."

Lone Coyote did not answer immediately. He looked at everyone present keenly and said: "Do you think we decided to wage war on you? Trouble has come to our lands. Since we ceased hostilities, more and more fair-skinned settlers have been arriving from the east. They began to settle on our lands. At first, we drove them out and killed them, but they kept coming. Now, a whole army is coming behind them, one that we cannot withstand. After losing several battles, we were forced to retreat. That's why we broke our agreement, because our horses need pastures, and our people need fresh food. I believe this danger will soon affect you as well. Therefore, I think it would be wise to unite and defend ourselves against this invasion."

"What do you say?" Keruk asked his tribesmen.

"Considering how many times they have broken their promises, what kind of alliance can we talk about?!" exclaimed the impatient Jakee, immediately drawing a reproachful look from Wikesa.

The young man frowned again and lowered his head.

"Yes, this young and fiery warrior is right," said Wikesa. "I remember several instances when you treacherously attacked us, breaking all previous agreements."

At that moment, angry shouts came from the other warriors, expressing dissatisfaction with the guests.

"I will never forgive them for my father's death!" shouted Geedzhii[44] and grabbed his knife.

---

[44] Geedzhii — raven.

To calm the rising emotions, Wikesa raised his hand to quiet everyone.

"But on the other hand, we face a significant threat from the fair-skinned people. Any hostility between us will only benefit those invaders," said the cassique, looking pointedly at those who had just shouted insults at the arrivals.

Silence fell in the tipi, and no one dared to break it. After a short pause, Keruk spoke: "We have heard you, Lone Coyote. I am curious to know what you propose?"

"We need to form a military alliance with you and the other tribes of your clan. Without this, it will be difficult for all of us to resist the fair-skinned invasion, as a great war is inevitable. We also agree to give you every fourth buffalo or deer we hunt on your lands as payment for the permission to live and hunt here. Additionally, we pledge to support you in any way and defend you at the first sign of need."

These terms were accepted. The tribal chiefs formed a military alliance and agreed to live peacefully and help each other.

Several years of peaceful life passed until shocking news reached Aponi's village. The fair-skinned people had attacked the horned ones' village, and many were killed. In the unequal battle, Lone Coyote, who fought desperately against the attackers to protect his tribesmen, was killed. Their village was plundered and destroyed, and the horned ones had to flee far into the mountains. This news greatly worried Keruk, who was too old for military campaigns, but his authority was unshakable, and no one even thought of reelecting a chief.

"We must send messengers to all the tribes of our clan and call them to join the war against the fair-skinned people. War is coming closer, and we must be ready. The horned ones have chosen Slippery Snake as their chief, who is not as reliable as Lone Coyote, but we must honour the terms of our peace treaty," said Keruk at the council of elders.

That same day, messengers spread out with a call to prepare for the campaign against the enemy. The village turned into a bustling anthill. The breath of war was felt in every dwelling. Warriors were preparing horses and weapons; women were making arrows. Even children were involved in these preparations. By that time, Aponi had turned eighteen. She was also preparing for war. The years spent alongside her father and grandfather were not in vain. She could ride and shoot a bow as well as any warrior. Her father taught her this. Sometimes Kwahu regretted that she was not born a man: anyone could envy such a fighting spirit. He imparted all his knowledge of martial arts to her. Over time, all the tribe's warriors began to respect his daughter,, but none dared to approach her.

One day, Keruk approached Aponi and, watching her tend to the horse, said: "My dear daughter. I want to say that I am proud of you. I know that war is not a woman's business, but I cannot prevent you from participating in it. The spirit of our ancestors lives within you, and now you cannot sit quietly aside. I bless you and will pray to our spirits for your protection. In the meantime, take this."

He extended his palm to the girl, revealing a small bone knife. The handle of the knife depicted a black wolf running across the prairie.

"Always keep it with you and never leave it behind. There may come a moment when it will be your only friend and hope for salvation," said Keruk, embracing his granddaughter.

"Thank you, Grandpa. I will call it Wolf and never part with it. I love you so much," the girl replied.

From her mother, Aponi learned to sew shoes and clothes. So she made a hidden pocket for the knife in her moccasin. From then on, it was always with her. Occasionally, she would take it out to admire the delicate beauty crafted by an unknown master. She looked at the pattern and imagined herself as a she-wolf racing through the prairie against the wind. In such moments, Aponi would delve into thoughts that took her far back into the depths of time to the days when her lineage was born.

Several hundred mounted warriors, adorned in war paint, stood still, gazing into the distance. The wind gently swayed the feathers in the warriors' hair. Everyone was silent, waiting for the scouts to arrive. Down below, on the land that belonged to Aponi's tribe, the fair-skinned people had built their fort. The girl looked around and felt satisfied. All the clans of the tribe had responded. Together with the horned ones, who had recovered from their defeat, the army looked formidable. A sea of spears pointed towards the sky, awaiting the command to battle. Just then, everyone saw three riders racing towards the lined-up army. They were the scouts. They rode up to the chiefs standing at the front and stopped their horses. Mimitech[45], the senior scout and Kwahu's younger brother spoke: "There are about a hundred soldiers in the fort. There are also civilian settlers. Cannons are stationed at each corner."

Hearing this, Slippery Snake grimaced. He was well aware of rifles' power and cannons' might. Their army was armed with spears and bows, clearly inferior to the fair-skinned people.

"We cannot attack head-on," he said. "The fort is too strong, and their fire sticks shoot very far."

"Then we'll wait for the night," responded Kwahu. "Night and the moon are our allies."

All chiefs accepted this decision. When the moon illuminated the valley, the detachment silently moved down to where the enemy fort stood. The attack was set to begin at once from all sides of the fort. The scouts silently killed the sentries, and the vanguard entered the fort without obstacles. Only the gates, guarded by several soldiers, remained to be opened. This time, it did not happen without noise, and a trumpet sounded in the fort. But it was too late. The gates were opened, and hundreds of riders burst into the fort with wild whoops, killing the bewildered enemies. In several places, fires broke out simultaneously. Aponi skillfully shot arrows at the enemies running out of their buildings, half-dressed and becoming easy targets for the attackers.

---

[45] Mimitech — new moon.

To take a better position for shooting, the girl dismounted and hid behind a wagon. From there, she targeted the fort's defenders, who were trying to resist. At some point, she heard a war cry nearby and, turning, saw an unfamiliar warrior armed with two tomahawks. He had dismounted and rushed into the thick of the battle. The girl froze momentarily, amazed at how enemies fell one after another around him, cut down by his deadly axes. Suddenly, the warrior turned to Aponi and, with all his might, threw a tomahawk at her. The girl screamed and closed her eyes, but the next moment, she heard someone gasping behind her. Slowly turning, she saw an enemy soldier clutching a tomahawk embedded in his chest with both hands.

Illustration by Artem Burlyk

"What are you staring at?" shouted the warrior, suddenly stopping.

He hadn't expected to see a girl on the battlefield.

"What's your name?" he asked her more calmly.

"Aponi," was all the anxious girl could respond.

"Be careful!" the stranger shouted to her.

Pulling the axe from the chest of the dead soldier, he rushed towards the source of the triumphant shouts of the attackers.

By morning, it was all over. The victors took a rich harvest of scalps. All the soldiers and settlers had been killed. The captured trophies were distributed among the tribes and clans. The heavy-loaded detachment set off homeward with war songs. Aponi rode alongside her father, silent. She couldn't get the stranger she met during the night battle out of her mind.

"Father," she said. "Last night, an unknown warrior saved my life. I will ride out and look for him, okay?"

"Alright, my daughter. I will wait for you," Kwahu replied, looking at Aponi with pride.

His only daughter had proven in battle that she was no less brave and skilled than the men. Aponi spurred her horse and galloped along the column that stretched for several hundred meters, moving slowly. The horses trudged heavily, laden with captured trophies and the bodies of the fallen. Aponi rode alongside this procession, scrutinizing the faces of the warriors, hoping to find her rescuer. Suddenly, she noticed some movement in the bushes and, drawing her bow, directed her horse towards the forest thicket. As she approached, she saw a man looking at her fearfully, his hands raised. He didn't resemble the settlers who had recently lived in the fort.

"Don't shoot! I beg you!" he shouted at her.

"How do you know our language?" Aponi asked, surprised, but did not lower her drawn bow.

"I am a priest. I bring the word of God to you. I spent several years among your people in the north, so I learned your language," the man replied, more calmly now.

For some reason, Aponi was intrigued by this man. She did not kill him; instead, she dismounted and tied his hands with a rope, ordering him: "You will come with me. Let the old Wekesa talk to you."

The whole tribe met the detachment, who returned after the victory. The air was filled with the joyful cries of women who met their husbands and the cries of grief and despair from those who had lost them. The entire village buzzed like an excited beehive, and no one remained indifferent to this event. When the noise had somewhat subsided, Aponi rode up to the cassique, pulling the bound prisoner towards her and said: "I have a gift for you. He says he is a priest among the fair-skinned people."

"Untie his hands!" commanded the cassique.

Aponi freed the prisoner's hands and stepped aside, observing him.

"So, are you a shaman among the fair-skinned?" Wekesa asked the man standing before him, rubbing his swollen hands.

"I am a priest, not a shaman. I serve our One God," the man replied, looking at the cassique with pride.

"How do you serve him?" Wekesa inquired.

"We build large buildings — churches and go there on Sundays to pray and read the Holy Scriptures," the priest answered calmly.

"So, to speak with your god, you need to build a big tipi and pray in it?" the cassique asked in surprise.

"Well, that's our custom. We conduct a special ceremony where we offer a sacrifice to our god, give communion to our believers and read from this book."

The prisoner pulled a worn book from his cloak and handed it to the cassique. Wekesa took the book, opened and looked at it from different angles. Then returned it to the priest, asking:

"So, you tell people only what is written in this book?"

"This is the Holy Scripture! Wise people wrote it over many centuries," replied the priest.

"Do you know the difference between us? We do not need to build a big tipi to communicate with the gods. We speak to them everywhere: in the forest, the prairie or the mountains. Our gods are where we are. We feel their presence in the rustling of the wind and trees, in the roar of mountain water and the silent sky. You believe in what someone wrote in your book many years ago. We trust what is in our hearts and what our ancestors passed down to us."

After a brief pause, the priest wanted to say something, but Wekesa waved to Aponi, standing nearby and said: "Take him to the edge of the village and let him go. He must return to his people. This man is not our enemy, but there is nothing for him to do here."

A few days passed since then. Aponi was sitting in the hut with her mother, sewing clothes. The cold weather was approaching, and they needed to prepare properly. Suddenly, Kwahu appeared in the doorway and, looking at Aponi mysteriously, said: "My girl, come here. We have guests from the neighbouring village. Someone wants to greet you."

Aponi looked at her father in surprise, put down her work and stepped outside. The bright sun hit her eyes, so it took her a moment to see the several riders standing behind Kwahu. One of them, seeing Aponi, immediately dismounted and approached her.

"Do you recognise me?"

"So it was you who scared me back then?" Aponi replied with a hint of a smile in her eyes and glanced at her father.

Kwahu stood nearby, watching the conversation.

"My name is Kakoannive[46]," said the young warrior.

Then he turned to Kwahu: "May I invite your daughter for a walk? I have been looking for her everywhere since we returned from the campaign. I visited

____

[46] Kakoannive — little wolf.

several villages until I found out yesterday where she was. Though until the last moment, I was not sure of it."

"I don't mind, as long as she agrees," Kwahu replied, looking at his daughter.

Aponi hesitated momentarily, then shook her head and said: "I agree. Let's go."

She brought her horse, jumped on it, shouted to Kakoannive: "Catch up!" and galloped away from the village.

The warrior was initially taken aback, as he did not expect such behaviour, but quickly recovered and gave chase. That day, they rode around all the nearby areas. Aponi enjoyed talking with him. He was different from the other warriors of the tribe, who, knowing about the combative nature of the chief's granddaughter, were afraid to court her. But this young man treated her freely and boldly. Aponi liked this; it was her first time comfortable with a stranger. She wanted to listen to him endlessly, so she was very upset when the sun hid behind the mountains, forcing them to return home.

"I will come tomorrow," said Kakoannive.

This was not a question but a statement that Aponi appreciated. To her surprise, she felt for the first time that she wanted to obey the man.

"Yes, I will wait for you," she replied with joy in her eyes.

The next day, as promised, Kakoannive came to visit her. Then he came again and again. Aponi's heart skipped a beat each time as she waited for his arrival, and she was saddened when they parted. The girl couldn't see herself being apart from him anymore. A day without Kakoannive seemed unbearably endless.

One day, the young man arrived not alone but accompanied by his father, Kichi[47]. Kwahu and Nizhoni met them. The guests dismounted, approached and bowed.

---

[47] Kichi — brave bear.

Kichi said: "My son Kakoannive wishes for your daughter Aponi to become his squaw. Would you object to this?"

"We do not object, as we know your son. He is a noble and brave warrior. But we must ask our daughter if she agrees to become his wife," replied Kwahu, calling for Aponi.

When the girl came outside, her father asked: "This warrior wishes to marry you. Do you object to this, my daughter?"

"I do not object, father. I will gladly become a faithful squaw to Kakoannive", Aponi replied, blushing.

After some time, Nizhoni and the groom's mother, Kizekochuk[48], covered their children with a blue blanket[49]. According to the traditions of the tribe where Aponi lived, Kakoannive came to live with his wife. Thus, another tipi appeared in the village, where two loving hearts settled. It seemed their happiness would never end.

"Also, tell him that if they destroy this tribe, we will allow them to live on their lands forever," said the officer in the red uniform to the interpreter.

The interpreter translated everything to Slippery Snake, who, along with three other warriors, had come to the newly rebuilt fort for secret negotiations. Slippery Snake did not bear his name without reason. Cunning and treacherous, he was a formidable opponent and an unreliable ally. The chief realised that the fair-skinned people wanted to use him to eliminate their enemies — his actual allies, whom he secretly always hated. Now, a thirst for profit ignited within him. Therefore, Slippery Snake decided to get as much benefit as possible from this offer and, at the same time, to deal with the hated tribe living on such fertile lands.

------

[48] Kizekochuk — morning star.
[49] Covering the children with a blue blanket during the wedding ceremony in some tribes signifies mourning for the years spent before marriage.

"That will not be enough," he replied to the interpreter. "This tribe is very strong, and it will be difficult for us to overcome them. We need horses, muskets, lead and gunpowder. Also, we will keep all the trophies and prisoners."

The interpreter conveyed his words to the officer. That frowned displeasedly but, having no other option, agreed to all the demands of the insolent chief. He only decided to deal with these horned ones in the future. The main thing was to weaken the alliance of tribes with which the fair-skinned people could not fight. His career as an army captain depended on the success of this operation. Therefore, he was forced to compromise his principles and negotiate with Slippery Snake, no matter how disgusting he found him. The officer had to follow the government's orders and clear these lands by any means for the settlers arriving daily from across the ocean.

Aponi woke up long before sunrise. She dreamed she was flying high in the sky while Kakoannive lay motionless on the green grass below. She called her beloved to join her and fly among the clouds, but it was in vain. The man did not respond to his wife's calls. Then, a black wave descended on the land, sweeping away the entire village. A bad premonition gripped Aponi. She got up and sat beside her peacefully sleeping husband. Above his head hung the dreamcatcher. Usually, still, the talisman was now spinning incessantly around its axis. Not understanding anything, Aponi got dressed and went outside. The sun had just begun to extend its warm rays from behind the mountains. Suddenly, the sound of galloping horses was heard. It was the scouts rushing back to the village.

The first scout shouted: "The horned ones are approaching! They have taken the warpath!"

The village instantly sprang to life and began preparing to repel the attack. Women gathered the children and the most necessary belongings to flee to the mountains, while the men organised to defend the village. However, there was no time left for proper preparation. A black, screaming wave swept over the settlement, destroying everything in its path. A bloody battle ensued, but the forces were unequal, and within a few hours, it was all over. The horned ones had won but paid a high price for their treachery. Many of them fell in battle. Cries of wounded attackers, whom no one intended to help, echoed from all directions. Everything was drenched in blood, but the traitors did not care: they scalped the fallen defenders, packed the loot and tied up the prisoners. Aponi found herself among the captured, watching through tears the horrors unfolding before her eyes. She had fought bravely alongside her husband. When an enemy bullet killed him, she was thrown to the ground; a lasso tightened around her neck.

Illustration by Artem Burlyk

As the evening fell, the detachment stopped at the edge of a steep canyon. The captives were gathered together and thrown to the ground. Three warriors were set as guards over them, grinning greedily and lustfully in their direction. A few more attackers began to build a campfire. Soon, the fire was blazing and illuminating the painted faces of those present. The flickering flames made them look even more fearsome and menacing. The horns they wore made them resemble wild and bloodthirsty animals. The horned ones gathered around the fire and began their dance. They circled, beat their chests and screamed wildly, making it seem like this dance of death would never end.

Slippery Snake approached the captives and examined them closely. Dressed in leather leggings[50], with his body shining from oil, he fixed his gaze on Aponi. Grabbing the woman by the hair, he dragged her and then threw to the ground a few steps away. Then he turned to his tribesmen, who were frozen in anticipation and shouted: "You have earned some entertainment, my warriors! So now they are yours!"

The excited horned ones rushed at the terrified captives, who awaited their fate with horror. Slippery Snake watched with satisfaction as the women were assaulted and screamed, torn apart by the horned ones. At that moment, Aponi quickly retrieved the bone knife hidden in her moccasin and discreetly cut the leather strap binding her hands. Hiding the knife in her fist, she resumed the same position she had been lying in. Slippery Snake turned back to her and began approaching slowly, with lust and animalistic rage burning in his eyes.

"Now I'll give you something you never got from your pathetic husband," he spat confidently. Smiling, he removed his leggings and leaned over the woman.

He reached out, trying to grab the captive by her hair. Rising sharply to meet him, Aponi grabbed the attacker's right hand with her left hand and, with the knife in her right, slashed the horned leader's throat with all her might. The rapist grabbed at the wound, trying to stop the bleeding and fell

---

[50] Leggings — leather trousers that were separately attached to the belt.

to his knees. His face turned red, his eyes bulged, and it seemed they would burst from the strain.

Aponi stood up and, looking him in the eyes with anger, said: "You have nothing to give me. For everything I needed, I already received from my husband, who died as a warrior should. But you will die like a dog at the hand of a woman!"

She then grabbed his hair and, with one swift motion, scalped him.

Slippery Snake gasped and fell helplessly to the ground. Aponi turned and ran to the place where the fire was burning, and the massacre was taking place. Raising her hands, holding the scalp and the knife, she shouted with all her might: "You can take our bodies, but not our souls! You will all face a disgraceful death, just like your leader, whom I, Aponi, daughter of Kwahu and Nizhoni, have killed!"

For a moment, silence fell around. The horned ones looked at the furious girl with horror as if she had emerged from the flames. Not waiting for the enemies to recover from their surprise, Aponi rushed at them with her faithful Wolf. In a moment, several of the horned ones were on the ground, bleeding, but there were too many enemies, and soon Aponi fell to the ground, pierced by an enemy spear.

Rada

There was nowhere else to run. They stood, holding hands, at the edge of the cliff. In front of them, far below, the sea sparkled with all the colours of the rainbow. The sun was at its peak, and it seemed that no one else was in the world except for these two. Rada[51] held Hojo[52] by the hand, and her heart trembled at the beauty that unfolded before their eyes.

The boy turned to her, hugged her tightly and said: "I won't give you to anyone. You are mine by right. No one can separate us. Only death."

"But my father and my uncles are already near. We have nowhere to run! They would find us anywhere!" the girl replied tremblingly.

"I don't care about all that enmity between our families. That was so long ago. I love you and only you. I'd rather die than give you to someone else. Do you hear me?" Hojo grabbed his beloved by the shoulders and looked straight into her eyes.

"I will die with you to be together forever," Rada whispered and hugged the boy.

---

[51] Rada — joy, happiness.
[52] Hojo — beautiful.

"Rada was talking in her sleep again last night. I listened for a long time, and it wasn't just nonsense," Shukar[53] excitedly said to her mother, Zora[54].

The old woman sat by the fire, smoking a pipe. A stew was simmering in the pot hanging on a tripod. The men would be back soon, and they needed to be fed a tasty dinner. Zora didn't seem to hear her daughter's words, but the old woman heard everything and was lost in her thoughts.

"She sees," Zora answered briefly.

"Do you think she has the same abilities as you?" Shukar asked.

"I don't even think, my daughter. I know. This gift is passed down through generations. You don't have it, so you are surprised by your child's abilities. But I can see it all. Rada has extraordinary abilities that she is not yet aware of. At the age of five, she can't explain much. Rada sees people, their past and future, and those who have passed away. I think she sees spirits, too. I once observed her from the side. Rada was communicating with beings invisible to us. She simply thinks that we can see them as well. But even I do not possess this gift," the old gypsy woman said calmly and released a thin stream of smoke.

"Mother, this scares me," Shukar whispered anxiously.

"It unsettles me too. I barely remember my grandmother. She also had the sight but didn't have time to pass her experience on to me. She left this world too early. So Rada needs to be very careful with this gift. For us, it is certainly a boon. We can make good money from fortunetelling. People love to pay for what they do not know. But on the other hand, the same gift could ruin her life. So we must handle your daughter carefully to avoid harming her," Zora replied.

Rada grew up in a large and friendly family. Their camp was always noisy and cheerful. They moved from city to city and never stayed in one place for long. After earning money, they buy food and necessary items and move on

---

[53] Shukar — beauty.
[54] Zora — dawn.

to the next town. This endless movement was the essence of their way of life — never settling in one place, always being on the move, in harmony with Mother Nature. From an early age, the girl loved to sing and dance, so no celebration was complete without her participation. The townspeople were incredibly fond of the little and vocal girl. Growing up among brothers, sisters and numerous cousins, Rada realised quite early that she was different from them. Initially, she tried to talk about her feelings with her peers, but after facing a misunderstanding, she decided to keep everything to herself. Her grandmother was the only one who fully understood her. The old fortuneteller knew everything her granddaughter told her.

Illustration by Artem Burlyk

When Rada was eight, Zora called her and said: "Dear, I have something to tell you. Sit next to me."

Rada sat down on the ground and prepared to listen.

"I look at you and see myself when I was little. It's as if I am living my life again. My brothers and sisters didn't understand me either. What I saw and felt was given only to me. I could see the future of people I met for the first time. For this, I was valued but also feared. I never made mistakes because the messages came from above, and those who send them don't make mistakes. I never used my gift against people or for someone's gain. Yes, I made a lot of money from it because people are curious to know their future and remember their past. They don't understand that it's not worth knowing what will come. Also, one shouldn't delve into the past. What was done can't be changed, and we don't control the future. We must live in the present and be grateful for what we have. Why am I telling you all this, dear? You must be careful with what you see and feel. Your gift is like a fire on which you can cook food but also get burned. I worry about you a lot because I know seeing people is difficult. It's as if you are living each of their lives, feeling their emotions and feelings. This is hard for ordinary people to understand. You must learn to protect yourself from people. From their destructive energy, and I will teach you this. Unfortunately, you are the only person I can't see in the world. You are stronger and, therefore, hidden from me. That's why I worry about you so much."

"Thank you so much for everything, Grandma," Rada said, hugging Zora tightly. "Yes, it's hard for me to communicate with other children. They don't understand me when I tell them things. They think I'm strange, but I see so much. When I sleep, I often travel to places where few have been."

"You also talk in your sleep," said the grandmother, laughing.

"Really?" the girl asked. "I wonder, what do I say?"

"Most likely, you are talking to those you see there."

"Maybe. The most interesting thing is they are not always people."

Zora looked at her granddaughter with surprise but said nothing.

Understanding her gaze, the girl continued: "Yes, sometimes I find myself in a world unknown to me and meet someone there who gives me advice or suggests a way out of a situation. Not always people, but some strange creatures I don't understand."

The grandmother listened to her granddaughter in amazement. No one in the world had ever told her anything like this. Zora felt as though she was speaking to an elderly person who had endured a difficult life journey and carried a wealth of human wisdom.

"Unlike you, I can tell you about your past or future," Rada suddenly blurted out, changing the uncomfortable topic.

These nightly journeys fascinated but also scared the little girl.

"Well, I don't want to know about the future. I don't have much time left to live anyway. But learning about the past from you is interesting," Zora replied, squinting.

"You know...," Rada said and paused for a moment. "That young janissary is still alive. Father did not kill him. He is alive but seriously wounded. You predicted that father would try to kill him, and he laughed at you."

"You see more than I could have ever imagined," Zora replied, not at all surprised, as if she had heard something ordinary.

The old gypsy woman lowered her gaze and fell silent. She remembered a summer day at the capital market and that young janissary she had met many years ago on the streets of a city across the sea. Back then, he was a small and helpless boy. Later, in the same place, she met his father, who was searching for his son in the streets of the burned city. That was a long time ago, and now her granddaughter has reminded her of the past. Zora closed her eyes, immersed in memories. Not wanting to disturb her grandmother, Rada quietly got up and left.

Time passed inexorably. Rada grew into a beautiful young woman. Grandmother Zora always stayed close by, observing and helping her granddaughter develop the girl's abilities, and teaching her how to protect herself from others. They kept this secret from their relatives for a while, but as time passed, Rada gradually began to practice her abilities. At first on family members and then on outsiders. Soon, word of the girl who could "read" people spread to the nearby towns and surrounding areas. Her father, Gazelo[55], was very pleased. As the camp leader, he was flattered that his beautiful daughter was becoming a local celebrity. Moreover, their income significantly increased thanks to Rada. Everything was going well for them, except for one thing: the longstanding feud with the Kaldaras family. Long ago, the father of their current leader, Manush[56], had killed one of Gazelo's uncles. Gazelo's father had vowed to avenge his brother's death, but the council of elders decided to accept a ransom for the sake of future peace. Since then, a quiet enmity had persisted between the families. The unresolved blood feud hung over them like a bloody sword, constantly reminding them of itself. The younger generation no longer knew exactly who killed whom and for what reason, but fear and hostility towards outsiders were instilled from an early age.

In those times, a wave of uprisings swept through the country. Many were dissatisfied with the Sultan's rule, and the country turned into a blazing bonfire. Bands of criminals roamed everywhere in search of loot. So, the camp stopped on the capital's outskirts for a while, waiting for the unrest to subside. There were always opportunities to earn money in the capital, especially since Rada had many people eager to learn about their future. One day, she and several women went to the local market to earn money through fortunetelling and buy food. On an autumn day, the market was, as usual, noisy but not too crowded due to the ongoing unrest in the country. Many merchants did not

---

[55] Gazelo — wise.
[56] Manush — man.

dare to travel to the capital. The women scattered among the rows of stalls, and Rada, along with her friends, stayed in the centre where a group of magicians was performing. The girl was so captivated by the performance of one of the artists that she didn't notice a group of young men approaching her.

"So this is the girl who can see the future?" one of them asked mockingly, looking at Rada.

"Well, for money, I can tell you your future too. Give me your hand, and I'll read your fortune," another said, laughing and mimicking fortunetellers.

The young men laughed, and the oldest silently looked into the girl's eyes. Rada was not at all intimidated and accepted the challenge. Crossing her arms over her chest, she squinted at the insolent boy.

"These are boys from the Kaldaras family. I've seen them before. We'd better leave here to avoid any trouble with your father," whispered her closest friend, Loly[57].

But Rada continued to look at the boy silently and then quietly replied: "Do you know, Hojo, that the horse you stole a week ago belongs to a very influential person? This person has already sent messengers all around to find his favourite."

The confident smile immediately vanished from the young man's face, and he looked around in fear.

"How do you know?" he asked fearfully, grabbing Rada by the shoulder.

"I know many things, so I advise you to get out of here with your cronies and not interfere with our work," Rada said with a deadly calm voice, removing his hand from her shoulder.

"Let's go, Hojo. Do you see she's a real witch," said one of the boys to his friend, and the company, caught off guard, hurriedly left.

"How do you do that? How did you know him?" Loly asked the girl.

"I saw him for the first time, just like you. But I'm sure it won't be the last. That I know for sure," Rada replied and fell into thought.

---

[57] Loly — lovely.

After earning some money that day, the girls returned to the camp. On the way home, they chatted and shared their impressions of what they had seen. Only Rada walked silently, thinking about her own things. The girl's only friend with whom she could talk about everything was her old grandmother, Zora. She had taught her granddaughter many tricks and secrets, but recently, she passed away, leaving the girl without guidance. So, Rada had to deal with her problems independently and improve her skills. In any difficult situation, the girl would seclude herself, immersing into that world where she found answers to all questions, but this time, she couldn't find them, which worried her greatly. The incident with that insolent boy didn't scare her but made her wary. Rada immediately sensed that the meeting was not accidental, but she didn't know what exactly was bothering her. The girl went to her mother to help prepare dinner to distract herself. Shukar, aware of her daughter's strange gift, tried not to interfere with the learning of her extraordinary abilities. Her late mother always said: "You have given birth to a priceless treasure. Support Rada in everything. Your child is wiser than many adults. So don't hinder her from developing her skills. The only thing she needs from you is your love and motherly warmth. Without it, she will wither."

"How are you, dear? Was everything alright? Did you see anyone in the city?" Shukar asked her daughter.

"Everything's fine, Mom! There were fewer people than usual because not everyone dares to come to the capital in these difficult times."

"But you seem worried about something. I can see it. What happened?"

"Well, it so happened that we ran into boys from the Kaldaras family. One of them was so insolent that I had to put him in his place.

"That's bad. I'm afraid that when your father finds out, we will have problems. The unresolved debt doesn't let him live peacefully."

"I know, Mom, but for some reason, this encounter worries me, and I don't know why."

A few weeks passed. Rada had almost forgotten about the incident at the market when she suddenly heard the voice of the one who had unsettled her so much during their last meeting.

"How do you do it? I haven't forgotten about you for a single minute since that day," Hojo was standing by the wagon, looking at the girl with interest.

Rada, as usual, was walking around the market, looking for people for whom she could read fortunes. His gaze was no longer as mocking as the last time.

"You returned the horse, so that's good for you. Otherwise, you would have had serious trouble," the girl replied calmly.

"I returned it, and you were right. I would have had extra trouble with it. My father even scolded me when he found out about that horse. But it was such a beautiful horse. It would have been a sin not to steal it," Hojo smiled, squinting dreamily.

Rada looked at the boy carefully. Today, he was entirely different. The insolence had disappeared. In its place stood a polite and gentle young man. This change pleasantly surprised the girl. More importantly, she felt a certain lightness as the tension from their first meeting had suddenly vanished. Rada wanted to talk. She cautiously asked: "You're from the Kaldaras family, right?"

"I know what you want to ask. My father's name is Manush, and my grandfather killed one of yours many years ago. Our families have been feuding for so many years," Hojo replied with sadness in his voice.

"That victim was one of my father's uncles. So, there is a blood feud between us," Rada whispered.

"Really?" the boy was surprised. "So many years have passed since then. Compensation was paid, yet the enmity hasn't disappeared."

"My grandfather swore back then to avenge us, but our family accepted the compensation and forbade shedding your blood for the sake of peace. He accepted the family's decision, but in his heart, he never reconciled with it."

Hojo exclaimed passionately:" In his place, I wouldn't have reconciled either!"

"You know, it's better if we don't see each other," Rada said nervously. "If my father finds out, it will be trouble for both of us."

"I understand your concern, but I want to see you again, and no one will stop me," the young man said firmly.

Rada looked up at him in surprise. The once overconfident braggart was nowhere to be seen.

In front of her stood a young man with a sense of dignity, which pleasantly surprised her.

"Alright, I will go," she said quietly. "I don't want to upset my family."

"Next week, I will be waiting for you at this place!" Hojo shouted after her.

Rada heard what he said but didn't turn around. She walked away silently, looking for other girls from her camp. The girl had already decided that she would come to the meeting, no matter what.

A few days later, Rada was at the same place again. From afar, she noticed the boy looking for her in the crowd.

"Good day! Are you waiting for someone?" she asked with a smile.

"Yes, I am waiting for a beautiful girl who has captured my heart," the boy smiled back.

"So, did you wait long?"

"Of course. Hello, beauty. I didn't come alone. I have a gift for you."

Hojo reached into his coat and pulled out a tiny ginger kitten, which was looking around fearfully. The girl took the fluffy creature and pressed it to her face.

"How lovely! I'll name it Khamalo[58]," Rada exclaimed joyfully.

"I knew you would like it. Moreover, I know cats can see things that ordinary mortals cannot. So now, this is your first helper," Hojo observed the girl's reaction.

---

[58] Khamalo — ginger.

Illustration by Artem Burlyk

They didn't notice how time flew by. Meetings with Hojo became more frequent, but Rada carefully hid them from everyone, knowing how it could all end. The ginger kitten settled well in the camp and became everyone's favourite. As Hojo had predicted, Khamalo grew devoted to his mistress and never slept away from her. Only the kitten stayed close to Rada during those moments when she embarked on her distant journeys in meditation. It seemed that Khamalo understood the girl better than anyone in the camp. In return, Rada shared her observations and impressions with him, and the cat seemed to understand everything.

"Do you see Zora too?" the girl asked Khamalo, who had jumped to his feet and was staring at the spot where the tent's shadow lay. "Don't be afraid of her. Grandma sometimes visits me to offer some comfort. Since she left, it has been hard for me to keep everything to myself because there's no one with whom to share my thoughts. Well, maybe only with you."

Rada smiled and stroked her pet's bristled fur on his back. The cat sat down on his hind legs and looked at his owner. He was still frightened, but Rada's soft voice calmed him. Within a minute, Khamalo closed his eyes and began to purr. The girl petted his back and pondered her thoughts. The spirit of her deceased grandmother didn't appear very often, but always before some events. Despite her abilities, Rada couldn't foresee everything, and this troubled her.

She once recalled sitting by the fire with her grandmother, discussing their worries. Suddenly, as if waking from a sleep, Zora said: "You know what, dear? I constantly think about you and your gift. The ability to read people isn't given to everyone. You can reach great heights in your development, but you can also lose everything in a moment and perish. This worries me greatly because I feel my end is inevitably approaching. You will be left alone, and no one can advise you. Your mother loves you deeply and feels with all her heart, but she doesn't fully understand your feelings. Therefore, it will be hard for her to help you."

"But what could ruin me, Grandma?" Rada looked into Zora's eyes.

The old fortuneteller looked intently at her granddaughter, paused momentarily, and said: "Love, my dear. It can ruin you. Your gift will disappear as soon as you love somebody with all your heart. This will be your price for a great feeling. A long time ago, I fell in love with a boy, but my father decided to marry me off to your grandfather. I couldn't go against my father's will and lost my love. Yes, your grandfather was wonderful, but I never loved him. This is probably my greatest pain, which no one knows about except you."

The old woman pulled the girl close and hugged her tightly. Shiny tears streamed down her wrinkled cheeks.

Rada remembered that conversation and thought about Hojo. Recently, this boy had taken over all her thoughts. She fell asleep and woke up thinking about him. In any situation, she would ask herself: "What would he do?" or "What would he say?" The feeling that had emerged in the girl's heart delighted and worried her. She still kept her relationship a secret, understanding the danger it posed for both of them, but all secrets eventually came to light.

"Rada, we need to talk," her mother's voice was troubled.

"What happened, Mom?" the girl responded.

"I was told you often see a boy from the Kaldaras family. Is that true?" Shukar asked.

The girl didn't hide it: "Yes, Mom and no one will forbid me from doing so."

"Do you understand that your father will kill you when he finds out? He will never allow his daughter to have a relationship with anyone from their family," her mother exclaimed in despair.

"Listen, Mom. I understand that we must adhere to traditions and customs, but the old sins of our ancestors should not poison the present and certainly not our future. Someone has to stop this cycle. Otherwise, our children and grandchildren will also live in hatred. My peers don't even remember what happened many years ago, yet they sincerely hate and fear everyone from the

Kaldaras family. Should the death of one person stand between us forever? Even if it was the death of our relative," Rada replied passionately.

Her daughter's words took Shukar aback for a moment. Then, extending her arms, she hugged her tightly and said: "I understand you, my dear. You must have met someone to whom you are ready to give your heart. I am happy for you, but we do things differently here. Your father is the one who should decide your fate."

"Were you also married off to him without your consent? Just like Grandma?"

Shukar silently nodded and pressed her daughter closer to her chest: "It's our tradition, and I couldn't do anything about it. Parents decide the fate of their children, and you know that well."

"I'm not going to go against my father, but I won't betray my feelings either. So, I will meet with Hojo no matter what."

"I understand and support you but cannot oppose your father. He is my husband, and I must obey him."

"Mom, everything will be as it should be. Don't worry about me. Even if I am expelled from the camp and have my hair cut off[59], I will not betray my feelings."

Some time has passed since that conversation, and Rada has begun to forget about it. She still secretly met with Hojo, and it became harder for her to part with him each time. When her beloved spoke with her nearby, her body seemed weightless. This new feeling was pleasant and calming. It carried her far above the clouds, where Rada forgot everything. In her thoughts, there was only Hojo.

That day changed her life completely. She was getting ready with her friends to go to the city market to buy some jewellery and tell fortunes for the locals and merchants.

---

[59] Cutting a woman's hair is the highest punishment among Gypsies, along with expulsion from the camp.

"Rada," her father's voice was stern. "Come here. We need to tell you something."

The girl turned around and saw her father and mother. Shukar stood behind her father with tears in her eyes. Rada approached and asked: "What happened? Why is Mom crying?"

"She is probably crying out of joy for you," said her father. "We have something to tell you. You have grown up and must get married. Every woman must have a husband and bear children. This is the meaning of her life. So, I have found you a worthy man from a respectable family who will be your husband."

Gazelo, smiling with satisfaction, watched his daughter's reaction. This was a significant day in every father's life, and he treated it with all seriousness. He expected his daughter to be bewildered by this news, which would be natural. However, her reaction puzzled him.

"Father, I will not marry a man whom I do not love and have never seen," Rada replied through clenched teeth.

Behind Gazelo, his wife burst into tears, unable to hold back any longer. He turned around, not understanding what was happening.

"Is there something I don't know?" he asked Shukar.

She silently shook her head and covered her face with a scarf.

"You will marry the man I have chosen for you. We have already agreed on everything with his parents, and don't you dare disgrace me. You will regret it!" Gazelo added angrily.

"Do whatever you want, but I will not marry him!" Rada shouted, turning around and running away.

She ran down the road, unable to see anything before her. Tears blurred her vision. It wasn't the day she was supposed to meet Hojo, so she decided to go to his camp and find him. Rada had never been there, but she roughly knew where it was. She saw several tents and wagons arranged in a semicircle from a distance. Slowing her pace, she saw a group of children playing nearby.

She approached and asked one of them: "Can you call Hojo for me? But do it so no one hears."

"Who are you?" the boy asked cheekily and defiantly. "What's in it for me?"

"I will tell your fortune if you do what I ask," the girl replied calmly, looking him in the eyes.

"Are you the one who can see people? I've heard about you. I don't need anything. I'll call him anyway. Besides, he's my brother," said the boy and ran to the camp.

The rest of the children surrounded Rada and began examining her curiously. Anyone else would have been bombarded with questions, but they regarded the girl who could see people cautiously. This didn't last long because she saw Hojo running towards her within a minute.

"What happened, Rada?" the boy asked anxiously.

Rada gestured with her eyes towards the children, who stood aside, watching them attentively.

"Hey, get out of here!" Hojo shouted at them. "Make sure no one knows you saw her."

"Alright, we're leaving," said his brother. "But you owe me now."

"Bachtalo[60], I'll talk to you later. Now get out of here and say nothing to anyone. Agreed?" Hojo cut him off sharply.

When the children left, Hojo turned to the girl: "Now, tell me."

"My father wants to marry me off. I told him that I won't marry someone I don't love," Rada said and looked at the boy with hope.

He hugged her tightly to his chest: "My dear! I won't let anyone take you away. Do you hear me? I can't imagine my life without you."

"But he said I would regret going against his will. Now I don't know what to do," Rada whispered and began to cry.

"Let's go to my father. He'll know what to do."

"Are you sure about this?"

---

[60] Bachtalo — happy.

"Yes, although the feud between our families has been going on for a long time, he always insists that it must end! I think this is the case where we can stop it."

Hojo grabbed the girl's hand and led her with him.

Trembling with fear, Rada followed him, trying not to look around. They walked to the tent where Manush lived under the watchful eyes of the camp's residents. Hearing the commotion, he came outside and meet his son with the stranger.

"Father, this is Rada from the Sheker family. I love her and want her to be my wife. I know about the feud between our families, but didn't you say the time has come for us to end it?" Hojo said to his father.

"Is this the same girl who is said to see people and tell fortunes?" Manush examined Rada closely.

"Yes, that's her," his son confirmed.

"She is the daughter of Gazelo, our blood enemy. His father swore to avenge us. That vow is still unfulfilled," Manush frowned. "But I will try to talk to Gazelo for your sake and your future. For now, Rada must leave; she cannot stay here."

During all this time, the girl did not say a word. She felt ashamed to look into the eyes of her boyfriend's father because she had gone against her own father's will.

"Thank you and forgive me for everything," was all Rada could say before leaving the camp.

"So you knew she was seeing a boy from the Kaldaras family?" Gazelo shouted and struck Shukar across the face with all his might. "You knew and said nothing to me?"

The blow knocked the woman to the ground, and she covered her face with her hands. She cried not so much from pain as from the insult. Never before had her husband laid a hand on her.

"Yes, I knew and kept silent because your daughter fell in love with a boy from the enemy family. She fell in love! Do you understand that? However, to whom am I telling this? You lived with me all these years without loving me. I was forced to marry you, too, and all these years, I've suffered because my heart still belonged to the one I once loved but had to leave to adhere to our traditions. However, your daughter won't do that. Remember that."

"What are you saying? You married me as a virgin!" Gazelo hissed in response.

"You won't understand. You don't know this feeling," Shukar replied calmly.

Gazelo raised his hand to strike her again, but at the last moment, he changed his mind and abruptly turned and left the tent.

Filled with rage, he didn't know what to do. His daughter, with whom he had placed so many hopes and expectations, had disgraced him.

"Gazelo, someone wants to talk to you," he suddenly heard the voice of his brother, Lolo[61].

"Who is it?" Gazelo asked.

"You'll see for yourself. Come, I'll take you to them."

They walked to the edge of the camp, where two men were standing, holding two horses by the reins. Gazelo immediately recognised the visitors. It was Manush and his brother Ilo[62].

"What did you want to talk to me about?" Gazelo asked instead of greeting them.

"It so happens that our children have fallen in love with each other. I think this is something we need to discuss. There is a great opportunity to end the years-long feud between our families finally. The dead cannot be brought back, and hatred poisons the lives of our children," Manush replied reasonably.

---

[61] Lolo — red.

[62] Ilo — heart.

"My father swore on blood to avenge the murder of his uncle. Though we took compensation from you, no one released us from that oath," Gazelo snarled through his teeth.

"Maybe it's time to do that? We belong to different families but to one people. We have no homeland, but we have what unites us. Our language, traditions, and culture. Should we live as enemies instead of uniting?"

"Unite with those who shed our blood?" Gazelo half-turned, showing his intention to leave. "We have nothing to talk about. Rada will marry the one I have chosen for her. Now get out of here and tell your son that if he comes near my daughter, I will fulfil my father's oath."

Manush and his brother mounted their horses without saying another word, and only dust rose on the road.

Rada slept restlessly. She had nightmares. She was flying like a bird through a desolate forest, and the black trees were trying to catch her with their branches. The girl tried with all her might to avoid them, but the trees grew more numerous. At some point, she felt someone touching her hand and woke up with a scream. Hojo stood beside her, placing a finger to his lips, signalling her to be quiet. Then he motioned for her to follow him. The night was dark, and the moon was hidden behind dark clouds. They left the camp unnoticed.

"What are you doing here?" Rada finally asked Hojo.

"My father couldn't agree with your father. On the contrary, Gazelo threatened to kill me if I dared to come near you. He also said that you would marry the one he has chosen for you," the boy replied.

"So what are we going to do?" Rada cried.

"I have only one choice left. To steal you away, but I want to know if you agree to be mine."

Hojo hugged his beloved by the shoulders and looked intently into her eyes. The moon peeked out from behind the clouds temporarily, and Hojo saw her eyes glisten.

"Yes, I want to be yours and only yours, but how will you steal me?" Rada asked in surprise.

"I've already stolen you. In the nearby forest, I've left two horses and some supplies we'll need for the first while. We'll have to run far away. Your father won't let you go so easily."

They set out into the night, choosing no specific path, just moving away from the place where danger awaited them. After a few hours, in the moonlight, the fugitives saw a half-ruined cabin.

"I think we can rest here until morning, water, and feed the horse," Hojo decided.

"Alright, I'll prepare us something to eat," Rada replied.

After a brief, late supper, Hojo spread sheepskins on the floor, took the girl by the hand, and sat her down beside him.

"On this first night of ours, I want to tell you that I love you so much. All my thoughts are with you because I can't imagine my life without you. I will never betray you and always be by your side until death," the boy whispered excitedly.

Pulling Rada close, he began to kiss her gently on the lips.

Illustration by Artem Burlyk

They made love all night, and it seemed as if no one else existed in the world. Then, they fell asleep in each other's arms as the first rays of the sun illuminated the old cabin, their last refuge.

Rada felt these embraces in her dream. They held her tightly and wouldn't let go. She felt cosy and yet anxious. In that dream, Rada seemed to see herself from the outside. There, she was being embraced by a large, furry wolf-man. Waking up from the nightmare, Rada looked around anxiously. Hojo was peacefully snoring beside her and seemed far away in his dreams.

"Hojo, they are close! We need to leave as soon as possible," she began to shake her beloved.

He instantly jumped to his feet and silently began to pack their things. When they rode up a hill, they saw several horsemen in the distance, racing in their direction.

"It's my father with his brothers. We need to run!" the girl shouted to Hojo.

"Follow me!" the boy yelled, spurring his horse and rushing down the hill.

The lovers raced as fast as they could, trying to escape their pursuers. The riders split into two groups and were almost upon the fugitives, pressing them closer to the seashore. Rada and Hojo were trapped like two wild wolves. Dismounting, they began to climb the cliff that towered above the sea. Reaching the top, they looked back. The pursuers were closing in, dismounting and starting to climb.

"I order you to return, you disgraceful girl," Rada heard her father's breathless voice. "I will kill you both if you don't come back."

"Then why wait?" Rada shouted back to her father and turned to face Hojo. "Are you ready?"

"Yes, my wife. Together until the end," Hojo replied in an unexpectedly calm voice.

Taking one last look at the beauty around them, the lovers ran, holding hands tightly and leapt into the abyss, their arms flapping like wings.

Luis

From the height of the hill, the enemy ranks were clearly visible. Flags and banners waved above them. Luis's army had won a series of battles in recent years, but this time, they were facing a strong opponent. Too many signs indicated this. Bad thoughts wouldn't leave him. Luis was noticeably nervous, and this was affecting his faithful mare, Tamira. To calm her and somewhat himself, Luis stroked the mare's neck, leaned towards her ear and said: "Calm down, my dear! Everything is fine! This isn't the first time. We've been through so much together. You and I, we are like one. I will be with you as long as my heart beats."

Then he remembered the dream he had a few months ago: the same hill with enemy ranks below, the same anxiety felt by the mare, and the terrible end from which he woke up in a cold sweat. Luis wiped his face with his hand as if shaking off heavy memories and then looked up. High in the sky, waiting for the imminent feast, a flock of black ravens circled. For a moment, his heart froze from the bad premonition.

Illustration by Artem Burlyk

"Mom! I saw the Moon so close it seemed to be hanging right above my head! This invention will change people's perception of celestial bodies!" Luis excitedly shouted to his mother when he returned from his teacher, Don Alberto.

His mother was preparing dinner in the kitchen. Luis was her favourite, so she always listened to him attentively and closely followed his life. The older sons were in royal service and rarely visited their parental home. Therefore, all of her maternal love was directed at the youngest son, the primary helper to the parents. His father worked as a chemistry teacher at the city university and was considered a respected person among his colleagues and students. After finishing school, Luis was determined to enter this university's mathematics department. He liked the exact sciences, such as geometry and arithmetic. The boy could sit for hours solving complex problems. Luis felt like he was on cloud nine when he managed to untangle a problem that initially seemed too complicated. Eventually, he developed an interest in astronomy. This interest was particularly encouraged by Don Alberto, who taught this subject at the university and, as a good friend of his father, often visited their home. He told the boy about the Solar System and what planetary satellites, stars and especially the Sun are. All of this was very interesting because at the school, which was under the patronage of the Church, Luis heard completely different things from his teachers. The boy felt as if he had already encountered the structure of the planets and knew what he was just about to study. Eventually, Luis began visiting Don Alberto at home, where a real observatory was set up. Today, for the first time, he saw the surface of the Moon through a telescope recently acquired by Don Alberto. The impressions from what he saw were bursting from within, and Luis wanted to share them with his parents.

"Dad, can you imagine? I saw the Moon so close that it seemed like I could hear some strange sounds from there. The entire lunar surface is covered with craters. Don Alberto says it's from meteorites," Luis babbled excitedly.

"Yes, Don Alberto told me about this device. However, he hesitates to bring it to the university. The Holy Church categorically denies the theory that Don Alberto supports. Therefore, to avoid trouble, he conducts his research at home. He has often emphasized how pleased he is to have a student and like-minded person like you."

It was evident that the father was proud of his clever son.

"I am equally very happy to be a student of Don Alberto and grateful to him for his teachings. I think that astronomy has a great future ahead. There is still so much unexplored," the boy said dreamily.

A year later, Luis finished school and entered the university. Here, new knowledge and friends awaited him. From now on, he could study his favourite subjects as much as his heart desired. Luis spent hours in the university library, which was considered one of the best in the country. And, most importantly, he wasn't constantly supervised by monks as he had been at school. Luis studied the works of ancient scientists and the creativity of artists and poets. The library became a place where the boy spent almost all his free time.

That evening, Luis was a bit late, having stayed, as always, at the university library. His parents were waiting for him at home for dinner.

"Luis, please run to Señor Jose's bakery and buy some bread before they close," his mother asked. "I didn't have time today!"

Luis saw that girl immediately. For a moment, everything in the bakery disappeared for Luis except her. The boy even forgot why he had come. After coming to his senses, he bought the bread and went home, thinking only about the stranger on the way. The bakery owner was a good friend of the boy's family: Luis and his brothers had been buying pastries from Señor Jose since they were little. Since then the boy started going to the bakery regularly to see this girl more often. From Señor Jose, Luis learned that her name was Laura, had already talked to her several times and today he intended to ask her out.

"Hello, Laura!" he said to the girl behind the counter. "I'll have your fresh, crispy bread as always."

Laura smiled warmly: "Good day! Just bread, nothing else?"

"Well, not quite," Luis blushed.

He was ready to sink into the ground from embarrassment but was not going to back down from his plan.

"Pastries, too?" Laura asked, not understanding.

"My name is Luis," the boy barely managed to say, looking around. "Would you like to take a walk with me in the park this evening?"

His heart was pounding like crazy, and it seemed she could hear it. The girl was flustered, surprised and confused by the sudden proposal.

"Well, I don't know. I have so much work."

"I'll wait as long as it takes. Señor Jose won't mind, even if you leave earlier. He's known me since childhood."

"Really?" Laura raised her eyebrows in surprise. "He never mentioned your name to me."

"He's just afraid I'll steal his favourite," Luis replied, laughing in relief.

"Alright. I'll stop by home after work and come to the park."

"I'll be waiting for you by the waterfall. It's very beautiful there in the evening," Luis exhaled and was about to leave when he saw Señor Jose in the doorway.

"Ah, I see. I knew it," Jose thundered. "You finally got to my girl."

Luis wasn't at all afraid of the frowning bakery owner.

"Señor Jose. If anyone knows, it's you that I'd never hurt Laura. You and my father would twist me into pretzels if I did."

"I know, I know," Jose threw back and, approaching the young man, playfully tugged his forelock. "If I didn't know, you'd be out of here faster than a shot!"

Then, calmly, he said to Laura: "You can leave early today. Claudia will take care of everything. Don't worry."

Luis was so nervous that his legs trembled. He had never asked a girl out on a date before. Now, he stood watching the water slowly fall, scattering a spray all around, playing with the sun's rays. He got lost in thought for a while and didn't notice Laura approaching him.

"What are you thinking about?" she asked.

He started in surprise and looked around guiltily: "Sorry, I didn't notice you coming. I like observing celestial bodies. There's so much mystery and unexplored things out there. These sprays reminded me of distant planets. Shall we take a walk along the river?"

Luis took the girl by the hand, and they walked along the shore, where swans were leisurely swimming. The sun hung high above the horizon, and the park was quiet. It seemed that nature didn't want to disturb the two young hearts getting to know each other. Luis talked endlessly about his studies, his plans, and how he visits Don Alberto, where they observe the celestial bodies together. Laura turned out to be an attentive listener. She was interested in everything Luis talked about. However, she decided to warn him: "You must be careful with your passion. I was at our church service last Sunday. Father Ignacio said that the Holy Church strictly condemns those who contradict its teachings. I really like what you're telling me. It's truly fascinating but also dangerous."

"Yes, you're right. I mentioned this to Don Alberto. He agreed with me. Moreover, the Church has begun to increase pressure on those who do not follow its teachings. It was so hard for me to study at school under the monks' supervision. Here at the university, I feel like I've spread my wings. My lifetime won't be enough to read all the books and learn everything I want to."

"The sun has already set. It's time for me to go home. I have to work again in the morning," the girl said, noticeably saddened by their imminent parting.

"I'll walk you all the way home. May I?"

"Yes, of course!"

The girl didn't hide the fact that she liked the boy. They started meeting almost every day. Now, Luis divided all his free time between Laura and the library. Eventually, he introduced his girlfriend to his parents, who had long known about their son's infatuation from Señor Jose. The lovers didn't notice how weeks and months flew by since they first met. Luis continued his studies, and Laura worked. Señor Jose increasingly left the bakery in her care. He was already advanced in years and had no children of his own. So he loved this girl like his daughter.

Everything seemed cloudless, but that black day shattered Luis's life. He was running to Laura and was already approaching when he noticed something unusual. People were crowding near the bakery, looking at Luis suspiciously. He went inside — there on a chair sat Señor Jose, barely breathing. Next to him stood the assistant Claudia, holding a pitcher of water.

"What happened? Where is Laura?" Luis shouted.

"She... they took her..." Señor Jose could barely speak.

"She was accused of having connections with the devil," Claudia said grimly. "She is now in the local prison. My nephew, who works there, said there will be a trial soon."

"What connections with the devil?! Have they gone mad?!" the boy looked around the bakery in shock.

Claudia just shook her head silently. He didn't remember how he got home. His mind stubbornly refused to comprehend this absurd situation.

Broken and desperate, Luis sought help from anyone he could but encountered a stone wall of indifference and fear. His helplessness maddened him.

The trial would be held in a few days, so the young man consoled himself: "They will sort it out! Laura is innocent. This can't be happening. It's some kind of misunderstanding."

The courtroom was packed. Laura sat on the defendant's bench, silently staring ahead. It seemed that she no longer cared about any verdict. The days spent in prison had completely killed her faith in justice.

"So, esteemed Don Pedro, you claim that this person," the judge pointed to Laura. "Had an intimate relationship with the devil?"

Luis craned his neck to get a better look at the man the judge was addressing.

"Yes, Your Honour, I do," the man replied.

"Please, tell us, how did you find out about this?" the judge continued.

"That evening, I was walking in the park and saw this girl. Her behaviour seemed suspicious, so I decided to follow her. I hid behind a tree and started observing. Suddenly, from the shadow of the trees, a demon appeared, and the girl engaged in carnal pleasures with him. Then, the demon turned into a large black raven and flew into the sky. In her turn, she transformed into a hare and ran deep into the forest," the witness said in a trembling voice.

At these words, Luis clenched his fists painfully. Tears welled up in his eyes.

One question pounded in his head: "How can he lie like this?"

"This is a lie! He's lying! It's a slander!" Laura shouted, jumping up from the defendant's bench.

The judge ordered her to sit down and continued: "Thank you, esteemed Don Pedro! We have no further questions. The court is adjourned for a few days. Remove the defendant."

"It's not true! Your Honour, you can't judge me based on this man's testimony," Luis heard Laura's voice, but no one was listening to her anymore.

The guards grabbed the girl and dragged her away.

"Laura, I'm here!"

She turned around, and their eyes met. Two loving people couldn't understand what was happening around them. Their eyes were full of tears, and their faces were horrified.

"I'm not guilty of anything!" the girl managed to shout, and the next moment, the doors closed behind her.

"I believe you, Laura!" Luis shouted after her, but she could no longer hear him.

He walked down the street, and all the passersby seemed to be looking at him with condemnation. Luis went to the park where their first date had taken place to avoid people. The boy sat on the riverbank and held his head in his hands. He watched the water and the leaves slowly floating with the current. A swarm of questions buzzed in his head: "How can this be? Where is the justice? Who is this person who slandered Laura so much?"

"If only I could turn back time, I would save her, but time is relentless. It's like fallen leaves floating down the river; they will never return to the tree from which they fell," the boy thought bitterly.

"Tomorrow, they will burn her in the central square," said Claudia. "My nephew asked me to tell you."

She had come secretly so that no one would see her. Luis looked at her with eyes clouded by grief and said nothing. After glancing around, Claudia didn't linger and quickly disappeared into the darkness.

By morning, the city square was packed with people. After all, such an event was not an everyday occurrence! They were going to burn a real witch who had caused so much harm to the townspeople. In the centre of the square stood a tall pole surrounded by wooden logs. Luis stood in the middle of the crowd and waited. He listened to what people were saying around him, and horror enveloped him. They all wished for his girl's death and eagerly awaited the execution of the sentence.

"Yes, she made our cow's milk disappear! Do you remember Doña Luisa fell seriously ill and suddenly died? They say it's all because of this witch."

Listening to these conversations, Luis felt like he was in a madhouse. How could he live among these people? They were about to execute his girl in a terrible way. He knew better than anyone that she was innocent. What had happened to these people? Where did this cruelty come from?

Suddenly, a murmur rose over the square.

"They're bringing her, they're bringing her!" came the cries.

He turned in the direction of the shouts and saw the procession — two men in black were dragging Laura over the cobblestones. She couldn't walk on her own because of her injured legs. The sight stopped the boy's heart for a moment, and his blood seemed to freeze in his veins. Tears welled up in his eyes, and his fists clenched in anger. They brought the girl to the pole and tied her tightly with ropes. She weakly raised her head and looked at the crowd, staring at her with hostility.

"Laura, I love you!" Luis shouted through the crowd.

He saw she heard him and whispered something in response, but he couldn't hear it. In despair, the boy bit his lips until they bled.

"By the decision of the Holy Inquisition, Laura from the Lopez family has been declared a witch. She confessed to connections with the devil and crimes against the residents of our city. The sacred court sentences her to purification by burning at the stake," proclaimed a man in black and signalled to the men with torches standing nearby.

They approached from different sides and set the wood on fire. The flames slowly crept towards the doomed girl, who awaited her end in horror. Luis rushed towards her, but the guards pushed him back, and he fell to the ground. Staggering, he got up and, through the smoke of the bonfire where his beloved was dying in agony, saw two people on a balcony. They stood next to each other, calmly watching the execution. One of them, Luis, knew very well. It was the local bishop, Antonio.

Illustration by Artem Burlyk

Several months passed after that terrible day. Luis could not return to his usual state. He abandoned his studies and isolated himself. His parents tried their best to support him, but it was all in vain. The boy was wasting away before their eyes and did not respond to their efforts. One day, his older brothers Gabriel and Miguel, who had long served in the royal guard and thus rarely visited home, came to the house. When their father sent them a letter, they urgently came because they loved their younger brother and wanted to help him.

"Get ready, Luis. You can't bring her back, but you need to live on. We have a proposal for you," said the eldest, Gabriel. "We hope you'll like it."

"Our good friend serves as a commander of a cavalry regiment. He will gladly accept you at our request," added the middle brother, Miguel.

Luis looked at his parents and said: "Father, mother, forgive my weakness. It might be better if I leave. I always wanted to be with you in your old age. But I can't live in this city. The city where people rejoiced at Laura's death. I will always remember the expressions on their faces during the execution."

Luis approached his parents, hugged and kissed them.

Captain Rodriguez, the commander of the cavalry regiment, warmly welcomed Luis into his unit. He knew the young man's personal tragedy, as Luis's closest friends — his brothers — had told him about it. The captain was glad to help the boy through this challenging period and to learn a new profession as a royal dragoon. Luis, who had dreamed of being a teacher, had to significantly change his lifestyle and start learning the art of war. He had never ridden a horse before, and now he had to learn to care for them and understand their quirks and habits. Over time, he learned to ride quite skillfully and could manage a horse alone and in a mounted formation. Military science did not come easily to him, but the boy endured all the trials and learned to fight. Luis diligently trained to shoot an arquebus[63] and fence with a one-

---

[63] Arquebus — a handheld firearm. By design, a long matchlock muzzle-loading rifle.

handed sword, the espada ropera[64]. He knew that his skill with weapons would determine his survival on the battlefield. Additionally, he learned to kill to avenge his beloved's death. Though he never mentioned this to anyone, not even his brothers, whom he trusted as much as himself.

Horses for the royal dragoons were supplied by horse farms from the kingdom and other countries. This was quite expensive, as the dragoons paid for these purchases themselves. Sometimes, they hired a trading ship for trips overseas to places where wild mustangs lived. These were beautiful and freedom-loving animals. They were difficult to catch and even harder to tame. Twice, Luis went overseas hunting and twice returned empty-handed. But this time, fortune smiled upon him. He managed to lasso a young filly. The captured horses were loaded onto the ship, and they set off. On the way home, Luis tried to approach his captive, but she neighed wildly and jumped, not allowing him to come near.

"Alright, alright. Don't worry. I won't hurt you," Luis said to her and walked away.

Upon arrival at the regiment's location, the captured horses were sent to the stable. Luis visited the filly every day to admire and talk to her. The first few days, she barely ate and became very emaciated.

"You need to eat. Please," he begged his captive, but she only snorted and shook her head.

But eventually, the time came when the filly allowed Luis to approach her and even stroke her neck. That day, he was on cloud nine.

"I'll name you Tamira! Yes, Tamira. My girl. You are so beautiful. I will never hurt you. I promise," he whispered in her ear.

Luis kept his promise. Until her last day, the filly never heard a harsh word from him. His loyal companion repaid him with devotion and tireless work. There was no better friend to him than she. More than once, Tamira saved

---

[64] Espada ropera — a one-handed sword used in the 15th - 17th centuries, often associated with Spanish fencing styles.

Luis's life on the battlefield, carrying him away from enemy fire on her swift legs. For this, he treasured her like the apple of his eye, having no one closer than his former captive. Luis often talked to the mare, and it seemed to him that she understood every single word. Since Laura's death, the boy had shut himself off and let no one into his soul. Tamira became the only friend with whom he shared his pain or joy. He also began having dreams he couldn't explain. Luis flew somewhere far away in these dreams, and upon waking in the morning, he didn't understand what had happened to him during these nocturnal journeys. Later, he would experience what he saw in his dreams, which amazed and troubled him. In these visions, Tamira played a special role. Therefore, Luis treated her uniquely, as if she were a human. This did not go unnoticed by his comrades.

"Are you brushing your favourite again?" he heard the voice of his friend Carlos. "She is a beauty."

"Well, of course. Such beauty needs proper care," Luis replied, continuing to brush Tamira's mane.

"This breed is very hardy and spirited. How did you manage to tame her?" Carlos asked.

"To be honest, it wasn't easy, but you know that love can work wonders. You didn't tame your Bianca right away, either. She was just as spirited," Luis said with a laugh.

"Yes, yes. It wasn't easy at all. I barely caught her back then, and let me tell you, there's no better friend to find. I took Bianca's freedom, and she saved my life in battle. It's strange if you ask me. But I see you talk to yours more than to any human. It seems she means more to you than just an ordinary warhorse."

"That's right, my friend," Luis replied, growing sombre.

He recalled a recent dream where he died in battle alongside his enemies. Tamira died with him, and the memory made his heart clench.

Autumn was approaching, and Luis finally decided to leave and do what he had dreamed of for many years. No one knew about his plans; only Tamira knew his intentions.

"Wait for me here, alright? I can't take you with me. It's too risky. Carlos will look after you," he whispered in the mare's ear, stroking her neck.

Tamira seemed to understand what he was saying and nodded. If she were human, she would have found the words to reply to her friend. But as it was, she could only silently agree to his request.

Claudia was walking home, lost in her thoughts. She had a lot of work today. Since Don Jose was no longer around, all the work fell on her shoulders. She had to hire workers to keep the bakery running.

"Claudia!" someone called softly from the darkness.

She flinched in surprise.

"Who's there?" she asked cautiously.

"It's me, Luis. I need to talk to your nephew," he said.

"Luis, you've changed so much over the years. You're unrecognisable. You haven't been home since..." she trailed off, understanding the boy's pain.

The relationship between the lovers had unfolded before her eyes, and Claudia, who had no children of her own, was very happy about it. Now, the only one left to her was her nephew Hernan, the son of her prematurely deceased sister.

"You understand: it's hard for me to return to this city. My parents sometimes visit me, but I can't come to them. It still hurts," Luis said, then added. "Does your nephew still work at the city prison?"

"Yes, he does. Why do you ask?"

"I need to meet with him, but it must be a secret. Even my parents don't know I'm in the city. Please don't ask why I need this meeting. Can I trust you?"

"Of course, you can rely on me. I won't ask anything. If you have nowhere to stay, you can stay with me. I'm at work most of the time anyway."

"No, it's alright. Tell Hernan I'll be waiting for him tomorrow after sunset outside the city gates," Luis said and disappeared into the darkness.

"So, two of them tortured her while Bishop Antonio watched?"

Luis and Hernan had been walking in the darkness of the city park for half an hour.

"Yes, it was Jorge and Umberto. Even the prison warden is afraid of those brutes," said Hernan.

"Do you know where they live?" Luis asked, boiling with rage.

"Yes, of course," Hernan explained in detail where they lived and then added. "They also like to wet their throats with freshly brewed ale at the local tavern."

"Is Don Pedro in the city? What's he doing?"

"That scoundrel who slandered Laura is now the lord mayor. I never believed his words from the beginning," Hernan said, lowering his gaze.

"Alright, I know his address. What about our bishop? Does he still live at the monastery?" Luis asked more calmly.

"Yes, he lives there. He's now an archbishop. They say he will soon go to the capital. A high position awaits him there."

Luis smiled maliciously and said firmly: "No, he won't go."

"There are some crazy rumours around the monastery, but you understand we can't talk about that in these conditions?"

"I understand everything, my friend. Thank you for your help. Do I need to remind you that you haven't seen me?" Luis asked.

Hernan nodded silently in agreement and disappeared into the darkness of the park.

Two men in black sat in the tavern, sipping ale. The few patrons tried to keep their distance from them. These were Jorge and Umberto, professional executioners.

"You worked well today," one said with a smile.

"Are you talking about that fool who screamed like a pig when I stretched him on the rack?" the other giggled, baring his rotten teeth.

"Yes. He should have confessed everything right away. Our archbishop knows how to get the truth."

"Yeah, but he only achieves it with our help."

Both laughed loudly, making the patrons shudder. The locals avoided talking to the executioners, knowing what they did, which filled them with horror and disgust. The executioners behaved arrogantly, knowing they had the support of the all-powerful Archbishop Antonio. They drank and laughed, not noticing the man in the black hood sitting in the corner, watching them closely. Quite drunk, they staggered home, supporting each other. Waiting until the two finally stepped outside, the unknown man slowly followed them. The executioners stumbled through dark alleys, shouting incoherently when suddenly a male figure loomed before them. They stared at the stranger in surprise.

"What do you want, poor fellow?" one of them slurred.

"I want nothing. I bring greetings from Laura. Remember that witch? You broke her legs before burning her at the stake."

"Who... are you?" the other stammered with a drunken tongue.

"I am your death, bastards!" the man hissed and, drawing a gleaming falcata[65] from under his cloak, slit both their throats with one swift stroke.

Don Pedro was hurrying home after the service. He was in an excellent mood. After all, the local beauty was coming over this evening to discuss opening an art gallery. During the service, he had claimed to be busy and invited her to talk at his home, eagerly imagining how he would untie her corset and let his hands roam her ample bosom. These thoughts made his

---

[65] Falcata — a sickle-shaped sword with an inwardly curved, mostly single-edged blade. Used in ancient Iberia.

head spin. Don Pedro rushed upstairs and took out his key, but the lock was already unlocked.

"Probably forgot to lock it in the morning," he thought and went inside.

He was in such high spirits that he didn't notice the man standing in the shadows behind the wardrobe. Don Pedro paced the living room, humming something under his breath, when he suddenly heard the latch on the door click. Since he was alone in the evenings, having dismissed the servants, he flinched at the unexpected sound and looked around. His heart clenched with fear. In front of him stood a stranger in a black cloak, his face hidden in the hood's shadow.

"Who are you?" Don Pedro stammered in terror.

"So, you say you saw her engaging in carnal pleasures with the devil?" the stranger said, ignoring the question.

"Who... who are you?"

"You say she then turned into a hare?"

Don Pedro's face momentarily took on a thoughtful expression as if recalling something long forgotten. Suddenly, that expression turned to horror.

"You misunderstood me. I tried to explain everything at the trial."

"I was at that trial and saw and heard everything. You, scum, sent an innocent girl, my fiancée, to her death, and now you will die."

"No, I beg you, have mercy," Don Pedro said, falling to his knees and reaching out his hands to the stranger.

The man in the cloak took a step forward and, with all his might, plunged a stiletto[66] into the villain's eye.

"Now you will never see anything again, bastard," the man said, turning and heading for the exit.

The evening service went smoothly. Archbishop Antonio was pleased with himself: his sermon had the desired effect on the congregation. They,

---

[66] Stiletto — a slender, pointed dagger.

as always, looked at him with fear and reverence the way he liked it the most. Archbishop Antonio could not tolerate any disobedience; everything had to be exactly as he wished. But now he was no longer thinking about his flock. The young chorister who had recently joined the church choir was disturbing his peace. The archbishop even faltered for a moment during his sermon, seeing the boy's face with plump lips, on which the down of future moustaches was already appearing. Remembering this, the archbishop smiled lustfully and quickened his pace.

"Leonardo!" he called to the monk who served as his secretary. "Bring me that new chorister. The fair-haired boy. I believe his name is Romero."

"Yes, Your Excellency. His name is Romero. I will call him right away," the monk replied, bowing and going to the exit.

The archbishop removed his mitre[67], placed it on the shelf, hung his mantelletta[68] in the closet and remained in his cassock[69]. He lit a candle and placed it on the table. The flame drew his attention, and the archbishop gazed at the light, entranced. Then, he seemed to hear a desperate scream. It was the scream of those burned at the stake. The archbishop shuddered, looked around and then fixed his eyes again on the flame, which burned steadily, sending a thin wisp of smoke toward the ceiling. Suddenly, the flame flickered from a draft. Someone had opened the door to the room. Without turning around, the archbishop asked: "Is that you, my boy?"

Not hearing an answer, he looked back in bewilderment. In front of him stood an unknown man in monastic garb, his face hidden in the hood's shadow.

"Who are you?" the archbishop asked sternly. "I see you for the first time. What is your business? My audience hours are over."

"You will make time for me," the man said and stepped toward the archbishop.

---

[67] Mitre — a ceremonial headdress of bishops and certain abbots in traditional Christianity.
[68] Mantelletta — a sleeveless vest-like ecclesiastical garment worn over the cassock.
[69] Cassock — a full-length garment of a single colour worn by certain Christian clergy.

"What is happening? Who are you? How did the guards let you in?" the archbishop shouted, looking around.

"Don't shout. The guards won't help you, and you won't see the boy, you lecher," the man said as calmly as possible, taking another step forward.

The archbishop stepped back and fell into the chair behind him. He gripped the armrests so tightly that his fingers turned white.

"Did you enjoy watching from the balcony as my fiancée died at the stake? The one you tortured with your accomplices? Do you come about to know what recently happened to them? Maybe they drank so much that the ale no longer went down their throats. Have you heard about your lord mayor? Such a tragic suicide. It's a wonder he managed to impale his eye on a stiletto," the man whispered menacingly, slowly approaching the archbishop.

"I'm not guilty of anything. The court made the decision, not me," the archbishop shrieked, his voice dry with fear.

"Of course, you're not guilty. Just like in the deaths of other townsfolk, you are tortured and forced to confess to fabricated crimes. You're filth that came straight from hell. An innocent sheep who preaches the Word of God by day and corrupts young boys by night. But every sheep has its wolf, and now you will die a terrible death."

Illustration by Artem Burlyk

The archbishop tried to get up from the chair but lost consciousness from a heavy blow to the head. The man approached, took a rope from his cloak and tightly tied the unconscious body to the chair. He uncorked a leather burdjuk[70] and poured oil, meant for city lanterns, over the bound man. After waiting for the oil to soak into the archbishop's clothing, he locked the door from the inside. Then, he securely fastened one end of the rope to a hook and threw the other end out of the open window. Everything was ready for the execution. The man walked to the table and picked up the burning candle. He stood silently in front of the bound archbishop for a moment, then brought the flame to the unconscious man, who burst into flames like gunpowder. The archbishop awoke in agony and began to scream inhumanly. The man, descending into the garden via the rope, calmly walked out of the city, never to return. He had fulfilled a dream he had harbored for many years. It seemed his soul should have found peace, but unfortunately, he felt no relief. The man understood that the deaths of the villains would not bring back his beloved. The only consolation was that the killed would no longer harm anyone.

The wind carried a rumble from the enemy's side. They were preparing for battle. Luis looked around and saw the lined ranks of the royal cavalry. They were to strike first, followed by the infantry. The dragoons were visibly nervous, waiting for the signal to attack. Suddenly, a trumpet sounded, and a flag was raised over the cavalry line, the signal to charge. The cavalry slowly moved forward, forming into battle formation. The cavalry broke into a gallop from a steady pace, and the entire mass surged forward, spears extended ahead. Luis peered into the enemy ranks, imagining himself breaking into their midst and slashing at the foe. A few dozen meters from the enemy line, he noticed some movement. The enemy's front row fell back a few steps, revealing the barrels of cannons aimed at the charging cavalry. Luis horrifiedly realised the enemy's plan, but it was too late. A volley rang out, enveloping the enemy lines

[70] Burdjuk — a leather bag designed to store liquids.

in cannon smoke, and the first ranks of cavalry were mowed down by fire. The battle formation was broken, but the cavalry still pressed forward. Another volley sounded, then another. The field was covered with the dead and dying, both men and horses. The screams of the wounded and dying echoed from all sides. But neither Luis nor his loyal companion Tamira heard them anymore. Only a flock of black crows circled the battlefield, waiting for their feast.

The Wolf

The wolf knew he could no longer escape the pursuit. Human voices and dog barking were approaching from all sides. They were closing in on him. The wolf ran into a sunlit forest clearing and looked around. There was no point in running any further. Ahead stood a tall, rocky mountain, too steep to climb. It was impossible to go around it, and the other paths were blocked. His pursuers knew their job well, having cornered the fugitive. The wolf ran to a small hill and crouched. His whole life flashed before his eyes from the moment of his birth. He remembered his parents, who gave him life. His brothers and sisters, with whom he grew up. His she-wolf, who had been a faithful companion until her death. His little pups, who never had the chance to grow up. The wolf's heart pounded with rage, and he bared his teeth. The enemies had taken everything from him, and now it was time to give them one last fight. Well, the humans would pay dearly for his life. The wolf would avenge all the wrongs they had done to him. After once more surveying the ambush, the fugitive was satisfied. He would meet them here. The narrow passage left no room for the pursuers to manoeuvre. The wolf pressed himself to the ground and began to peer into the forest thicket.

A few weeks had passed since the wolf pup was born. Those weeks went by in complete silence and darkness. Finally, its hearing developed, and its eyes opened. The pup curiously and cautiously observed the other wolf pups wriggling alongside it in the den. Its mother, the she-wolf, who was always nearby and sweetly smelled of milk, especially caught its attention.

The pup grew quickly, causing trouble for his parents, brothers and sisters. The mother had the most challenging time feeding the little ones from morning until evening. Every time they gathered to eat, the pups would jostle fiercely for her teats. Only when they had had their milk fill and fell asleep at the bottom of the den did the she-wolf have time to rest. Then, she would go outside to nourish herself. The den was located near a mountain stream, and the she-wolf would greedily drink the cold water to quench her thirst.

The faithful male wolf was always nearby, except when he went out to hunt for food. The forests where the pack lived teemed with wildlife, so obtaining food was not a problem for an experienced hunter like the family's father. The pup noticeably differed from the pack's grey members in its fur colour. Its black coat shone in the sun like coal, making him almost invisible at night.

The pack's way of life was strict: every wolf had its role. The father, the pack leader, strictly maintained order. Young and strong wolves served as fighters and guards. The old and sick stayed apart, protected and fed by the pack. Last year's young ones looked after the pups born this year. Only the youngest had no responsibilities, playing from morning till evening.

The little wolf was growing and becoming increasingly independent. He was curious about everything around him, whether it was worms living in a rotten tree or birds chirping in the treetops. Squirrels living in a tall tree nearby particularly caught his attention. He would often invite them to play with his whining, but they were afraid to come down to the ground. However, the butterflies, which were incredibly numerous in the forest, were his favourite plaything. The pup could spend hours watching and chasing them.

The mother wolf always stayed nearby, carefully watching over the pups. The forest, as wonderful and mysterious as it was, also concealed dangers. At any moment, the she-wolf could signal the pups to gather together and follow her back to the den. She would carry the most disobedient one in her jaws. The pup stood out not only because of his fur colour. From a young age, he began to show traits of a true leader. His brothers and sisters silently acknowledged his dominance and always listened to him. He was a born hunter: he learned faster than anyone else when his father took the pups hunting. Skills like hiding, sneaking silently, recognizing smells or sounds and, most importantly, suddenly attacking the prey. He learned all of this from his father. Learning was easy, and sometimes it seemed to him that he had already hunted before.

The pup honed his skills daily by tracking small animals in the forest. Adult wolves always hunted as a pack, each with a specific role, but the little one was not yet ready for this. He was growing up and gradually becoming a young, strong wolf, a worthy pack member.

Two harsh winters were behind them, which the wolves survived without much trouble. Plenty of deer and roe deer were around, so the pack did not suffer from hunger. Now, the young wolves began to take their places in the hierarchy, looking after the pups born last year.

The young wolf was fascinated by watching the pups play among themselves and gain the experience necessary for life in the pack. He often liked to be alone with nature. One day, while running around the outskirts, he came across a herd of horses grazing in the steppe beyond the forest. He liked these graceful and strong animals. Therefore, he did not come close to avoid scaring them.

One night, he had a strange dream that felt very real. The wolf even woke up and stood on his paws, looking around. In that dream, he came, as usual, to the edge of the forest to watch the horses. Soon, he noticed a young black filly playing not far from the herd. As his father had taught him, the wolf approached from the downwind side to not frighten the stranger. Soon, she was joined by a black raven. The filly raced with the raven across the steppe. Then the raven perched on her back, and she slowly carried him. The wolf also wanted to run with them but understood it was impossible. He was so captivated by the young filly that he came out of his hiding place, and she saw him. They met eyes and stood still momentarily, looking at each other. Then, the young horse turned and slowly ran to the rest of the horses grazing in the valley.

When the wolf woke up, he wandered around disappointedly, looking hopefully at the surrounding area. He felt that this dream was a reality he had once lived.

Illustration by Artem Burlyk

The pack he belonged to was not the only one in that area. They had their territory, which they fiercely guarded against enemies. The wolf knew that another pack lived beyond the mountains. Everyone strictly adhered to their territories, never crossing the borders. During difficult times, the wolves would unite into one large pack to hunt big game. This time, members of both clans gathered to hunt the giant bison, which passed through these areas twice a year. The wolves always took advantage of this opportunity to hunt this beast, but a bison is neither a roe deer nor a deer. It is a strong and resilient animal that cannot be hunted by just one pack. So the wolves gathered together and set off for the hillside, where they observed the massive bison herd.

After a long observation, the leader separated from the rest of the wolves and went around the animals peacefully grazing in the valley. Two more strong and agile wolves ran after him. They were to set up an ambush in the valley, where the bison would be driven by the wolves remaining on the hill. Some time passed, and the wolves, as if on cue, set off towards the herd. At first, they moved calmly, hugging the ground. Then, fanning out into a semicircle, they started running and, no longer hiding, rushed headlong, trying to steer these giants into the valley where the ambush awaited them. Seeing the rapidly approaching wolves, the bison were startled and began to flee in the opposite direction, towards their doom. The chase lasted several minutes. The wolves had already chosen a few bison as their prey, which had strayed from the herd and began to separate them from the rest of their companions. Next to the wolf was a young she-wolf from the other clan, chasing one of the bison. The distance between her and the prey was gradually decreasing. They were close to the ambush site when suddenly one of the bison running with the main herd sharply turned and charged at the she-wolf. She saw the danger too late as it rapidly approached. This giant, the prairie king, would have crushed the she-wolf in another moment. Suddenly, she felt rather than saw a shadow flash in the air. The bison slowed and spun around on the spot. Clinging tightly to its neck with his teeth was the black wolf. To help her rescuer, the she-wolf ran and bit into the giant's neck from the other side. After a few minutes of struggle, the bison, weakened from blood loss, fell to its knees and then collapsed on its side. The wolves finally let go and jumped away from the dying beast.

Their eyes met, and it seemed as if everything around them had disappeared momentarily. There was no chase, no thunderous hooves of the massive bison, no growling of wolves. There was nothing and no one — just Him and Her.

The joint hunt was successful. The wolves had brought down several bison and were enjoying the fresh meat. That day, the she-wolf did not return home with her pack. She followed the one who had saved her life because she felt her place was now beside this strong black wolf.

The pack accepted the new member cautiously but without aggression. Beside her was a wolf with a certain authority, and no one dared to stand in his way. Moreover, his father, the powerful old pack leader, approved his son's choice.

Several months passed in the pack. The she-wolf was now regarded as one of their own. The wolf never left her alone for a moment. They were always together. After a long and snowy winter, spring arrived. The snow began to melt. Mountain streams gurgled, and flowers reached up to the sun. Buds swelled on the trees, and bird songs came from all directions. Life, dormant during the winter, began to stir again. Looking at his mate, the wolf realised he would soon become a father. It was time to leave the pack because only his mother had the right to bear offspring for the clan. One morning, they bid farewell to all the members of the large family and set off. The couple did not know where they were going. The she-wolf ran obediently behind her wolf into the unknown. This did not frighten her because she knew no one was more loyal than her chosen one in the world.

Soon, they found a good place for a den at the foot of an old oak tree growing on the slope of a ravine. The tree had leaned over time, exposing its roots and forming a spacious burrow. The entrance was concealed by thick brush, making it an ideal spot for their future litter.

Days and weeks of their new life stretched out. The wolves hunted together and enjoyed playing in the forest glade, basking in the sun. The couple gradually explored their new territory in search of food. There was plenty, so they didn't worry about the future. The only thing that concerned them was the presence of humans. At the edge of the forest stood a solitary cabin. However, the wolves tried to avoid it, sensing a certain danger that these two-legged creatures carried.

In a short time, the den became crowded. The she-wolf had given birth to six pups, filling their home with whimpering. Now, the wolf had to go hunting alone. He needed to care for the she-wolf, who fed the pups almost around the clock. He rarely entered the den now, sleeping outside to guard the entrance. When the pups slept, the she-wolf would come out to stretch her muscles, eat and drink from the stream that flowed from the ground near their home. By the end of summer, the young wolf family had grown stronger and began to leave the den to explore the area. At first, the pups were frightened by the new sounds coming from the forest, but over time, they became bolder and ran around the den energetically. The mother always watched over them, ready to hide the children under the oak roots in case of danger. Watching the pups, the wolf remembered his childhood and the pack where he grew up. He was attentive and gentle with his extended family, and it seemed that this would last forever.

"Master! Are you home?" a voice called from outside.

A young man with a rifle in his hand stepped out onto the cabin's porch. Six horsemen were riding around the yard.

"Greetings! What brings you here?" he asked the visitors.

"Our hunters have spotted a wolf family that has recently appeared near the ranch," replied the eldest of them. "So we need to kill them because they could be a threat to our livestock."

"But they haven't come near our land," the man replied.

"Well, it's only a matter of time. The cold will come, and they'll approach our homes. Besides, they've recently had pups. A large family always needs a lot of meat," said another of the horsemen.

"We already know where their den is. We've tracked them. So it won't be difficult to finish them off in one go," added the eldest.

The man thought for a moment and didn't respond immediately. He hunted to obtain fresh meat out of necessity, but he didn't enjoy killing animals just for the sake of it. However, he understood that the visitors were right. Having wolves nearby posed a certain danger to his farm. Also, his daughter often stayed home alone.

"Daddy, who is it?" a voice came from inside the cabin.

The man turned and said: "It's our neighbours, dear. Don't worry. I need to go away for a while. You'll stay home alone, okay? Just don't go far."

"Okay, daddy. I'll wait for you," the girl said, disappearing back into the house.

A few years ago, he settled on this land with his wife. They built a spacious house, cleared a field, and planted corn. Recently, they began raising livestock. The farm, which was rapidly growing and becoming profitable, now had several dozen sheep. But last year, his wife suddenly fell ill with an unknown disease and soon passed away.

Since then, the man had been running the farm and raising his daughter alone, who had recently turned ten. He loved her with an endless love, ready to give his life for her without hesitation. The little girl reminded him of his beloved wife, who had left this world so untimely. The man had no relatives, so his daughter was the only close person he had in the whole world.

That day, the wolf family woke up, as always, with the first rays of the sun rising over the forest-covered mountain peaks. The wolf pups scattered around the den and began playing with each other. The wolf approached the she-wolf, rubbing his nose against her neck. She turned to him and, closing her eyes, gently rubbed her head against him. The wolf needed to go hunting to feed his growing family, which was becoming increasingly demanding. This time, he had to run a lot. It seemed as if the animals had conspired and hidden from him. Still, eventually, the wolf caught a muskrat that had carelessly climbed onto the riverbank and hurriedly carried it back to his waiting family. As he approached the den, the wolf felt a sense of unease. Birds were flying above the trees, squawking loudly. He dropped his catch and rushed headlong into the forest. Usually, when he returned from hunting, a crowd of wolf pups would run to greet him. This time, he was met with silence. At the entrance to the den lay the she-wolf and all the pups. Blood no longer oozed from their bodies; it had dried and now gleamed in the sun with a crimson sheen. The wolf approached, sniffed the bodies, and let out a howl of agony, a pain tearing from deep within.

"Daaaaddy! I'm scared. Daddy!" the little girl walked through the forest, crying.

So many times, her father had left her alone at home with strict instructions not to wander far, and she had never disobeyed. But this time, she got caught up chasing a bright butterfly and didn't notice how far she had gone into the forest. At first, she didn't panic and confidently headed in the direction she thought would lead her home. After a while, she realised she had taken the wrong path and decided to turn back. Eventually, it became clear she was completely lost. The evening was inevitably approaching. The darkness and sounds of the forest made her unbearably scared. The girl sat down at the base of a large tree, hugged her knees and cried.

The wolf heard the child's crying from a distance and decided to get closer. Since his family had been killed, he hadn't left his territory, seeking revenge and looking for an opportunity to make humans pay for the pain they caused. But the wolf was cautious, knowing the cries could also be a trap. He carefully went through the underbrush towards the source of the sobbing. After a few minutes, he saw the girl sitting under the tree. The wolf silently stepped into the clearing and took a few steps toward the child. The girl looked up and screamed in fear, covering her eyes with hands. The wolf came even closer. He sniffed the air and bared his teeth as he recognised a familiar scent he had remembered for the rest of his life. He had first smelled it near the lifeless bodies of the she-wolf and the pups. Now, the killer's child sat before him, trembling with fear. The wolf took a step forward, ready to avenge their death swiftly.

The wolf's menacing advance halted as he sensed the girl's vulnerability. Despite his grief and anger, something inside him hesitated. He remembered his pups, their playfulness and innocence. The girl's sobs reminded him of the helplessness of his own lost family. The rage began to wane, replaced by a complex mixture of emotions.

Instead of attacking, the wolf circled the girl cautiously, studying her. She stood frozen, too terrified to move. Now just inches away, the wolf sniffed her again, trying to make sense of this human child. Her scent was saturated with fear but also carried a faint trace of the same tenderness he remembered from his pups.

Suddenly, the girl pulled her hands away from her tearful eyes and, looking into the wolf's eyes, stammered: "You won't kill me, right?"

The wolf stopped and carefully looked at the defenceless and weak human child. An unfamiliar feeling stirred within his wounded soul. Without taking his eyes off the girl, he began to realise that he didn't have the heart to kill a vulnerable child. Only those beasts who killed his family were capable of such a thing. Remembering his pups, he growled furiously, causing the lost girl to cover her eyes with her hands again. The wolf approached and lay down beside her. The girl sat there for a while, holding her breath, afraid to take her hands away from her face. But eventually, she couldn't resist and peeked through her fingers at the beast lying peacefully at her feet. Her fear subsided slightly, replaced by curiosity and confusion. She cautiously reached out a hand, trembling but brave. The wolf, sensing no threat, allowed her to touch his fur.

They slept together until morning. The girl snuggled closer to the wolf in her sleep to keep warm from the night chill. When they woke up, the sun was already breaking through the treetops. The wolf stood up, looked at the sleepy girl, and slowly walked across the clearing. After a few steps, he stopped, turned, and silently looked at the girl.

"Do you want me to follow you?" asked the small one as she got up.

As if understanding her words, he turned and silently continued. The girl slowly trailed after him. He walked without haste, occasionally turning to make sure she wasn't lagging behind. They had already covered a considerable distance when the outline of a cabin appeared between the trees.

The wolf emerged from the forest thicket and stopped. On the porch sat the man with a rifle. He had his head in his hands and wasn't moving. Suddenly, feeling someone's presence, he lifted his head and saw the black wolf standing openly at the edge of the forest, just a few meters away. The man jumped to his feet, aiming the rifle at the beast. At that moment, he heard a familiar voice: "Daddy, don't shoot! He saved my life!"

Illustration by Artem Burlyk

He flinched and lowered the rifle. His daughter ran out from behind the wolf.

"Daddy, my dear! I'm sorry I disobeyed you and got lost. I will never do it again. This wolf kept me warm all night so I wouldn't freeze, and he brought me back to you. Don't kill him," the girl cried, choking on her tears.

The man threw the rifle to the ground and rushed to meet his daughter. For a moment, they stood silently, hugging each other and barely breathing. Then, the father lifted his head and looked at the wolf, still standing at the forest's edge. Man and beast locked eyes and stood frozen. The man's gaze met the wolf's, whose eyes seemed almost human and filled with reproach. The realisation of what had happened shook the man to his core. He groaned and fell to his knees, clutching his head in his hands. When he looked up, the wolf was gone. The man stood still, holding his daughter's hand tightly, staring into the dark forest. Soon, a long wolf howl echoed from within the trees.

The enemies were close. He could hear the branches of bushes and trees breaking as the pursuers advanced. The wolf tensed and prepared to leap. Suddenly, a dog emerged from the bushes, charging straight at him. With a leap, the red dog was left lifeless on the ground. The wolf rushed forward, encountering another dog, which also fell motionless with a severed throat. At that moment, another dog lunged at him, meeting the same fate. After dealing with the dogs, the wolf dashed into the thicket and lay in wait.

Soon, two pursuers emerged from the bushes, calling for their dogs. The wolf let them get closer before attacking. One of the pursuers barely had time to turn before the wolf's jaws clamped onto his throat. The man fell dead, not even raising his rifle. The other pursuer, seeing this, immediately fired at the wolf. The bullet grazed his shoulder but did not stop him. He leapt and bit into the man, who desperately tried to fend off the wolf's teeth with his hands. After overcoming the enemy, the wolf jumped back and looked around.

Suddenly, a shot rang out from behind the bushes. The wolf was thrown back. He managed to get up, but another shot brought him down for good.

The wolf was still breathing when several armed men stepped into the clearing. They stood silently, afraid to approach the formidable beast who had fought so fiercely for his life. The wolf lifted his head and, seeing two ravens slowly circling in the sky, closed his eyes. The next moment, he was already flying after the ravens into oblivion.

Raivo

Father Raivo noticed the flower kiosk from afar. He walked leisurely towards it and saw a young girl arranging flowers in vases. He admired the scene for a few minutes: a sunny day, bright flowers with butterflies fluttering around and the young girl who reminded him so much of his first and only love. Then Father Raivo remembered why he had come, and a sad expression crossed his face.

"Louisa?" he called softly.

She startled and looked up.

"Yes, it's me. What do you need, Father? Do you need flowers?"

Father Raivo silently approached and handed her a folded piece of paper.

"May the Lord accept his soul," he said, then turned and walked towards the park.

"So you say you will always love me?" Martha playfully asked the young man, sliding her hand under his shirt.

"Yes, always. Do you doubt it?" Raivo replied, pulling her closer and starting to kiss her gently.

"Then prove it," she whispered passionately, responding to his caresses.

Martha was a few years older than him, but this didn't bother Raivo at all. She was his first woman, who opened the door to adult life for the young man. He was infatuated with her, living from one meeting to the next. She liked him too. Martha was attracted to his youthful zest for life and emotionality. She had been with enough men to compare them to this young and naive boy. Yes, those men were wealthy, but they lacked the wild energy radiating from Raivo. That's why sex with him was simply insane. At the beginning of their relationship, he seemed a bit clumsy, but he learned quickly. Now, as an experienced woman, she increasingly asked him for a break to calm her racing heart.

Illustration by Artem Burlyk

The only thing that overshadowed their meetings was the secrecy. In a small town, rumours spread quickly, and Martha didn't want anyone to find out about her relationship with the young man. She knew all too well the trouble that gossip could cause. Raivo, on the other hand, insisted that their relationship should be as open as possible. Martha was his first love, and he couldn't imagine his life without her. Seeing his youthful fervour, Martha sadly understood that they had no future. Sooner or later, he would grow up and change his outlook on life. There were so many young and beautiful girls around who could be a worthy match for him. Besides, Martha had an illegitimate daughter who lived with her grandmother in a small fishing village by the sea. She hadn't told anyone about the child and kept it a deep secret, fearing societal judgment. The strict religious traditions did not recognise extramarital relationships. Martha had long intended to talk to him about the child, but she forgot everything in his arms. It was beyond her control. Sometimes, she felt as if the devil himself was controlling their feelings. With Raivo, no one else in the world existed for her. Martha constantly and unbearably desired his body. Just thinking about him ignited a burning flame, and a sweet languor spread in her lower abdomen.

There was a knock at the door. Martha looked at the wall clock in surprise. Raivo was supposed to come later. Not understanding what was happening, she went to the door and turned the key in the lock. Two unfamiliar men stood silently in front of her.

"Are you looking for someone?" she asked.

Without a word, they pushed her aside, entered the house and locked the door behind them. Martha pressed against the wall in fear.

"Alright, no panic. If you behave, nothing will happen to you," said one of the men.

"What do you want from me?" she whispered.

"Recently, our younger brother has been visiting you very frequently. At first, we thought it was just a physiological need and didn't pay much attention, but a few days ago, he confessed to us that he wants to marry you. Listen, don't ruin the boy's life. He has a great future ahead of him. Our family will never accept this decision. So, it would be best for both of you if you just disappeared," the second man said calmly.

"We also think that your daughter misses her mother. How old is Louisa now?" the first man winked, indicating that the guests were well-prepared for their visit.

"Louisa will be five soon," the woman whispered and sat on a chair.

"Girls at that age need their mother's attention to avoid making mistakes later. The Holy Church teaches this. You have an hour to pack your things. We will take you to your mother. You can leave a letter for Raivo at the door, but no hints about future meetings. Say goodbye once and for all without explanations. That's it, don't waste time," the second man said sharply.

Raivo walked down the dark street, quietly humming to himself. He was already beside his beloved in his thoughts, imagining how he would press Martha close and slowly undress her. Her voice aroused him, and her moans of pleasure lifted him to the sky. He felt like a man with unlimited power over his beloved woman in such moments. Today, Raivo was determined to talk to her about their future together because these secret meetings had started to irritate him. He didn't understand why she was hiding their relationship from others. Last week, Raivo had told his older brothers that he wanted to marry Martha. It seemed to him then that they understood his decision and promised their support.

Raivo grew cautious as he approached Martha's house. Usually, he was greeted by the light of a candle shining through the lace curtains. This time, however, the windows were dark. Not understanding anything, the young man approached the door and reached for the handle. Suddenly, he noticed a piece of paper sticking out of the crack. Pulling out the note, he unfolded it but couldn't make out the letters in the dark. So, he walked over to the streetlamp and began to read. From the very first lines, his head started to spin.

"My dear boy! It is hard for me to say this, but the time has come for us to part ways. I have tried to explain everything to you for a long time, but emotions always got in the way. Believe me, this will be better for both of us. You will always leave the brightest and most pleasant memories in my heart. I want you to remember my tenderness and love for you. Please, do not look for me. Farewell. Yours, Martha."

Raivo read the letter several times. Tears blurred his vision, and he kept staring at the piece of paper, unable to understand what had occurred. Everything happened so suddenly, like a lightning bolt from a clear sky. The young man walked home through the dark streets, not seeing the road. All his hopes and dreams dissolved in an instant.

A few weeks passed, during which Raivo tried to discover something about Martha's mysterious disappearance, but all was in vain. She had vanished without a trace. One day, after yet another fruitless search, he walked along, gloomily staring at his feet. Without realising it, he found himself standing in front of the local church doors. Raivo came from a very religious family whose members regularly attended this church. He pulled the door, and it opened. The young man walked inside and sat on the nearest pew. He had been here since his baptism and knew everyone who served here, especially the elderly Pastor Edwin, who had baptised Raivo and his older brothers.

He sat silently, gazing around. Everything was familiar — the altar, where the clergy conducted services. The old organ was built into the church walls during its construction. The harpsichord played during the services. The stained glass windows through which the sun shone. Everything seemed the same as usual, but Raivo felt he had come to the church for a reason. Suddenly, he heard footsteps behind him. The young man turned around and saw Father Edwin slowly walking between the rows of pews. He noticed the young man and smiled: "I'm glad to see you, Raivo! What brings you here today? The service isn't until Sunday, or did you want to confess?"

The young man stood up and said: "Good day, Father! No, I'm not ready for confession. I just found myself here. I don't understand how it happened."

"Then it must have been necessary for you to come here. Would you like to help me with the service this Sunday?" he asked the young man.

"I would be happy to, Father! What should I do?" Raivo asked.

"Come earlier than usual. You'll see for yourself," said the pastor as he walked away.

The following Sunday, Raivo arrived at the church early. The boy was a bit nervous, and Father Edwin noticed it. He smiled and reassured him: "Don't be nervous! Everything is fine. This is God's house. No one will harm you here."

"I'm just worried about whether I can do everything right. There will be many people in the church," Raivo admitted.

"Come on," the pastor nodded. "You should change your clothes to look like a real acolyte."

That service remained etched in Raivo's memory for life. He felt a sense of ease and peace during it. He had never thought he could serve as a priest. One thing is to attend church as a parishioner and quite another to stand next to the altar. The young man felt support not only from the pastor but also from the congregation in the church. He was a bit embarrassed by the attentive gazes directed at him.

"You did everything well," smiled the pastor at the end. "If you want, come next Sunday as well."

"Thank you very much, Father. I will definitely be here," Raivo replied excitedly.

Thus began the young man's journey toward God. He started reading much literature on religious topics and asked the pastor about the church's structure and hierarchy. He was particularly interested in the history and development of the Church. Father Edwin was very supportive of this enthusiasm. One day, he asked Raivo to stay after the service.

"I see you enjoy helping me, and you're not just doing it for its sake. You're genuinely interested in everything related to the Church. I'm too old and it's becoming harder for me to conduct services. The congregation needs a new pastor, just as every flock needs a shepherd. If you want to replace me, we can discuss this matter at our community's general meeting in due course," Father Edwin said to the young man.

"Yes, I truly enjoy it because I come to the service with joy and anticipation and return home reluctantly. I grew up under your guidance at this church, but I never imagined I could one day become a pastor," Raivo replied.

"I will give you this Bible," Father Edwin handed him a thick book with a black cover. "You have a Bible at home, but I don't think you've studied it thoroughly. I studied it while preparing to dedicate myself to God, and I want this particular book to help you. The Bible was written over fifteen centuries in different languages, some of which no longer exist. For us, it is the foundation upon which our faith rests. You can influence people by holding a whip, or you can do it with the help of this book. So, study it meticulously and ask me if you have any questions. You will find many things in it that may seem contradictory. Therefore, you must know everything perfectly to be a worthy guide for your flock. Although, of course, we are not meant to know everything."

Two years flew by quickly, during which Raivo was always by Father Edwin's side. One day, the church community gathered for their regular meeting to elect a new pastor.

"Dear brothers and sisters," Father Edwin began his speech. "For a long time, I have been your pastor. I have dedicated fifty years of my life to this position and have served you faithfully and truthfully. Over these years, our community has grown and strengthened significantly. But now, the time has come for me to retire. My health has deteriorated significantly, and it is very difficult for me to fulfil my duties. I knew this time would come, and I prepared a replacement for myself. You may have noticed that Raivo has been constantly by my side. For two years, he has been my assistant, so there is no need to introduce him specially. Moreover, you all know this young man from his childhood."

Father Edwin gestured for Raivo to come to the podium.

The young man addressed the congregation: "Dear community. I never thought I would want to dedicate my life to serving God, but they decided otherwise up there (Raivo pointed to the ceiling). Two years ago, with a broken heart and in despair, I stumbled into this church. Father Edwin met me and gave me hope for healing through faith in our Savior. He has been my first advisor and good teacher all this time. I hope he will never be disappointed in me as his student. For the past two years, I have dedicated myself to studying the Holy Scriptures, the rules and traditions of our Church, theology and the history of the Church. If you choose me as your pastor, I promise to serve you faithfully and truthfully, just as my teacher did."

Father Edwin pointed him to a place in the hall and approached the podium again.

"Dear brothers and sisters, I propose this young man as my successor, in whom I have as much confidence as in myself. Do not be concerned about his youth. When I began my service to God, I was not much older than he is now. At that time, I had to learn everything on my own. But before you stand an already prepared priest, to whom I have imparted all my knowledge and experience."

On that momentous day for the young man, the community unanimously elected him as their pastor. Father Edwin sent a letter of recommendation for Raivo's approval as the community's pastor to Archbishop Raoul, the head of the local diocese. Soon, a letter of approval arrived, and the new pastor officially took up his duties.

Time passed, and Raivo gained more experience as a priest and head of the religious community. He turned out to have a remarkable talent for oratory. The city municipality often invited Raivo to various events. His sermons touched the hearts not only of community members but also of those who did not belong to it. Thanks to this, the community grew year by year.

"Many years ago, our Church embarked on the path of Reformation to cleanse itself of everything that defiled the holy faith. Unfortunately, the Holy Church became mired in intrigues, luxury and other indecent things. Therefore, our task is to make our faith crystal clear, to separate the wheat from the chaff. We must always remember the shameful practice of granting indulgences and torturing and executing innocent people in the name of the Lord. Therefore, I urge you, brothers and sisters, to unite around our Church because only strong faith will bring us salvation in the future and cleanse our thoughts from the unnecessary," Father Raivo spoke to the townspeople at the annual harvest festival organised by the local authorities.

Raivo had the talent to speak and persuade people, and despite his fairly young age, he quickly gained the respect and admiration of the townspeople. He gladly responded to everyone who sought his advice. With his sincerity and zeal, Raivo easily opened people's hearts, and they confided their innermost secrets to him, firmly knowing that the pastor would keep their confidences.

"Father, what will happen to me after death? What will happen to my estates and properties?" asked Raivo, one of the town's wealthiest residents.

Raivo had often interacted with such people, so he already knew how to deal with them. The wealthy live for their wealth and forget that earthly life is fleeting. However, he hadn't known this man for long, although he had seen him in church several times. The man had significantly helped with the church building's repairs and purchasing gifts for orphans last Christmas.

"I will be honest with you. Perhaps my words will seem somewhat cynical," Father Raivo began after a brief pause. "When you die, your relatives and loved ones start fighting over your wealth. Your possessions will pass into the hands of other people. Those who love and respect you will mourn you, but it will not last long. At first, they will think of you often, then less frequently. In a few years, they will remember you only on your birthday and the anniversary of your death. Eventually, human memory will fade so much that people will completely forget about you, even if you once did something for them."

"So, should I not do anything for those who need help?" the man asked, surprised.

"No, you are doing everything right, and this help is invaluable. Just ask yourself: 'Am I happy right now?' Understand one thing — you should never forget about yourself. If you are happy, you make those around you happy too. Conversely, your sadness is the sadness of your loved ones. You cannot change the past. We have no control over the future. We often forget that we must live in the present moment. Not sometime later, but right now. Because the dreamed-of tomorrow may never come, someday, looking back at your past life, you will realise with horror that you spent it trying to achieve some specific result. But in doing so, you were not happy for a single moment. Try to find your happiness in faith, and you will discover a new world," Raivo replied.

A few years later, a great and senseless war began, claiming the lives of millions of people. It did not spare Raivo's family. His two older brothers were drafted into the army. Soon, one of them died, and the other went missing. The news caused his mother to fall ill suddenly, and she passed away within a few months. His father held on for a while but soon also passed away. Alone, Raivo increasingly fell into despair. Accustomed to being a helper for his parishioners, he sorrowfully realised that he needed help himself but had no one to turn to. He placed all his hopes and aspirations in the Almighty and spent much time in prayer, but he still lacked someone to whom he could pour out all his years of pain. Throughout his service to God, he never managed to get married, although church rules allowed him to have a wife. However, he never met a woman who could replace the one who had disappeared many years ago. His heart held only Martha, whom he had once loved with all his heart and who had remained in it forever.

After the war ended, his country declared independence, and Raivo played a significant role in this act. With his immense authority, he often spoke at rallies, convincing citizens of the need to fight for independence.

"We have a God-given land. Our grandfathers and their ancestors lived on it. Since immemorial times, we have cherished our native language, traditions, and culture. We have the sacred right to have our state and be equal among equals in the united family of nations. No one can tell us how to live on our land. Only we know how to manage it. We must protect our sons and daughters so that no empire can throw them into the hell of war. Therefore, I urge you to support the Declaration of Independence prepared by our local council," he passionately addressed the citizens.

Several years passed, and life gradually began to improve. The country gained the long-desired freedom and started building its institutions. The Church played a very active role in this. Many had lost faith in God and themselves after the horrific war. Here, Raivo had an enormous amount of work to do. The issue of pastoral work was very pressing, and the priest had to work within the limits of his physical and spiritual strength to help everyone in need. He organised a shelter for children orphaned by the war. The church's kitchen was set up to prepare meals for the homeless. Raivo regularly visited the hospital where former soldiers were being treated. He gave himself entirely to the people, not caring for himself. However, the time came when he had to consider his own health.

"Father," the doctor said in a concerned tone. "It's very good that you listened to me and went to the capital for an examination. I received the results this morning."

"What do they say?" Raivo asked grimly. "I hope I'll live a bit longer?"

"You are close to the truth, Father," the doctor replied, looking up from the papers. "You have a rare congenital heart defect that hadn't manifested until now. With normal conditions, you could have lived quite a long life, but you've overworked yourself with excessive physical and psychological stress. Your heart beats like an old man's, even though you are still quite young."

"How long can I live, doctor?" Raivo asked calmly.

"That will depend on the lifestyle you choose. You must understand that everything now depends on you," the doctor said.

"Also on the will of our Savior," Raivo added. "Thank you. I will try to take care of myself. I still have many unfinished tasks."

Raivo heeded the doctor's advice and delegated some of his charitable duties to church community members. He focused all his efforts strictly on church matters, knowing no one else could perform them. The Holy Service, Confession and Communion remained his direct responsibilities.

"Father," Raivo heard the voice of his assistant, Kalju. "A young woman has come for confession. What should I tell her?"

"Lead her to the confessional. I will be there shortly," Raivo replied.

He put on the alba[71], girded himself with a rope and looked at himself in the mirror. For a moment, he silently stared at his reflection, then, smiling to himself, turned and headed to the confessional. Raivo walked, sensing that this confession would be unusual. He immediately noticed a young woman by the wall behind the partition with a small window. Her face was partially obscured by a light haze, and she held a handkerchief in her hands, covering

---

[71] Alba — a long white liturgical robe. Wearing an alba is mandatory for a cleric performing the liturgy.

her mouth with it. Raivo sat on the chair, took the rosary, and closed his eyes. After a short prayer, he turned towards the confessional, trying to see her through the small holes in the window.

"What brings you here, my child?" Raivo asked. "I haven't seen you in church before."

"Father," the girl began and then hesitated. It happened that I hadn't been to church since my baptism. It's a long story, but now I am in such despair that I need your advice and help. I am very frightened and ashamed, so I desperately need to repent of my sins. I don't know what to do and why this happened to me."

"My dear child. You have nothing to fear. You are in the temple of our Heavenly Father. He is always near and ready to help at any moment. It's a pity that you didn't come to us earlier. Perhaps I could have prevented what has frightened you so. If you are ready to repent of your sinful actions and open your heart to me, now is the best time to do so. Everything you tell me will remain within these walls. Only you, He and I will know," Raivo said, raising his index finger upwards.

The girl remained silent for a while, gathering the courage to begin her story. The priest waited patiently, not rushing her, seeing how difficult it was for her.

"Father," the girl finally began in a voice dry from anxiety. "I fell in love with a man and lived with him outside of marriage. I know the Church condemns such relationships because it is adultery. It all started the year before last. We met and soon started living together. I am illegitimate, born out of wedlock. I never knew my father, and my mother recently died from a severe illness. So, I have no one in the whole world. This man was the only one I trusted, although he rarely talked about himself, citing a difficult childhood and complicated relationships with his family. I didn't insist because I felt happy and needed. Very often, he would leave me, explaining it as work-related trips. Yes, he didn't lie to me. It was indeed his job, but I had no idea what

Illustration by Artem Burlyk

it actually involved," here, the girl fell silent, and tears started to flow thinly from her eyes.

She wiped them with a handkerchief and continued: "A few weeks ago, the police arrested him. He turned out to be a hitman who had taken the lives of dozens of people and was wanted in many countries. I feel betrayed because I loved and trusted him. He was my first and only man, whose real name I only learned now, during the trial. I can't imagine my life without him, but the realisation that his hands are covered in blood makes me break out in a cold sweat. Those hands held me so tenderly and tightly."

The girl fell silent and stared at the floor.

Raivo waited a bit and then said: "It is very good that you came to us. No matter how we live, we come to God sooner or later, whether in this life or the one after. Everyone has their understanding of sin. One person will suffer from a lie, while another won't consider even murder a sin. I understand your feelings. Do not regret loving him, for love is the highest emotion a person can experience. Long ago, I also loved a woman who suddenly disappeared. Since then, I know nothing about her, but my love still lives within me. What happened to you is your own experience. Only the Creator and our Father knows why it happened. It is very difficult for us to understand what happens in our lives because, often, the Lord works in incomprehensible ways. You did the right thing by daring to tell me what troubles you because it is never too late to repent of your sins.

"In the name of the Father, the Son and the Holy Spirit, I absolve you of your sins. Go with God and do not forget Him because He is always with us."

The girl rose from the chair, bowed to the priest and staggered towards the church's exit.

Before reaching the door, she turned and said: "Thank you, Father. I hope He will accept my repentance."

Raivo remained in the confessional for some time, reflecting on what he had heard. Her story deeply moved him. However, something else troubled the priest. He felt this was not their last meeting and the next one would be fatal.

Father Raivo paid great attention to the religious upbringing of the youth: he organised the teaching of the Catechism in primary school. He was often invited to meet with students at the capital university. He also established spiritual care for the prisoners in the local prison. Occasionally, Raivo visited there to give talks or speak one-on-one with those who needed spiritual help. He had a trusting relationship with the prison warden, who occasionally attended Sunday services at the church. One day, Raivo received a letter from him asking to come and hear the confession of a condemned criminal. As a priest, Father Raivo had confessed a death row inmates several times and each time, he prepared very carefully. However, this time, he approached the sacrament with double attention. Raivo knew in advance that this would not be a simple confession. The premonition of his own impending death made him view the condemned man differently, as the man was heading to the place where Raivo would soon follow.

The next day, the priest knocked on the gate early in the morning. After a minute, a small window opened, revealing a guard's face. Recognising the pastor, the guard opened the gate and let Raivo into the prison yard. He was escorted to the warden, who rose from his desk and greeted him.

"This is a very difficult criminal," said the warden. "He has dozens of victims on his conscience in various countries. I don't think he is inclined to repent, but according to the rules, we must give him this opportunity. So now you will be taken to him, and from there, it's up to you. Our guards will be nearby."

"Alright. I will do everything I can," Raivo replied.

The warden signalled the guards, and they led the priest through narrow corridors to the death row cell. On the way, Raivo tried to imagine what the man who would be hanged in the prison yard in an hour looked like. He was convinced this was the man the young woman had spoken about in her confession. Now, the priest had to guide him to the other world. They reached the cell door, and one guard opened it and gestured for the priest to enter. A young man sat against the wall in the small, windowless room. He squinted at the newcomers. It was clear that the prisoner had become unaccustomed to light, having spent a long time in darkness.

"Son, today you will stand before our Heavenly Father. Wouldn't you like to confess your sins?" Raivo asked the condemned man.

The young man silently stood up and looked the priest directly in the eyes. A chill ran down Raivo's spine from that gaze. Never in his life had he encountered such eyes. They were both captivating and terrifying at the same time.

"No, holy Father. I don't need intermediaries in my communication with God. Since I will meet Him today, I will personally tell Him everything," he tried to smile, but a pained grimace appeared on his face instead of a smile.

"Well, as you wish, my son," Raivo replied, turning to leave.

At the doorway, he stopped and, turning back, said: "When you see Him, give my regards!"

"Ok, I will," the prisoner tried to smile again, but it didn't work once more. "Father, may I ask you to fulfil one request? A final request?"

"Yes, my son, ask."

"Do you have a paper and a pencil?"

"No, but I will ask the guard," Raivo left the cell and returned a minute later with a sheet of paper and a pencil, handing them to the man.

He sat at the table and began to write something slowly. Then, he folded the paper in quarters and handed it to the priest.

"At the corner of the main street, near the park entrance, there is a flower kiosk. The florist there is called Louisa. Please give this note to her."

"Very well, I will do as you ask," Raivo said and left the cell.

Illustration by Artem Burlyk

In the corridor, the priest saw the prosecutor holding a document with the court's decision. The prosecutor silently nodded in greeting and entered the condemned man's cell.

Stepping outside the prison, Raivo looked back at the prison walls. The sun rose above them, and its rays cut through the clouds, creating a unique pattern in the sky.

"This is the last morning of his life. One day, my last morning will come too, but unlike him, I won't know when it is," Raivo thought.

Clutching the Bible, he quickly walked away from that dreadful place toward the local park.

After giving the letter to Louisa, he decided to walk through the park and breathe in the fresh air. There were too many emotions this morning. The pain in his chest was becoming more frequent, a constant reminder. Father Raivo had long since come to terms with it and tried not to pay attention. His heart had endured too much personal and human sorrow and could no longer bear the strain. Now, all that remained was to wait for the call to the other world. He, more than anyone, understood this well and was ready for it. Reaching the end of the park, he sat on a bench. A fresh breeze blew from above, bringing some relief. The priest took off his clerical collar[72] and unbuttoned the top button of his shirt. He closed his eyes and, for a moment, imagined himself as a small, carefree child. Childhood memories carried him far beyond the horizon. Drawing a deep breath of fresh air, Father Raivo held it briefly before slowly exhaling. His head spun slightly, but only for a moment. His mind cleared, and Raivo opened his eyes. Yes, it was the same girl who had come for confession last week. He hadn't asked her name then, nor had he managed to get a good look at her. But he realised she had recognised him, though she pretended to see him for the first time. The sudden thought

---

[72] Clerical collar — a white collar worn by Catholic priests and clergy of some Protestant and Orthodox communities. It is one of the most recognisable elements of clerical attire.

flashed through his mind that if he had met this girl earlier, perhaps her fate would have been different. Although he was certain that everything was in God's hands and trying to change someone else's fate would only be foolish in the eyes of the Creator. Everything had to happen exactly as it did. Father Raivo vividly recalled that confession. He had been deeply shocked by what he heard and couldn't respond immediately. Since then, he hasn't seen her until that day. He was sure it was the same girl because he remembered her voice well. It couldn't be confused with any other, as it reminded him of the one he had always remembered. He once again plunged into memories of distant years, and suddenly, a sharp pain pierced his heart. The air became scarce, and Father Raivo clutched his chest with his hands. Then his hands fell to his sides, and his head dropped onto his chest. He remained sitting on the bench, and to the few morning park visitors, it seemed as though the man was simply sleeping, exhausted from hard work.

Petro

Petro stood motionless by the bed where Nastya lay. It seemed as though she was sleeping. Holding his breath, he looked at her, waited for his wife to open her eyes, and habitually ask: "How are you, dear? Are you alright?"

The realisation that Nastya had passed into the other world was slowly breaking through his consciousness. Still, Petro stubbornly refused to believe it, as he couldn't imagine his life without her. After standing silently for a while, he took his wife's cold hand, kissed and gently placed it on her chest. Then he stepped out onto the porch and looked at the horizon, over which the bright yellow sun was slowly rising. The thought that one day there would be a morning he wouldn't greet didn't sadden him at all. Petro was ready for it.

"Mom! We want to eat," Petro looked at his mother with desperate, hungry eyes.

Myroslava took her son's hand and pulled him close. Her mother's heart was breaking from the pain. They hadn't eaten in several days. While she could somehow endure the hardship, she couldn't bear to see her children suffer. It might have been easier for Myroslava if her parents were alive, but they had died shortly before the great famine began. They had been her primary support in all matters. Now, their help would have been invaluable. The old folks had been so happy with the children, but only Petro had the chance to spend time with them.

Myroslava's husband had been taken away by those who came to seize food from the peasants. Several months had passed since then, and no word from him had been heard. During all this time, Myroslava had tried to feed the children with whatever she managed to hide from the raiders, but those meagre supplies had run out. Now, they had to search for edible roots or beg for food from neighbours. She was grateful even for potato peels, from which she could make soup. But now, even those were gone. Enemy forces had seized the entire summer harvest. Every day in the village, they buried people who had died in every corner. Their bodies lay unburied for days, as a cold and hungry autumn approached.

"Petro. We cannot stay here," Myroslava said to her son. "We need to head south, closer to the sea, where your father's relatives live. Maybe we can survive this winter there. Dress the little ones. We must leave as soon as possible."

Petro gathered his younger brother and sister, who were one and a half and four years old. He was the primary helper for his father and mother. Last year, he had turned just ten, but he was as responsible as an adult. Since they had been left without their father, their mother relied on Petro to care for the younger ones. The little ones, seemingly sensing the absence of their father, obeyed their older brother in everything. Recently, Katerynka has often cried from hunger, and the younger Tarasik has been lying silently on the bed, not even moving.

Myroslava packed the necessary things into bags, tied the younger child to her back with a scarf and shut the door. The family set off on the road heading south. Petro held his sister's hand. When they encountered bodies of the dead on the roadside, he would hug and press Katerynka to himself so the child would not see the horror. They asked to spend the night in the first village they came across. Initially, the hosts did not want to let them in, but seeing the small children, they relented and offered them shelter. They prepared breakfast for the guests in the morning — a few boiled potatoes. The older children ate greedily with their skins on, and it seemed that nothing in the world could be more delicious than those potatoes. Myroslava tried to feed Tarasik, but he was so weak that he could only swallow a small piece.

"Are you heading south?" the host asked Myroslava.

"Yes, I hope it will be easier there because I can't feed them here," the woman nodded.

"Don't go by the road. It's better to go through the steppe. They have patrols on the roads, and you might get detained. Try to travel as much as possible at night, although sleeping in the steppe with children is very difficult right now," the man sighed.

Myroslava followed the advice, and they left the road to travel through the steppe. Trying to avoid open areas, they moved through ravines and gullies. At night, they asked for shelter from people in the villages they passed. Everywhere, they saw hardship and hunger. Despite their own difficult circumstances, people helped as much as they could with food, sincerely sympathising with the mother and her children. They travelled through the steppe for quite some time, constantly looking around to avoid running into enemy patrols. Suddenly, they saw a few stone statues standing alone in the middle of the steppe.

"Mom, what is that?" Petro asked his mother in surprise.

"These are stone statues left to us by our ancient ancestors," she replied.

"Can we stop and rest a little? It's very interesting here. I want to look at everything. I feel like I've been here before."

"Alright, son, but not for long because we need to reach the nearest village to spend the night. For now, let's eat what the kind people gave us."

Myroslava took Tarasik off her back, laid him on the ground and began preparing their simple meal. Petro walked through the steppe, observing everything around him. The light wind made the steppe grass sway in waves, and it seemed to him like he was walking on water. The stone statues silently watched him, and he became more convinced that he had been here before. He had never felt such a strange sensation and didn't know how to react. A peculiar lightness enveloped him. The boy walked among the stone figures and seemed to hear them whispering. He felt as if they wanted to tell him something. Returning to his mother, Petro saw that she was kneeling and crying. Next to her stood Katerynka and, beside them lay Tarasik, motionless.

Illustration by Artem Burlyk

They buried him in the steppe, next to the silent statues. Myroslava dug the grave with a knife, wrapped her son in a scarf, and laid him on the damp ground. After covering the small body with earth, she placed a stone on top. The mother took her children's hands and continued south. She needed to get there as quickly as possible, not to lose those she was now holding tightly in her hands. They were the most precious thing she had in her life.

A few days later, they finally reached a large city. Thanks to a stroke of luck, they were fortunate to find shelter in a house where a large family lived. The mother left the children on a bench in the park while she went to look for distant relatives of her husband who lived in the city.

"Are you waiting for someone?" Petro heard an unfamiliar voice.

A girl about his age stood nearby, looking at Petro intently.

"Yes, my mother. What's it to you?" the boy grumbled angrily.

"Where did you come from?" the stranger persisted.

"What's it to you? Go away!" the boy frowned.

"Well, I must care if I'm asking. Do you have nowhere to live?" she said, not as a question but as a statement.

Petro remained silent. Of course, he understood they urgently needed a place to stay because they couldn't remain outside in the cold. However, he decided to wait for his mother. The stubborn girl didn't leave and also waited. How could the boy have known then that she would be his guardian angel for the rest of his life?

"I couldn't find them. The neighbours say they moved away a few years ago. I don't know what to do. Who is this? Your new friend?" Myroslava asked worriedly, pointing at the girl before turning to her. "What's your name?"

"Nastya. I live nearby. My dad works at the factory, and my mom is a seamstress; she sews clothes at home. Times are really hard now. We must find ways to survive," the girl replied with mature wisdom.

"Do you know where we could find shelter? For me and my three..."
Myroslava hesitated, then quietly added. "For my two children."

"We have a big room with a separate entrance. I need to ask my dad.
Come to our house. He'll be home from work soon," said Nasya and with a
wave of her hand, she led them down the street.

She brought Myroslava and the children home and introduced them to
her mother, Lyubov, and her two younger brothers, Mykyta and Ivan. Soon
after, Mykhailo, the father of the family, arrived. After a brief conversation
with Myroslava, he agreed to give them the large room for free. He was familiar
with hunger firsthand. Every day, people fleeing from famine arrived in the
city, but not everyone was as lucky as Myroslava and her children. Many died
on the way or were detained by the military. The omnipresent and merciless
hunger loomed over the country like a bloody sword.

To survive, Myroslava immediately began helping Lyubov with sewing.
The children quickly became friends, and over time, the house turned into
a bustling hive of activity. Mykhailo helped the new residents as much as he
could, unexpectedly finding himself the head of a large and friendly family.

Several months passed unnoticed despite shared concerns. Slowly, the
hunger began to recede, and life returned to the land. People, still recovering
from the horrors of recent years, gradually returned to their usual routines.

"I suggest you stay with us for a while. There's a school for the children,
and you can find work here. There's no point in returning home since who
knows what might happen soon. There's no trust in the new government,"
Mykhailo said to Myroslava, looking around cautiously.

Many of the townsfolk who opposed the new regime had been arrested and
executed, so talking about such things was dangerous. Myroslava understood
this very well, as her husband had never been found. This could only mean
one thing: he was no longer alive.

"Alright, Mykhailo. If we aren't a burden to you, we will stay a bit longer.
Besides, our children have become so close that I sometimes mix up which

are mine and yours," Myroslava smiled. "We'll see what happens next. Thank you for your hospitality."

So they lived as one big family until Lyubov suddenly fell seriously ill. Mykhailo took her to doctors, but it was all in vain. The illness did not retreat, and within a few months, Lyubov passed away. Mykhailo took his wife's death hard, especially since he was left with three underage children. He continued to work at the factory, but now he had to take on household chores that his wife used to do. Nasya helped as much as she could, but she was still a child. Mykhailo increasingly had to ask Myroslava for help. She gladly helped with the household, having long regarded his children as hers.

About a year after his wife's death, Mykhailo came home one evening, gloomy and visibly upset.

"What happened?" asked Myroslava as she set the table.

"A few workers at our factory have been arrested," Mykhailo replied, taking a bite of bread. "These are ordinary people with families and children, yet they stand accused of working as enemy spies."

"You know we can't trust the authorities," Myroslava lowered her voice.

"I feel for the children. God forbid something happens to me. How will you survive?"

"Don't say that. Everything will be fine. We have to raise them," Myroslava reassured him.

Mykhailo finished his meal, pushed the plate away and fell silent. He stared at the table, avoiding eye contact with her.

"Myroslava," he finally spoke. "I've been wanting to tell you something for a while."

"What is it?" she asked, suddenly alert.

"It's hard for me to live without a wife. Ever since Lyubov passed away, I've been overwhelmed by the work that she used to do. The children aren't that young anymore, but they're still children. You and your kids have become part of our family. Sometimes, it feels like we've always lived together. The children have grown so close that I've started to consider your children as my own."

Myroslava dried her hands with a towel and sat across from him.

"Your children have also become dear to me, and I know what you want to say. There's no time for contemplation in these tough times," she said.

Mykhailo nodded: "Yes, I was thinking... maybe we should unite our families officially. This way, we can better support each other and provide a stable home for all our children."

Myroslava looked at him thoughtfully and said: "You're right. It makes sense. Together, we can give them a better future."

"So, we'll live together as husband and wife? I think our children will understand. I will never hurt you and will treat you as my wife. But if you want to become my wife officially, I would gladly marry you," Mykhailo said, hope shining in his eyes.

"I think it's better not to rush. Although the chances that my husband is alive are very slim, legally, I am still married," Myroslava replied calmly.

A few years passed after this conversation. Myroslava was officially declared a widow, and they got married. The children understood their parents' decision. For some, it meant finding a mother, while for others, it was gaining a father. Together, the large and friendly family faced the difficult and joyful moments of their challenging life. Over time, the terrible memories of famine and repression began to fade, and the children grew up, ready to pursue their own plans.

"I like it here. This place is perfect for planning our future and reminiscing about the past. What are you thinking about right now?" Nastya asked Petro.

He didn't respond immediately. The teenagers sat by a cliff, looking out at the sea from a height. The sea shimmered in the sunlight with various colours. Seagulls circled above the waves, occasionally diving into the sea to hunt for fish. The summer sun stood at its high, warming the children with its heat. A gentle breeze brought refreshing coolness from the sea.

"You're right. This place does feel magical and brings back memories. I'm thinking about what lies ahead for us. For example, what do you want to become?" the boy asked.

"I want to be a history teacher. There's so much we still don't know. It's wonderful to teach children and to learn at the same time. Right now, I'm rereading the history of the ancient world. I have more questions than answers," Nastya replied. "What about you? What do you want to be?"

"I want to be a military pilot," Petro answered. "Aviation has a great future. It's a profession for brave people. Also, there's so much romance in it."

"You'll be a great pilot. You're so determined and romantic, too," the girl laughed and tousled the boy's hair.

The boy was used to this kind of behaviour. Nastya was a year younger than him, but he listened to her in everything as if she were older, allowing her to take charge. He felt an unconscious, boundless trust and deep respect for her. Petro had grown accustomed to her always being by his side, helping in everything, whether with actions or advice. In return, with his strong fists, he was her personal protector and had defended her more than once from local bullies. They seemed to be inseparable. Even their parents no longer separated them.

"Nastya, tell Petro..." or "Petro, when is Nastya coming?" were common phrases in the house.

Everyone was so used to their friendship that they didn't notice how it blossomed into love over time.

"You know, I feel like I've known you since birth," Petro said to Nastya.

They were sitting in their favourite spot by the sea as usual. Petro hugged the girl, and she leaned closer, resting her head on his shoulder. They sat for a long time, watching the sunset over the horizon. Petro was agitated, nervously fidgeting with his fingers on his leg. He didn't understand his feelings, as this was a first for him. Recently, Nastya's presence affected him so much that he forgot everything else. When he touched her, it felt like an electric shock ran through him. He held the girl tightly in his arms and felt her heart beating dully.

"Nastya. This is the first time I've felt like this! I don't know how to describe what happens to me when you're near. Sometimes I even feel like I can't breathe," he said, pulling away from her and looking into her eyes intently.

He ran his fingers through her long, light-brown hair. Nastya looked at him attentively, breathing heavily. She trembled and waited silently for him to share what was troubling him.

"I drown in your eyes. I want to melt into them," Petro said, pulling the girl closer and passionately kissing her on the lips.

They kissed clumsily, long and sweetly, unable to pull away from each other. When he finally stopped kissing her, he still pressed his face against hers for a while.

Gently kissing Nastya's neck, he whispered, his eyes closed: "I love you. Do you hear me, my girl? I love you madly. I want you always to be near. I can't get enough of you."

"My dear! I've been waiting for this for so long. I feel so at ease with you. When you touch me, tenderness spreads throughout my body. I love you with all my heart and promise to be faithful until death," the girl replied passionately.

Their relationship didn't go unnoticed by their mother. She was the first to notice that the children had fallen in love with each other. On a dark winter night, she and Mykhailo lay in bed, listening to the wood crackling in the stove. Outside, the wind howled, and the snowstorm raged. The children were already asleep, peacefully murmuring in their sleep.

"It seems we'll have to move the older kids to a separate room," Myroslava said with a smile.

"What do you mean?" Mykhailo asked.

"Don't you see? Our children have fallen in love and spend all their time together."

"In love? How? I mean, I understand a man and a woman... but they are still children."

"Listen. Petro is already eighteen, and Nastya is seventeen if you've forgotten. They're not such children anymore. You haven't noticed how they've grown up because of your work."

"You're right. I was already married at eighteen. Kids grow up so fast. What do we do now?"

"Nothing. They're a good couple. We'll have a wedding in the spring and let them live and give us grandchildren," Myroslava laughed.

The following year, at the beginning of June, Petro and Nastya got married. The room where Myroslava once lived with her children was given to the newlyweds. They immediately began to settle into their new home. They had many plans for the future, but a few days later, a terrible war erupted.

The fourth year of the war, which had claimed millions of lives, was passing. Petro was one of the first to volunteer for the front lines, joining a reconnaissance company. Clever and physically strong, he immediately caught the eye of an experienced captain who arrived at the recruitment centre. Selecting a few young men, the captain brought them to the training base and lined them up in the yard in front of the barracks.

"From now on, I am your father, and you are a big family. You will be issued new uniforms and provided with quarters today. Tomorrow morning, we begin training. In three months, we will make real scouts out of you. Those who pass the tests will join special units. Those who fail will be dismissed and sent to the regular army. Every offence will be severely punished. There will be no rest. The enemy continues to advance, and we have no time to waste," the captain told the new recruits.

Three months flew by so quickly that Petro hardly noticed when the day of the exams arrived. During this time, he and the other soldiers studied hand-to-hand combat and the use of cold weapons. They learned to camouflage themselves in any season and received training in marksmanship, fortifications and sapping. Petro was very well physically prepared and had quick and unconventional thinking. He easily passed all the exams and was soon sent to a military unit. Thus began the young man's combat path, who later carried out several successful operations behind enemy lines and was considered one of the most experienced soldiers in the reconnaissance company.

This mission behind enemy lines did not go well from the start. The enemy spotted the group as they crossed the front line, but the commander had orders to complete the mission at all costs — to blow up a railroad bridge. So, he decided to press on and try to evade the enemy's pursuit. They wandered through forests for several days, covering their tracks and setting mine traps for their pursuers. Eventually, they reached their target and took cover. In front of them was the bridge they were supposed to destroy. After waiting a while, the group commander gave the order to move forward and neutralise the bridge guards. However, this time, they were met with failure. The enemy feigned a lack of vigilance but had actually set a trap. As soon as the scouts approached the bridge, machine gun fire erupted from all sides. Petro, who was at the rear, saw his comrades fall under the enemy fire. He managed to drop to the ground and crawl back. The enemy did not rush out of their ambush, fearing that some scouts might still be alive. Alone, Petro began to crawl back toward the safety of the forest quickly, but luck was not on his side. The enemy had thoroughly prepared to guard that bridge. Petro stumbled into another ambush and, despite his attempts to fight back, was captured and bound. He was taken for interrogation by an enemy officer. The officer tried to extract any information from the prisoner, but his efforts were fruitless. Petro remained silent, even though he understood the enemy language from school. The prisoner was thrown into a shed, and a guard was posted outside. He had been searched hastily, and, luckily, they did not find what he had carefully hidden. Scouts have many different hiding places for emergencies. Petro had been taught many hidden weapon techniques. He had small blade knives concealed in his belt, under the buckle and in the sole of his boot. The belt was taken during the search, but they didn't check his boots. Now, that small knife was his last hope for escape. His hands were tied behind his back, but Petro managed to remove a boot and retrieve the knife despite the restraints. Slowly, he cut through the ropes. Now, he just had to neutralise the guard.

Petro waited for nightfall and began to listen intently. When everything outside became quiet, he pushed over a ladder, leaning against the wall. The door swung open within moments, and the guard burst in with his rifle ready. That was all the scout needed. He struck the guard in the throat with the knife, and that one fell to the ground without a sound. Grabbing the guard's rifle, Petro took his belt, a pouch and a water flask and slipped into the night like a shadow.

Petro had been walking through the forest toward the front line for several days. Hungry and emaciated, he resembled a lone wolf prowling the woods searching for food. As he approached the front line, he stumbled upon an abandoned farmstead surrounded by cornfields. The owners had evidently managed to plant the corn but had to flee before they could harvest it. Petro tore off a young cob, stripped it of its leaves, and bit into the juicy kernels. He ate greedily, ignoring the corn milk that dripped down his chin.

Illustration by Artem Burlyk

Suddenly, he heard a wolf's howl emanating from the forest. Petro turned and cautiously walked toward the sound. Soon, he saw the wolf standing at the forest's edge, with a person lying nearby. He looked around and, trying not to make any unnecessary noise, moved toward the person. The wolf, seeing Petro, stood still for a while. When it realised Petro was headed in the right direction, it ran back into the forest.

In front of Petro lay an enemy soldier with a severe wound on his forehead. He was breathing heavily, and blood covered his entire face. After a moment of hesitation, Petro took a bandage from the wounded man's first aid kit and carefully wrapped his head. With a bit of water left in his flask, Petro gave the injured man a drink. The man took a few sips and slowly opened his eyes. His clouded gaze cleared a bit, and he tried to say something but lost consciousness again.

Petro spent the night in the forest beside the wounded man. He couldn't leave him to die, even though he was the enemy. It was one thing to kill an enemy in battle but quite another to finish off a wounded man. So Petro decided to carry him across the front lines. In the morning, Petro woke up and nudged the injured man. He opened his eyes and looked questioningly at Petro.

"What's your name?" Petro asked, suddenly remembering that the man didn't understand him.

"My name is Petro. Peter, in your language, understand? What about you? What's your name?"

He repeated the question in the man's language and poked him in the chest with his finger.

Then he tapped his chest and said again: "Peter, Peter!"

The wounded man remained silent. Petro pulled him up to a tree. Leaning him against the trunk, he gave him a few more sips of water. The man then raised his hand, placed it on his chest and whispered: "My name is Michael."

"Michael, then. Alright, Michael, get up and let's go to our side."

Petro dragged him for several kilometres until they were behind the front lines. There, he handed the wounded man over to scouts, who transferred him to a prisoner-of-war camp. Petro stayed behind to report on the failed mission and the loss of his comrades.

"Maybe you betrayed your comrades and deliberately led them into an ambush?" a powerful blow to the head knocked Petro off the chair where he sat with his hands tied.

"Maybe that's why you didn't kill the enemy but saved his life?" he heard the same voice and simultaneously received a kick to the stomach.

Petro was interrogated for several hours, yet he stubbornly remained silent. The pain from the torture and the injustice overwhelmed his body and mind. Exhausted, he lost consciousness. He dreamed of Nastya. They walked through a field, holding hands, with colourful butterflies fluttering around. Suddenly, Petro felt the sky open, and water poured on him. Nastya disappeared, leaving him lying in a puddle of water.

"Well, he's alive. I told you to go easier on him," Petro heard another voice. It's a good *thing we revived him with water. What if he had died?"*

"What can happen to him, the bastard? He betrayed his comrades," replied the one who had been torturing Petro.

"Well, let the tribunal decide that. Tell the guards to take him back to the cell and clean up here. You made a mess with all the blood, Sergeant," the superior officer added disgustingly.

The trial was swift. Petro was found guilty of causing the death of his comrades and was sentenced for treason against the Motherland to fifteen years of hard labour followed by ten years of exile. While still in the military detention cell, he wrote a letter to Nastya and secretly passed it to a familiar guard to deliver.

"My dear girl. My heart breaks in two over what has happened. I am innocent of any wrongdoing. I have been condemned for a crime I did not commit. Tomorrow, I will be sent to the labour camp. The thought of never seeing you again terrifies me. Forgive me, my love. Believe me, I will endure all trials and return to you. Just wait for me. I hold you tight, my dearest. Your Petro."

Nastya received the letter when the convoy with the newly convicted had already reached the location of the high-security camp. She sat down on a chair and buried her head in her hands. The terrible news overwhelmed her, and she wept bitterly.

The train screeched to a halt, and the guards began opening the doors of the carriages.

"Line up outside!" came the shout from outside, and the prisoners shuffled toward the exit.

They were herded into a wide square and lined up. After a roll call, a military officer in a pea coat stepped into the centre of the square and addressed the newcomers: *"I am Lieutenant Colonel Nikolai Vasilyevich Bernikov, the commander of this colony where you will serve your sentence. From now on, you are nobodies. Your task is to atone for your crimes through hard labour. I do not advise you to try escaping. If our guards don't catch you, the local hunters will be rewarded for each caught prisoner. A week ago, several convicts attempted to escape. Today, they returned. In part, that is."*

He gestured with his hand, and a nearby soldier approached him with a bucket. The lieutenant colonel nodded, and the soldier emptied the bucket onto the ground, spilling out bloody human hands.

After sorting and sanitation, the prisoners were distributed among the barracks. Petro stood in the middle of his barrack, looking around. Dozens of hungry eyes stared at him intently.

"Look at this! A nice coat just my size," one of the convicts approached Petro with a sneer. *"What are you looking at, you traitor? Take it off!"*

"This is my coat," Petro replied calmly.

"What did you say, you scum?" the man said, grabbing Petro by the collar.

Without a word, Petro struck the man under the ribs with two fingers, causing him to collapse to the floor, gasping.

"Anyone else cold and wants to warm up?" Petro said calmly, looking around.

Here, his skills from the scout school were very useful. He instinctively sensed danger and was ready for the next attack.

"Hey, soldier! Come over here. We're all on the same side," Petro heard a deep voice and turned around.

On one of the bunks, a sturdy man sat watching Petro closely. Around him were several other men who were also observing Petro with keen interest.

Petro approached and greeted them: "My name is Petro. Where's my spot?"

"Sit here. We're all military, so it's better for you to stay with us. The criminals try to dominate, but we've already put them in their place several times, so they don't mess with us anymore. I'm Mykola," the man said, extending his hand to Petro.

Petro noticed an anchor tattoo on his wrist.

Noticing Petro's glance, Mykola added: "Marine Corps."

"How did you know I was military?" Petro asked.

"Listen, we can spot each other a mile away. The training, the look in the eyes... And the way you took him down tells a lot. You served in reconnaissance?" Mykola guessed.

Petro nodded silently. He didn't want to talk about how he ended up there.

"Alright, relax. You're among your own. Stick with us, and you'll be fine. Rest up because tomorrow morning we go to work."

Petro took a seat with them, feeling a slight sense of relief. Although he was in a harsh place, he had found some allies. He lay down on his bunk, mentally preparing for the challenges ahead.

The long, bleak days in the colony began and seemed to stretch on endlessly. Sometimes, he felt that time had stopped there. Constant hunger, cold, diseases, hard labour and the guards' abuse took their toll. Many prisoners couldn't withstand it, and almost every morning, someone didn't wake up. But what weighed most heavily on Petro was being cut off from the outside world. Correspondence was forbidden, and he couldn't send any news of himself to his family or Nastya. Over the years, he managed to send out letters twice secretly, but he never received a reply. Thoughts of escape increasingly filled his mind.

"Petro. We need to talk," Mykola whispered.

Their bunks were next to each other, allowing them to converse secretly.

"Speak. I'm listening," Petro turned to face him.

"We're planning an escape. Are you in?" Mykola looked calmly into his eyes.

"How? When?" Petro sat up quickly.

"Quiet. You'll find out everything tomorrow. Just don't tell anyone, understood?"

"Of course!"

Petro, covered with his coat, tried to sleep, but he couldn't close his eyes until it was time to get up. He dreamed of freedom and the moment he could embrace Nastya. It seemed like he touched her for a fleeting moment, but the guard's shout interrupted his dream, and he had to get up for work.

The next day, Petro was restless with anticipation. Mykola and a few others gathered discreetly during a break to discuss the escape plan. They had been carefully plotting for weeks, noting the guards' routines and identifying potential weaknesses in the camp's security.

"A month from now, when the snow melts, we plan to escape. We've prepared hiding spots at the logging site where we can stay for a few days.

Once things calm down, we'll head south. We've already made some stockpiles of supplies and food there. So, are you with us?" Mykola asked Petro again.

"Yes, I'm with you. What do you need from me?"

"Start gathering food and pass it to me. I'll hide it. Since you don't smoke, you can trade your cigarettes for bread. We need to prepare well for the long journey," Mykola said.

"Alright, agreed," Petro nodded.

For the entire month, Petro, trying not to draw attention, traded cigarettes for bread, matches, clothes and other items that could be useful to them. He counted the days and hours until the moment when he could breathe the air of freedom.

However, fate had other plans. A day before the planned escape, a local woman who worked in the colony called out to him while he was being escorted from work. Unthinkingly, he took a step toward her, which led to him being knocked down by the guards and later thrown into solitary confinement.

The dark, cold cell of the punishment block seemed to crush Petro's hopes. That night, as he lay on the hard floor, he resolved not to give up. He might still have a chance if he could get out of the punishment block in time. Petro knew he had to stay strong and be ready for any opportunity to join his comrades. He could hear the distant sounds of the camp and felt the weight of the isolation. His mind raced about the escape plan and whether Mykola and the others would proceed without him. The only connection to the outside world was a small hole someone had made in the tin window cover. Through it, Petro could distinguish between day and night. Once a day, a piece of black bread and an aluminium mug of water were handed through the window in the door. Walks were forbidden, so Petro performed various exercises to maintain his physical condition. The reconnaissance school had taught him how to endure cold and thirst. However, it was difficult to stay warm in the cell. The battle with the cold turned into a struggle for survival. Each day, it became harder to resist this invisible enemy. The solitary confinement stretched on, each day blending into the next. Despite the harsh conditions, Petro clung to the hope of escape. He kept his body and mind as sharp as possible, knowing he needed to be ready for any opportunity.

From the beginning of imprisonment, Petro found a friend with whom he talked and shared his bread. This rat, probably used to the prisoners, wasn't afraid of them. At first, Petro was wary of his new neighbour, but over time, he grew fond of it and even missed it when the rat didn't come for long periods.

"Where have you been so long? Come here, I'll give you some bread," Petro told the little creature.

As if it understood, the rat scurried closer, stood on its hind legs, and waited for a treat.

Illustration by Artem Burlyk

They communicated this way until the cell door opened one morning, and Petro heard: "*Prisoner, out!*"

He got up and stepped outside. The morning sun was shining. Petro squinted and shielded his face with his hand.

"*Move it!*" the guard yelled from behind.

"*Look at that. He's still alive. I thought we'd have to drag him out of the cell,*" said another guard.

"*Yeah, this bastard is tough as the oak tree,*" added the first.

When Petro arrived at the barracks, he realised that his comrades had not waited for him and had escaped from the camp. In their places were new prisoners he had not seen before, but Petro's spot was still vacant. He first sat down and then collapsed onto his bunk. After the punishment cell, it felt like the most comfortable place on earth. No one questioned him, as everyone knew where he had come from.

The next morning, the prisoners were lined up in the yard. The colony commander stepped forward.

"*I remind those still restless that they can escape from here. You can run, but you won't get far!*" he gestured to a guard.

The guard approached and dumped severed hands from a bucket onto the ground. Petro stood in the front and clearly saw an anchor tattoo on one of the hands.

"Please, I beg you, pass him this note," Nastya pleaded, looking into the young guard's eyes. "Petro needs to know that I'm nearby."

"I'll be shot if I do this! Do you understand that?" he replied, looking around fearfully.

"Ivan, you're from our hometown. Don't you know what's happening there?" she asked.

"I know, but I'm a man under orders. I have family back there. If something happens to me, they'll come for them," Ivan responded.

"Ivan, you're rarely allowed to leave the camp. I don't know when I'll see you again. Take the note, I beg you. I tried to do it through the woman who works there, but she couldn't manage it. You're my only hope. Petro will feel better knowing I'm here, close to him," Nastya implored.

She had met Ivan a few months ago in the village store, where guards from the local colony came to buy unavailable goods behind the barbed wire. By some miracle, Nastya received a letter from Petro and, without wasting time, came and settled in a village near the colony.

"Alright," Ivan glanced around fearfully again. "I'll give him your note."

"God bless you!" Nastya thanked him, placing a small piece of paper in his hand.

"You too. Now go away from me!" Ivan urged.

"This is for you," she handed him a small package.

Ivan initially refused, but Nastya insisted so persistently that he finally took it and tucked it into his coat.

The next day, when the prisoners were being lined up for work, Ivan managed to slip the note to Petro under the guise of handing out tools. After noticing the familiar handwriting, Petro quickly hid the note in his clothes and waited for a moment to read it in private.

Later, when he finally had a moment alone, Petro unfolded the note: "My dearest Petro, I'm here, close to you. Stay strong, my love. We will be together again soon. Yours forever, Nastya."

The note brought a surge of hope and strength to Petro. Knowing that Nastya was nearby gave him the courage to endure and the resolve to survive whatever lay ahead. Petro's head was spinning. He just couldn't seem to come to his senses. He read the note several times and secretly burned it to avoid putting the guard in danger. His Nastya was just a few kilometres away! She had been living nearby for a while, and he had just found out about it. Suddenly, he remembered the escape plan and felt a chill. If he hadn't been thrown into solitary confinement, he might never have found out about his beloved. Now, he had hope for a reunion and a goal to strive for, no matter what. His Nastya was nearby! What else did he need? He could endure any trials and return to her.

Two more years passed, during which Nastya managed to get a few more letters to Petro. In one of them, she informed him that his mother had died and her father had been killed in the war. She had lost contact with their younger brothers and sister while searching for Petro.

One day, Petro, waking up in the morning for work, felt an unusual stir in the camp. Soldiers were running around the area, dogs were barking excitedly, and someone was shouting incomprehensible commands.

"What happened?" he heard one of his comrades ask.

"I can't understand. Maybe someone tried to escape?" Petro guessed.

Later, they learned the reason for the commotion. The leader of the country, who had been one of the organisers of the network of prison camps, had died. Everyone now anticipated an amnesty or at least an easing of the conditions. The news came sooner than expected. A few weeks later, Petro was summoned to the camp commandant, where he was read a court decision about his amnesty. His former merits and a good recommendation from his commander were considered. The news made his head buzz. He couldn't fully grasp what had happened.

Petro was in a daze as he was released, his mind racing with the thought of reuniting with Nastya. Stepping out of the camp gates, where he had spent a long ten years, he was overwhelmed by the fresh air and the feeling of freedom. Everything he owned fit into a small duffel bag slung over his shoulder. He was forbidden to return home for ten years, but what mattered when his Nastya was by his side? He knew exactly where he needed to go.

Reaching the village where Nastya lived, Petro's heart pounded with anticipation. He knocked on the door of the small house she had described in her letters. The door opened, and there she stood. They stared at each other for a moment, then she rushed into his arms, and they held each other tightly, tears streaming down their faces.

"I'm here," Petro whispered. "I'm finally here."

"I'll never let you go," Nastya replied, holding him more tighter.

They knew they had endured the worst and could now look forward to building a future together.

The couple settled in a small town with a factory and a sawmill. The little room with a bed and a wardrobe seemed like a paradise on earth. Soon, Petro started working at the sawmill, and life gradually began to improve.

"It's okay. Over time, we'll rent a separate place, but for now, this is enough for us. Right, my dear?" Petro asked Nastya.

"Of course. As long as it's just the two of us, what more do we need?" Nastya laughed and nestled close to her husband.

"In time, we'll go back home. I can't live here. Everything reminds me of the camp and the horrors that happened there. Also, the people, do you see how angry and unkempt they are?"

"Are you asking me?" Nastya smiled sadly. "I had to see a lot in the village where I lived. Our pigs lived more tidily. Have you ever heard of a 'snohach'? I had a landlord who was one. He courted me until he got a good beating."

"Snohach? What's that?" Petro asked in surprise.

"It's a father-in-law who sleeps with his daughter-in-law while his son is away!" Nastya grimaced in disgust.

"That's so disgusting," Petro replied. "How can they do that? What kind of customs do these people have? As long as I've been observing them, all they do is steal, lie and fight. They need nothing else in life."

"What can we do? We must endure these ten years, and then we'll go home."

Year after year passed in exile. Both worked and eventually lived in a separate rented house. Nastya put a lot of effort into making it neat inside and out. Keeping the home cosy was one of her priorities. Petro tidied up the yard, fixed the fence and laid a stone path to keep mud from being tracked into the house during bad weather. Almost at the end of their term, their only son, Oleksiy, was born there. When the boy turned one and a half, they finally returned to their homeland. The journey home was long and arduous. Upon arrival, they settled in a small village, using their savings to buy a spacious house with a beautiful garden. Surrounding them were growing mining towns, so there were no issues finding work, and Petro immediately started working at the mine. Little did he know that one day, it would take away the most precious thing he had.

"So, what's under your eye, and why are your hands bruised?" Petro asked his son with surprise.

"It's nothing," Oleksiy replied gloomily.

"Don't play dumb with me! Come on, spill it. Your mother will find out anyway. You know how she is. So it's better if we face her together. It'll be easier that way."

"Well, it's at school. A few guys there think they can do whatever they want. Their parents have important positions in the city, so they think they're untouchable. They bully everyone, even the teachers. Today, they called me a convict's son. Sorry, Dad. I couldn't hold back. Even though they're older than me, I gave them a good thrashing. Your lessons came in handy."

"Ah, a fighter for justice," Petro ruffled his hair. "You did the right thing. Just try to avoid fights in the future. I understand you very well because I'm the same way, but you need to focus on your studies, and such incidents can harm your future. I taught you to fight for this very reason: to protect your honour and the honour of those you respect and love. These scumbags think we're nothing, but we know our worth. For the future, remember the words of ancient sages: "The best fight is the one you avoided." Also "The true hero is not the one who won a thousand battles on the field, but the one who conquered himself.""

The couple loved Oleksiy very much, but Nastya was more severe in upbringing due to her strict nature than Petro. The father and son obeyed her in everything. They were like two brothers. The teenage Oleksiy would ask his father everything he knew. Together, they repaired an old motorcycle, went fishing, hiking and did carpentry. While in exile, working at a sawmill, Petro learned to work with wood. Now, he had a small workshop. Almost all the furniture at home was handmade by him. Oleksiy loved working with his father. The smell of wood was unmistakable. One day, Petro carved a small idol out of wood. When Oleksiy saw it, he asked: "Who is this, Dad?"

"A long time ago, gods lived on this land, and people revered them. They lived in peace and harmony with Mother Nature. But then they were destroyed, and misfortune came to our land. The last ten volkhvs[73], those who preserved ancient knowledge, were executed. Before their deaths, they cursed this land, each for a hundred years. Since then, there has been no peace on this land. However, our ancient faith was not completely destroyed. Its traditions intertwined with the new faith, and some people still preserve our faith in its purity. Your great-grandfather had an idol like this one, but much taller. He made it himself in the forest near his house. Unfortunately, I didn't get to talk much with my grandfather; he died when I was younger than you. But I remember well his stories about the warriors who, many years ago, came on boats to our ancestors. About how our princes fought and strengthened our state, earning respect even from enemies. He told me about the old beliefs and traditions. About our ancient gods who lived among us then. My grandfather taught me to pray to them and make offerings. I remember what I felt when we visited that idol together. I had a strong conviction that I had done this before. I told my grandfather about it, and he only smiled mysteriously at me. Then, one day, he suddenly died, and soon after, a great famine began. We had no time for it then, and I forgot many things. I regret it so much. I

---

[73] Volkhvs — a practitioners of pagan rites in ancient Rus. They were primarily keepers of religious knowledge, wise men and healers.

Illustration by Artem Burlyk

only remember the names of a few of those gods, such as Perun, Dazhbog, Svarog, Veles and Lada."

"Who might know more about this?"

"I don't know, son. They say our molfars[74] preserve that ancient knowledge and beliefs. But who knows if they are still alive."

Oleksiy grew up, and after finishing school, he entered an automotive mechanical institute with a military department. He successfully graduated and, having a military rank got a job with the paramilitary mining rescue unit at a mine. Later, he got an apartment and moved to the city but visited his parents as often as possible. They missed him very much. Besides him, they had no one else in this world, as they never found their younger brothers and sister.

"I think our Oleksiy is in love," said Nastya, making dumplings.

"Why do you think so?" Petro was surprised.

"When he came over for the weekend, he seemed agitated and didn't stay for dinner."

"So what? Maybe he had some business to attend to?"

"No, I feel in my heart that our boy is in love."

"Well, that's great! I shouldn't be the only one in love," said Petro, and they both laughed

A mother's intuition proved to be right. One day, Oleksiy visited them, and after dinner, he said: "My dear Mom and Dad. I have something to tell you. I met a girl whom I value and love very much. We have already started living together. I know this is a bit against our traditions, but it is not considered improper nowadays."

"What did I tell you?" Nastya looked at Petro triumphantly.

"When will you introduce us to her?" he asked Oleksiy, avoiding his wife's reproach.

---

[74] Molfar – a person attributed to supernatural abilities. Combines the traits of a healer, sorcerer and soothsayer. To some extent, they are descendants of the Cossack characternyks,

"Well, that's why I came, to arrange a day and time," Oleksiy replied.

"We are retired, so we are free any day. Right, Petro?"

"Yes," Petro agreed with his wife. "Son, you tell us when you can! You both work, so maybe on the weekend?"

"Okay, Dad, it's a deal. This Saturday we'll be here at two o'clock. So, expect us."

On Saturday, as planned, Oleksiy arrived with a young, beautiful girl. At first, she was shy, but soon, seeing the friendly and pleasant relationships in the family, she relaxed and began to talk. The girl's name was Svitlana. She worked at a city bank. Svitlana had no brothers or sisters. Her mother had been living abroad, and her father had died few years ago. Her paternal relatives lived far away, and she visited them when she could. So, apart from Oleksiy, Svitlana had no one here. Petro liked the girl very much. He was cracking jokes as if he had become twenty years younger, for which he received a few reproachful looks from Nastya, and then he began to behave more reservedly.

Oleksiy and Svitlana started visiting the village more often and soon got married. Both parents liked the daughter-in-law. She had grown up without a father, and her mother only cared about herself. So Svitlana greatly lacked parental warmth and wise advice. She gravitated towards her in-laws with all her heart, and they treated her like their own daughter. So, the old couple received the news of Svitlana's pregnancy as if it were an event of global significance. From then on, all conversations revolved around the future family member. The baby's gender, name, nutrition, clothing, and many other things became the main discussion topics between parents and children. Svitlana looked at them with tenderness but brushed off the premature advice: "Let me give birth first, and then we'll decide what to do and how."

"You don't understand anything. This needs to be approached with full responsibility. It's not every day that I have grandchildren. I'll make a true Cossack out of him," Petro said, pacing the room from corner to corner.

"What if it's a granddaughter? What will you do?" Nastya asked, laughing.

"A granddaughter? What are you talking about?" Petro stopped in the middle of the room.

"Well, look: women give birth to both girls and boys. That's how it is. So what will you do if we have a granddaughter?" Nastya asked again.

"I don't want to hear it. I already know what I'll do with him. We have so many things ahead of us. So do whatever you want, but give me a grandson," Petro said, scratching his head and went outside.

The universe heeded Petro's wishes, and in due time, Svitlana gave birth to a baby boy whom, after a family council, they named Yaroslav. It was a true joy for the parents and the grandparents. Petro felt such tenderness for the little one that his voice would change when he held the grandson in his arms. Nastya looked at him with amazement, realising that even after decades together, she had not fully known her husband. The boy grew up mainly in the village, where his parents often brought him. Oleksiy and Svitlana were working, and the elderly were retired, so they gladly cared for Yaroslav. Moreover, the fresh village air and homegrown produce benefited the child. When the boy started school, he only visited the village during holidays. Petro eagerly awaited each time he would see his grandson again. They were true friends who missed each other and rejoiced at every meeting. Feeling his age, Petro hurried to pass on all his knowledge and skills to his grandson. When Yaroslav was about five or six, his grandfather carved a wooden flute and taught him how to play. The boy was very talented and quickly picked it up. Later, Petro taught him to play the mandolin, which he had brought back from his distant exile. But when Yaroslav turned ten, tragedy struck the family.

"Petro!" Nastya was sitting on the bench, breathing heavily. "Something's wrong with Oleksiy."

"What is it? Why do you think so?" he asked her.

"You know I can sense things from a distance. It felt like an electric shock. It's Oleksiy. Something bad has happened to him," Nastya replied, distraught.

Petro, knowing her ability, dressed silently and left. As he approached the city, his heart clenched with a sense of foreboding. Ambulances and fire trucks were speeding through the streets, and a siren wailed in the distance.

"What happened?" he asked a passerby at the bus station.

"An explosion at the mine," the man replied and walked away.

The miners and rescuers who died in the mine accident were buried in closed coffins. Only Petro came to the funeral. The death of their only son devastated Nastya, and she couldn't even get out of bed. They stood together: Petro, Svitlana and Yaroslav, who was holding his mother's hand and silently crying.

"Svitlana," said Petro. "We are your family. You can always count on us. Don't worry about Yaroslav. As long as I have strength, he will be taken care of."

She turned to him, hugged and burst into tears.

Calmed down a bit, she whispered: "Thank you so much. I don't know what I would do without you."

Several years passed since that terrible day. Nastya gradually recovered from Oleksiy's death and returned to her usual life. Now, all the attention and love of the old couple were devoted to their grandson. Petro, having lost his only son, focused all his efforts on raising his grandson. He was afraid of taking with him to the grave the knowledge and experience he carried within. Yaroslav's friends also grew fond of Petro, who was always ready to help and offer sound advice. When he started his stories, the children would gather around him and listen with their mouths open, like wide-eyed fledglings waiting to be fed.

Petro, by nature, was restless and always got into some mischief, for which his wife scolded him.

"What, are you going to steal corn with your grandson again? Don't embarrass me! How old are you, you old stump?" Nastya berated her husband.

But he would look guilty and secretly wink at Yaroslav.

The villagers often teased him for these antics, but it did not prevent them from respecting him for his sincere soul and difficult life. In his workshop, Petro made many things. Despite instilling a love for music in his grandson, he also wanted to teach him how to handle weapons. First, it was a slingshot carved from a cherry branch. Then, a bow and arrows. Later, as Yaroslav grew older, Petro taught him how to make a homemade gun. This was done secretly from Nastya because they would both be in big trouble if she found out. He paid special attention to exercises with cold weapons. Petro had a whole collection of knives, homemade or purchased. He taught the boy knife fighting techniques and how to throw knives from any position.

"Never play with a weapon. It does not take jokes lightly and never use it to harm others. But if you decide to use it, do it only for a just cause. Feel the blade with your body, embrace it with your soul, and feel the cold of the metal, its weight and its centre of gravity. Never throw a knife into a living tree because it, like a person, has a soul. In a tough situation, a knife can be your only friend. Never neglect it and always treat it with respect."

Illustration by Artem Burlyk

One summer, when Yaroslav was with them during the summer holidays, Petro sat on a bench smoking his favourite pipe. The tobacco had turned his grey Cossack moustache brown, giving him a rather colourful look. Yaroslav had set up a small drum orchestra with jugs and glass jars that Nastya had hung out to dry on the fence. He was drumming on them with carved sticks, trying to create some kind of melody. But he miscalculated his strength and hit his grandmother's favourite jug hard. It cracked in half and fell to the ground. The boy, frightened, sat down on the ground and looked at his grandfather. Petro, startled, stood up from the bench just as Nastya appeared from around the corner with a bucket of milk.

"Run!" Petro shouted to his grandson, and they dashed out the gate.

The escapees ran down the street until Petro stopped, leaning on his knees and said: "Son, have some conscience; don't run so fast. I'm almost eighty years old."

"Grandpa, why did you run? It's my fault," Yaroslav replied.

"There's a saying, my boy: 'Perish yourself, but save your comrade,' " Petro said with difficulty, struggling to breathe.

"Grandma wouldn't have killed me over that pot. It's not that scary. How are we going to face going home now? Though, it really is a pity about the pot. It was so old. They don't make them like that anymore."

"I don't even know why I started running. Old reflexes, probably."

"So what are we going to do? It's almost night. We have to go home anyway."

"Let's go to my godfather's, take some potatoes from him, and go to our spot. We'll make a fire and bake them. Look what a beautiful evening it is! Just lie on the ground and look at the sky."

Godfather Ivan gave them not only potatoes but also some bacon and bread. They built a fire, and as it started, they talked nonstop. That evening, Petro told his grandson about his entire life: from a hungry childhood to the war and the camps. The boy listened intently, afraid to forget even a single detail of his grandfather's life. He was amazed by everything he heard from his grandfather. Yaroslav wouldn't have learned such things from anyone else. Petro didn't stop for a moment. His eyes sparkled, and his hands occasionally clenched into fists. They roasted bacon and bread over the fire, burning their fingers and ate charred potatoes while talking incessantly.

"*Grandpa, does God exist?*" the boy suddenly asked Petro.

The grandfather paused for a moment.

"Look at the sky! Do you see how many stars there are? Now, for a moment, imagine the entire Universe. Can you grasp infinity? No," Petro answered himself. "It's the same with God. He exists, I know it, but He is not like how various clergy depict Him. We cannot understand Him just as we cannot imagine this infinity. Although everyone sees it, they can't even touch it."

"*But what about Hell and Heaven?*" Yaroslav continued to ask," *Do they exist? What happens to us after death?*"

"I don't know, my boy. Someday, everyone will find out. As for Heaven or Hell, I can tell you one thing..."

Here, Petro's throat tightened, and he paused as if recalling something.

Gathering his strength, he said: "I have seen so much in my life that it seems to me that Hell is here on Earth and only after our death we will find freedom and eternity."

"*Do you believe in life after death?*" the grandson persisted.

"Nobody knows what will happen to us after we leave this life. I know that the end of anything is the beginning of something else. It's like sunset and sunrise. You watch the sunset and think your day is ending. But for someone else, it's a sunrise, and their day is just beginning."

Yaroslav went silent, pondering what he had heard, and then asked: "*Grandpa, why are you so afraid of grandma?*"

Not expecting such a question, Petro laughed so hard that tears even appeared in his eyes.

"I'm not afraid of her. I just love and respect her very much. I love her so much that my heart tightens with tenderness for her. We've been together for over sixty years. She saw me off to war, then travelled with me across the north while I was shuffled between camps. If it weren't for her love, I probably wouldn't have survived. She is like the air to me. I can't breathe without her. So, it's not that I'm afraid of her. Simply because I love my Nastya very much."

For a while, the grandfather and grandson watched the fire and the embers, which glowed with different colours in the light breeze and remained silent.

"*Grandpa, why do we speak different languages?*" the boy finally broke the silence.

"Over three hundred and fifty years during the occupation, our native language was banned many times. Gradually, it was pushed out everywhere and remained only in the villages. We still learned in our native language, allowing it to take a small breath. Your parents caught up a bit of that time, and almost all schools switched to a foreign language. Higher education was always taught in another language. It's good that now our country has gained independence and our native language is gradually returning. But it's a very long journey."

"*Why was it banned?*" Yaroslav asked, puzzled.

"Ancient people said that — if you want to conquer a nation, you must take away their language. So they were right. Our language was almost destroyed, as well as our memory, because the genetic code of a people is stored in its language. People without memory are easier to govern. So learn our native language, son. It is our soul and what identifies us as a nation."

"*But that was in the past, and now we live in peace with them. Also, we have a lot in common with them,*" the boy insisted.

"Remember, son: sooner or later they will go on war against us. I spent twenty long winters there. I know them very well."

"*War? Why? What for? What do we have to divide?*"

"Yaroslav! They are a completely different people. We have nothing in common with them except a bloody history. Everything they have, they stole from us: language, culture, religion, history, traditions. Stolen and appropriated. We forgave them because we forgot our history. But even so, we have not lost our desire for freedom because freedom is the most valuable thing a person has. I say this as someone who spent ten years in camps. It's like breathing: as soon as you can't breathe, you immediately understand how happy you were before when you could breathe freely. We are a freedom-loving people, and they are slaves. A slave who does not want to be freed from slavery will never forgive another slave who has become a free man. He will try to make him a slave again. Understand, he will do everything to make others as enslaved as he is instead of freeing himself. They are accustomed to living in slavery; it suits them. But we need freedom; we cannot breathe without it."

Petro remembered that evening until his death. He felt immense relief from pouring out his soul to his only grandson. He did not know how prophetic his words would be and that Yaroslav would have to defend his homeland from an enemy invasion with a weapon in hand in a few years.

One morning, Nastya couldn't get out of bed for the morning milking. Petro had to milk the cow himself and drive it to the herd. When he returned, Nastya was awake, looking at him.

"Petro. My love. My time has come. I feel the breath of death. It is near. Don't mourn for me. We will see each other again soon," she whispered to her husband.

Petro sat next to his wife, stroked her hair and, leaning down, kissed her on the lips.

"Do you remember that seaside and our first kiss?" he asked, and his tear fell on Nastya's cheek.

"Yes, my dear. I remember everything. I love you just as much as I did then," Nastya said and closed her eyes.

He stayed by her side the entire day. The next morning, she didn't wake up.

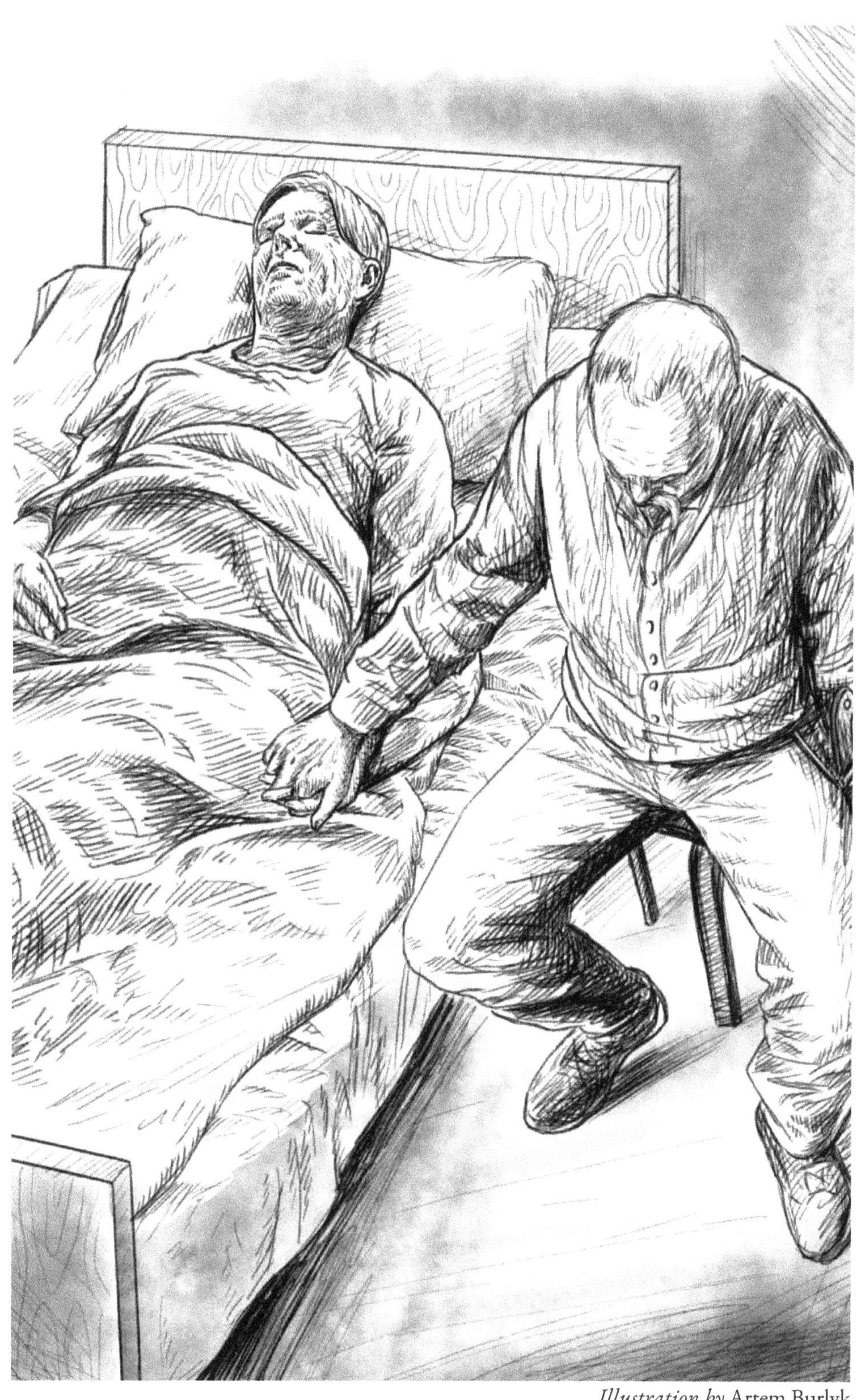

Illustration by Artem Burlyk

Petro stood on the porch for a while. The sun had fully risen above the horizon. He put on a clean shirt with his favourite sweater. Then he went to the neighbours to tell them what had happened and asked them to call Svitlana and Yaroslav. Returning to the house, he approached his wife, who seemed to be sleeping peacefully on the bed. Pulling a chair close, Petro took Nastya's hand with one hand and rested the other on the hilt of the knife always strapped to his belt. With a deep breath, he closed his eyes and drifted into sleep. Petro dreamed of a summer forest where hundreds of colourful butterflies danced in the sun's rays. He felt like a light butterfly fluttering in the air with the others. Flying over the ground, he saw Her. She sat on a flower with her wings spread, looking like a flower herself. Two pearlescent spots on her back shimmered with all the rainbow colours, magically drawing him to her. He couldn't take his eyes off such a beauty and stayed with her ever since. They flew together from flower to flower, rising high into the sky, swirling in an unparalleled dance. This went on for some time until one morning, his beauty did not wake up. He circled around and touched her with his wings, hoping she would wake up and fly with him into the celestial heights, but it was all in vain. She slept the eternal sleep. The butterfly sat next to her, folded his wings, and waited for the morning when he would not wake up as well. That morning was not late and came inevitably.

Petro exhaled one last time, his head bowed to his chest. His hand slipped from the knife's hilt and hung down.

Epilogue

The feeling of incredible lightness did not subside. He moved forward towards the bright radiance. Strange and unknown creatures flew around. The silence was so profound it felt as if he had gone deaf. The air was filled with unfamiliar, marvellous scents that made his head spin.

"How are you, my son?" suddenly, he heard the Creator's voice, which seemed to come from everywhere.

"I feel good, Father. Never in any of my lives have I felt so light and uplifted," he replied.

"Finally, you are home. You have walked your path with dignity, and now your experience will be passed on to the Treasury of Memory. To where knowledge transitions upon completion of passages. Now, the Guardians will take you there, and then you will go where you are awaited."

"Alright, Creator. I am happy to accomplish the purpose for which I have walked such a long path. In my thoughts, I often imagined this meeting, but it has exceeded all my expectations."

"Everything in its time, my son. If you had known everything, your life would not have been so rich, and our Treasury would not have waited for the invaluable experience you brought with you. Step by step, you walked towards your goal. With each step, you gained new experience and knowledge."

"By the way, I sent you a greeting through someone condemned to death. Did you receive it? At that time, I wanted you to know about me as soon as possible. Although, what am I saying? You have always known about me."

"No, he has not finished his journey yet, but you will meet soon. I have always known about you. Every thought of yours, every experience, was known to me. I saw your path and rejoiced at every success. Now, rest. You have earned the peace and joy that lie ahead. So, don't delay, my son. The Guardians are waiting for you. I wish you a pleasant reunion."

He turned and headed towards where two Guardians were waiting for him. They led him to the Treasury of Memory, where he imparted everything he had brought with him: all his experiences, feelings, and observations. He felt even lighter, as if he had shed a heavy burden. Now, he wanted to flutter like a butterfly. After this, the Guardians took him to a place where unknown life teemed. Everywhere, he saw others like himself. They didn't walk but seemed to glide through space. Plants of strange shapes intertwined with each other, and beings of otherworldly beauty moved along them and through the air. New scents and colours created a magical atmosphere of tranquillity. He wanted to dissolve into this marvellous world. Suddenly, he saw Her. There was no doubt that it was Her. A stunningly beautiful butterfly fluttered around him, gently flapping its iridescent wings.

He raised his hand, and the butterfly gently perched on it, softly fluttering its wings.

"You didn't wait long for me, my dear! Everything happened as you said it would. I couldn't stay long without you. Now, infinity awaits us. Will it be enough for us to be together? So, let's not waste any time. Let's fly right now."

Illustration by Oleksand Prodan

The end.
Serhii Adamenko
Ireland, 2023

Illustration by
Arten Burlyk and **Oleksandr Prodan**